Hens
and
Chickens

Hens
and
Chickens

a story
about love by
Jennifer Wixson

Published by

White Wave™

For more information contact:
White Wave, P.O. Box 4, Troy, ME 04987.

10 9 8 7 6 5 4 3 2 1

ISBN 978-0-9636689-8-1

eBook ISBN 978-0-9636689-7-4

Hens and Chickens is a work of fiction. Names, characters,
(most) places, and incidents are the products of the author's imagination
or are used fictitiously. Any resemblance to actual events, locales and
persons, living or dead, is entirely coincidental.

This book is dedicated to:
my husband, the Cranberry Man, who
loves me despite my odd ways and ill humors
AND the late Miss Bess Klain of Norway,
Maine, who inspired four generations of "children"
with her zest for life and love of music.

Acknowledgements

The author would like to thank the following for their generous contributions of time, love and support for *Hens and Chickens*: my parents, Rowena Palmer and Eldwin Wixson; my sister, Cheryl Wixson, and my mother-in-law Bessie Luce; my awesome editorial team of Stanley Luce, Marilyn Wixson, Christin Chenard, Rebecca Siegel, Robert (Bruce) Johnson, Jessica Wixson Shaw, Emily McFarland, Ellen Gibson, and Elizabeth Schoch; my nit-picky proof-reading nieces (the Oxford comma —say, what?) Joanna and Laurel McFarland; my amazing artist and design specialist Peter Harris Creative; my review readers, Carrol Patterson, Carrie Reed, Susan Palmer, Brenda McKenzie and Carrie Deak; my marketing support person Cody Mayhew; and the members and attenders of the First Universalist Church of Norway, Maine and the West Paris Universalist Church, who experienced the embryo chick of *Hens and Chickens* from the pulpits of their lovely churches.

Table of Contents

Chapter 1

·······

"You'll Be Back!"

I'm not sure why we 21st century pips isolate ourselves from the joy we need to thrive; but we do. It's almost as though a new breed of genetically modified humans (GMH) has evolved out of the prior century, humans with hearts that cleave apart from our flesh as easily as freestone fruit. Some of this evolution can be blamed on forces beyond our control, such as the Great Recession. And some can be attributed to our own feelings of powerlessness, which became pervasive after 9-11.

But powerlessness, my pips, is an illusion. What *is* doesn't necessarily have to *be*, as my story—a little tale about hens and chickens; pips and peepers; love and, well, *love*—hopefully reveals. But maybe I should start at the beginning, before I clamber up onto my soap box. There will be plenty of opportunities for *that*, later on.

Although I wasn't present at the beginning, I was told later in sacred confidence (not now betrayed—I've been authorized to share this tale) that our story begins in Boston, Massachusetts, on a Friday in late February, 2012. It was a damp, chilly day, with that wet-dog smell characteristic of an early New England spring. The train was late ("as usual," my source tells me) but our heroine, 27-year-old Lila Woodsum, pushed spritely through the shiny glass doors of the downtown office building, *chugged* up the tired old elevator to the 5th floor, and cheerfully presented herself at her outdated cubicle in the insurance office of Perkins & Gleeful, Inc. at 8:51 a.m.

"You're late," teased Rebecca Johnson, Lila's motherly co-marketing manager, from the conjoining cubicle.

"No, I'm not—I'm nine minutes early," Lila corrected. The waifish twenty-something shrugged out of her Boston pea coat and pulled off her black cashmere scarf. Her skinny-leg jeans and oversized wool sweater made her appear even taller than her 5-feet, 7-inches. Lila tossed her outerwear over the side of the cubicle and shook free her chickadee-like cap of shiny black hair. She turned around and grinned at her older co-worker. "BUT I would've been late if I'd stopped for my usual coffee. I hate it that I'm soo conscientious!"

"That's what I meant; you're late for *you*," said Rebecca. She was a short, pleasingly plump brunette in her late forties, with a pretty face framed by soft, copious curls. "Did you get my text?"

Lila fished in her coat pocket for her smartphone. "Oh, yeah. I just forgot to look at it. What's up, Becca?"

"I'm not sure. Cora's been locked in her office since I got here."

Instinctively, Lila turned to examine the closed wooden door of a small side office allotted to the Perkins & Gleeful office manager, "Queen" Cora Batterswaith. A venerable insurance company, Perkins & Gleeful, Inc., was founded in 1889 and currently employed 1,136 people in the New England states. In the forest of insurance companies serving the Greater Boston area, Perkins & Gleeful was the oak. However, since (and perhaps prior to) the Great Recession, the company, like many others in the insurance industry, had been experiencing an internal black-rot, a crumbling of values and practices, which threatened to destroy the company from the inside out. (That the rot was wholesale throughout the entire financial services industry in the dawning days of 21st century did not justify the dissolution, much as the comfort in numbers might help the upper echelon sleep at night.)

However, if Perkins & Gleeful was the oak, Lila Woodsum – young, flexible, unorthodox – was the birch, not the delicate paper birch but the pert silver birch that tenaciously fights for its rightful place in the sun against the larger trees of the forest. Lila, honest by nature, would also admit that her own personal history contributed greatly to her present dissatisfaction with life in the 21st century.

Lila's hazel eyes narrowed perceptively. "Queen Cora's here on a Friday?" she asked.

Rebecca, who did not like Lila's derogatory nickname for their su-pervisor, nonetheless let the slur pass. She bit her naturally ruby lip. "I know; strange, isn't it?"

Lila registered her best friend's slip. She also noted the worry in the usually serene face of her motherly co-worker. She knew only too well that a regular paycheck was an absolute necessity for Rebecca, who sup-ported a daughter in college, as well as herself, on her modest (by Boston standards) salary. Examining the office manager's closed door, Lila felt her own anxiety begin to rise, swirling upward like the winter mist from the Charles River. Automatically, Lila clamped her feelings into lockdown mode, a necessary technique she had unfortunately learned at a very early age.

"Cora's been in there with the door closed since I got here at 8:30," Rebecca whispered. "She's arguing on the phone with someone. I hope we're not ..."

"Omigod, not the pink slips, again!" Lila interrupted. She plopped down into her cheap office chair and offered her partner a reassuring smile. "Please, Becca – the Recession is soo over!"

"Shhhh, dear! They'll hear you!"

"WHO will hear me? Look around you, Becca. In case you hadn't noticed, there's nobody else here. You and I, we MADE it. Our jobs are safer than they were five years ago when I was hired onto the marketing team—what were there then? Seven of us? And now we're down to TWO? They can't afford to let any more of us go or there won't even be a marketing department. SOMEONE has to promote Perkins & Gleeful—the Queen sure isn't going to do it." Despite the emotional lockdown, Lila was unable to keep a rising modicum of anger and scorn from her voice.

Rebecca glanced doubtfully around the huge, empty floor, now peopled with vacant cubicles. She sighed. What Lila said was true: once there had been seven employees in the marketing department, now there were only two: herself and Lila. "They do outsource a lot of stuff nowadays, though," she added, apprehensively.

"Outsourcing is soo 20th century," said Lila. "Really, Becca, you've got to get with the times."

"And that's part of the problem," Rebecca cried, seizing her opportunity. "I'm old and you're young! Companies like ours want young people to work for them because they think young people are up to date with the modern technology." She paused for a fraction of a second. "Do you think I should dye my hair?" she added, anxiously.

"Yeah, and they think they can pay young people a lot less, too," said Lila. "That's really what is driving employment these days—the Almighty Dollar! That's why companies like ours try to squeeze more and more work from FEWER employees." She flipped open her work laptop and powered it up.

"At least we have a job; I'm grateful for that!"

"And that's what they want—they want us to be very, VERY grateful," Lila said, scrolling down through her email. "Just for the record, I thought you DID dye your hair," she added, without looking up.

"You did *not*! Don't you see all the gray ones?"

"Nope," said Lila. She shifted in her seat in order to give her partner and best friend her full attention. "Look, Becca, I think you worry too much about getting laid off," she continued, honestly. "Cora can't write code; she doesn't know HTML and she's probably never even heard the term *metadata*." Lila glanced back at her screen, momentarily distracted. "Omigod; I'm up to 2,000 followers on Twitter @PGleeful!"

"Two thousand followers!" Rebecca exclaimed. "You're amazing, Lila! Two thousand Tweeps following an insurance company? What could be deadlier, more boring than us!"

"Tell me about it. I don't know how I make the company sound so interesting!"

"Lie?" suggested Rebecca.

Both women giggled, and Lila was gratified to see her friend begin to relax. Surreptitiously, she breathed a sigh of relief.

Suddenly, Rebecca's cubicle phone buzzed. Startled, both women jumped. Rebecca answered the call mechanically, and Lila watched as the blood drained from her friend's already winter-pale face. She could hear the tell-tale, high-pitch voice of Queen Cora on the other end.

Rebecca dropped the phone back onto the receiver. "She wants to meet with me in her office," she said. "Now!"

Lila clenched her fists under her desktop so that Rebecca couldn't see. "Don't panic," she advised her older friend. "Cora probably just wants to vent. Some numbers came in and she caught hell from Kelly. Obviously, they're not looking at MY numbers on Twitter."

Rebecca smiled weakly and rose from her outdated office chair. "I really think this is it. I could tell by her voice."

Lila tittered in a vain attempt to laugh it off. "Well, then, it's been nice to know ya—I'll see you in the unemployment line!" She watched as her professionally-dressed, 5-feet, 2-inch friend straightened her back and walked woodenly toward the side office.

Lila turned to her laptop and pretended to read her tweets, but all the time she was keeping an eye on Cora's office. She was startled, therefore, when someone tapped on her shoulder. She hadn't even heard

Hens and Chickens

Vice President Joe Kelly coming up behind her. She jumped slightly, and cursed herself inwardly for revealing her anxiety to him. "Joe, sorry, I was concentrating on my emails and didn't hear you. Would you believe—we're up to 2,000 followers on Twitter!"

"Can I see you in my office for a minute, Lila," her gray-suited boss replied blandly. "Now, please."

Without waiting for her answer, Kelly turned on his heel. Lila watched him walk quickly back to his office, obviously expecting Lila to jump up and follow him. "Now, please," she mimicked.

Lila felt an intense longing to rebel. She glanced at the side office. No sound, no movement. No nothing. *Was this … IT?*

Lila rose reluctantly and followed Kelly down the corridor past the empty gray cubicles of the marketing department. Her mind flashed back to her early days at Perkins & Gleeful five years ago. When she had begun working at the insurance company, the cubicles had been full of laughing, joking, hard-working Bostonians, a vibrant collection of humanity of all ages, shapes and sizes. There was Black Irene, rotund, jolly; Silly Billy Timms; Susan Medley – the list went on and on. She remembered thinking to herself that first day: *"Omigod, I feel soo out of place! Everybody knows everyone else! I'll never be able to remember all their names!"*

But within three months, Lila not only knew all their names, she had come to know and love most of them intimately. When Lila's mother and step-father were killed in a boating accident in 2009, it was to her office family that she had turned for much-needed emotional support. There was Shelly Thompson, with her excessively-spoiled Siamese cat that was always escaping when it came into heat, Shelly, who had helped her pick the outfit for her mother to be buried in; and then Carl Esler, the gay water cooler gossip, who had held her hand through her mother's funeral service. And now—now there was dust, deathly quiet, and decay. *Welcome to the New World Order of corporate America,* Lila thought. *Welcome to the 21ˢᵗ century! What am I DOING here?!*

She hesitated in the oversized doorframe of Kelly's large corner office, unwilling to be trapped inside. Kelly was Queen Cora's supervisor, and one of Lila's least favorite people at Perkins & Gleeful. He was short, crisp-speaking and neatly clipped (like a show dog, Lila often thought). Kelly was a typical micromanager, frequently stooping down into the trenches to dictate to the underlings, including the diminished marketing department, countermanding many of Cora's directives.

"Sit down," Kelly said, waving a neatly-cuffed wrist. "Shut the door."
Lila saw the flash of a gold cufflink and felt a momentary blind rush
of anger. She groped for the nearest leather chair. *WTF! Perkins & Gleeful
was paying Kelly so much he could afford GOLD cufflinks?!*

"Would you like a cup of coffee?" Kelly's hand hovered over the
desk phone, where a front office secretary (who Lila knew would do his
most menial bidding) was only a push button away.

No pink slip, then!

Strangely, Lila experienced an intense disappointment. "Nope, thanks.
Had my coffee limit on the way to work," she lied.

"We thought it best to bring you in here while Rebecca collected her
things," Kelly continued.

Lila felt a savage twisting of her gut. Once again, she tried the lockdown technique. This time, however, she failed.

We who? she thought, sarcastically.

"What?" said Kelly. "Did you say something?"

Lila hadn't realized she'd mumbled out loud. "What happened to
Rebecca?"

"We needed to downsize again. Congratulations, Lila. You're getting a
promotion. You're now the new Marketing Director at Perkins & Gleeful."

Unconsciously, Lila clenched her fists. "What's that mean?" she challenged. "That now I'll be doing the work of seven people and getting
paid half a salary?"

"Think what you're saying before you say it, Lila," Kelly cautioned.
"Don't say anything you'll regret."

Lila leaped to her feet, her pent-up passion finally boiling over. "Like,
take this job and SHOVE it?! Like, you made a big mistake, Kelly; you
fired the WRONG person!"

Kelly leaned back in his chair. He pressed his fingertips together in a
tent formation. "Do you think this is easy for me? Rebecca has been with
Perkins & Gleeful longer than I have."

"Yeah, I DO think it's easy for you! That's what you were hired for—
and you've had plenty of practice over the past few years!"

"Calm down, Lila. You're just angry because we let your friend go.
Take the rest of the day off. Go shopping or whatever you women do to
blow off some steam. Things will look different on Monday."

"You're right they'll look different, because I won't be HERE on
Monday!"

Hens and Chickens

"Lila, Lila. You know that's an empty threat. What about those student loans? Who's going to pay those for you? Not Mommy and Daddy, now are they?"

Enraged, Lila wanted to lean over the polished mahogany desk and slap the Perkins & Gleeful Vice President. *How dare he?* She choked back tears. *How dare he!*

"There, there. Things will look better in the morning, honey."

Lila drew herself up to her full height, which was in fact three inches taller than Joe Kelly. "Screw you!" she said, looking down upon the Vice President; "I quit. Have a nice life!"

Lila turned on her heel and stalked out the door. Kelly twiddled a pencil on his desk, an amused smile upon his closely-shaven face. "You'll be back!" he called after her, confidently.

Chapter 2

· · · · · · ·

The Plan

My source tells me that Lila did not condescend to answer the parting shot of the Perkins & Gleeful Vice President as she stalked out of his airy corner office. "I will NEVER come back to this place!" she swore under her breath.

She rushed down the empty corridor and back to her cubicle, but she was not in time to catch Rebecca. The cubicle that conjoined with Lila's own, usually decorated with dozens of photos of Rebecca's 21-year-old daughter, Amber, was now empty and colorless. All signs of Lila's co-worker had vanished from the vacant 5th floor office of Perkins & Gleeful. "It's like she was never here at all!" Lila marveled.

Lila picked up the few personal photos and silly sentimental objects decorating her own cubicle and stuffed them into her purse. She threw on her scarf and coat and quickly headed for the elevator, punching the ground-level button in anger. She paced back and forth restlessly, listening to the lurching sounds of the tired elevator *chugging* back up the elevator shaft.

When Lila finally exited the office building, the sidewalk was largely empty. A car with a shot muffler blasted by and she smelled the vehicle's foul exhaust. She grabbed for her phone and punched in Rebecca's name. The call went straight to Voice Mail; her friend had shut her phone off.

"Becca, I know you're upset, but don't do anything, yet, O.K.?" Lila said, into the impersonal VM box, as she walked mindlessly toward the train station. She stopped, and glanced over her shoulder at the steps to the T. "Wait. Don't even go home. Meet me at Grass Roots Café as soon as possible. I'm going to get myself that coffee after all. I've got something IMPORTANT to tell you."

Lila dropped her phone into her purse and pulled out her CharlieCard. Within half an hour, she was settled comfortably with a large cup of steaming coffee into a quiet corner of Grass Roots, a boutique café situated in the ground floor of an office building on Arch Street. Lila inhaled the comforting scent of the hot Arabica bean coffee. "Ahhh! Life is good!"

Lila practically grinned with satisfaction. *Who knew? Who knew quitting a job could feel so good!*

But what to do next? What should she do? How could she help Rebecca?

Lila was aware that her financial situation – which was actually the polar opposite of that described by Joe Kelly – gave her opportunities that her older, widowed friend did not share. Rebecca's daughter Amber still had a year left at UMass and Rebecca's home in Roxbury was heavily mortgaged to pay for that education. Lila knew that Rebecca lived closely, almost paycheck to paycheck. Lila, on the other hand, was single, debt-free, and rented a modest condo that could easily be given up—and had a bank account with more than $250,000, thanks, sadly, to the proceeds from her mother's life insurance policy.

What do I REALLY want to do with my life?

Lila tried to imagine a future for herself and her motherly friend—and failed. An imaginative, creative person, she normally turned to her daydreams for inspiration. But lately Lila's daydreams had all been nightmares.

Maybe I should put the question out to the Twittersphere? Maybe some of my Tweeps will have some good ideas?

She tweeted her situation to the 2,000+ followers @PGleeful, cheerfully taking advantage of the social media avatar she had created for her former employer. "Heck, they won't know what's going on for weeks at Perkins & Gleeful," she muttered aloud. "I don't think Kelly even knows what Twitter is, and Queen Cora still thinks Facebook is where it's at."

Within minutes, Lila had several replies from Twitter, but one in particular, from @MissJanHastings, stood out.

"Old house next door falling down; take a chance – move to Maine. What have you got to lose, darling? We'll show you how to raise chickens."

We'll show you how to raise chickens.

Lila felt the hair on her arm stand up. The image of herself gathering eggs and scattering grain to a flock of clucking chickens revived a faint, happy memory from her childhood and struck Lila now as something, well – *something she would really like to do.*

Hens and Chickens

"Omigod, I can see it," she said, laughing aloud, hand tightening around her cup of coffee. "I can totally see it!"

"I'm interested," Lila tweeted back to @MissJanHastings. "What next?"

Seconds later came the reply: "Come visit; this weekend. You and your friend can stay with me. I'll put you up in the Rose Rooms."

The Rose Rooms ...

Lila pictured in her mind an old New England farmhouse with faded, rose-figured wall-paper and the scent of lavender potpourri wafting through the upstairs bedrooms. *What have we got to lose? An outdated paradigm that isn't working anymore—except for corporate America?*

Lila felt more hopeful than she had since her mother's untimely death. A few more tweets and a couple of Direct Messages to @MissJanHastings settled it. If Lila could convince her former Perkins & Gleeful marketing partner, they would venture to Maine that very afternoon to check out Miss Jan Hastings' offbeat proposal. What better way could they possibly spend their weekend?!

"O.K., I'm here under protest," Rebecca said, sliding into a seat opposite her young friend. She plopped her over-sized faux leather purse on the floor. "I'd rather be throwing myself under a train but I thought I might as well get a coffee first. And congratulations, by the way. Cora told me about your promotion while she helped me box up my stuff. Would you believe it? She even helped me lug everything to my car—bless her!"

"I didn't get the promotion," Lila said, quickly. "Are you alright?"

"W-h-a-t?!" exclaimed Rebecca. "Cora promised me the job was yours – that's what kept me from falling apart. That, and I was afraid my mascara would run."

"I quit, Becca."

Rebecca sucked in her breath sharply. "You ... quit?"

"Walked out on Kelly. Didn't even slam the door."

Alarmed, Rebecca reached across the table and clasped Lila's slim arm. "Be serious," she pleaded. "You can't *quit*. Companies don't hire unemployed people; I saw it on *60 Minutes*!"

"Screw corporate America—sorry!" Lila automatically apologized. "I've got a plan—if it all works out. I'm going to Maine and raise chickens. Or eggs. Or something like that. And you're coming with me!"

"Oh, you're only doing this to protest my firing!" said Rebecca, pushing a soft brown curl back from her face. "And while I love you for it, I think you're foolish. It's not too late; Kelly will still take you back."

"Most likely. But I'm not going back—I'm liberated. I always wondered what it felt like for those women's libbers in the '60s, burning their bras and all. Now, I know. It feels totally mind blowing; it really does. Who does corporate America they think they are, anyway? The only game in town? No way! We're gonna get a NEW life."

Rebecca sank back into her seat. "I think I need something stronger than coffee," she said, weakly.

"They make a really good chocolate croissant here."

"I was thinking of something a little stronger than chocolate!"

Lila groped for her wallet and drew out a $20 bill. She tossed the money at her friend. "Here, get whatever you want. It's on me," she said.

"Lila! That's $20!" Rebecca eyed her friend with horror. "You won't even get unemployment because you *quit* a perfectly good job."

"Chicken feed," Lila retorted. She giggled at her own joke. "Ha, ha. Chicken feed. Go get your coffee, Becca, while I find out how much organic chicken feed costs."

Rebecca's daughter, Amber, had recently introduced Lila to the organic food movement. Lila didn't know much about the growing movement, but Amber's enthusiasm had piqued her interest. She turned to her phone, and within a minute had discovered the answer to her question: a bag of certified organic feed cost about $25. "No joke," she said. "I wonder how much those things eat?" She jabbed away at the phone.

When Rebecca returned with a coffee and croissant, Lila set her phone on the table. "Here's the plan," she said. "You're gonna rent out your house, and we're gonna move to Maine, buy this rundown old place next to Miss Jan Hastings, and make a new life. We're gonna live off my mother's life insurance money until we can make a living from our chicken and egg business. I've got enough to carry us for a couple of years, no sweat. In the meantime, you can send your unemployment money to Amber. She'll love the plan 'cause we're gonna be organic!"

"We're going to sell … chickens?" Rebecca said, skeptically.

"Raise chickens and sell EGGS," corrected Lila. "ORGANIC eggs. In Sovereign, Maine."

"You've arranged all this with a Twitter person?"

Lila nodded, beaming. "@MissJanHastings," she said.

"*Who* is *she?*"

"Miss Jan Hastings is a retired music teacher who loves children and chickens," Lila answered, excitedly. "She's got a pet chicken, actually—Matilda. I've seen pics. We've been following each other on Twitter for a couple of years."

"But you don't really *know* her?"

"I know more about Miss Jan Hastings than I do Cora Batterswaith, and I've known Cora five years! Miss Hastings is pretty old now—probably late sixties or early seventies. She's never married, loves donuts and kids, and hates what the banks and corporate America have done to this country. She lives in this really neat town called Sovereign—which is somewhere near Unity or Liberty, Maine. I think there's a small college nearby."

Despite herself, Rebecca was intrigued. "Unity College," she mused.

"It's called Unity College. I've actually been to Unity, believe it or not."

"Omigod, no way!"

"Yes, way. Unity was one of the colleges that Amber considered. There's an annual organic fair in Unity every fall; I went there with Amber two years ago." Rebecca looked thoughtful. "I can picture the area in my mind."

"S-o-o-o? What's it like?"

"Well, there's a lot of farmland," Rebecca replied. "I can't recall Sovereign, but Unity is sort of a one-horse town. Actually, it's more than a one-horse town because the Amish have a settlement in Unity, I remember."

"This is TOO good. The Amish? It's perfect! What's not to love about moving to the sticks of Maine and raising chickens?"

"But what about Ryan?" Rebecca asked, anxiously. "What will Ryan say?"

"Puh-leeze. We're just friends—we're not even having sex."

Rebecca blushed.

"Sorry, I forget you're from another generation," said Lila. "Hey, if Ryan MacDonald wants to come to Maine to see me, I won't send him packing. But I'm not staying in Boston just to be near the Perkins & Gleeful corporate attorney!"

Unconsciously, Rebecca sat up straighter in her chair. "Well, I don't seem to have any bright ideas myself," she said, gamely. "I can't promise you I'll commit to anything at this point – especially with Amber still in college. But I'm willing to take a look. Let me go home, feed my cat and pack my overnight bag. I'll pick you up at one o'clock. That way we'll be able to get to Sovereign before dark."

"Becca, this is amazing!" cried Lila, who, although not normally demonstrative, leapt up and gave her friend a quick hug.

"I'm not promising anything, remember!" Rebecca cautioned, familiar with Lila's youthful exuberance.

"I know; I know! We're just going to Sovereign for a look. You won't regret it!"

"I haven't got much to regret at this point," replied Rebecca, wryly. She leaned down to pick up her purse. "But I might soon—God help us!" she added, under her breath.

Chapter 3

. . . .

Rebecca

*A*t 48, Rebecca Johnson had experienced her share of life's little disappointments. And while the loss of the marketing job with Perkins & Gleeful was certainly a major stumbling block at this point in her life – especially with Amber only a junior in college – it was not one of her top five disappointments. Those would be marrying an abusive (lying, drunken etc. etc.) husband, losing their son Thad in a motorcycle accident, caring for a parent with Alzheimer's; and, well, why bring them all back?

Rebecca's past disappointments flashed briefly before her soft blue eyes while she sat at the Grass Roots Café and listened as Lila outlined a possible new future for the two women. But it had not always been that way. Rebecca was one of the popular girls in high school; not the most popular, true, but popular enough to make everyone believe that she would lead a charmed life. She was a pretty, friendly brunette, and, although short, she had a good figure and a warm, compassionate nature.

Rebecca was a cheerleader; not the Captain of the cheerleading squad, no, but one of its solid members, necessary for the middle of the pyramid. A natural homemaker, she sewed most of the costumes for the drama club, and always carried spare sanitary pads, tampons and ibuprofen. She was the girl next door, the girl Anthony Trollope wrote copious 19th century love stories about.

Rebecca's childhood and young womanhood were largely serene and uneventful, until she had married her college sweetheart. On that day, the storm clouds began building on an otherwise cloudless sky.

Rebecca's husband, who would always remain nameless (unless "your father" could be considered a name), was a confident, charming sweet-talker who talked the comely co-ed right out of her tightly-held virginity. (Even now Rebecca was embarrassed to admit to Lila that she'd never been with another man.) Amber's father was a salesman, a

15

top-earner for a growing insurance company—none other, in fact, than Perkins & Gleeful, Inc. When his sales crumbled after the death of their son, Rebecca had taken a job at the front desk as a receptionist. By the time her husband had drunk himself into a casket, Rebecca had been promoted to the marketing department and was left as the sole provider of eight-year-old Amber Joy.

For many years, Amber, now 21, was Rebecca's reason for being. Amber, a delightful, caring child, was a more modern and lankier version of her mother. She was a daughter of whom every mother could feel proud, and Rebecca was certainly no exception. But Amber had grown into an inquiring, passionate teen and naturally separated from her mother to bond with younger, more progressive friends. When Rebecca had first noticed her chick try to leave the nest, she had felt incredibly terrified and sad; but she did not prevent her daughter from forming new attachments. Instead, she had stepped aside, and had courageously given her daughter the slight push necessary to send her solitary chick out into the world to create a meaningful life for herself. Amber's latest passion was the blossoming organic movement.

"It's a lot harder to be a good parent than a bad parent," Rebecca's mother had allowed two years ago, before Mom forgot who this short, professionally-dressed brunette was who visited her every weekend and sometimes on weeknights. "You've done a good job with her, Rebecca."

It was probably the last coherent praise Rebecca ever received from her mother. She leaned over and kissed the elderly woman's waxy white face. "I love you, Mom," she said, choking back tears.

Once Amber had flown from the nest to UMass, Rebecca found herself drawn even closer to her motherless coworker, Lila Woodsum. Everyone in the office liked and admired Lila, who, fresh from college, had been hired to liven up the group and to provide new tech savvy to the company. (Rebecca had been right about that.) Those were the good days, when money seemed to drop from the heavens and every $1 Perkins & Gleeful spent on marketing seemed to return $100 in sales. But then the Great Recession hit, and in the fall of 2008 the first layoffs had begun. Once there had been seven of them in the marketing depart-ment—now there were, well, none!

Even now, motoring up the Maine turnpike, Rebecca could not be-lieve that after all these months of worrying about losing her job the axe had finally fallen. She who had faithfully attended the office at Perkins

Hens and Chickens

& Gleeful every work day (except for a few vacation and sick days) for the past 16 years, now had no place to go on Monday (or Tuesday or Wednesday …). She had lost not only her gainful employment, she had lost also part of her identity. True, she was still Amber's Mom and Lila's Best Friend. But who *was* she – Rebecca Johnson? And what did she really want for her life?

The last few hours seemed surreal to Rebecca. The firing from Perkins & Gleeful. Coffee at Grass Roots Café in the middle of a work day. Lila chattering about hens and an offbeat stranger she'd met on Twitter. Her young friend pitching a plan to move to Maine. It was almost like a dream!

To Rebecca's credit, she had not agreed to consider the Maine adventure from any self-interest. Much as she loved Lila and shared with her a deep sense of "family" connection, she would never be comfortable "living off" her young friend. No, if Rebecca acceded to the plan – and that was a *big* IF – it would be simply to keep a watchful eye on Lila.

From outward appearances, Lila appeared to be a light-hearted, confident young woman. But Rebecca, who was no stranger to caregiving or sorrow, noted the deepening shadows beneath her friend's eyes and her thinning figure. Lila wasn't happy – hadn't been happy – at least not since her parents were killed in that terrible boat crash in late 2009. Lila's flippant remarks and her joking and teasing belied her true feelings. But Rebecca sensed that a heart-wrenching pain was hiding not far beneath the surface, and suspected that the slightest scratch would bring it up.

And why not? Rebecca wondered. *Why shouldn't she feel the loss of her parents, still? What could be more natural?*

But natural or not, that terrible loss – or *something* – was harming Lila's health; physically, mentally and spiritually. Rebecca also noted with seasoned awareness that Lila seemed to be afraid of a committed romantic relationship. When pressed by Rebecca about it, Lila defended her single lifestyle by claiming "all the good men are gay" and "I'm going to focus on my career, first." Even now, Lila had formed a new "friendship" with the perfectly eligible (and extremely handsome, Rebecca thought) corporate attorney, 32-year-old Ryan MacDonald. Yet it appeared to Rebecca that Lila was going to run away to Maine simply because Ryan might be pressing her for more of a commitment.

I can't believe he's still hanging around and they haven't even had sex yet. He must be more of a White Knight than I thought!

"Hello, hello – Rebecca, you soo totally haven't heard a word I've said for the last 10 miles!" accused Lila. "This is our EXIT!"

Automatically, Rebecca glanced in her rear view mirror to check the traffic situation. "I'm not ignoring you – I'm driving," she said, defending herself. The green and white Exit 113 sign loomed large, and Rebecca switched on the car's directional signal.

"You'd be halfway to Canada now if I wasn't with you," continued Lila. "Where were you, anyway?"

Where was she? In the past? No, she wouldn't be feeling so hopeful if she was stuck in the past. "Just thinking about your plan," Rebecca answered, lightly. "Wondering if it *is* possible to pack up and relocate. Start a new life in Maine." She hesitated. "Did you text Ryan about it?"

Lila bristled. "Why should I tell HIM? What does he care?"

"Oh, Lila, I think Ryan does care! I think he cares a great deal."

"OK, well, so maybe I'm the one who doesn't care," Lila said, defensively. "I don't want to feel like I've got to tell someone what I'm doing every minute of the day. Especially a man. Anyway, he'll know soon enough that I've left the firm, 'cause Joe Kelly will tell him."

Rebecca knew it would be useless to continue the "Ryan cares for you" conversation, even in a more-subtle form. Lila was smart, sometimes too smart for her own good. Lila was also stiffnecked and stubborn. If she thought Rebecca was pushing her toward Ryan MacDonald, she would almost necessarily turn and run in the opposite direction. Rebecca allowed the subject to drop. "Which way do I go off the exit?"

"We can only take a right off this exit," Lila said. She shifted in her seat. "We've got to get a brand name for our new business," she continued, intently. "What do you think of *The Egg Ladies?*"

Rebecca thought a moment. "I always liked the word 'ladies' – it's so old-fashioned," she said.

"That kills it, then." They both laughed.

"Thanks a lot," said Rebecca. "You had me picturing myself all laced up in a Gunne Sax gown, collecting eggs from our adoring chickens. I knew I'd never get to own a Gunne Sax!"

"What's a gunny sack? Some type of a grain bag, isn't it?"

"You don't know Gunne Sax?!"

"Totally clueless."

Rebecca was momentarily transported to the charm of a past life, a bygone era. She happily described the hippy-style gowns from the '70s and '80s to Lila. "The dresses were romantic; long and flowing, made with calico and lace and velvet, especially around the bodice," Rebecca elaborated. "I always dreamed I would wear a pink and ivory dress with a black bodice and go tripping through a green pasture with Prince Charming."

"Sounds, um, sweet."

"It *was* sweet. But it was a very sweet time back then." Rebecca sighed. "I couldn't afford a Gunne Sax, though – they were terribly expensive. So I tried to sew one, but the dress ended up looking like something Lily Munster would wear. Plus those long dresses look much better on taller girls, like you, dear—doesn't Route 202 take a turn to the left soon?"

Lila glanced down at her phone. "Not yet – three more miles. Mmmm, Lily Munster. Not sure I like that image, but I'm seeing the long dress picture. It's not bad. I almost think it's something we can work with."

"I sewed most of Amber's baby clothes, you know. I love to sew."

At the mention of Amber, Lila gave a little start forward in the passenger seat. "I can't believe we're doing this! So, what did she say? I bet Amber loved the idea of an organic egg farm in Maine!"

Rebecca hesitated. "I told Amber we were going to Maine for the weekend, but I didn't tell her I lost my job. I didn't..."

"What?! You didn't tell Amber 'The Plan?'" Lila interrupted. "I was counting on her support. I know how conservative you are, Becca!"

"I wasn't sure what was going to happen, and I thought ..." Rebecca broke off lamely. "I don't know what I thought."

"She's going to have to know sooner or later," said Lila. "Especially about the losing-your-job part."

"Well, let it be *later*," replied Rebecca, with a small but determined shake of her head. "At least until after the weekend. Do you think we should bring a hostess gift to your Twitter friend?" she asked, changing the subject. "That's what I do when I go to visit someone."

"Of course you do; that is so totally 20th century! My aunt used to bring my mother a set of peach-colored bath soaps. She brought the same set every time," said Lila. "But, hey, why not? Let's get Miss Jan Hastings something. Who says we have to live in the mean and nasty 21st century?"

"Who says the 21st century has to be mean and nasty?" countered Rebecca. "Who says we can't make the 21st century what we want it to be?"

"R-i-g-h-t," said Lila, dryly. "What should we get for a hostess gift?"

"Oh, I don't know; I don't know your Twitter friend. Plus I'm not sure how many shopping opportunities we'll have before we get to Sovereign." Lila regarded the rural landscape with a wry grin. "Good point," she said. "Let's just stop at the next store and see what they've got, OK?"

"Sounds like a plan."

"You're going to love Miss Jan Hastings, Becca," Lila continued, her enthusiasm waxing as the distance to Sovereign waned. "I just know it!"

Rebecca smiled. "I'm prepared to fall in love with her immediately."

"I've been reading her tweets for a couple of years, feeling the envy grow inside me, hating my job; hating everything about my life—except you," Lila added quickly. "Wanting to kiss corporate America good-bye, yet not knowing where I wanted to go or what I wanted to do. Feeling as though I didn't belong, that I was lost in a world that was growing stranger and stranger …"

" 'curiouser and curiouser' like *Alice in Wonderland*…"

"Exactly! Except whenever I followed Miss Hastings' tweets, and then I felt as though I belonged in her little world, and that I should be the one taking her and Matilda to school to see the kindergarteners, or stopping in at Ma Jean's Restaurant to get a piece of apple pie and learn the local gossip, or worrying about the foxes…"

Lila broke off and gazed out the window.

Rebecca glanced at the pensive face of her friend, and knew Lila wasn't seeing the snow-covered landscape that whizzed past. The pine trees. The frozen lake. The empty cottages, waiting for summer visitors. "I hope you're not going to be disappointed, Lila," she cautioned.

Lila shook herself back to the present. Her laugh had a sharp edge to it. "Of course I'm going to be disappointed – we're all going to be disappointed! That's the way of the world, these days. EVERYBODY is disappointed in life."

"It doesn't have to be that way," said Rebecca, quietly.

"No?" challenged Lila.

"No."

"Prove me wrong, then. Do this with me, and I'll never ask you for anything else again. Please, Becca!"

Rebecca was thoughtful. "You know I'd do this crazy adventure and a whole lot more to make you happy, and … and … to maybe help you find some sort of a settled life."

Hens and Chickens

"Translated from Rebecca-speak: 'Find a man and settle down and have babies,'" Lila said, drily. "I know, I know what you're thinking – you think I might find love and romance in Sovereign, Maine. You just can't stay away from that 'Lila needs a lover' mantra!"

"Lila needs a solid, steady partner, not a lover," Rebecca corrected. "And if he happens to turn out to be a lover—well, so much the better!"

They both laughed. Suddenly, Lila spotted the junction sign for Route 9/202. "Turn left up there," she said, pointing to an upcoming intersection.

Rebecca slowed her vehicle, and pulled over into the left-hand turn lane. "Is this it?"

"This is it!" said Lila. "Let's go see what Sovereign, Maine can do for BOTH of us. Who knows, you might even find a 'solid, steady partner' yourself!"

"Me?!" Rebecca said, blushing. She felt a thrill of … what? … pulsating through her. Hope? Excitement? New life?

Funny, it had never occurred to Rebecca that she might find love and romance in Sovereign, Maine!

Chapter 4

. . . .

Sovereign, Maine

$\mathcal{A}$s Rebecca Johnson and Lila Woodsum turn onto Route 9/202 to wend their way up through the picturesque central Maine towns of Albion, Unity and Troy – shaking the dust of corporate America off their feet (and possibly their old way of life) – perhaps this is a good time for us to take a little turn ourselves. Perhaps, my pips, you'll allow me a fleeting divergence as I describe to you their destination, Sovereign, Maine, and the way of life toward which they are motoring.

In beginning, I must point out that there is no longer a town center in Sovereign, so if you are expecting to see a country village with charming shops and brick houses, such as in neighboring Unity, for example, you'll be disappointed. For public buildings, the town of Sovereign now boasts only four: the post office, the elementary school, the Union Church, and the volunteer fire station. Each of these four establishments stands independent like sentinels on four different corners in town. There is also Gilpin's General Store, situated halfway through Sovereign on the Bangor Road, which acts as the glue that holds the community together.

Sovereign, like its neighbors Troy and Thorndike, is a farming community, with the prospect of miles of rolling pasture ground relieved only by private and town wood lots, a brook or two (and more than the requisite number of vernal pools and frog ponds) and a few rolling hills on the Dixmont side of town. A long-shuttered pea canning factory lingers near the abandoned train station, as though hoping to hear the revived *hiss* from the steam engines. I will not say that Sovereign is NOT picturesque – especially in the sweet greenery of June when the scent of fresh-cut hay is in the air and the dairy cows lounge in the cool shade of gray clapboarded barns. But natural physical beauty is not that which has put Sovereign on the map. No, it is the character of Sovereign's residents – an inner beauty – for which the town is known, and which has ensnared many wandering hearts (including my own).

Jennifer Wixson

There are places in the world populated entirely by good people—people whose natural inclinations are compassionate, kind and thoughtful. Evil does not exist in these communities, having never been able to get a toehold here despite many varied and numerous runs at it over the centuries. These places are like frost-pockets of goodness, where the killing frost comes just in time to quench all budding attempts at small-mindedness and mean-spiritedness. No one knows for sure what has allowed these few places in the developed world to flourish in their innocence and decency, but most of us believe that – somewhere – these places exist. Sovereign, Maine, home to Miss Jan Hastings and 1,047 other souls, is one of these places.

If you were ask Wendell Russell, 64, a direct descendant of the original 18th century settlers of Sovereign (and Miss Hastings' neighbor to the south on the Russell Hill Road), Wendell would probably credit this phenomenon to something special in the soil – the soil which fed the trees and the corn and the cattle and ultimately the people of Sovereign that contributed to (or maybe even caused) this "kindness gene" in the good-hearted DNA of Sovereign descendants. "Wal, you know, they was all eatin' the same peas, beans and corn when they stahted out," Wendell would explain. "Or maybe 'twas the apples, 'cause, you know, they all shared the same pips back then."

They all shared the same pips back then.

I have often wondered over the years if perhaps the early settlers of Sovereign shared back then because they had to share. Perhaps those folks necessarily learned to squash the natural greedy instincts with which we are all encumbered, and, by such squashing, the less-hardy traits of self-denial and grace were enabled to grow. Perhaps the early settlers, who, in 1790, pushed the boundary of white civilization when they moved out past Fort Halifax into the wild, unorganized territory of the District of Maine, recognized that they were dependent upon one another. They knew that fellowship mattered; that one man by himself would likely fail in this wilderness environment – especially in the God awful winters – but that a community might survive if they stuck together. Perhaps during one long, forsaken winter they awakened to the universal truth (which is so often overlooked or discarded) that it doesn't matter which man owns the most oxen or which woman has the prettiest ribbons on her bonnet or which child is the smartest—no. None of that matters in the end. What matters in the end is how many times in this life

Hens and Chickens

we have said "*I love you*," how many burdens carried by others we have offered to share, how many kind words we have bestowed upon children, the downtrodden and the elderly.

There are those, of course (especially in neighboring Unity), who claim that religion is at the root of the modern day conviviality and goodness of the citizens of Sovereign. Some of these diviners point out that Sovereign was settled by Universalists (such as Miss Hastings' family), whose steadfast belief in the doctrine of universal Christian salvation for all mankind likely encouraged the humanist notions of empathy and charity to abound. There are other oracles, however, who swear that the first settlers in the area were Quakers (Wendell Russell's ancestors), who migrated to Sovereign from Philadelphia via Massachusetts and who brought with them into the wilderness brotherly love and acceptance of all.

But despite what some might think (given my sacred profession), I don't believe that organized religion has had a hand in creating the benevolence that exists today in Sovereign. I believe it was more likely a smaller appendage, the pint-sized hand of a trusting child tucked inside the calloused paw of a parent or friend or neighbor, which beget the goodness of this community, a community in which kindness, forbearance and mercy have always been—sovereign.

You might suspect, then, that Sovereign folks are vigilant against marauding bands of evil and greed, and are quick to bolt their doors lest one snake in the garden despoil the whole spot. But if you think that, "you'd be wrong," as Wendell Russell would say, chuckling at the notion of locking his door, which doesn't even have the hardware for such a queer operation.

Sovereign folks have always been welcoming folks (and I know this from personal experience). It doesn't matter who you are or where you harken from or even how often you beat your dog or curse your wife – you are gladly received into communal fellowship. For Sovereign folks know that Evil cannot stand and look Good in the face. Wickedness always averts its eyes before the divinity of Love, which is Lord of All. Evil requires fear upon which to feed, much like a vampire requires fresh blood, and when a soul seeks shelter in love it has nothing to fear.

Therefore, miraculously, the thieves who move to Sovereign become philanthropists, giving away 10 times all they ever thought to steal; the swindlers revert to upstanding citizens and members of the Board of

Selectmen; the gossips and back-stabbers transform into harbingers of good news, ferreting out all the spots in Sovereign where the fiddleheads and mushrooms are hiding and sharing that precious information with their neighbors; and the liars and the cowards convert to Methodism and develop altruistic and self-abnegating streaks that occasionally have to be treated with doses of blackstrap molasses, especially in February (so perhaps there is some small validity to the theory that organized religion has benefited Sovereign).

When the hippies arrived en masse from the Eastern cities in the '70s, Sovereign folks found their alternative, back-to-the-land lifestyle refreshing and rejuvenating. Instead of driving the young people away or shunning them like some other Maine communities, residents of Sovereign welcomed the hippies, enjoying the opportunity of revisiting the forgotten arts of homesteading – the cabin building, the root cellaring, the butter churning, the maple sugaring – arts that had been passed down by their ancestors for nearly 200 years but which had been in danger of becoming extinct in the 20th century. Sovereign folks, especially the old timers, thought it was a "darn good chance" to have the hippies homestead in Sovereign, bringing the past back to life, and thus once again the town's open-door policy enlarged the general goodness of the community.

Perhaps, at this point, you might be raising "a doubter of truth," as Wendell Russell would say; a yellow caution flag. Perhaps you might be secretly suggesting to yourself something such as: Why – if the town of Sovereign is so truly good and gracious – why aren't more than 1,048 souls living there? Why doesn't *everybody* live there?

Why doesn't everybody live there?

Unfortunately, this is not a question I can answer. For I do live in Sovereign, now (in an old homestead on the Cross Road). But if you don't inhabit our benevolent community, perhaps you can answer that, or answer the even more germane question: *Why is my town not more like Sovereign?*

You might also be conjecturing to yourself: If goodness and mercy are as catching as the storyteller claims (like the measles), why has charity not infected every community throughout the world?

Alas, I can't answer that question, either. I myself have often wondered why everyone has not cast aside smallness and meanness of spirit and embraced unconditional love. I suspect, however, it's because we are humans, and for some reason, we humans are more attracted to the glitter of gold than to the dull grunge of charity.

(Forgive me; I *am* now stepping briefly up onto my soap box…)

Even as I write this little tale, I can hear fear-mongers beating the drums of bigotry and narrow-mindedness so loudly that some citizens have armed themselves with pistols and semi-automatic weapons to use against one another. My Quaker spirit revolts thinking that brother is now preparing to rise up against brother, and father against son! What is this: *what is this*, I ask, if not the sly, sneaky hand of greed at work broadcasting ignorance and fear, so that the purveyor of this distress might benefit from fear's largess?

But fear cannot – *will not* – gain its desired end. For evil has a way of swallowing itself up completely, like the Cheshire Cat, and someday – SOMEDAY, I promise! – evil will disappear altogether from the face of the earth!

But we must help, my pips; we must help.

We must be kind. We must be compassionate. We must be thoughtful. We must be just. We must not be small-minded or mean-spirited. We must not give evil a toehold in our communities. We must act in a communal spirit of love and fellowship that acts as a killing frost. We must create our own frost pockets of goodness.

With our help, the tide will turn. Already, there is an undertow of mercy at work scrubbing evil from our hearts, washing the meanness of the 20th century – the greed, the self-indulgence, the fear – safely out to sea. This sandblasting of a new heaven and a new earth in the 21st century will take some time, requiring from all of us patience, courage, hope, forbearance, love, black flies—and a sense of humor.

And in the meanwhile, the folks of Sovereign will keep their doors unlocked.

Chapter 5

· · · · · · ·

Mike Hobart

$\mathcal{S}$hortly before dusk on that same Friday, our hero, 30-year-old Mike Hobart, pulled his late model baby blue pickup truck into the near-empty parking lot at Gilpin's General Store, a 110-year-old mercantile situated, as I have mentioned, about halfway into the bounded settlement of Sovereign on Route 9/202. During Sovereign's heyday of 1910-1950 (when the population broke the 2,000 threshold), five general stores operated in strategic locations around the 10-square-mile settlement, including two near the old train station. Now, however, only Gilpin's remained. Yet sadly even this legendary landmark was threatened with extinction, thanks to the advent of big box stores and the ever-widening shock waves of the Great Recession.

Hobart, a self-employed carpenter who lived "off the grid" in Sovereign in a post and beam cabin he built himself, hopped from his 4-wheel-drive pickup. The six-foot, well-muscled Hobart, a hand-some, steady man, inhaled deeply, drawing the pleasant scent of wood smoke deep into his lungs. He pulled his denim jacket closer around his muscular chest and tugged his Boston Red Sox cap down over his neatly-cropped, dark-blond curls. The February sun had set, and he felt the winter chill creeping into his jean-clad legs. Hobart kicked a frozen snowplow remnant out of his path sending shards of icy snow scattering like marbles across the parking lot. "Score!" he said aloud.

Hobart strode confidently through the double-glass fronted door of Gilpin's and called out a greeting to the owner. "Hey, Ralph! Where are ya?" The store smelled like Murphy® Oil Soap, and Hobart knew that business must be slow since Ralph Gilpin was cleaning again. He took off his leather gloves and stuffed them into his back pocket.

"Ain't likely to be too far off," replied the wizened shopkeeper, hustling up to the front with a floor mop in hand. Ralph Gilpin, 76, great-grandson of the original Gilpin's founder, kept the store pretty much the same as it was during Charlie Gilpin's time, with a few exceptions, most notably electricity. A true general store, Gilpin's still sold everything from hardware to dry goods to wedding dresses. Ralph's rubber sole shoes squeaked on the wet wood floor as he advanced. "Haven't seen ya in a while, Mike," Ralph said, extending an arthritic right paw. "Watch the floor." The two men shook hands.

"I been working, Ralph. How's Maude?" asked Hobart, easily.

Ralph leaned the mop against a shelf of canned peas and corn, and settled in for a friendly chat. "She's Maude! Cookin' up a storm for some church fundraiser goin' on tomorrow. They're tryin' to get money to replace them pew cushions. She's doin' jest fine; but I ain't so good," he added, plaintively.

"Anything serious?"

"Jest the rheumatism. But it's to be expected in February, I guess."

"Sorry to hear it," Hobart replied, sincerely. "Seems like spring's gonna be early this year, so hopefully we'll all feel better soon."

"Ya ain't got no reason to feel poorly—yer just a kid!" Gilpin scoffed.

"Don't try to make me feel sorry for you, Ralph; it won't work. You haven't aged a day since I moved down from Maple Grove 12 years ago," Hobart rebutted, easily. "Tell Maude I said 'hello' and that I'll stop in for some of her bread pudding soon."

"Ya better come ovah for suppah tomorrow night and tell Maude yerself," the wiry shopkeeper suggested. "She misses having a handsome face around."

"I thought that's why she kept you," joked the carpenter, hooking a thumb into the belt loop of his jeans. "Five o'clock on Saturday, still?"

"Ayuh," said Ralph. "Show up then and there might be some dessert left."

As if on cue, a wall-clock melodically chimed the rural Maine supper hour. "Hey, do you still have some drill bits back in Hardware?" Hobart said, turning to business.

"Think I might," replied Ralph. "What big project ya got goin' on now, Mike?"

"Aw, nothing major; just finishing Joe Cooley's sugar house up on Common Hill," said Hobart. "He wants it done before the sap starts to run, which looks like it could be any day now. I broke my bit earlier. Cheap piece of junk from the big box store."

"Tut, tut," said Gilpin, a bit gleefully. "Ya get what ya pay for. What size ya need?"

Hens and Chickens

Hobart glanced around the thinly peopled store. He had been planning to buy just the one drill bit, but he changed his mind. "I'll take a complete set, if you've got one," he answered.

Ralph Gilpin grinned and twisted adroitly like a player on an old timers basketball team. "Follow me, Mike," he said, threading his way among half-empty but neatly-stocked shelves to the back of the store where the hardware department was situated. "Let me see – ah, here she is. Complete set of drill bits; only $32.95."

Hobart knew he could purchase the drill bits much cheaper at the big-box store in Bangor, but then, as Ralph said, you get what you pay for. Plus Hobart regularly tried to support Gilpin's dwindling business. "I'll take 'em," he said, reaching for the plastic package and stuffing it into his jacket pocket.

"Anything else ya need?"

Hobart was about to reply in the negative, when a movement two aisles over caught his eye: a waif of a woman with a shiny black coif like a chickadee was carefully examining a display of old-style kitchen items. She was a stranger to Hobart, who knew everyone in Sovereign. The carpenter thought she was the freshest, most natural-looking girl he had ever seen. *What was SHE doing in Sovereign, Maine?* Unconsciously, he caught and held his breath.

The old shopkeeper followed Hobart's stare. "Pretty gal, ain't she?" said Ralph, in a confidential tone. "The two of 'em came in the store a short while ago, wantin' somethin' for a hostess gift."

Hobart only half heard the shopkeeper. His gaze was arrested by a set of defensive dark eyes – brown? hazel? – which had discovered his open admiration. On a subconscious level, Hobart knew that he was being rude. But on the physical level, he discovered that he couldn't – wouldn't – look away. Her appearance in Sovereign was so unexpected and sweet, much like the first bright crocus blossom that thrusts up through the deep, white snow in March. The young woman dropped her eyes first. Hobart exhaled, and only then realized that he had been holding his breath.

Who WAS she and where did she come from? More importantly, where was she going and when could he see her again!

"T'other one said they was goin' to spend the weekend with a friend up on Russell Hill," Ralph Gilpin continued. "Maybe I better go see if they found what they was lookin' for."

"Stop," said Hobart, putting out his arm and catching the skinny shopkeeper by the chest. "Let me go. It might be something heavy."

"I kin still throw a bag of grain, Mike," said Gilpin, slightly offended. "I might be feelin' poorly but I ain't dead yet."

"Listen, put the drill bits on my tab, Ralph, and shut up already. I'll see you and Maude tomorrow night."

Hobart felt a strong magnetic pull toward the girl, much like the undertow of a full-moon tide. He practically floated into the aisle where two women – the mysterious girl and an older female companion with shoulder-length brown curls – were openly admiring the general store's line of vintage kitchen utensils. Hobart watched the waif examine a wooden rolling pin that was crafted by a local woodworker. She rolled and twisted the polished honey-colored wood from one slender hand to the other, and he knew he would never think of a rolling pin as ordinary ever again.

"Can I help you?" Hobart offered, putting himself forward.

The young woman looked at Hobart's ball cap and denim jacket, and then regarded him with suspicion. "You work here?" she challenged, a slight flush spreading across her cheeks. She lightly placed the rolling pin back on the shelf and turned to face him.

"Lila," her companion whispered. "The man is offering to help!"

Lila! Hobart whispered the name to himself. Was there ever a more perfect name than *Lila?*

"I worked here when I was at Unity College," Hobart answered, ingeniously. "Sometimes I still help out when Ralph is busy."

The girl glanced around the empty store. "Right. Busy, like … tonight?"

Hobart blinked.

An impish look appeared in the girl's hazel-gray eyes. "Hey, maybe you COULD help us," she said. "Maybe you could help us find a BRASSIERE for my friend?"

"*Lila!*" exclaimed the motherly brunette, blushing. "Pay no attention to her," the woman continued, hastily, taking Lila's arm and pulling her close. "It's a private joke. We're looking for a hostess gift. For a friend."

Unabashed, Hobart tried to recollect what special item from Gilpin's would make an appropriate "hostess gift." He pushed his baseball cap back a bit and scratched his head. Hobart surveyed the nearby shelves helplessly to see if he could find a suitable suggestion. A bachelor who lived alone, Hobart's familiarity with household accessories was limited.

Hens and Chickens

"Uh, sure, give me a minute," he said.

The young woman, Lila, regarded him with growing impatience. "He's clueless," she said. "Let's go, Becca."

"Wait!" It occurred to Hobart that if he knew to whom the gift was to be given, he would have a better shot at finding a suitable item. "Who're you visiting?"

The motherly woman spoke up. "We're spending the weekend with Jan – well, perhaps you know her? – Jan, uh, Jan – Lila, what's Jan's last name again?"

"Miss Hastings?!" exclaimed Hobart, relieved. "Oh, everybody knows Miss Hastings. You're … friends?"

"She's one of my Tweeps," said the girl. Her voice held a hint of boredom. "One of my followers on Twitter," she added, as an explanatory note.

Hobart felt his masculine hackles rising. She had pre-judged him and dismissed him! She thought he was a clodhopper who chopped wood (well, he did chop his own wood) and lived under a rock (he did not) and who didn't know anything about social media or smartphones or designer coffee (he did know all about it, and that's some of why he lived in Sovereign). Hobart's pride was nicked, and for a moment he wanted to play the *doofus*. But the carpenter's better nature prevailed and he shrugged the slight off. Unfortunately, some of the shine dissipated from the young woman, as well.

Hobart felt himself sinking back down to earth. The sparkling light seemed to get sucked out of the shop. He even noticed a dust bunny that had eluded Ralph trying to sneak under the nearest shelf.

Hobart turned away from the waif to address her much more pleasant companion. "I'd take Miss Hastings a bag of black oil sunflower seed if I were you," he said, kindly. "Matilda loves bird seed – and Miss Hastings loves Matilda, as do most of the children in town."

"You know her?" the woman asked.

"Everybody knows Miss Hastings."

"Of … course."

"I hear she has about 4,000 followers on Twitter, now." Hobart couldn't resist letting the girl know that he wasn't a complete idiot.

"Hmmm," said Lila, with the faintest interest.

"Sounds perfect," interjected her friend. "Bird seed it is – OK, Lila?"

Without waiting to hear Lila's reply, Hobart strode over to the 'Seed and Feed' aisle, and hefted a 50-pound sack of black oil sunflower seed onto his shoulder as easily as though it was a small child. He carried the bag up to Ralph Gilpin, who was now awaiting them at the checkout counter.

The girl, Lila, reached the counter next, and pulled out her wallet to pay for the birdseed. "How much?" she asked Ralph, ignoring Hobart. She smiled sweetly at the apron-clad shopkeeper.

"Twenty-five dollars," replied Ralph, grinning, a bit foolishly. Hobart noticed he altogether neglected the register.

"Plus tax," Hobart added.

"Right—plus tax," said Ralph, hastily. " 'Twould make it $26.25." The shopkeeper rang the sale into the register and the drawer *chinked* open.

Lila pulled two $20 bills slowly from her wallet. Hobart waited patiently, shifting the heavy weight of the birdseed on his back. As the girl reached over the counter to hand the money to the skinny shopkeeper, he caught a whiff of some kind of natural soap scent. Hobart took the opportunity as she leaned closer to examine her face. Her smooth skin was pale and wan, and dark shadows ringed a set of pretty hazel eyes. *So, things were not as they appeared on the surface!*

Transaction complete, the girl pocketed her change. She smiled again at Ralph, this time more naturally, and Hobart, who was still assessing her, caught the edge of her smile and felt the sun burst through the clouds. She moved toward the glass door with the grace of a white tail deer and Hobart felt his innards tighten and his hopes begin to rise again.

Wake up, Mike, he cautioned himself, feeling bedazzled. *Don't do anything stupid.*

Behind him, Ralph slapped the register drawer shut, breaking Hobart's heady trance. The carpenter waved a parting salutation at the shopkeeper, and exited the store.

The girl reached the car first, and pulled her navy wool jacket closer against the dampness of the evening. She shivered slightly. "You can put it in the backseat," she said. "Our stuff is in the trunk."

Hobart shifted the birdseed to his left shoulder and opened the car door with his right hand. He tossed the 50-pound bag into the back seat, straightened up and brushed off his front. "Tell Miss Hastings I'll stop by in the morning and unload the bag for her," he said.

Lila started to protest, but her companion stopped her. "That would be lovely; we'd appreciate that," she declared. "Thank you … Mr. …?"

Hens and Chickens

"Hobart. Mike Hobart," he said, offering up a firm hand.

The motherly-looking lady shook his hand in a friendly fashion. "I'm Rebecca Johnson and this is Lila Woodsum," she said. "Thank you so much for helping us, Mike. We city girls really appreciate it!" She glanced at Lila, but the younger woman had already retreated to the passenger side of the vehicle and clambered inside. Rebecca sighed, but gave Hobart a reassuring smile. "See you tomorrow, then," she said.

"You can count on it," said Hobart. He backed up deliberately in the direction of his pickup, and nearly tripped over a bag of Ice Melt the shopkeeper had just set outside. "Dammit, Ralph!" Hobart ejaculated under his breath. But he recovered himself enough to lift a hand in a farewell salute as Miss Hastings' mysterious visitors – Lila Woodsum and Rebecca Johnson – pulled out of the parking lot and motored off in the direction of Russell Hill.

Life is looking up! Hobart thought to himself. Then he hopped back in his truck and drove home to his cabin in the Sovereign woods.

Chapter 6

• • • • • • •

Miss Hastings

Lila affected not to see the friendly wave offered by the good-natured Mike Hobart, whom they had just left at Gilpin's General Store. Instead, as the two friends motored back onto Route 9/202, she stared out the passenger's side window pretending to be engrossed by the view. Within moments – and almost despite herself – Lila felt herself falling under a sort of a trance produced by the rolling central Maine farmland. The area was white and fresh from a recent snowstorm, which looked in the gathering dusk as though a rapid hand had indiscriminately unrolled a thick layer of cotton over everything: trees, rocks, old haying equipment, and pregnant hay bales. It was a surreal-looking world, almost the polar opposite of what they had left behind in Boston: noisy, rushing, with concrete and steel cityscapes.

Rebecca accelerated onto the gray ribbon of road. "I don't understand why you're so *mean* to men, Lila," she said. Her tone was gentle, but there was implied criticism in the remark. The car passed through a puddle of melted snow and water *plashed* against the underside.

Lila absently ran her fingers through her short black locks. "Am I?" she said. "I guess I am," she continued, without waiting for a response. "Guys bug me. They always look at me like I'm some kind of raw meat."

Rebecca sighed. "Men admiring women is a very natural thing," she said. "How else do you ..."

"Puh-leeze, Becca," Lila interrupted, hazel eyes flashing. "Spare me the, 'How else do you expect to find a husband?' lecture. Why can't men just like me for ME?"

Rebecca almost pouted. "Well, maybe because you don't give many men the *opportunity* to get to know you for *you*," she pointed out. "Like that Mike back there; he was perfectly friendly and helpful and ..."

"And practically jumped my bones on that old hardwood floor!"

"I didn't see it," said Rebecca, somewhat primly.

"You weren't standing in my shoes," Lila said. "Listen, I'm sorry if I was rude and embarrassed you."

"You didn't embarrass me – well, not much anyway. I'm just worried about you for your sake, Lila dear!"

Humbled, Lila realized that it was true – Rebecca's concerns were never for Rebecca, they were always for Lila. Since Lila's mother had died, Rebecca had stood the place of parent to her, a fact for which Lila was eternally grateful. *It's about time I started acting grateful, instead of fighting her like an immature child all the time!*

"I'm sorry," Lila apologized. "I promise—I'll try to do better."

Mollified, Rebecca fell silent, allowing the subject to dissipate naturally on its own accord. If she had known the jumbled mass of thoughts and feelings in Lila's breast, however – feelings of anger, confusion, and frustration – perhaps she might have continued the conversation.

There were times – such as this evening – when it infuriated Lila that she was born a woman, not a man. She regularly threw on oversized clothes or tried to hide her sexuality beneath a man's shirt, desperately wanting to be treated as a person first and foremost, not as a desirable woman. Unfortunately, no matter what she did, Lila couldn't disguise her vulnerable feminine allure from any man aged 12 to 112. Sometimes she longed to go and live someplace where she could just be known for herself – Lila Woodsum – not as a sexual being. *But unless I move to a place without any men at all,* she thought, *that isn't likely to happen.*

"Isn't this beautiful countryside?" Rebecca gushed. "I love the fields; the farm land. It's so romantic, isn't it, Lila?"

"Uh, totally. Just what I pictured . . . oops," Lila said as they drove by the intersection for Route 7, the Moosehead Trail. "I think we've gone too far." Lila regarded her phone. "We should have taken a right turn a couple of miles back onto Russell Hill Road, sorry—I spaced it."

Rebecca turned around at the next driveway and within five minutes they were lumbering slowly up the Russell Hill Road, a secondary back road that was lined with snow-covered stone walls and ancient maple trees. The sun had set, and Rebecca proceeded cautiously as the light quickly evaporated from the evening sky. "I didn't realize how dark it is in the country without street lights," she said, laughing nervously.

Lila spotted the shoulder of a full moon pushing its way up the eastern horizon. "Don't worry, there's a full moon on the way up," she said.

Hens and Chickens

As Lila gazed at the ethereal moon, all her negative thoughts evaporated. Instead, she felt a germinating sense of wonder and belonging.

"How do you know the moon is rising, Ms. Nature?" Rebecca teased.

Lila tittered, like a jubilant chickadee. " 'Cause I can see it through trees!" She pointed to the crest of the moon now clearly visible through a stand of pine trees halfway up the hill. The waxen moon was rising fast, and looked like a roving spotlight as it glided up the hill. Lila's heart skipped a beat. "Stop a sec, will you?"

Rebecca obliged, and Lila rolled down her window and breathed in a lung-full of sharp, fresh winter air. "Ahhhh!" she exclaimed. "Now THAT is the smell of liberty!"

"It's certainly a far cry from Boston," agreed Rebecca. "Or even Roxbury, for that matter."

While the two friends sat companionably in the parked car, the fat moon slipped up beyond the outstretched fingers of the treetops and floated majestically in the night sky. Lila spied a pair of white tail deer cavorting under a gnarled crabapple tree in the sparkling snow-covered field to her right. She pointed the deer out to Rebecca, exclaiming; "I haven't seen a deer since I was a kid!" The two deer, hearing Lila's high-pitched voice through the open car window, scampered off to the safety of the thick woods that lined the far edge of the field.

"Omigod, look at that tree, Becca!"

A hundred yards up, on the left hand side of the road, an ancient maple tree was split dramatically in half and stood like a sentinel, with one thickset arm raised to the sky and the other bent graciously to the ground. Into the devastated grounded limb, some imp had carved steps into the wood, creating a set of stairs that led up into the leaf-less canopy of the tree.

"The tree is welcoming us!" cried Lila.

"It *is* very unusual," said Rebecca, putting the car in gear and proceeding cautiously up the hill toward the split maple tree.

"Hey, there's a big old house in back there," Lila continued eagerly, leaning forward in her seat. "I don't see any lights, though. Maybe it's a foreclosed home?"

Rebecca's gaze moved beyond the broken maple to examine the darkly-shadowed mass of multiple large buildings set back fifty feet from the road. "It looks pretty run down," she said, hesitantly.

"Omigod, this must be the old homestead Miss Hastings wants us to buy! Pull in the driveway!"

"Oh, do you think we should? Isn't Miss Hastings expecting us?"

Lila felt a struggle within herself. Part of her wanted the immediate gratification of seeing the possibilities that awaited them. The other part, however – Lila's better nature combined with her long-standing habit of timeliness – won out. "Keep going; we're late already," she said, dropping back into her seat. "I told Miss Hastings we'd be here by 5:00 and it's nearly 5:30, now!"

"I think it's best to see the place tomorrow, in the daylight. Maybe it will look … better. And we certainly don't want to keep Miss Hastings waiting."

"You're right, Becca, as usual."

A half mile further up the road, just beneath the crest of Russell Hill, Miss Jan Hastings' shingled two-story cottage hove into view. The former music teacher's residence was an awkward design, looking as though two very different houses had grappled for the same foundation, and, neither having won, agreed to share the same spot, cold-heartedly embracing one another. Frozen snow *crunched* beneath the car tires as Rebecca pulled carefully into the narrow curved driveway. Light spilled cheerfully from multiple windows in the antique cottage as though a merry party was underway inside. Rebecca parked the car next to an attached side shed near an obvious break in the snow bank, which – although not the front door – signaled the common entrance. Before she and Lila could unbuckle their seatbelts, however, the side door flew open allowing bright light to escape and spilling a short black shadow across the white snow.

"Hello, dahrrrlings!" a full-bodied woman's voice called, by way of a greeting. "I'd offer to help you with your things but I've got my slippers on!" Loud gleeful laughter followed. "Come in, come in, you DAHRRRLINGS!"

Lila and Rebecca exchanged glances. Was this—Miss Jan Hastings?

Rebecca obediently picked up her purse, exited the car and *crunched* up the snowy path to the shed. Lila, however, took a moment to gather her overnight bag from the trunk, and, as her eyes became accustomed to the light, surreptitiously examined her Twitter friend. If this was Miss Hastings, the woman was nothing like Lila had pictured! Jan Hastings was closer to *80* than 60, with an elfin frame and wiry gray-black hair that looked like wriggling worms trying to escape a fork of turned up earthen sod. Most astonishingly to Lila, Miss Hastings was dressed in a smart black wool suit complemented by a frilly white blouse, and sported oversized chicken slippers on her nylon stocking feet. Miss Hastings was so obviously a singular character that, even if Lila hadn't known anything about her at all, she would have warmed to her immediately.

"You must be SO tired, poor dahrrrlings," Miss Hastings gushed, shooing Rebecca into the house. She stood vigil at the door stoop, however, awaiting Lila. "Matilda and I thought you'd nevvver get here!"

When Lila reached Miss Hastings' outstretched arthritic hands at the shed door she was moved by an inexplicable feeling of tenderness. She dropped her bag on the shed floor, reached down and hugged the tiny woman. "I'm so glad to meet you, at last," Lila said, sincerely.

"Dahrrrling!" cried Miss Hastings, squeezing Lila's cold fists affectionately with her warm, knobby hands. "Let me look at you—you're even lovelier than I thought! Come in, dahrrrlings! Come in!"

Lila felt hot tears fill her eyes, and she brushed them away. *I'm home,* she thought. *I'm safe!*

"Here's Matilda, waiting for you!" said Miss Hastings, leading them from the shed into a small mudroom.

The shed had been bright, but the mudroom was lit by a single 40-watt incandescent bulb and Lila blinked to help her eyes adjust to the sudden dimness. She noted a Shaker-style coat rack, draped with several scarves and shawls, and a large dark object in the corner. The room smelled like sweet sawdust.

Miss Hastings pulled a dark cloth from the object in the corner, and a faint *chirping* could be heard. "Wake up, dahrrrling – we have visitors!" A caged, black and white hen blinked once or twice, and then hopped down from her perch onto the sawdust.

"Oh, she was asleep!" said Rebecca. "You shouldn't have woken her up on our account!"

"Well, we won't spend too much time with her because I just know you're hungry and tired! But I just couldn't resist introducing you."

"Hey, Matilda," said Lila, schootching down on the floor next to the large wire cage. "I've seen your picture and heard all about you!" The hen began hopping and clucking in response, sending sawdust flying everywhere. "Omigod, she's so cute," Lila added.

Lila stuck her finger into the cage and waggled it in a friendly fashion. Matilda cocked her head sideways and eyed the worm-like digit. She clucked disapprovingly, then darted forward and attempted to grasp Lila's finger with her yellow beak. "Hey, she BIT me!" Lila said, withdrawing her finger quickly with a disconcerted laugh.

"She probably thought your finger was a worm," said Rebecca quickly, excusing the chicken.

"Poor dahrrrling! Did she hurt you? She just wants some treats— I've spoiled her. Here, like this," said Miss Hastings. She mysteriously produced a shiny black seed from her suit pocket and pushed it through the wire bars. Matilda leaped forward, grasped the seed as though it was a bug, and immediately gobbled it down. Miss Hastings cackled with laughter; "Matilda LOVES sunflower seeds!"

Her words reminded Lila of the 50-pound bag of black oil sunflower seeds that the friendly Mike from Gilpin's General Store had slung effortlessly into the back seat of the car. "I almost forgot – we brought you a hostess gift," she said.

"You dahrrrlings! You didn't need to bring me ANYTHING – just your wonderful selves!"

"It's for Matilda," Lila said. "A bag of sunflower seeds. Some guy named Mike – Mike Hobart – is going to come by tomorrow and unload them."

"Mike Hobart—what a dahrrrling boy! He built the most WONDERFUL cabin in the woods on the other side of town. We're so fortunate that he's stayed on in Sovereign after he graduated from Unity College!"

"He built his own cabin?" asked Lila, becoming interested, in spite of herself.

"Oh, yes! From pine trees that he cut all from his very own land! He's so industrious, just like the boys used to be in MY day," said Miss Hastings. "Now THAT was a VERRRY long time ago!" Once again, she broke into a gale of hearty laughter.

Rebecca nudged Lila, her blue eyes carrying an unmistakable communication: *See? Maybe you shouldn't be so quick to judge him!*

"He seemed very nice," said Rebecca.

"A simply DAHRRRLING boy," repeated Miss Hastings. "But tell me again, why is Mike stopping by tomorrow?"

"To unload the bag; it's pretty heavy – 50 pounds," said Lila.

"OOoo, my goodness, 50 pounds – haaaahaaaa!" Miss Hastings burst into laughter again. "OOoo, I see – well, it's perfectly understandable!"

"Not to me," said Lila, confused.

Hens and Chickens

"I'm sorry, I'm not following, either," added Rebecca.

"Dahrrrling, that 50-pound bag of birdseed will outlast both me AND Matilda!"

Lila felt herself blushing. *He had made them buy a 50-pound bag just so he could have an excuse to come over tomorrow!*

Embarrassed, Lila leaned forward to hide her blush. She picked up a few black seeds that had somehow escaped onto the mudroom floor and tossed them back into the cage. Matilda immediately jumped on the sunflower seeds. The bird swallowed the seeds whole, cocked her head at Lila and squawked for more. Lila laughed. "Totally cute," she said. "I can see why you love her!"

"Back to sleep, you little rascal!" said Miss Hastings, draping the black cloth over Matilda's cage. "Come into the kitchen, dahrrrlings, and we'll get you poor things something to eat, too!"

In the large, eat-in kitchen, Rebecca and Lila were met by a blast of dry heat from an antique black wood cookstove. A copper tea kettle steamed merrily atop the stove, while a pot of corn chowder, which had been set expectantly on the bun warmer, sent the sweet scent of buttery corn throughout the kitchen. A round oak table with matching pressed-back oak chairs was set cheerily for three diners.

Lila dropped her overnight bag onto the aged-gold linoleum floor, and leaned toward the scorching woodstove. "Ahhhh, I could get used to this!"

Miss Hastings wagged a knobby index finger toward a Canadian rocker, judiciously situated between the woodstove and a kitchen window. The rocker was piled high with soft green cushions. "Sit right there, Lila," said Miss Hastings. "You'll have toasty toes in no time!"

Without waiting to be invited twice, Lila unbuttoned her pea coat, slipped it off and plopped into the rocker. "Wake me when it's breakfast time," she said.

"Shouldn't we take our boots off?" worried Rebecca.

"OOoo, don't be silly! I want you to be perfectly at home, dahrrrling," said Miss Hastings, as she moved about the kitchen, preparing to put the meal on the table.

"Rebecca DOES take her boots off at home," interjected Lila.

"Rebecca! Yes, my poor dahrrrling," said Miss Hastings, removing a pitcher of cold milk from the fridge and setting it on the table. "I know all about you! Well, you can take your boots off if you want to."

Rebecca stepped onto a red braided rug, pulled off her neat ankle boots and set them next to the front door. "Oh?" she said, in a curious manner. "What has Lila tweeted about *me*?" She shrugged out of her coat, and draped it over the back of a kitchen chair.

"OOoo, I know EVERYTHING, don't I, Lila?!" said Miss Hastings, cackling gleefully again. "I know all about that mean old boss, calling you into her office this morning and giving you the boot! After 16 years!"

"At least she helped me carry my things to the car," Rebecca said smiling. "That's more than Joe Kelly, our vice president—he didn't even say 'goodbye'!"

"Tight-fisted old twit!" empathized Miss Hastings. "We'll show him, won't we, Lila?"

"Totally!" said Lila. She stretched her long legs luxuriously, like a cat, and contentedly surveyed the mustard-colored room. The kitchen sported brightly figured red and yellow curtains that matched the table cloth, and was decorated with chicken and rooster themed knick-knacks and tchotchkes. Lila felt completely at home.

"Isn't there *something* I can do to help, Miss Hastings?" asked Rebecca. "We didn't mean for you to go to so much trouble for us!"

"OOoo, please call me Jan, dahrrrling!" replied Miss Hastings. "Nobody calls me Miss Hastings, except for my former students – which – haaahaaa! - are most of the people in Sovereign!" She cackled again. Her voice had the full-bodied richness of an opera singer.

"Mike Hobart told us EVERYONE calls you Miss Hastings," Lila said.

"That dahrrrling boy!"

"And I think 'Miss Hastings' is lovely," added Rebecca. "It has such old-fashioned charm to it—that's what I'm going to call you!"

"Me too," said Lila.

The modest meal went off splendidly. Homemade corn chowder was complemented by a loaf of Amish-made whole wheat bread and farm butter. When the supper things were cleared away, Lila retreated to her rocker by the stove while Rebecca and Miss Hastings settled in at the kitchen table over dainty teacups of black tea.

"Lila says that you were a music teacher in town, Miss Hastings?" Rebecca said, stirring a large dollop of raspberry honey into her tea.

"OOoo, yes!" Miss Hastings exclaimed, joyfully. She waggled her knobby finger at Rebecca. "I know every single child in town by name

Hens and Chickens

– AND I know their children and grandchildren!" She burst into gales of laughter again.

"Are you still teaching?" Rebecca asked.

"Thank goodness, NO! I retired YEARS ago. I should really be dead by now — haaahaaa! – I'm 87!"

"Omigod!" cried Lila, who had only been half listening, but now was startled by this piece of information into sitting upright in the rocker. "Eighty-seven? That is totally amazing!"

"Lila!" expostulated Rebecca.

"Don't stop her—I ADORE honesty! That's why I ADORE children. They're nothing BUT honest! Just the opposite of all those mean, nasty politicians and corporations!"

"You got that right," agreed Lila.

"Matilda and I still go to school two or three times a year, just to get our honesty FIX!"

"You take Matilda to school?" Rebecca said. "Oh, I bet the children love that!"

"OOoo, the dahrrrlings; they do get SO excited when they see Matilda! We sing. We dance. We parade! We do WONDERFUL things!"

Lila sank back into the rocker and closed her eyes, listening abstractedly to Miss Hastings and Rebecca chat about children, teaching and music. Lila had formed an image of her Twitter-mate in her mind over the years, and she had discovered during the last hour that Miss Jan Hastings was soo NOT the masculine, work-booted chicken-lover she had imagined but a petite, educated, dynamo of a woman who definitely marched to the beat of her own drum.

I wonder what I'll be like when I'M her age? Lila mused to herself. *Will I be even half as lovable and fun?*

Lila's thoughts wandered of their own accord back to the unexpected meeting with Mike Hobart, who had tricked them into buying the largest size of birdseed so that he could have an excuse to see her again. Lila tried to convince herself that she was mad at him, but she failed. *Neat trick,* she said to herself, impressed by his ingenuity.

But … would someone like Mike Hobart – if he did come to love her – still feel the same way in ten years? Twenty years? Thirty years? Forty years? Lila wondered.

At this point in her life, Lila wasn't interested in any kind of romantic relationship. Still less was she interested in casual sex. She had her reasons, and they were good reasons. Lila believed that her attitude toward sex, romance and dating was nobody's business but her own (not even Rebecca's). She was aware that most men thought she had a chip on her shoulder. But if they only knew! The burden she was carrying was more like a mountain, than a chip!

A tangled mess of painful thoughts and feelings rose up in Lila as she toasted her waif-like frame by Miss Hastings' cookstove. While half-listening to the conversation between Miss Hastings and Rebecca, Lila flashed back to a recent "dating" experience from the winter, just prior to her friendship with the new corporate attorney Ryan McDonald. After much encouragement, Lila had accompanied some young friends to a bar, friends who had been pushing her to "get out and meet some men." When her friends abandoned her for the dance floor, Lila was approached by a well-dressed, well-heeled accountant, who, with gin and tonic in hand, confidently appropriated the vacated seat next to her.

After the usual blather of introductions, the accountant smirked and offered to buy Lila a drink. Bothered by the whole "dating" charade, Lila decided to put her cards on the table. "Look, if you're just here for sex, don't waste time on me," she said, honestly. "I don't care what happens tonight, I'm not going to have sex with you. So, if sex is all you want— feel free to go find someone else."

No sooner were the words out of Lila's mouth than the accountant stood up, collected his drink, and hustled off after another prospect. He never said "goodbye" – and he never looked back.

Lila cringed at the recollection. *What would Mike Hobart say if I threw the same announcement at him? Would he, too, pick up his "toys" and walk away?*

Or maybe – just maybe – might there be HOPE here in Sovereign, Maine?

Chapter 7

·······

The First Day of
the Rest of Her Life

ila awoke early the next morning to the sound of—quiet; complete and absolute stillness. It was almost as though the cozy corner bedroom was soundproofed, and for a few moments the quiet had an unsettling effect on her.

But as Lila snuggled deeper into the generous featherbed of the Rose Room – enjoying the smell and sensation of the crisp, clothes-line-dried sheets on her brass bed – she gradually came to hear a most amazing sound: the beating of her own heart! Lila listened to the regular *thump-thump-thump* of that steady organ and wondered: *When was the last time I listened to my heartbeat?* A thrill of happiness pervaded Lila's being, and her heart picked up its tempo in response.

The Rose Room was every bit as lovely as Lila had pictured. The wallpaper was a blushing antique ivory, strewn with bouquets of wine-colored roses that trailed fragile, fairy-like green stems. A ruby red paint-ed floor peeped out beneath a multi-colored, hand-braided rug, and the painted trim around the ceilings and windows was a muted off-white. Old-fashioned lace curtains adorned the two matching windows, one of which – the tall one – faced east, and the other was a smaller, dormer window facing south. The corner room had a slanted ceiling into which the dormer was set, and the room was sparsely but tastefully furnished with two antique chairs and a pine dresser with matching, attached mir-ror. A blanket chest, which was tucked under the slanted ceiling, boasted several black and white framed family photos and a dish of rose-scented potpourri. Enchanted, Lila lay back upon the feather pillows and tucked the pink patchwork quilt up under her neck.

I wish I was a kid again! Lila thought. Hot tears filled her eyes, tears for the innocence she had lost in childhood. She dashed them away, angrily, but not before tasting the warm wet salt of despair.

I'm not going to feel sorry for myself anymore! Lila vowed. The time-worn (but no less useful) quote popped into her head: "Today is the first day of the rest of your life!" Lila repeated the phrase several times to herself until she gradually came to believe that its meaning might just possibly be relevant, even for her situation.

Maybe it's not too late to be a kid again. After all, look at Miss Hastings! She's still a kid – and she's 87!

A faint knocking at the bedroom door interrupted Lila's musings.

"Lila? Are you awake?" whispered Rebecca. She opened the door slowly and peeked inside. "Isn't this wonderful?"

"Totally awesome," said Lila. She saw that her barefoot friend was shivering in her white cotton nightgown. Lila patted the spot in bed next to her. "Quick, get in here before you freeze to death!"

Rebecca scooted into bed and the two women giggled as they pulled the covers up to their necks. The sun was just beginning to send searching golden rays over the swaying tops of the pine trees, which were visible through the eastern-facing window.

"I feel like I went to sleep and woke up in Never Never Land!" exclaimed Rebecca. "Do you think Miss Hastings will let us live here forever?"

"The question is," said Lila, "will Miss Hastings LIVE forever!"

Both women giggled again. "She already has, hasn't she?" replied Rebecca.

"Can you imagine anything more totally amazing!"

"How does she do it, I wonder? Do you think she eats a lot of honey-bee propolis? I've heard that's supposed to have wonderful medicinal effects?"

Lila absently traced the outline of a rose on the wallpaper above her head. "I think she's just a kid that never grew up," she said. "Miss Hastings is the female version of Peter Pan." Lila paused, her hand dropping to the quilt. "Do you think we get a chance to start over in life, Becca?" she asked, earnestly.

Rebecca laughed, her tousled mop of loose brown hair making her appear 10 years younger than her 48. "I hope so, because I already have!"

"No, seriously."

"Seriously! But let's not go there. It's such a lovely start to the day and I don't want to dredge up old stuff—for either of us. Let's just agree

Hens and Chickens

that 'starting over' is a necessary and welcome part of the human experience and decide – to – start – over – today!" Rebecca emphasized her statement by pulling her feather pillow out from under her head and lightly bopping Lila over the head with it.

"PILLOW FIGHT!" exclaimed Lila. She responded by whacking Rebecca over the head in return and a playful battle ensued. White down feathers flew like fat April snow.

The house beneath them had been quiet, but, suddenly – in the midst of the pillow fight – a muted sound of music was heard from a distance below. "That sounds like someone practicing their scales," said Rebecca, pillow arrested in mid-air. "It's coming from the studio, that funny-looking part of the house where Miss Hastings used to give piano lessons."

"Omigod, do you think it's her?" said Lila. "Her hands are sooo arthritic."

"Where there's a will—there's a way," replied Rebecca. "It's either Miss Hastings or a ghost playing her baby grand piano since there's nobody else but us in the house! Shhh, let's listen." Rebecca clutched her pillow to her chest and sank down onto her knees on the thick mattress. The scales ended abruptly, and were soon replaced by a light-hearted and lively piano concerto. The two women listened in worshipful silence.

"Oh, my goodness! That's 'A Midsummer Night's Dream'," gushed Rebecca. "It's Rachmaninoff's arrangement of Mendelssohn's Opus 21!"

Lila nodded, dumbly. The exquisite music had unlocked something deep inside her, something that had been hidden away for nearly 20 years. A little girl was slipping out from behind iron bars and moving ethereally from Lila's flesh into the dusty motes of light that expanded through the eastern window. Lila's heart hurt, and she pressed her hand to her chest to keep her heart from breaking.

Oh, no! Oh, no! she cried, silently. *Don't go! Don't leave me!*

The vision – an eight-year-old dark-haired, pony-tailed girl in a red sweater and Oshkosh B'Gosh® blue jeans – turned and lifted her chubby hand to Lila in a cheerful greeting.

Why, she's saying, 'Hello!' noted Lila to herself. *She isn't GOING; she's COMING—coming home to me!*

There are very few of us who remember the day, the moment, when our childhood ends. For most of us, the sun sets on our innocence gradually, sliding down over the western horizon like a toboggan run down over a long, steep slope. We are never really conscious of the moment we reach the bottom of the slope; we just know that one day we wake up and the toboggan ride is over. For a few unfortunate children, however, the loss of innocence is so tragic and dramatic, that it is a miniature Hiroshima which is etched upon the back of their eyelids forever. Alas, our heroine Lila Woodsum was one of these children!

However, whether or not the loss of childhood innocence is duly noted and recorded in our diaries, the day in our adulthood in which our childlike sense of trust and wonder is reborn is always remarkable, a truly momentous day – and one that we will never, ever forget. Today was THAT DAY for Lila Woodsum.

Lila closed her eyes, and allowed her heart to be healed by the sound of the music. The piano acted as a cauterizing agent, singeing evil memories from her heart and replacing them with a cool, deep well of goodness. The healing was so powerful, so real, that Lila could feel a sort of harmony welling up like water in the inner most core of her being. She felt herself floating, as the water buoyed her up, propelling her forward. The water parted like a prayer from her skin. She was cleansed; reborn, an innocent child of God once again.

The music stopped. Lila caught and held her breath, willing the piano to begin again.

"Do you think we should get dressed and go down, now that she's done?" Rebecca asked, tossing the covers aside in answer to her own question.

Lila was unwilling to shake off her dreamy state. "You go," she said. "Use the bathroom first. I'll be down in a few minutes."

She lay back in bed, savoring the moment. Yes, it was a red letter day. And the day was only just beginning!

When Lila cheerfully joined Rebecca and Miss Hastings in the kitchen 15 minutes later, she discovered a bowl of hot oatmeal awaiting her on the bun warmer of the wood cook stove. She pulled up a chair, and helped herself to a slice of buttery toast.

"Dahrrrling, there's a pot of coffee on the stove and some hot water for tea, if you prefer," said the good-hearted spinster. "I told Rebecca that you've now seen the extent of my cooking abilities!" Miss Hastings burst into gales of laughter. "Corn chowder and oatmeal!"

"You don't cook?" said Lila, surprised.

"Never got the hang of it – I was a working gal! I took my noon meals at school, and then most of the rest of my meals came from Ma Jean."

Hens and Chickens

"Who is Ma Jean?" asked Rebecca, curiously.

"She runs the local restaurant—she and I are two peas in a worn out old pea pod! She's still cooking, and she's 82! We'll go down and see Ma Jean for lunch today – she cooks out of a renovated farmhouse on the Bangor Road – and then you city people can see how good food SHOULD taste!"

"Oh, it sounds lovely!" said Rebecca. "We'll treat! And don't you worry about any more meals while we're here, Miss Hastings. I may not be Ma Jean, but I'm a pretty good cook, if I do say so myself!"

"When do we meet with Mr. Russell about the house?" Lila asked, anxiously.

"Don't you worry, dahrrrling, you won't be able to sneak out of town without meeting Mr. Wendell Emerson Russell! He's more excited about your visit than I am! I told him you'd be down around 9:30 a.m., and you don't have far to go—he's just down the road!"

"We saw an old house on the way in last night – with a neat tree out front," Lila said. "It had steps in it! Is that the place?"

"That's it—the old Russell homestead! She's even older than I am and so is that tree! The children call that the Staircase Tree!" said Miss Hastings. "Would you believe, that poor maple tree was struck by lightning 15 years ago but like some of the rest of us old fools around here simply refuses to die!"

"Looks like a stairway to heaven," said Lila; "for us, anyway."

Rebecca nodded. "I'm starting to think it *is* a sign," she said, taking a sip of her coffee.

"Well, it'll be a GIFT from heaven for Wendell if you two take over that mausoleum," said Miss Hastings. "I told him I wasn't going to get involved in this transaction in any way, shape or fashion – except to get you up here to meet with him – BUT dahrrrlings, don't do anything you don't want to do!"

"That's my job," Rebecca spoke up, quickly; "to counterbalance Lila's enthusiasm." She smiled. "But I think I'm falling under Sovereign's spell a little bit, too."

"Hallelujah!" said Lila, reaching for a second piece of toast.

A loud double knock on the shed door startled the three women.

"My goodness, I didn't hear anyone drive in," said Miss Hastings, turning half-way around in her chair. "Come in, dahrrrling!" she called, toward the mudroom.

"It's just me, Miss Hastings—Mike Hobart," replied a husky masculine voice. "I'm here to unload that bag of birdseed."

"OOoo, dahrrrling! Come in; come in! We're just finishing our breakfast."

A freshly-shaven Mike Hobart entered the kitchen. "I hope I'm not too early," he said, standing sheepishly on the entryway rug in order to keep from tracking up the kitchen with his wet boots. "Am I interrupting?"

"I'm done," said Rebecca, flashing the handsome young carpenter a welcoming smile.

"Me too," said Lila, cheerfully. She wolfed down the last crust of toast, and pushed her oatmeal bowl away.

Rebecca glanced at her young friend in surprise. She had been expecting more of the same cold-shoulder treatment from Lila, but this was almost, well – friendly!

"I'll help you, Mike," said Lila, rising from her chair. "Where do you want us to put the birdseed, Miss Hastings?"

"OOoo, there's a big old aluminum can in the shed, dahrrrling, where I store the birdseed to keep it away from the mice and squirrels. There's plenty of space in it! Haaahaa!" Miss Hastings made a vain attempt at containing her laughter. "Take your time, dahrrrlings!" she added, winking meaningfully at Rebecca.

Once in the shed, Lila opened up her budget of concerns. "I wanted to help so I could apologize for last night," she said, holding the door as Mike Hobart passed through with the birdseed on his shoulder. He plopped the 50-pound bag onto the wooden shed floor with a *thud*. "I was kind of bitchy, and I'm sorry," she continued.

"I didn't notice," Hobart lied, generously. He pulled out his pocket knife and slit open the plastic bag.

"Thanks, but I know you're lying."

"You do not," he said, smiling. He dumped the bag into the aluminum can and a shower of dust floated up into the air. "You don't even know me."

"Maybe not, but I'm pretty good at recognizing liars," Lila said. "Not that I think you lie regularly," she added hastily, "but that's how I can tell. Real, regular liars have a 'just-washed-my-face' look of innocence that is so fake. I can spot it a mile away!"

"Sounds like you've had a lot experience with liars."

Hens and Chickens

"Too much," said Lila. She grimaced slightly, and shook her head.

As Lila tossed her head, shiny black feathers of her hair floated up and then settled back down in disarray. Hobart wanted to lean over and push the feathers back into place. His hand moved toward her head instinctively, but he stopped himself just in time. "Well, you won't have to worry about *that* if you stick around Sovereign," he said. "It's just the opposite around here. Folks in Sovereign are so brutally honest that sometimes I wish they *would* lie, at least enough to save my pride once in a while."

Lila tittered, which sounded to Hobart like the cheerful chuckle of a bird. Once again he was reminded of a black-capped chickadee, the Maine state bird. Hobart's heart lifted in response and he wanted to make her laugh again so that he could hear it once more. Her cheeks – so pale yesterday under the harsh fluorescent lights of Gilpin's General Store – were flushed rosy this morning. Her hazel eyes, which yesterday flashed warningly 'STAY AWAY,' now twinkled with the openness of friendly interest.

Hobart folded up the plastic bag and tucked it onto a gardening shelf in Miss Hastings' shed. "How long are you staying in town?" he asked, hopefully. He pushed his baseball cap back on his head and looked around for something to lean against.

"We're not sure, actually. We're thinking of buying the Russell place and raising chickens – selling eggs – something like that."

Hobart whistled, long and low. "The old Russell place! That would be great. It needs some work, but she's a beautiful old post and beam." He leaned against the potting bench and folded his arms.

"Post and beam?" said Lila, hazel eyes fixing earnestly on Hobart's ocean-blue ones. "What's that?"

"Timber framing; it's a type of construction," he replied. "The old timers around here built their houses using trees they cut off the land. They hand-hewed thick beams from the logs and hooked 'em together like this," he said. He used his hands to demonstrate the interlocking construction.

"Seems like you know a lot about it?"

"I built a post and beam cabin 10 years ago, when I was in college. I learned a lot from my mistakes! My cabin's a lot smaller, but it's the same general principal."

"Have you ever been inside the Russell place?" Lila asked, wistfully.

"Yep, a couple of times. Not long after I first moved here, and then last fall Wendell showed me around again. I know he's tried to sell the house and some of the land, but – and I probably shouldn't be telling you this – with the economy and all, I don't think he's even had an offer."

"Do you think the place can be repaired? Tell me the truth—I know you will," Lila said, lightly touching the carpenter's arm, seeking reassurance.

Her touch electrified Hobart's arm. For a moment, the wood shed floor beneath his feet drifted away from him. "Maybe," he said, steadying himself. "The main house is solid, but the hen pen needs work, especially if you're planning to raise chickens. It's definitely worth saving, though."

"Omigod, that is soo great!" Lila exclaimed. She let go of Hobart's arm and clasped her hands excitedly. "Can you come with us today and look at it?"

Hobart hesitated. "I want to—but …" he broke off.

"But what?"

"But I really shouldn't get involved at this point, as much as I'd like to help you. You and, uh, your friend …"

"Rebecca," said Lila.

"You and Rebecca should let Wendell show you the place and then – if you're still interested – then I'll help you in any way that I can."

"We'll pay you, of course," said Lila, quickly.

"Well, we can talk about that later, too."

Lila cocked her head sideways and regarded him carefully. "You're not one of those guys that go around rescuing damsels in distress, are you?" she asked, pertly.

"I could be," admitted Hobart, slightly abashed. "Is that a bad thing?"

"Not if you give the damsels a chance to rescue YOU once in a while," Lila retorted.

"Oh, that's easily arranged," he replied, "if you stick around long enough."

"It's a deal, then!" said Lila. She stuck out a thin white hand for the carpenter to shake.

Hobart chuckled, a deep husky sound. "You're pretty confident," he said. He grasped Lila's outstretched hand but instead of shaking it, he held it securely in his callused paw. "Must be you're not afraid of spiders and mice," he added, teasingly. "You do know that place has been empty for something like – 10 years?"

Hens and Chickens

"Seven," corrected Lila. She unhurriedly pulled her hand away him. "But who's counting?" She leaned down and scooped up a small handful of sunflower seeds from the storage can. "Come with me," she said suggestively to the carpenter.

Hobart needed no further encouragement. He followed Lila back into the mudroom, where she uncovered the cage containing Matilda. She dropped to her knees and made soft *cluck clucking* noises. Matilda responded eagerly, hopping down from her perch and over to the side of the cage.

"Here you go, Sweetie," Lila said, holding a sunflower seed through the metal bars. Matilda snapped up the seed and greedily returned for more. Lila laughed happily, and repeated the process until her handful of seeds was fed out. She stood up, brushed herself off and regarded Hobart proudly, as though she had just scaled Mount Everest.

"You really like chickens, don't you?" asked Hobart, marveling at the difference between this radiant young woman and the surly chit with a chip on her shoulder whom he had witnessed last evening at Gilpin's General Store.

"Allow me to introduce myself, Sir," she said, with a theatrical flourish. "You are now addressing one of *The Egg Ladies* of Sovereign, Maine!"

Chapter 8

·······

The Old Russell Place

Lila was correct in her numbers—the old Russell place had been vacant for seven years. The locals tell me that if the house hadn't had such a good roof on her she would have been down into the cellar years ago. And if Pappy Russell had known the deal he was getting in 1956 when he complained about the price of that standing-seam metal roof, my sources say he might not have complained so loudly. (Although the old timers say that Pappy always did need something to grumble about, he being the most malcontent Sovereign ever produced.)

But these days the old Russell place was "leaning towards Sawyers," as Wendell Russell, Pappy and Addie Russell's grandson, would say, a tongue-in-cheek way of inferring she was pretty run down. It's a long story why the place has been empty so long, but the short version is that because nobody in the direct Russell line wanted to live at home after Addie Russell died (Pappy being long gone by then), especially not the eldest son George, who inherited the place. So Addie's booming egg business was sold off and the house was left vacant. When George Russell died and his only child Evelyn Russell didn't want the place, Cousin Harold moved in for a short while (but apparently he didn't stick), and eventually one after another everyone died, until Wendell – who was the last of Addie and Pap Russell's grandchildren still standing – finally inherited the family homestead.

By the time of his grand inheritance, Wendell Russell was 62-years-old. All the glorious dreams he had once husbanded of reviving the old egg business had long since evaporated. Wendell had joined the U.S. Navy and had travelled the world. He calculated that – although he loved the egg business – he was probably too old now and certainly not rich enough to start a new farming operation, let alone restore a run-down house, attached hen-pen and various out-buildings. "Wal, you know, it's all I kin do to keep my pickup runnin' nowadays," Wendell said to Ralph Gilpin when he first came back to live in Sovereign two years ago.

But Wendell, a bachelor now retired after 35 years in the service, figured that he would like to live a quiet life in Sovereign, Maine on the old homestead. If he could find someone to rent or buy the old house and a few acres, he could afford to finish out his days comfortably in Bud's place, a three-room outbuilding set back in the woods 100 feet from the main dwelling that the hired hand Bud Suomela had built. At the time our tale begins, Wendell had been installed in Bud's place for two years, however, he had yet to find anyone foolish enough to consider taking the old home place off his hands. Until now.

Now, Miss Hastings had scratched up a possible candidate for the place – "a young gal from Massachusetts," he'd been told – and if she was interested, Wendell, who was raised on the farm by Grammie Addie, was to teach her the egg business. Wendell Russell, always the optimist, thought that life might be taking an altogether advantageous and interesting turn.

The great meeting was scheduled for 9:30 a.m., and needless to say, Wendell sauntered over to the house more than an hour early. He'd kept the old place plowed out and left his truck parked in the driveway in winter, shoveling a winding, narrow path around the back of the house to the hired man's cabin.

After Wendell received Miss Hastings' initial telephone call yesterday morning, he worked at the house most of the day, replacing books and knick-knacks onto the shelves from which the winter squirrels had knocked them, and just generally putting the house in order for today's viewing. There was no electric service to the house (the power had been turned off before Wendell's time) so instead of running a vacuum Wendell took the smaller rugs outside and shook them. He swept off the larger braided rugs and pushed the broom over the wide pine floors. He started the wood cookstove in the kitchen and ran it all day – trying to remove some of the musty odor – burning up left over maple firewood from the woodshed as well as a pile or two of old yellowed papers and envelopes that had been stacked on the kitchen table. Wendell also kept the pot-bellied parlor stove in the great room burning, and, with both wood stoves working in tandem, was able to bring the temperature up to 70°F, on the ground floor, anyway. The upstairs, well, the upstairs with its three full bedrooms and attached open chamber was still chilly, but it

Hens and Chickens

was Maine and it was February, and Wendell, who could remember when a glass of water froze one winter upstairs when he was a child, thought altogether it was pretty warm up there.

Instead of driving, Lila and Rebecca elected to walk the half mile down Russell Hill to the old Russell place. Rebecca had done up the breakfast dishes so that Miss Hastings, who had reiterated that she was NOT getting involved in the transaction in any way, shape or fashion DAHRRRLINGS, was able to retire cheerfully to her computer room at her usual time to send out a few tweets to her followers on Twitter.

"Take your time, dahrrrlings!" she called out, as they were dressing for their walk.

"Be sure and tell your Tweeps what we're up to!" cried Lila back. She pulled on her boots and looked up at Rebecca. "I can't believe we're actually doing this," she said.

"Me either!" replied Rebecca, grinning. She stuck her wool hat firmly on her head, and together they marched off.

Although technically still winter, the bright sun had begun its annual tilt toward the northern hemisphere, casting lukewarm rays over the snow-covered countryside. The two women promenaded down the paved road, talking and laughing, enjoying their escape from the city and their former servitude with Perkins & Gleeful, Inc. An agitated red squirrel scolded them noisily from the branches of a maple tree, and the white smoke from Miss Hastings' wood stove danced its way up into the atmosphere until it vanished into thin air.

Lila noted the chattering squirrel, the dancing wood smoke, the cloudless blue sky and felt irrepressible excitement. "There's so much LIFE here!" she cried, twirling about in a little circle.

"It's wonderful! I bet you can get a lot of great tweet ideas. Did you update your status on @PGleeful?"

Lila skipped ahead, and spun around to confront her former partner. "I DID NOT!" she said, wagging a finger. "I don't give 'two hoots and a holler' about @PGleeful, as Miss Hastings would say! I'm gonna create our own avatar on Twitter and steal all my Tweeps from Perkins & Gleeful! It's all part of The Grand Marketing Plan—I've been thinking about it all morning."

"All morning? It's only 9:30 a.m.!" said Rebecca, smiling. "By the way, dear, can we tweet from here?" she added. "Do our cell phones work?"

"Yep. Don't worry, Becca; Amber can still reach you."

Rebecca, who had not been thinking of her daughter but of the possibility of Ryan MacDonald trying to contact Lila, didn't reply.

"By the time Kelly and Queen Cora get around to hiring a social media coordinator, @PGleeful won't have any followers at all!" Lila exulted. "And THAT will cost 'em some big bucks to remedy."

Wendell, always on the alert, heard their chatter and laughter before Lila and Rebecca turned into his plowed driveway. He pulled a small black comb from his jeans pocket and leaned over to glance at the image offered up by the round shaving mirror hanging judiciously next to the black soapstone kitchen sink. Wendell dragged the plastic comb through his gray hair, which was long enough to tickle the collar of his plaid flannel shirt, and checked the results. Satisfied, he went to the shed door to greet the two women.

After general introductions in the shed, Wendell ushered Lila and Rebecca into the traditional country kitchen of the Russell homestead. " 'Tain't like 'twas when I was a kid," he apologized, in his drawling laid-back voice. Thirty-five years of travel around the world in the U.S. Navy had not been able to scrub the peculiar Maine accent from his voice. "But, you know, she's still got some life left in her; if you use her right."

"Omigod!" said Lila, overcome by an amalgamation of eagerness and intoxication. Agitated, she surveyed the antique farm kitchen, uncertain where to begin poking and peering first. The cupboards? The drawers? The upstairs?! The sheds! She felt like a kid at Christmas, and worked hard to quash an impulse to run around the sprawling house yelling, "Yiiipppeee!"

"You don't live here yourself, Mr. Russell?" Rebecca asked politely, pulling off the blue, hand-knitted wool mittens that Miss Hastings had given her to wear on her walk.

"No—oh; I live next door in Bud's place," replied Wendell, jerking his thumb over his shoulder in the general direction of his residence. "He was the hired hand here for, oh, perhaps thutty years. Bud – course, he didn't have no family of his own – he helped Grammie Addie with the egg business, 'specially after Pappy died."

"Do you mind if I look around by myself?" Lila interjected. "I don't mean to be rude, but …" she broke off, her eager, beseeching eyes pleading with the old bachelor.

Wendell chuckled, low and cheerful. "Ayuh, you go ahead. I ain't got nuthin' to hide," he said. "And if you got any questions, I'll be right heah."

Hens and Chickens

"Coming with me, Becca?" said Lila, flashing her friend a backward, thoughtless glance.

"No – you go ahead, dear," responded Rebecca. "I've got a few questions for Mr. Russell." She took off her jacket and draped it over the back of a chair. Lila, without waiting for further permission, disappeared into the bowels of the house.

Wendell chuckled again, and turned his bright blue eyes upon Rebecca. "You kin call me Wendell," he said, bashfully. "Nobody ever called me 'Mister Russell.'"

Rebecca smiled. "Then, I'm 'Rebecca,' please." There was an awkward pause, but she soon latched onto a comfortable conversational course. "Miss Hastings said you were in the service, Wendell?"

"Ayuh; retired Navy." Wendell pulled chair out from the table and brushed off the cushioned seat with the palm of his hand. "Wouldja like a cup of tea? I brought some tea bags and some water ovah from Bud's place."

"I'd love some," said Rebecca, gracefully taking the proffered chair. "You had to carry water? There's no running water in the house?"

Wendell set a nickel-plated tea kettle onto the wood stove to boil. "Wal, the pump is shut off—course. It's a private well, with awful good tastin' water," he said. He hitched up his pants and lowered his solid six-foot-plus frame into the chair opposite his guest. "But there ain't been no powah turned on in this house …" he paused to reflect; "wal, not since Cousin Bob left seven years ago, I guess."

Surprised, Rebecca glanced up at the darkened electric lamp dangling above the kitchen table. "I didn't even notice there *was* no electricity!" she said.

"Wal, you know, the place was built before there WAS powah, and so they was pretty particular 'bout where they put their windows."

"Did you grow up here, Wendell?" encouraged Rebecca. "I'd love to hear the history of the place."

Pleased with Rebecca's friendly familiarity, Wendell Russell flashed a wide grin, revealing a gold upper incisor. "Wal, I sorta growed up here. This was my grandparents' place, and their grandparents' before 'em. I stayed here summers and holidays when I was a kid – my Dad was Grammie Addie's youngest – and then I lived here 'n helped Grammie Addie with her egg business after Pappy died. She kept 400 laying hens— Rhode Island reds, mostly. She supplied all the local general stores with eggs and she also had a regular egg route. She was awful shaap, Grammie Addie. 'Twas quite a real business, you know; 'twarn't no pin money thing," he concluded, proudly

"Oh, my goodness—400 laying hens! That seems like an awful lot!"

"Old Pappy – before he died – he designed the hen pen jest for Addie's egg business," said Wendell, jerking his thumb over his shoulder again, this time in the direction of the attached shed. "Pappy and Bud built the shed into thet little hill out back so there was lots of protection for the hens on the Noth side. And on the South side he put in all them tall windows you kin see from the driveway. There was always lots of light down in the hen pen—chickens need 'bout 14 hours of daylight to lay good," he instructed. "They could git out into the outdoor pen into the sunlight anytime they wanted to, 'cause it was all fenced in. Course, Addie did need to put in some artificial light in wintah. She wanted to git the most she could out of them hens as long as possible, and she darn near made every one of 'em go the full two years."

"Two years?"

"Thet's pretty much what you get from a laying hen," said Wendell. He was interrupted by the shrill whistle of the teakettle as the water on the wood stove began to boil. Wendell got up to make the tea, hardly missing a beat. "Grammie Addie had a system; every year in the spring – 'bout Patriot's Day – she'd staaht 200 replacement chicks, and by the time fall rolled around and the new hens was ready to lay, she'd thin the old ones out and move the new ones into the hen pen. Course, there was a time in between when we had to clean the hen pen out—we did thet in summer. Now, THET warn't my favorite job! I never could stand the smell of ammonia," he added wryly, wrinkling up his nose at the offensive memory.

"I bet not!" Rebecca said, laughing. She accepted a cup of hot tea from his hands, and set it quickly down onto the shiny figured oilcloth. "What did your grandmother do with all the old chickens she took out?"

"Wal, we mostly et 'em," replied Wendell, flashing another toothy grin. He hitched his jeans up and sat back down. "Bud and I chopped their heads off and they went into the freezer. We give a lot away, too. They warn't much good, though. I never knew what real good chicken tasted like 'til I joined the Navy. All I ever et when I was a kid was one of Grammie Addie's played out old hens."

Rebecca giggled at the imagery.

Hens and Chickens

"Cookie?" Wendell asked, reaching for the bag of oatmeal cookies he had placed on the countertop earlier. He helped himself to a thick stack and pushed the bag temptingly across the table to Rebecca.

"Thank you," she said. Rebecca carefully selected one cookie from the bag.

"You ain't gonna stay alive thet way," Wendell commented. "You'll probably need at least four of them cookies to git back up to Miss Hastings' house."

Rebecca made a little face. "In the city, I'm generally regarded as being on the heavy side," she admitted. "I've been on a diet since I was 10, I think."

"Wal, you ain't in the city now, you're in the country—and you look jest the right size for a country gal," Wendell said, gallantly.

Rebecca actually blushed. She put her hands up to her red cheeks. "My goodness, I think the tea is a little hot," she said, trying to cover her blush. "Not that I'm complaining – Oh, dear! – we certainly appreciate you going to all this trouble for us, Wendell!"

"Wal, when Miss Hastings told me 'bout you gals driving up here all the way from Massachusetts to see the place, you know, I got pretty excited. I'd like to see someone livin' heah, maybe fixin' up the old place as time and money permits. I ain't lookin' to git rich, neither," he added, hastily.

"I'm sure you're not!"

"It jest hurts me to see the old place go downhill, year after year. And I don't want to be the one to have her fall down on my watch," he continued, seriously. "Miss Hastings said yore little friend might be interested in raising chickens and there ain't no better place in the state of Maine to raise hens and chickens than right heah! I know that for a fact," he stated, shaking his index finger in affirmation. "And, thanks to Grammie Addie, I probably know jest as much 'bout the egg business as anybody teachin' poultry husbandry up to the University – and I'd be glad to help you gals out."

"Well, we'd need all the help we could get, that's for sure!" said Rebecca. "I don't know if I should be asking this, but … Do you have any idea what you'd want for the place?"

"Wal, I'd sell the house and the 10-acre field for forty thousand dollars."

"Forty thousand dollars!" repeated Rebecca, astonished.

"And I'd be willing to hold the note," Wendell added, hastily. "Is thet too much?"

"That's not *enough*!" exclaimed Rebecca. "Why, this place must be worth a hundred thousand, at least!"

Wendell shook his head, sadly. "Not nowadays," he said. "One realtor I talked to told me to rip the whole thing down and jest sell the land. Course, I couldn't do thet."

"No, no, of course not," sympathized Rebecca. "But … forty thousand dollars? Are you sure? Of course, I don't know what Lila will think; I don't even know where she's disappeared to …" Rebecca broke off. She put her hand to her flushed cheek in order to cool it. "I'm rambling, aren't I?" she asked, embarrassed.

"Yep," said Wendell. "But you go ahead and ramble. I ain't got no place to go today and nuthin' to do when I git there."

Rebecca regarded him with dawning wonderment. "Me either," she replied, almost giggling. She sank back into the padded kitchen chair in pleasurable relief. "In fact, I think I *will* have another cookie!"

Wendell Russell slid the cookie bag closer to her elbow. "Take two—they're cheap," he said, flashing his gold-toothed grin.

Rebecca was reaching for the cookies when Lila burst back into the room. "Look what I found!" the younger woman exclaimed.

Chapter 9

· · · · · · ·

Discoveries

Lila carried into the kitchen a long gown of blue satin as carefully as though it was a sick child. "Look at this!" she repeated, to Rebecca and Wendell Russell. "I found it hanging in an upstairs closet—in a zipper dress bag. Isn't it awesome? There are four or five of 'em altogether. They're just like those dresses you were telling me about, Becca – Gunne Sax! I brought this one down to show you. I hope you don't mind," she added, turning anxiously to Wendell.

"I don't mind," he replied. "They was probably my great-grandmother's. She was quite a looker and was pretty proud of the way she got herself up, according to Grammie Addie, anyway. She was a skinny little thing, kinda like you," he said, referring to Lila. "I never knew her, but I've seen pictures."

Lila lay the silky, midnight-blue gown onto the kitchen table and slowly unfolded it. The smell of cedar pervaded the air. Despite the fact that the dress had been stored away for decades, and that there was only natural light in the kitchen, the blue satin shimmered gloriously on the table like a pool of water. The ankle-length gown was trimmed with a dainty burgundy ribbon, so delicate it could have been cut from the same spool as the fine bookmarker ribbon found in expensive Bibles. The bodice was tight-fitting, and trimmed with several yards of the burgundy ribbon in an exquisitely-designed pattern.

"It's gorgeous," gushed Rebecca, reverently examining the elaborately trimmed sleeve lying on the table next to her. "This dress is all handmade, and the stitching is beautiful—the best I've ever seen, personally!"

"She sews," Lila said to Wendell, by way of an explanation.

"Ayuh," he replied. His bright blue eyes flashed in unconcealed admiration.

"Yes, but my handiwork isn't *this* good," said Rebecca, quickly. "This dress came from a real, old-fashioned honest-to-goodness *seamstress*. You don't see this kind of work anymore unless you can afford haute couture. It used to be that a good seamstress was an integral part of city or village life, but those days ended, Oh! a hundred years ago when the assembly line and mass production came into being. Now, we're so overwhelmed with cheap clothing that has been cobbled together in China or Mexico or Thailand – or maybe all three countries at once – that we don't even know what *quality* is anymore! Well, this, *this* is an example of how great our country used to be—back when we did our own work for our own people!"

"I've never heard you talk like this before, Becca," said Lila, somewhat taken aback.

"I've never had occasion to!" cried Rebecca. "It's a shame that the days of quality craftsmanship in this country are over, whether it's sewing a dress or building a set of table and chairs."

"Wal, there's an Amish fellow down to Unity who builds pretty good furniture," interjected Wendell. "He makes coffins, too. I was thinkin' of goin' down and talkin' to him about makin' up a wooden casket for myself; jest in case. Maybe you'd like to go with me when I go?"

"I'd love to!" said Rebecca. "Well, if we're around, that is. I'd love to see his furniture."

"And Mike Hobart is a carpenter, too," added Lila. "I don't know how good he is, but he built his own post and beam cabin."

"Ayuh, he's a pretty shaap fellow," agreed Wendell.

Rebecca offered a small, embarrassed laugh. "I guess I'd better get down off my high horse then," she said. "It's just always been a pet peeve of mine that nobody seems to care about the quality of anything, anymore. All people seem to care about is price! Do you know, they don't even teach home economics in the schools these days?"

"Um, what's that?" said Lila, reaching for a cookie from the bag that had mysteriously moved back in front of Wendell. She held her hand under her mouth as she crunched the cookie to prevent the crumbs from dropping on the gown.

"See what I mean!" said Rebecca. "Home Ec was my major in high school and college, and now – now not one person under the age of 40 knows what I'm talking about!"

"Isn't it like, how to bake a potato and do laundry and that kind of stuff?" mumbled Lila, mouth half-full.

"How to sew, budget, cook, plan, organize, keep house," listed Rebecca, earnestly; "and many, many *wonderful* skills that are much more useful throughout our lives than how to create an avatar on Twitter or how to download an app for our cellphones or how to ..." she broke off, suddenly. "I'm preaching, aren't I? I'm sorry; I'm not sure what's going on with me this morning! I feel like someone let the genie out of the bottle!"

"Wal, put the cap back on the bottle, quick!" said Wendell, with an unusual burst of energy. Surprised, Lila stared at the old chicken farmer. "I kinda like the genie being out," he added, lamely.

Lila's eyes narrowed as she turned to examine her friend's flushed face. "You know, so do I!"

The next discovery of the morning occurred when Wendell Russell gave Lila and Rebecca a tour of the old "hen-pen," the family nickname for Grammie Addie's egg operation, which was an attached wigwam-looking, two-story shed that housed the 400 laying hens. The hen-pen also included a separate egg sorting station, situated just outside the caged area on the ground floor, accessed by an unusual spiral steel-and-wood staircase. There was also the cold storage room, a 10X10 space hollowed out of the damp musty earth that kept the boxes of eggs naturally cool during the hot Maine summers. The coop and nest boxes were located on the ground floor of the hen pen, and on the upper floor wooden grain and sawdust bins were strategically situated so that measured amounts of sawdust and grain could be easily dropped to the hens below. In addition, the building included a unique Pappy-designed ventilation system that automatically – by way of natural convection – replaced the ammonia-laden air of the chicken coop with fresh cool air so that, according to Wendell, "Ain't nobody that evah see the hen pen could believe there was 400 laying hens inside!"

The tour of the hen pen consumed nearly an hour, and Wendell was a thoroughly honest guide. "She's got quite a few windows broke," he admitted, when the three were once again ensconced at the kitchen table. "And most of them nest boxes will likely need to be rebuilt, too. You'll need to upgrade the electrical service—she's only 60-amp and ain't up to code. But altogether the hen pen ain't ready to be tore down, yet."

"How much do you think it will cost to fix everything?" asked Rebecca.

"Wal, you know ..." Wendell began.

"Don't worry, Becca," said Lila, impetuously. "Mike Hobart has offered to help us."

Wendell straightened up in his chair. "Course, I'd like to help, too. I kin do the electrical work; 'twas what I done in the Navy. Shouldn't cost much for electrical supplies—a thousand or two at most," he said, reassuringly to Rebecca.

"We'll pay you," Lila offered. "I'm going to pay Mike, too."

"Wal, you know, what you do with Mike is between you 'n him. But I don't really need any money," the old chicken farmer drawled.

"But we couldn't let you help us without paying you!" said Rebecca.

"Wal, you know, I might be coaxed into a suppah or two now 'n agin," he said. He flashed a shiny grin.

"Oh, my! That's not very much," said Rebecca.

"Wal, maybe you could also try to bake me some of 'Euna's Hot Water Gingerbread'. Euna Crockett—she was my grandmother's best friend, lived over on the North Troy Road near where Ralph Gilpin's got his house. She made the best hot water gingerbread I ever et!"

"I'd *love* to try and bake Euna's gingerbread," said Rebecca, enthusiastically. "Do you know where I could get the recipe?"

"Ayuh," replied Wendell. He rose from the table, opened a white cupboard to the left of the cook stove, and pulled out a dirty tan book stuffed fat with newspaper clippings, recipe cards and various other papers. "This is Grammie Addie's cookbook, her *Bible*, she used to call it. She's got a copy of 'Euna's Hot Water Gingerbread' in heah."

Wendell handed the cookbook to Rebecca, who took it with sparkling blue eyes and eager anticipation. Rebecca gingerly opened the fragile cover and turned to the title page. "Oh, it's the 1914 edition of *The Boston Cooking School Cookbook* by Fannie Farmer!" she said. "This is very collectible!"

"How do you know THAT?" asked Lila.

"This is the *last version* of this *very famous cookbook* that Fannie Merritt Farmer edited herself," Rebecca explained, seriously. "Fannie died in 1915, and after her death members of her family edited her cookbook. In 1959, Fannie's niece, Wilma Perkins, took over the so-called editing, but unfortunately it was almost a re-writing at that point." Rebecca gave a little sniff. "Some people say that Fannie wouldn't even recognize her own cookbook after her niece got done with it!"

"You are REALLY into this stuff," said Lila, eyes open wide with wonder.

"I told you, I majored in home economics," Rebecca said. She turned to Wendell. "This cookbook is worth at least $100 dollars. In fact, I'll give you $100 for it right now!"

Hens and Chickens

"Wal, you know, I couldn't sell it; course, 'twas Grammie Addie's."
Rebecca looked crestfallen. "Of course, I'm sorry. I shouldn't have asked."

"Wal, maybe we could work out some kind of temporary loan," suggested Wendell.

Rebecca brightened. "That would be lovely!" She slowly and carefully leafed through the yellowed pages of the cookbook "Look at these wonderful, inspirational newspaper clippings that she collected!"

"Wal, you know, Grammie Addie liked down-home, cheerful kinds of things," Wendell explained. "The newspapers was full of it in those days; not like nowadays when all there is in the paper and on T.V. is BAD news and sex," he added. "Grammie used to go around sort of half singin' stuff. Like this," he continued, breaking into a full-throated, deep baritone:

'When all the world is dark and gray, keep on hoping!
When bad things sometimes come your way, no sense moping!'

… I forget all the words exactly," he continued, in his normal voice; "but 'twas something like thet."

Lila was so startled by his singing that she stared blankly at Wendell like a child woken up from a deep slumber.

"Your grandmother sounds like a lovely woman!" Rebecca interjected, quickly. "I never knew either one of my grandmothers. I'm very envious."

"Omigod, I just had a GREAT idea!" cried Lila. "We should use Grammie Addie in the marketing of our egg business! We could be *The Egg Ladies* of Sovereign, Maine – and she could be our avatar!" She turned to Wendell excitedly. "Do you mind? Do you have a picture of your grandmother that we could use?"

Wendell didn't have the least notion what an 'avatar' was, but he liked Lila's enthusiasm. "I don't know why I should mind. So long's the photograph is one of Grammie Addie in her good dress; course, she'd probably want thet. In fact, I think I got a black 'n white of her 'n Euna Crockett in the bedroom."

"Both of them together? That would be perfect!"

"Thet's what I thought. Lemme git it." Wendell hauled himself up out of the chair and exited the kitchen to retrieve the old photograph.

Lila looked meaningfully at her friend. "Well, Becca?" she demanded, in a lowered voice so that the chicken farmer wouldn't overhear. "What do you think?"

Rebecca gave a little laugh. "I'm sold!"

"I knew you would be!" Lila exclaimed, triumphantly. "I just knew you wouldn't be able to resist!"

"I wouldn't have believed it possible when we left Massachusetts, but now I can't imagine any other course of action than moving to Sovereign!"

"You won't regret it, I promise!"

"No, I don't think I will," Rebecca affirmed.

Wendell returned with a 5X7 black and white framed photo of Grammie Addie and her best friend, Euna Crockett. The two women were standing side by side on the shed step of the old Russell homestead. Grammie Addie was holding a woven basket the size of a watermelon, filled with eggs.

"This is too much!" said Lila, taking the photograph from his outstretched hand. "It's perfect for our avatar."

Wendell reclaimed his seat. "Ayuh," he said. "Thought 'twas what you was lookin' for."

"You're sure you don't mind?"

Rebecca coughed politely, securing Lila's attention. "Isn't there something we need to do before we start marketing a company we don't have yet?" She looked pointedly at her young friend.

Lila stared blankly. Her nimble young mind had already leaped ahead to future possibilities. "What?" she said.

"Some, ah, *financial business* we need to take care of with Wendell, before we appropriate his house, his grandmother and everything?"

"Omigod," said Lila, laughing. "I totally forgot! I thought it was a done deal."

Wendell grinned. "Wal, you know, I think *'tis* pretty much a done deal," he said.

And the major discovery of the day was how easy it was to do business in Sovereign, Maine!

Chapter 10

· · · · · · ·

Settling In

The next few weeks skipped by as Lila wrapped up her old life in Massachusetts and relocated to the old Russell homestead in Sovereign, Maine. Despite pleas from both Lila and Rebecca, Wendell would take no more than $40,000 for the house and 10 acres of field, carving out for himself the hired hand's house – Bud's place – and the balance of the 110-acre woodlot. He even brushed off an initial down payment.

"If you put in a separate driveway entrance for me ovah to Bud's place, thet'll be enough for a down payment," Wendell said.

"But I have PLENTY of money," Lila protested.

"Wal, you know, there ain't nuthin' I need to buy that I ain't already got," Wendell replied. "And thet driveway entrance won't come cheap. Them aluminum culverts cost 'bout $800. Plus I'm thinking you'll find plenty of things to spend money on around heah pretty quick."

And so the entire purchase price on the old Russell Place was to be paid in monthly installments of $300 for 15 years. "That's not even a third of what I pay for rent!" Lila chortled to Rebecca, after Miss Hastings retired for bed that second evening in Sovereign.

Rebecca was a bit more circumspect. "But you had a regular job with Perkins & Gleeful in order to pay that rent with," she pointed out. "Now we're depending on …"

"… on our own smarts and hard work paying OUR way, not THEIRS," finished Lila with satisfaction and not a little triumph. "If we get the axe this time, we've got nobody to blame but ourselves!"

Wendell was to remove all personal items of value (except Grammie Addie's cookbook, which was to remain on loan), and Lila would take immediate possession of the house. She and Rebecca were to dispose of any items left in the house that they didn't want. Wendell was leaving the furniture, dishes, bedding and even the silverware. Lila could hardly believe their good fortune.

"Wal, you know, I ain't got no more room in Bud's place," Wendell said, simply.

Within two weeks of returning to Massachusetts, Rebecca had contracted with the parents of a friend and neighbor, who wanted to be close to their grandchildren – but not *too* close – to rent her house. The new tenants took a year's lease on the property, paid in advance, and the monies would be enough for Rebecca to pay her mortgage, property taxes, insurance and still have money left over for minor repairs.

The new tenants wanted to move in by April 15th, however, which sent Rebecca into a frenzy of packing, sorting and storing, and resulted in several weekend visits by her daughter Amber. "She's bringing some friends to help every time she comes," Rebecca reported to Lila, "otherwise I don't see how I could possibly get everything done in time!"

Lila quickly gave notice and packed up her condo (which was nothing as compared to Rebecca's breaking up of the Johnson family home), then returned to the old Russell homestead to prepare the hen pen for the arrival of the 100 certified organic laying hens she had purchased as a starter flock from a farmer in southern Maine. In addition, she had taken responsibility to coordinate the legal paperwork involved in the real estate transaction, both Wendell and Rebecca suggesting she take the lead. One sore spot cropped up almost immediately, however. Since Lila insisted on being the one responsible for paying the mortgage, Rebecca refused to have her name put on the deed. This was troublesome to Lila, who was conscious of how necessary Rebecca was to the success of the entire operation.

"She thinks because she's not giving me money toward the mortgage, she doesn't have an equal right of ownership," Lila confided to Mike Hobart one sunny afternoon in early April. A trusting relationship had replaced their fledgling friendship as the two of them had spent the prior three weeks working shoulder-to-shoulder cleaning, rebuilding and retrofitting the old hen pen. "But she doesn't realize I couldn't do this whole egg business thing WITHOUT her."

"Mmmhmm," Hobart mumbled. He took the short yellow pencil out of his mouth, and jotted down a figure in a small notebook. "Two inches by three-quarters," he said. He glanced up at Lila, curiously. "She sounds old school to me; pretty much what I would expect from Rebecca," he continued. He pushed his cap back on his head. "Does it bother you that much?"

"That's the point! It's soo old school," Lila proclaimed. She was removing the compacted, cruddy sawdust from the nest boxes with a gardening trowel, but paused to wipe her face with her hand. "I know so many women who've helped men buy and fix up a house or build a business, and then, 10 years later – when the guy replaced them with a younger version – they got NOTHING! Why? All because they never insisted on legalizing their partnership!"

"Sounds like you knew the wrong kind of men," said Hobart, calmly. He leaned over and brushed a piece of dirty sawdust from Lila's cheek.

"I didn't say that happened to ME," she said, blushing.

Their eyes locked and Lila experienced a hyper-awareness of his presence. Moist body heat emanated from his muscular chest and shoulders. She felt the ground spin and heard a ringing sensation in her ears.

Hormones at work! she cautioned herself. *Beware!* Instinctively, she retreated closer to the double-row of whitewashed wooden nest boxes.

Hobart observed Lila's retreat with amusement. "I'm not going to eat you," he said, closing the pencil into the fold of his notebook and placing the book upon a nearby sawhorse. He took off his cap and ran his fingers through his matted hair. He reached for a bottle of spring water, tipped the bottle up and took a long drink. The fresh water gurgled down his throat. Hobart set the bottle and his cap onto the sawhorse, and wiped his mouth on the sleeve of his gray sweatshirt. "Listen, I don't know what crappy stuff men have done to you in the past, but I can guarantee you that this is one man who only wants good things for you. I don't have any ulterior motive here except to help you and Rebecca get this egg business off the ground."

Lila, a little taken aback, could think of no immediate retort. Instead, she tried not to notice how strong and capable his hands were as he reached for the tape measure. But the more she attempted NOT to focus on Mike Hobart, the more her brain honed in on minutia like the boyish curl of hair growing on the nape of his neck and the peculiar ironbark brown of his eyelashes.

"And since I seem to be on my white horse at the moment," he continued, hearing no response to his prior declaration; "I want to know if you've taken a close look at the financials for this egg business. Do you know what your expenses will be? Who your market is? How much you can sell the eggs for? Do you know what it takes to get an organic certification in Maine?"

Facts, figures, numbers, marketing—these were all Lila Woodsum's territory. She was an expert at business matters however much she might be deficient in other areas. His questions instantly pushed her hot buttons. "Of course I have!" she retorted, hazel eyes flashing. "I don't have all the answers to your questions at the tip of my fingers, but I've run enough numbers to justify *The Egg Ladies.*" She admonished him with the garden trowel. "Not that it's any of your business, but I can show you those numbers at lunch!"

"Whoaa!" Hobart said, with a smile in his eyes. He took a half-step back and raised his palms in mock defense. "Don't hurt me! I was just asking a few questions; as a friend."

Embarrassed, Lila laughed shortly, and dropped the trowel into the nest box. "Sorry, I'm a little defensive," she admitted. "I have a Master's in Business and I'm not used to having my projects questioned."

"I can see that," Hobart said. He paused. "Wendell said you were the marketing manager of some big insurance company in Boston?"

Lila nodded curtly. "Rebecca and I shared the marketing director job until she got downsized," she said. "Then our boss offered it to me, as a PROMOTION—sarcasm intended. That's when I told him to take the job and shove it. Sorry," she added quickly; "I'm trying to clean up my potty mouth. Bad for business, you know."

"No problem," Hobart said, reassuringly. "I used to be pretty rough around the edges when I was first self-employed."

"When was that?" asked Lila, eager to learn more of Mike Hobart's history.

"When I had my paper route," he replied. He grinned. "I was the toughest, 10-year-old dude in Maple Grove."

They both laughed. Hobart sensed Lila relax. *Sensitive area avoided,* he thought. *At least for now.*

"You seem to like your own way pretty well," Lila agreed. She leaned back against the row of faded, white-washed nest boxes and regarded the carpenter with a challenging smile. "So do I."

"Well, that's not going to be a problem," he said, stretching a long arm out and leaning against the nest boxes, perilously near Lila.

"Why not?" she asked, in a low voice. She felt the pull of his mesmerizing blue eyes cinching her closer, and could practically taste his earthy scent. Lila closed her eyes and swayed toward the inevitable.

Hens and Chickens

"Because I'm going to do exactly what *you* want me to do," he replied, in a matter-of-fact tone. "You get to call the shots, Lila—not me."

Startled, Lila opened her eyes, and blinked.

Hobart pushed away from the nest boxes and straightened up. "Here you go," he said, reaching for the trowel and tossing it to her. "Shouldn't we go back to work now, *boss?*" he asked.

An astonished Lila caught the gardening tool automatically. "Umm... yeah," she said. "Sure."

Lila felt a momentary sinking feeling of disappointment. That certainly wasn't the outcome she'd expected! But what was she hoping would happen? What did she want from him? Was it more than friendly advice, support and his carpentry help?

Someday – soon – she would need to take a look at those questions. Because they were every bit as important as the questions Mike Hobart had asked her about *The Egg Ladies!*

"So, what DOES it take to get an organic certification in Maine?" she asked him, unwilling to let their conversation drop.

Hobart finished his next measurement before answering. He let the end of the yellow tape go, and it *zipped* back into the silver metal case. "I don't know," he replied, honestly. He reached for the short pencil, which was now stuck over his ear. "You should talk to Tom Kidd. The locals call him 'The Organic Kidd.' Tom's a big mover and shaker in the organic movement in Maine and with MOGG."

"MOGG?"

"The Maine Organic Growers Group," he replied, jotting his measurement in his book. "Tom Kidd is on the MOGG certification committee. He might even be the head of it, now." Hobart hesitated. "Tom and I went to college together. We're not exactly friends, but we're not enemies, either. He lives in Unity. I usually run into him at Gilpin's a couple of times a week—want me to ask him to stop by sometime and talk with you?"

"That would be awesome," said Lila. "Rebecca's daughter Amber has been involved in the organic movement for years, but I'm, well, pretty clueless."

"If you're absolutely sure you want to go the organic route ...?"

"Totally sure," Lila affirmed.

"Then Tom Kidd is the man to talk to. Just as long as you stick to business with him."

"That sounds like a warning," said Lila, raising a dark eyebrow.

"It is. Tom Kidd is not a man I would recommend to my sisters."

"Or a friend?" suggested Lila.

"Or a friend. Just keep your eyes open, and you'll be alright. Tom Kidd doesn't kiss with his eyes open."

"You, you …!" Lila scooped up a handful of dusty gray sawdust from a nest box and hurled it good-naturedly at Mike Hobart. "Don't think I was going to kiss you, because I wasn't!"

Hobart shielded his eyes from the sawdust, and smiled, disarmingly. "I know you weren't. I was just teasing," he said. He brushed the sawdust from his curly blond hair and sweatshirt. "But not about Tom Kidd," he continued, seriously. "Tom has a reputation of being charming with the ladies. A little too charming, if you ask me."

Mike Hobart's warning had an interesting effect on Lila. The rest of that day she found herself contemplating what might be behind the handsome carpenter's heads-up.

Was Mike Hobart jealous? Or was there something about Tom Kidd that really would bear watching?

Or both?

Chapter 11

· · · · · · ·

"The Organic Kidd"

Tom Kidd had been a major player in the Maine organic movement for the past 12 years, since he'd arrived from New Haven, Connecticut with his shoulder-length black hair not exactly wet behind the ears. Kidd landed on the doorstep of Unity College to major in environmental studies and to make Tom Kidd a name in the blossoming national organic movement. Not coincidentally, Unity was also home to the Maine Organic Growers Group (MOGG), one of the earliest organic associations in the country.

Tall, thin and devilishly handsome, the Organic Kidd had begun his working career as a MOGG apprentice. But Tom Kidd didn't intend to work as an apprentice for long, slogging away at weeds in hot, dirty fields that smelled like cow shit. No, actual physical *work* was NOT his strong suit. Utilizing his natural sales abilities, a charming smile, coaxing brown eyes and a marketing finesse (for which Maine farmers, even organic ones, are not known) which WAS his strong suit, Kidd soon landed a desk job with MOGG. Once he was graduated from Unity, Kidd secured an advanced degree in organic marketing from a mail-order college, and before long he was promoted to the MOGG certification committee where he quickly became the "go-to guy" for organic certification in the now-exploding Maine organic movement.

"Hey, hey, hey Hobart—whaddaya say?" Kidd greeted Mike Hobart when they ran into each other Sunday afternoon at Gilpin's General Store, a few days after Hobart's conversation with Lila. "Met the new babe up on Russell Hill yet?"

Hobart stiffened instinctively at the allusion to Lila. He didn't like the way Tom Kidd had chosen to live his life, but he tried not to let it affect the way he treated his former Unity College classmate. "Yeah, I'm helping renovate the old hen pen," Hobart replied, pulling a gallon jug of milk from the cooler.

"Hen pen, my ass," said Kidd. "I heard she's a young *chick*. I should've known you'd be onto her like a guinea hen onto a tick, Hobart. You never did miss an opportunity."

Hobart let the cooler door drop with a *whoosh*. "I think the only opportunity for me with Lila is …"

"Lila?!" Kidd interrupted. He whistled through a mouthful of white teeth, which he never hesitated to show off. "Hey, we're on a first name basis, are we? Good job, buddy!"

"… the only opportunity is to help her rebuild the hen house and pens," Hobart calmly continued. "It's a long time since anybody raised chickens at the old Russell Place. By the way, Tom, she's interested in becoming certified organic."

Kidd fingered his fainéant black goatee. "Hey … maybe I should drop by?" he mused, almost to himself.

"Maybe you should," said Hobart. "In fact, I told Lila if I saw you I'd point you in that direction. She wants to know what it takes to sell organic eggs."

"Well, I'm not used to taking pointers from you, Hobart – especially about women – but you could be onto something this time if all I hear about your friend Lila is true. Pretty hot, is she?"

Hobart winced. "She's pretty, anyway," he admitted lamely, beginning to feel uncomfortable. "Why don't you go see for yourself? Her name is Lila Woodsum."

Tom Kidd slapped Hobart on the back. "Hey, buddy, you're the man!"

Hobart moved away from Kidd and toward the cash register, where Ralph Gilpin was warily eyeing the two men. Hobart thought his old friend and former employer looked as though he expected a dog fight to break out at any moment. Tom Kidd queued up behind Hobart with a single can of cold beer.

"What's the best time for me to drop by?" Kidd asked, as he carelessly flipped through a selection of candy bars at the counter.

"Lila's around most days," Hobart replied, opening his wallet to pay for the milk. Hobart should have let it go at that, but the guy on the white horse couldn't resist affixing a note of warning. "So am I," he added, with a meaningful look at Ralph Gilpin that stopped the old shopkeeper's open mouth.

"Hey, thanks for the heads-up, buddy. I'll be sure to drop by at night!"

Hens and Chickens

Mike Hobart mentally kicked himself. *Dammit! Now, I've let the wolf in the door!*

Hobart exited Gilpin's without uttering the biting response to the Organic Kidd that was perched on his lips. Lila would have to fight her own battles—plus she had never said she wanted him to protect her in the first place. It wasn't his job. He had said he would help her rebuild the chicken house, and that's what he was going to do.

Unless …

But, no. It was no good speculating on what hadn't happened, might not happen.

Hobart's philosophy was that life – and love – would take their natural course. He just hoped that in Lila's case that natural course wasn't like the course of water—taking the lowest route.

Hobart alerted Lila that he had seen Tom Kidd, and that the MOGG certification "go-to guy" would be stopping by imminently to see her. But Tom Kidd knew how to play his cards better than that. He knew that he could make more of an impression with Lila if he didn't make an appearance TOO soon. Kidd also was pretty sure that longer he waited the more likely he was to catch her *without* her carpenter-bodyguard.

As the Organic Kidd had calculated, Lila noticed his absence more than she might have been impressed by his presence. In fact, as the week progressed, Lila was beginning to think that she had met everyone in Sovereign and most of the neighboring towns BUT the Organic Kidd!

Word about the sale of the old Russell homestead and *The Egg Ladies* had spread via the local grapevine like news of an open house at which free coffee and donuts would be handed out. Neighbors, relatives of neighbors, friends of relatives of neighbors and the just plain curious stopped in daily to introduce themselves, offer assistance and see how the work progressed. Ma Jean sent up homemade pie from the restaurant by way of various couriers on a regular basis; the entire board of selectmen visited (as well as the planning board); and the code enforcement officer (who was also the fire chief) and his wife came by to say "hello" and put the rubber stamp on Wendell's re-wiring of the hen pen. And Miss Hastings, who no longer drove and had in fact sold Lila her 1964 Pontiac LeMans, telephoned at least once a day. "Dahrrrling, I don't want to bother you," she said to Lila. "But if you get lonely, you know where we live! Matilda and I LOVE your tweets about *The Egg Ladies*!"

On Thursday afternoon, Ralph Gilpin, whom Lila had met upon her arrival in town and several times since at the general store, motored up Russell Hill to formally introduce his wife. Gilpin looked like a pole-bean next to his amply-endowed wife, Maude, and the couple instantly reminded Lila of the child's nursery rhyme: *"Jack Spratt could eat no fat and his wife could eat no lean."* Ralph and Maude arrived when Lila and Mike Hobart were knee-deep in removing old soiled sawdust from the hen pen.

Without even waiting to see the state of the house or kitchen, a horrified Maude Gilpin issued an invitation to Lila for supper on Saturday night. "You need some good food to put some meat on those bones!" she cried. "You, too, Sweetie," she added, including Hobart in the invitation.

"I don't want to impose," Lila said; "but I'm starving, so I won't refuse. Thanks."

"She can't cook," explained Hobart, leaning on his shovel. "So 'til her friend gets here, she's living on nuts and yogurt."

"Heavens!" exclaimed Maud, to whom the thought of going a day without a piece of homemade pie was a tragedy. "We'll fix you right up with a welcome basket, Sweetie! Trudy Gorse mentioned to me just yesterday that she'd met you, and that the Welcome Wagon Committee ought to put something together for you BUT I've been so busy I haven't had a chance to cook a single thing since I saw Trudy, except the roast chicken and biscuits I cooked for supper last night, of course, and the custard I baked with duck eggs for Ralph's dessert last night, too."

Lila was so overwhelmed by Maud and her culinary accomplishments that she hardly knew how to respond. "You make custard with—duck eggs?" she said, in wonderment.

"Only 'til ya git yer egg business off the ground," Ralph interjected, squeezing his wife's fat hand fondly. "Then – I project – my Maude's gonna be yer best customer!"

Maude beamed proudly, as her husband steered her out of the hen pen toward the car. "See you Saturday, kids!" she called, with a friendly wave.

It was late Friday afternoon before Tom Kidd finally stopped in to see Lila. He had cruised the Russell Hill Road several times earlier in the week, but each time he had spotted Mike Hobart's baby blue truck parked territorially in the yard. This time, however, Lila was left undefended.

"Hey, hey—whaddaya say? I'm Tom Kidd," he said, by way of an introduction when Lila answered the knock at the shed door.

Lila, however, who had glanced out the kitchen window prior to answering the knock, needed no introduction from him. Mike Hobart's casual description of the Organic Kidd, combined with his gentle warning, had helped her form a pretty accurate picture in her mind of Tom Kidd. She recognized the type of man he was instantly. "Lila Woodsum," she replied, hesitating momentarily, unsure as to whether or not she wanted to shake hands with him.

Kidd, quick to pick up on her hesitation – and suspecting Hobart had warned this slim pretty creature to beware of him – boldly stuck out his hand, and Lila had no choice but to shake it.

Lila unconsciously compared the organic farmer's soft, supple hands with those of the sturdy carpenter's. And unfortunately for Kidd, there was no comparison. *Why, his hands are more like a pampered woman's than a farmer's!*

Lila tugged away from his handshake, and the Organic Kidd took the opportunity to step over the faded green doorsill into the shed.

"Hobart said you're interested in having a certified organic egg business," Kidd continued, pulling a sheaf of white papers from under his arm. "I brought you some info and the MOGG grower application – mind if we sit down and go over 'em?" The Organic Kidd flashed his notorious dimpled smirk, which, framed by his pencil-thin mustache was always successful with the ladies, whether they be eight or 82.

Lila, however, noted that the "spontaneous" smile did not reach Tom Kidd's brown eyes. Instead of being open and honest, his eyes were narrowed with keen observation and speculation. Lila suspected she was being carefully played by this dark stranger, a pawn on a chessboard that promoted the self-aggrandizement of the Organic Kidd.

"Mind if we sit down and go over these?" he repeated, gesturing toward the kitchen table, which was visible through the open connecting door.

Normally, Lila would have risen up in rage at his arrogance; however, something in his aggressive action combined with the dark threat of his predatory visage, triggered a terrifying flashback to her childhood. Suddenly, she was an eight-year-old again, cowering beneath her bedclothes in her solitary, isolated bedroom. The color drained from her face. Beads of sweat popped out on her forehead, and she felt as though she was going to faint. She retreated into her kitchen and clasped the back of a wooden chair to steady herself.

Not now! she silently beseeched herself. *Please ... not now!*

"Hey – are you OK?" asked Kidd, concerned, following her into the kitchen. He didn't want her to topple over on him; might be bad for the organic certification business!

"Um—sorry, give me a minute," Lila said. She sank into the solid oak chair, and covered her face with her hands. Unwanted, icky memories overwhelmed her like a bad movie that kept playing inside her head. *Omigod; make it stop!*

Tom Kidd set his papers on the table atop a pile of chicken magazines. "Hey – why don't I give you some time to check these out," he said, suddenly anxious to make his escape. "I'll stop by in a week or so to see if you've got any questions. It's all pretty straightforward – really."

Kidd's cheap aftershave permeated the kitchen and almost overpowered Lila. She put her head on the table. *I will not faint!*

"The papers are right there," the Organic Kid said, inching toward the shed; "on the table."

"Thanks," she mumbled, from inside folded arms.

"See you later," he called, from the shed door stoop. "Hope you're feeling better real soon!"

"Uh-huh," said Lila.

Moments later Tom Kidd scooted into his truck. He switched on the ignition and reached for his half-drunk can of beer.

Jesus! Hobart's got a whacko on his hands with THAT chick! he thought, taking a long draught from the bitter beverage. *No wonder he didn't try to discourage me!*

Lila lay as she was, head on the table, and listened with intense relief as Kidd roared off down the hill. Despite the damp April breeze that blew up the hill, she left both the kitchen and shed doors open a full 15 minutes after his hasty departure. The refreshing air swept through the room – cleaning out his stench – and gradually restoring her to her normal senses. She lifted her head from her arms and surveyed the old farm kitchen; finding comfort in the worn, wide pine floor and honesty in the solid thickness of the 6X6 hand-hewn beams that supported the second story. Here was truth! Here was goodness! Here was peace, safety, security! Here were ALL the elements from Lila's childhood that—*that she had always longed for and never had!*

"That went well," she said aloud, recovering herself. "What kind of self-respecting villain would run away just when the damsel in distress was about to capitulate?!"

Unwittingly, Lila pictured an episode from *The Perils of Pauline*, in which poor Pauline was tied to a railroad track as a chugging steam engine loomed large. The top-hatted villain rubbed his hands together in glee as Pauline wriggled helplessly trying to free herself.

Hens and Chickens

Lila recalled, with some embarrassment, her pert question to Mike Hobart that second day in Miss Hastings' shed: "You're not one of those guys that go around rescuing damsels in distress, are you?"

"I could be," he had admitted.

I could be.

Lila smiled somewhat sadly at the sweet memory. *Ah, but there are some situations from which Pauline has to rescue herself!*

Chapter 12

. . . .

Lila's Conundrum

"Omigod; I wonder if this is a DATE?" Lila said aloud, as she prepared for the Saturday night supper engagement with Maude and Ralph Gilpin—and Mike Hobart. "What a silly thing to worry about!"

Lila found herself wandering around the house for the better part of an hour in the late afternoon wondering whether or not the event with the carpenter could actually be construed as an official date. True, each of them had received a casual invitation from Maude, however, after the Gilpins departed Mike Hobart had gallantly offered to pick Lila up in his truck and escort her to the Gilpin's home, which was situated on the other side of town.

"It certainly wouldn't make the 'date' cut by Boston standards," Lila said to herself, as she checked her hair in the bathroom mirror. She pushed her bangs to the left, then, dissatisfied, moved the shiny hair to the opposite side. But … things were different in Sovereign, and what was a casual night out in Boston might be a date in Maine. "I think once they get you in their truck up here it's a date," she instructed her mirror image; "either that, or you're a dog."

In the fervor of her anticipation, she accidentally knocked over an uncapped bottle of herbal shampoo sitting on the vanity top and the scent of rosemary and lavender wafted through the bathroom. Lila cleaned up the mess, and confronted herself again in the mirror. "Get it together, Lila!" she instructed her reflection. She bent closer to check her pearly white teeth. "Good to go."

When she stepped back from the mirror Lila realized she was wearing the exact same skinny-leg jeans and oversized wool sweater she had been wearing the day she had walked out of Joe Kelly's office and into liberty. Now, however, thanks to weeks of physical labor and a lack of fast-food restaurants, her formerly skin-tight jeans drooped slackly from her thin hips, and the heavy black sweater swallowed her figure as completely as the whale swallowed Jonah. "I've got to do better than THIS or people WILL think I'm his dog!" she exclaimed.

Lila retreated to the first-floor bedroom, which she had appropriated for her own use. Here, her clothes and personal items were scattered throughout the room, spilling from boxes, draped on chairs and piled high on the old pine dresser. Lila picked through the jumble of clothing until she found a black silk skirt and a modest grey blouse with a V-neck ruffle that were both small enough for her to wear.

She donned the new outfit, smoothing the wrinkles away as best she could, and then re-checked herself in the larger bedroom mirror. "Not the best I've ever looked," she remarked, "but at least I won't be mistaken for a black lab!"

Lila rifled through the top dresser drawer until she located a pair of nylons. She sniffed them to make sure they were clean, and having satisfied herself pulled them on. She fished a pair of black flats from the floor of the closet and plopped onto the disheveled brass bed to slip into the footwear. To complete her toilet, Lila carefully retrieved a pair of ruby studs from a cedar keepsake box she kept on her dresser. The earrings, her birthstone, were a 21st birthday gift from her mother, and were Lila's most prized possession.

She hesitated before closing the lid of her keepsake box, her eye tenderly lingering on a slightly yellowed envelope bearing a cancelled 44¢ stamp. Her own name and her last Massachusetts address were penned on the envelope in her mother's familiar hand.

I can do this! Mom would WANT me to do this! she encouraged herself.

Lila snapped the box shut, and stuck the studs into her ears. The rosy sparkle of the earrings illuminated the tiny flecks of burgundy in her hazel eyes, which were now eager with anticipation.

Over the past few weeks Lila had learned to recognize the peculiar hum of Hobart's truck, and she heard the carpenter motoring up the hill toward her house. As he pulled in the drive, she peeked sideways out the kitchen window to see how he appeared. Was he any different?

Lila watched as Hobart let himself out of the driver's seat and then turned to retrieve something – a bunch of flowers! – from the passenger's side. Lila pulled back quickly from the window.

"It's a date!" she said. Her heart did a little back flip.

Hobart knocked on the shed door, and politely waited on the stoop for Lila to answer. She paused on the other side, her hand on the iron

Hens and Chickens

knob, attempting to control her racing heart. Then Lila swung open the door and tried to act nonchalant.

"Hi," she said. "Right on time – a man after my own heart."

Hobart heard the words "heart" and "man" somewhere in the back of his brain, but the front of his brain was concentrating on the vision before his eyes. She was almost ethereal, graceful, *beautiful* – like a delicate silver birch swaying in the April breeze, tossing its dainty branches back and forth as a woman seductively tosses her hair. Her radiant gaze invited him into a personal space he had never been with her before and—he choked.

Hobart thrust the handful of spring flowers at her like a schoolboy. "Here," he said. "These are for you."

Lila accepted the bouquet of yellow daffodils automatically; her happy eyes never leaving his face. She read his frank appreciation, and responded with a warm rush of gratitude. A tingling sensation spread from the center of her being down to her the very tips of her toes. "They're beautiful," she said, dipping her pert nose into the bouquet to inhale their natural sweet scent.

"So are you," Hobart said, leaning gawkily against the roughly painted door frame in an attempt to steady himself. "You're beautiful, *Lila*."

Lila's heart fluttered at the sound of her own name on his lips. Should she invite him in? What was the country protocol?

"Come in a sec while I put these in some water," she said finally, retreating into the kitchen to the relative safety of the soapstone sink. She opened the cold tap and pulled a quart canning jar from the bottom cupboard. Hobart followed her inside and stood awkwardly on the entry rug. "You didn't have to do this, Mike," she continued, gently fitting the flowers into the jar and fanning the yellow trumpets in a clumsy attempt at a floral arrangement. "It's not really a ... date."

He regarded her, bemused. "No? How come you're all dressed up then, if it's not ... a date? I've never seen you out of your jeans since you came here, *Lila*."

There it was; that name again. *Lila!* Why did it sound so different tonight? They had been on first name basis for weeks, but *Lila* had never sounded so *magical* before!

Lila set the jar of daffodils on the kitchen table, and straightened up. She leaned back, feeling the coolness of the soapstone through her thin silk clothing. "What are we doing here, Mike?" she asked, almost trembling. "I'm confused. I want this to be a date – but I don't want this to be a date. Look at us – how silly we're acting!"

Hobart tugged at the collar of the blue dress shirt that peeped out from the neck of his wool sweater. "I do feel kind of foolish," he admitted, grinning; "like an eighth grader on my first date."

"Maybe this whole thing is a mistake," said Lila.

"Maybe we should just not worry about it – what it is and what it isn't – and take the evening as it comes tonight?"

Lila picked up the light-weight spring coat she had draped over a chair earlier. "Why not?" she said. "Why not!"

Hobart helped her up into his truck and closed the door behind her. Then he jumped into the driver's side, started the engine and backed out into the road. Within moments they were headed across town to Ralph and Maude Gilpin's home on the North Troy Road.

The sun had not yet set – Daylight Savings Time having kicked in a few weeks earlier – but the finer features of the Maine landscape were slipping away in the fading April twilight. The red maples had budded out and lent a rust color to the dull rift of leafless trees in the distance. A patch of yellow willow shoots, near Black Brook, which shortly would be lost in a sea of green from its neighbors, shone like canned sunlight in a thicket of ordinary gray-brown stems.

Hobart, eager to share his love and appreciation for the area, highlighted items of natural interest as he carefully negotiated the back roads. "There's the beaver!" he pointed out excitedly, as he spied the familiar brown nose leading an expanding pool of ripples in its watery wake. "He's out early tonight."

"I see him!" cried Lila, the tip of her nose touching the cold glass of the passenger window.

Hobart pulled into a dirt turnout beside Black Brook, gravel *crunching* beneath the truck tires. He stopped the truck and switched off the ignition so that Lila could watch the beaver glide through the black water. "He's headed for those alders over there," Hobart said, leaning across Lila to point to the fledgling trees. "He's building up his dam. Beavers don't like the sound of running water – the tinkling and trickling noises that most of us humans find soothing – they try to stop it up where ever they are."

As he reached in front of her to point, Lila caught a whiff of his natural masculine scent, which was strong and reassuring – just the opposite of Tom Kidd's cheap cologne. "I never thought about why wild animals do what they do," she mused.

He pulled back and regarded her meaningfully. "Animals are no different than people," he said. "We all have a purpose for why we do what we do. We might not know it, but we have our reasons all the same."

"And what's the purpose of you getting all duded up and bringing me a bouquet of flowers?" she asked lightly.

"To impress a pretty girl that I admire and want to get to know better," said Hobart. He reached for her slender hand and held it gently within his own. "Is it working?"

Lila's first instinct was to retort with a flip remark, but to her embarrassment two giant tears welled up in her eyes. A flood of hot water threatened to follow. Mortified, she tugged away from him and covered her face with her hands. Despite valiant efforts, a sob escaped from her locked box of emotions.

Hobart's heartstrings tugged painfully in response. "Go ahead and cry," he encouraged. "Don't mind me."

His words and affectionate tone had an immediate effect and her thin chest heaved for several minutes with unmitigated feelings of grief and loss. "Ahhhnnnn, ahhhh, uhhnnn," she cried.

Unfazed, he rummaged around the seat of his truck and located a blue bandana. He held cloth out to Lila. "Here," he said. "Use my handkerchief – it's pretty clean."

Sniveling, Lila accepted the bandana without looking at him. Between tears and dilatory sobs she dried her eyes. "Sorry," she said, wiping her face. "That was stupid of me." She blew her nose into the handkerchief.

"Don't worry about it; I have three sisters," he said. "I'm used to it. Feel better?"

She inhaled a deep, wobbly breath and exhaled slowly with a new sense of serenity. "I do, actually," she said with a smile. "You have three sisters! I'm so envious—I'm an Only Child."

"Yeah, I have an older brother, too. But I'm the baby. One of my earliest memories is being decked out in a pink frilly dress and paraded around downtown Maple Grove in a doll carriage. My sisters tried to convince everyone I was a girl. I was three or four at the time, though, so not many of 'em bought it."

Lila laughed heartily. "That's too funny!" she said, daubing tears of laughter from her eyes. A thought popped into her head. "I wish I'd known you when you were a kid, Mike."

"Aw, you didn't miss much. I was a late bloomer."

"Me too," said Lila.

"You're blooming now; I can see it. You've changed—this place is good for you, Lila."

A Canada goose flew low overhead honking a warning to the beaver, and Lila leaned forward craning her neck to catch a glimpse of the fat gray bird through the top of the windshield. "I love it here," she said, dropping back against the seat. "I feel like I'm home. I never want to leave it." She shivered slightly.

"Cold?" Hobart said, anxiously. He switched on the truck's engine, and turned up the blower on the heater. "What an idiot! I forgot you're wearing those thin clothes."

"It's not the cold, it's … well, it's something else," Lila broke off lamely. She looked forlorn; lost.

Hobart thought she resembled an abandoned chick, unsure how to go about finding its mother. "If there's anything you need to talk about, feel free. I'm not the smartest guy in Sovereign, but I'm smart enough to shut up and listen."

Lila shook her head, wordlessly. She unconsciously ran her hand through her hair.

Hobart caught the fresh herbal scent atomized by the movement of her hair and had an overwhelming desire to crush her to his chest. He wanted to hold her; protect her; care for her *forever*. Instead, he gripped the steering wheel and shut his eyes, willing himself to maintain the respectful distance between them. He didn't want to rush in and take advantage of Lila in her vulnerable state. It wouldn't be the right thing – for either of them.

Moments later, he drew in a deep breath. "We better get going," he said, in a controlled voice; "or we're gonna be late."

Lila glanced at the dashboard clock. "It's five o'clock," she said. "We ARE late."

But instead of putting the truck in gear, Hobart sat stupidly gazing at Lila with yearning eyes. She was still clenching his blue bandana. He couldn't leave it like this. The guy on the white horse just wouldn't allow him to drive off without another word, as though nothing had occurred between them.

Maybe she had expected him to kiss her? Maybe she *wanted* him to kiss her? Maybe he was making the biggest mistake of his life by NOT kissing her?!

Hens and Chickens

Lila noted his hesitation, and correctly read in his unguarded eyes the tug of war that was ensuing in his breast. She felt a large measure of gratitude toward him. Not many men would have acted as he did – most, she felt sure, would have taken advantage of her vulnerable condition.

"Thanks for being such, such ... a gentleman, Mike," she said, regaining her composure. "It's kind of a corny, old-fashioned word – gentleman – and nobody uses it anymore, but it suits you." Lila refolded the blue bandana and proffered it to him with a hopeful smile.

"Keep it," he said, huskily. He gently pushed her hand back into her lap. "You might need it again."

She gave a little light-hearted laugh. "Omigod, that is so true! Thanks."

And then Hobart did put the truck in gear, glanced over his shoulder and pulled back out onto the tar road. Not another word needed to be said; even the guy on the white horse was satisfied.

Chapter 13

·······

Maude's Little Suppah Party

In rural Maine, the supper hour (or "suppah" as it's fondly known) is at 5 p.m., except in deep winter when the hour of repast dips in conjunction with the temperature and could be as early as 4 p.m. Supper is a small meal; on Saturday night it's typically baked beans and corn bread; other nights "suppah" might be chicken soup or venison stew or even Saltine crackers crumbled up into a bowl of fresh milk. Historically, "dinner" was always the big meal of the day, served up at noontime (when Maine's thousands of small dairy farmers were freed up from the twice daily chore of milking) with ham butts bigger than plates, roast chickens bursting at the seams with stuffing, and plenty of mashed potatoes, peas, hot biscuits and gravy. Food was – and still is – a central part of life for the rural Mainer, especially the family farmers, most of whom scratch out a subsistence living from the land, and, if nothing else, get to enjoy the earth's bounty and the fruit of their labors.

Maude Gilpin (nee Hodges) hailed from a dairy farm in Winslow (about 25 miles southwest of Sovereign) and was expertly trained in all the rigors and mysteries of a farmer's wife, including animal husbandry, domestic economy and larder management. The only problem was— Maude Hodges didn't marry a farmer! She had met Ralph Gilpin when he stopped by the farm one May afternoon in 1960 to sell kitchen wares (his grandfather wanting to indoctrinate Ralph well by starting him in the business as a travelling salesman), and Gilpin not only made his sale, but also, as he says, "carried off the best heifer in the pasture!"

Financially, Maude probably had a better life in Sovereign as the wife of a shopkeeper than she would have enjoyed if she had stayed down on the farm with one of the local boys. However, she not-so-secretly hankered for the life that might have been, and attempted to fill that longing through her baking. Ingredients never being in short supply in the Gilpin household, Maude became a legend in the little community, leading the charge of every bake sale, every fund-raiser, every benefit supper, in addition to stuffing her scanty household (comprised of a scrawny husband and two skinny children) with pies, cakes, cookies and homemade donuts.

Maude, now 71, was fat, pretty, gregarious and kind-hearted. Despite her size, Maude was light of foot and loved to twirl around the oversized kitchen that Ralph had ordered remodeled especially for her, most generally when she was in the throes of cooking for friends or loved ones. She put her precious Nat King Cole 33RPMs on the ancient stereo, turned up the volume, and sang and danced her way through her recipes as happy as a schoolgirl skipping school. Maude was adored by her husband, emulated by her daughter (who was now married to a dairy farmer and lived in neighboring Thorndike) and respected by the citizens of Sovereign. Altogether, Maude Gilpin was a happy woman.

Nowadays, nothing made Maude more jubilant than fussing over her grandson, Grayden ("Gray") Gilpin, age 15, who (like Ralph before him) helped his grandfather out in the store and was currently living with them while his father was off fighting the war in Afghanistan. Gray's parents were divorced, and his mother was re-married (for the second time since her divorce from Bruce Gilpin); and since both Gray and his mother were satisfied with the current living arrangements, the boy was likely to remain with his grandparents—forever, if Maude had her way, especially since his mother was not exactly the kind of role model she wanted for her grandson.

The other venture that made Maude's simple heart sing was meddling in the romantic affairs of young people. Ralph, who was by no means obtuse and who was also on close terms with his former employee, had dropped a hint to his wife as to the significance of this supper "date" for Mike Hobart and Lila Woodsum. Instantly, Maude's plans for a casual pot roast "suppah" (with potatoes, onions, turnip and biscuits) ripened into a formal standing rib roast dinner, with a locally-raised piece of prime rib the size of firewood to be saddled with boiled onions and winter squash dripping with freshly-churned butter, a garden salad (with organic greens and tomatoes from her daughter's hothouse in Thorndike), baked potatoes and gravy, yeast rolls, and the piece de resistance – a hot apple pie smothered in homemade vanilla ice cream.

"Fill the water glasses, please, Grayden," Maude instructed her grandson, as she expertly sliced the standing rib roast.

Hens and Chickens

"They ain't even here yet, Maude," said Ralph, worriedly. "Ain't ya cuttin' that roast a bit early?"

"Do I go down to your store and tell you how to run things?" Maude countered, without taking her eye off her task. "I do NOT. Please, don't tell me how to run my kitchen, dearie."

"It ain't like ..." Ralph began, twisting a dish towel in agitation.

"Stop it," said Maude, shaking the carving knife at him. "The roast has rested, and I need the juices to make the gravy. Besides, I hear Mike's truck, now."

Gray, a youthful replica of his bean-pole grandfather, pushed the country curtains aside and peered out the window. "It's Mike, Grandpa. Wow! He's holdin' the door for his chick, too! No wonder – she's pretty hot!"

"Is that any way to talk young man?" said Maude.

"Aw, c'mon, all the guys talk like that, Grandma."

"Well, you're not 'all the guys,' you're my grandson. And while you're living in this house you'll talk like a gentleman."

Ralph and Gray exchanged empathetic glances, and Ralph went to the front door to welcome Mike and Lila into the living room. He took Lila's coat and Mike's jacket, and handed them wordlessly to the slim shadow at his heels. Gray, despite having been instructed beforehand by his grandmother to remove the guests' coats to the bedroom, required a slight shove from Ralph to point him in the right direction and to keep him from outright ogling Lila.

"C'mon in," Ralph said, welcoming Lila and Hobart into the pleasant seating area. "Maude's cooking up a storm in the kitchen."

"I am NOT!" she called, from the other room. "I'm just making gravy."

"Smells awesome," said Lila, glancing around the cheerful 1920s two-story house, comfortably furnished in a modern country motif. "What a lovely home," she added.

"It's a 1918 Sears® manufactured home—my Grandpa bought it straight out of the *Modern Home* catalog," said Ralph proudly. "It's the Greenview Model; he paid $1,462 for it back then. Got himself quite a deal, didn't he?"

"This is a Sears® kit house?" asked Lila, lightly touching the walnut-colored wainscoting in obvious admiration.

"Ralph still has the guarantee certificate that came with the house," Hobart said, seating himself familiarly on the sofa. "I've seen it." He slung one arm over the back of the couch, and patted the vacant spot next to him. Lila sank down beside him.

"I'll show ya," the shopkeeper said. He approached an antique secretary, and eagerly rummaged through the top drawer. "Here – look at this!" Ralph brought an official-appearing paper certificate and handed it to Lila. "Whaddaya think of THAT?"

Lila curiously examined the aged, green and white certificate. "I've never seen anything like it," she said. "Look! It says, *'Full refund if customer is not satisfied',*" she read aloud. She handed the paper back to Ralph with a smile. "Seems like your grandfather was satisfied!"

"I should think so," Ralph exhorted. "He had the house built 94 years ago for his bride – and now I live here with MY bride!" He returned the certificate to the drawer and perched himself on the edge of the recliner that was situated across from the couple.

"You and Maude are newlyweds?" asked Lila, curiously, looking at Hobart for confirmation of this interesting fact.

Gilpin guffawed, and Gray tittered.

"I heard that!" said Maude from the kitchen.

Lila appeared confused, and Hobart dropped his arm to squeeze her hand reassuringly. "It's just a figure of speech," he explained. "Ralph and Maude have been married 52 years."

Ralph leaned forward and spoke in a stage whisper to Lila: "She's still my bride, though." He straightened up and raised his voice: "Didja hear that too, darlin'?"

"I heard you, dearie! Now, bring those kids into the dining room 'cause suppah's on the table!"

Maude was proud of her formal and thus rarely used dining room, which featured a rectangular solid-maple table, matching upholstered chairs, a glass-fronted hutch and serving buffet. Tonight the table, which was large enough to serve 12 comfortably, had been reduced to create a more intimate atmosphere and was laid with a floral-print linen cloth and complementing pastel green napkins. Gray had polished his grandparent's wedding silverware, and the multiple knives, forks and spoons gleamed in the soft amber light provided by eight beeswax candles that had been strategically placed for romantic efficacy on the table and throughout the square room. Crystal water glasses captured the flickering flames and they winked at one another like a field full of fireflies on a hot June night.

Hens and Chickens

"Cain't hardly see what I'm eatin'," complained Ralph, after the first heaping bowls of food had made the rounds.

"Shushhh, now," said his wife; "don't ruin things by complaining."

"Pass the salt, Grandpa," said Gray, smashing down a mountain of mashed potato.

"When do you expect you'll have your first eggs for sale?" asked Maude, anxious to steer the conversation into convivial territory.

Lila perked up. "I'm getting my first 100 laying hens next week—the day before Rebecca arrives," she answered. "Hopefully, by this time next week the hens will be settled in and we'll be open for business!"

Maude, who was not familiar with the finer details of *The Egg Ladies*, did not know who "Rebecca" was. A congenial hostess, however, she would not ask any impertinent questions. She smiled and nodded amiably. "Well, put me down for a standing order of four dozen eggs a week," she said. "I'll need more when the fiddleheads come in."

"Who's Rebecca?" interjected Gray, hopefully. "She your daughter?"

Lila's eyes twinkled with youthful understanding. "Sorry, Gray, Rebecca's my partner," she replied. "I came up from Massachusetts a month ahead of her to get the hen pen ready for the chickens. She's moving up on Wednesday—boy, I'll be glad when she gets here!"

"Your *partner*?!" squealed Maude, casting a horrified glance at Mike Hobart, whom she had seated deliberately next to Lila in order to facilitate his romantic endeavors.

"Business partner," explained Hobart, hastily. "Lila and her friend Rebecca Johnson are business partners in the *The Egg Ladies*."

Maude visibly relaxed. "More potato, Sweetie?" she said, rewarding Hobart by proffering him a bowl piled high with white fluffy Maine spuds. He took a second helping and passed the bowl over to Gray, who was eyeing the dish hungrily.

"I don't think I would have had the courage to move to Maine on my own, without Rebecca," continued Lila, unconsciously setting her knife down across the edge of her plate so she could use her hands while she talked. "I'm in charge of the chickens, the hen pen and most of the marketing," she enumerated; "and she's in charge of everything else, which means running the household, keeping our business accounts straight, AND keeping our customers happy."

"It must be *wonderful* to have another pair of hands to help with a project like that!" said Maude. "I always wondered what it would be like to have someone help me in the kitchen, especially when I'm working on preparing all the food for a big fundraiser."

"Pshaw!" exclaimed Ralph. "Ya wouldn't even let me help ya tonight!"

"Shushhh," said Maude. "Don't spoil the mood!"

"Did you find out where to get organic baby chicks yet, Lila?" asked Hobart, smoothly changing the subject.

"I found out better than that!" Lila exclaimed. "I read the information Tom Kidd gave me and discovered that I don't need to buy organic chicks to be certified – I just need to take possession of the chicks by the second day of their life, and then raise 'em organically."

"Great!" he replied. "I'm glad Kidd was finally good for something."

"You're going to sell organic eggs—that's wonderful!" said Maude.

"Do you think people around here will pay $4.50 a dozen for organic eggs?" Lila asked, worriedly.

Ralph leaned forward. "Ya jest charge what ya need to charge to pay yer bills," he instructed; "and some folks will buy, and some folks won't. I predict my Maude will be yer best customer – and if ya got any extra eggs ya cain't sell, I'll take 'em off yer hands down to the store!"

"How manby chickbens ya gonna hab?" mumbled Gray, attempting to dispose of a pile of lettuce.

"Don't talk with your mouth full," said his grandmother. "Where are your table manners tonight, young man!"

"My goal is to have 400 laying hens on-line, year-round; just like Wendell Russell's grandmother did," answered Lila, speaking more to the table at-large than to Gray. Her hazel eyes glowed with excitement. "That's what the hen pen is designed for. I'm starting with this flock of 100, and adding 200 replacement chicks this spring, and 200 more next spring. We'll have to make a few alterations to become organic certified, but by and large we're keeping the operation the way it was 50 years ago!"

"Do ya think ya might need someone to mow ya yard this summer?" asked Gray. "Cause I'm available."

"Ain't ya workin' for me this summer, young man?" asked his grandfather. "I thought that's what I was gettin' that old Ford back on the road for!"

"I gotta buy gas," retorted Gray, buttering a third yeast roll. "Plus I gotta save for college. I can work for ya AND mow on the side, Grandpa."

"Grayden's a worker," Maude said proudly to Lila. "No shillyshallying at the Mall for him, like *some* teenagers. More meat?"

Hens and Chickens

Lila politely declined the second helping of meat, and turned her friendly attention back to the teenager. She smiled at him across the table. "As far as I'm concerned, you're hired, Gray. Wendell said there's an old John Deere® riding lawn mower that comes with the place, and if you can get it going, you can use that to mow."

"Awesome!" exclaimed Gray, his eyes lighting up. "Hey, if that John Deere® don't run good, Mike, can ya help me fix it up?"

"You bet, buddy," said Hobart, who was fond of Ralph and Maude's grandson. "You certainly don't want your grandfather helping you – he's all thumbs when it comes to mechanics."

"I ain't all thumbs—I'm jest particular," muttered Ralph. "That's why I always hire stuff done."

"Yeah, right," said Hobart, winking at Gray.

"That's sweet of you to help Grayden, Mike," said Maude. "Just so's you know, I feel a batch of bread pudding coming on real soon!"

"Hey, have ya seen Tinkerbell this year yet, Mike?" Gray asked Hobart, taking a gulp of milk.

"Tinkerbell?!" exclaimed Lila. Her startled fork *clinked* against the water glass. "I KNEW this was a Peter Pan kind of a place! Why doesn't it surprise me that there are fairies in Sovereign!"

"Tinkerbell's an albino deer," Gray corrected, setting down his glass. "She ain't no fairy. I saw her last summer in that big field out behind ya place. Miss Hastings was the one who named her Tinkerbell, not me!"

"Tinkerbell is actually not an albino," said Hobart; "but a white-colored, white tail deer. And just between you and me, Gray, Tinkerbell is actually Tinker*beau*—she's a HE, not a doe. But don't tell Miss Hastings. I know she'd be disappointed."

"A white deer!" said Lila, shaking her head in amazement. "I never knew there WAS such a thing."

"It's a genetic quirk," explained Hobart. "There's a long history in Sovereign of a herd containing white deer. Hunters used to come from all over the United States to try and bag one. I heard of the white deer long before I went to Unity College, but I never got to see one until last year, when Tinkerbell surfaced."

"But don't you people hunt deer up here, Mike?" asked Lila, worriedly.

A look of discomfort crossed Hobart's face. "Well, I don't hunt anymore, but ..."

"I do!" interrupted Gray. "My Dad bought me a 12-gauge shotgun for Christmas and Grandpa said I could hunt this year." He turned to his grandfather for confirmation. "Right, Grandpa?"

"After ya take — and pass — that hunter's safety course," Ralph reminded him.

"Don't you worry, Sweetie," Maude said to Lila; "nobody in Sovereign would shoot Tinkerbell. Everyone knows how fond Miss Hastings is of that white deer! And if *you* post *your* land to hunting, just like all your neighbors, the white deer will be protected from hunters from Away."

"Well, there's no guarantee of that, unfortunately," Hobart said, uneasily. "Hunters don't have the *esprit de corps* they used to. Plus there's so much posted land nowadays that many hunters can't find a place to hunt, so they just ignore the signs and hunt where the deer are."

"I'll definitely post my land AND keep my eyes peeled," said Lila, firmly. "No one's going to shoot Tinkerbell on MY land!" Lila unconsciously pushed her empty dinner plate away from her. Maude was quick to catch the signal, and she rose to clear the table.

"I just hope I get a chance to see Tinkerbell!" Lila added, excitedly.

"I'll help ya keep an eye out when I'm over there," offered Gray. "I'm pretty good at spottin' deer."

"If yer wanting to help someone, why don't ya help yer grandmother clear the table," Ralph directed his grandson.

"Let me help," said Lila, half rising from her chair.

"No, no; you and Mike just sit right there, Sweetie, and make yourselves comfortable," urged Maude. "My two boys can help me." She winked obviously at Ralph and indicated with a little nod of her fat head that her husband, as well as Gray, should follow her through the swinging doors into the kitchen. "We won't be but a few minutes and we'll be back with the dessert."

A pleasurable, companionable silence ensued after the three Gilpins departed from the candlelit dining room, leaving Lila and Hobart alone together. Lila sat staring at the crystal glasses, mesmerized by the flickering lights.

Hobart spoke first. "Having a good time?" he asked.

Lila nodded, eyes glowing. "What an amazing family! I'm so glad I've had the opportunity to meet them," she said. "Too bad Gray isn't a little older; he'd be perfect for Rebecca's daughter, Amber."

"I'm glad the kid's not any older or he might give *me* a run for my money," said Hobart, emphatically. He placed his linen napkin on the table not far from Lila's hand. "You seem to like him pretty well!"

Hens and Chickens

"He's totally cute," said Lila. Of its own volition her fingers crept toward his hand like a sand crab seeking shelter. Within moments, they were holding hands.

Hobart toyed with her feminine palm, leisurely rolling and unrolling her delicate fingers. "I could sit like this forever," he said, lazily.

An absurd contentment pervaded Lila's being. "You wouldn't get much work done that way," she said, lightly.

"All work and no play might make Lila go away," he said, leaning closer to her.

"I'd like to learn how to play," she said. "I never played much as a kid – the Only Child thing, you know."

"I can teach you," he murmured into her ear. His lips brushed her hair.

"I bet you can!" she giggled.

Gray peeked out through the swinging doors. "Geez, Grandma, they're holdin' hands!" he whispered loudly.

Hobart sat bolt upright in his chair. "Not anymore, though," he called. "You can come back in, now!"

Chapter 14

·······

"Something New…
In Those Eyes"

Maude's little "suppah" party broke up about 9:30 p.m. On the drive home, Hobart pulled the truck into the same turn-out where they had spotted the beaver earlier in the evening. He switched off the headlights, turned up the truck's heater and rolled down his window. His handsome face was barely visible in the celestial rays of the moon. "Close your eyes and listen," he directed Lila. "Tell me what you hear."

Lila shut her eyes dutifully and concentrated. At first, all she heard was silence billowing in on the ethereal mist from Black Brook. But as her hearing became more acute, she picked up a faint intonation from the swamp – *peep, peep, peep!*

"A baby chicken!" she cried, opening her eyes in amazement. "What's it doing here? Where's its mother?!"

"It's actually a spring peeper; a tree frog," Hobart replied, with satisfaction. "What you're hearing is a mating call from a small brown frog not much bigger than the tip of your thumb. It's one of the first sounds of spring around here."

"I've heard of peepers," said Lila, "but I never knew what they were."

"There's a vernal pool in the woods above your house," continued Hobart; "you've probably got some peepers of your own up there. In a few days there will be a whole chorus of peepers and they'll sound like sleigh bells off in the distance."

"I'm going to sleep with my window open from now on!"

"That will work – until the bull frogs and the wood frogs come on line – then you'll have to shut your window or the noise will drive you crazy. I'm not kidding."

Lila laughed. Her eyes had grown accustomed to the dim moonlight, and she deliberately sought his steady gaze. "Thank you for an amazing evening, Mike," she said, simply. "I never knew I could be so happy!"

Hobart felt an unusual tightness in his chest as his heart swelled beyond the bounds of normal felicity. He reached over and took her hand. "Let's see if we can keep it going," he said, suggestively.

"That shouldn't be a problem, since both my chickens AND Rebecca arrive next week!"

"That wasn't quite what I meant," he said, drily. "Score *one* for Sovereign honesty, and *zero* for the male ego!"

"Oops," said Lila, giggling. "Sorry!"

"Don't apologize; I wouldn't want it any other way." Hobart closed the truck window. "There's a deer," he said, quickly. "I can just make it out. It's drinking on the other side—see it?" He directed her gaze across the moonlit brook, where the mist had now evanished as discreetly as a curtain on a darkened stage.

"I see it!" she said.

"This place is a regular wildlife corridor. You never know what you're going to see when you stop for a while."

"Or hear," Lila said, as the frogs' volume had increased. "I get what you mean about the noise!"

"Mmmhmm," he said. "Frog mating calls are one of my favorite sounds."

Lila giggled again. She started to say something, but hesitated. She gave Hobart a measured look.

"What is it?" he asked.

"Since you seem to be sincere about this honesty stuff," she said; "there IS something I'm curious about."

"What? I don't have many deep, dark secrets."

"Why were you so uncomfortable talking about deer hunting at dinner?" she asked, frankly. "And what made you decide to stop hunting?"

Hobart was slightly taken aback. "I didn't realize I was so obvious," he said.

"Maybe not to everyone; but I noticed that you seemed sort of …" she broke off.

"Tortured?" he finished. "I don't have many deep, dark secrets, but that's one of 'em. I've never told anyone why I stopped hunting; not even my Dad, although he stopped hunting years ago himself."

Lila instantly regretted her forwardness. "Oh, don't tell me, then!" she cried.

Hens and Chickens

But Hobart was not going to let this opportunity for deeper communion slip away. He wanted an honest, open and caring relationship with Lila, and he was willing to bare his soul to secure it. Whether she was ready or not, well, only time would tell. "I *want* to tell you, Lila," he said, meaningfully. "I don't want to have any secrets from you."

Lila shivered at the implied intimacy of his remark. She closed her eyes, hiding from him the hunger for love that reciprocated his own.

Taking her silence for assent, he reached out and tenderly drew her into his arms. Lila sighed with pleasure, and nestled against his warm, sturdy chest. He rested his chin on top of her head and breathed in the sweet scent of her hair. She felt his heart skip a beat beneath the rough wool of his sweater. They sat blissfully together in the moonlight as time slipped away like a sunset.

"It's kind of a long story," Hobart said, after several minutes of refreshing silence.

"I've got all the time in the world," Lila replied, snuggling against his chest. She exhaled contentedly.

Hobart gathered his thoughts. "I grew up hunting and fishing, just like most boys in Maine," he began. "We lived next door to the largest wilderness east of the Mississippi, after all. My father bought me my first gun – a 20-gauge shotgun – when I was nine. I killed my first deer, an eight-point buck, when I was 10. In fact, I picked Unity College so I could study conservation law. I wanted to be a game warden in Maine when I grew up."

Surprised, Lila opened her eyes and looked up at him. "That didn't happen!"

"No, that didn't happen." Hobart paused for reflection.

"Because ..." she encouraged.

"Because I had sort of an Aldo Leopold moment my freshman year while I was out deer hunting with a college classmate. I stopped hunting as a result, and changed my major to earth science. I fell in love with trees, and became a carpenter."

"Who was this Aldo Leopard guy?" Lila asked, jealously. She wanted to know who it was that had so much influence over him.

Hobart groaned in disbelief. "You've never heard of Aldo Leopold? Pioneer of the modern environmental movement! Author of *A Sand County Almanac*?"

Lila trailed her fingers lightly across his chest. "Nope."

"Let me guess—they didn't teach environmental ethics and wilderness conservation in that marketing Master's program?"

"If they did, I skipped class that day."

"That would have been a big mistake," he assured her. "Someday, I'll read you some of Leopold's writings. I think you'd like them."

"I think I'd like anything YOU like," she said. "But there's more to your story, right?"

"There's more. Sure you want to hear the details? They're pretty gruesome," he said, anxiously.

"Don't worry about me," she said. "I want to hear everything."

Hobart took another minute or two to collect his thoughts. "We were hunting on some of the town owned woodlots that day," he continued, in a more distant tone of voice; "in that wilderness area that butts up against Wendell's woodlot." Lila closed her eyes again as he reminisced, and imagined that she was tramping through the woods with Hobart and his friend. She could almost smell the musty scent of the forest as he spoke.

"We jumped a couple of skippers, yearlings, in the cedar swamp near the Troy town line. My college classmate was a beginning hunter and he got buck fever—kind of a nervous over-excitement at seeing a deer. His hands shook so much he could hardly keep his gun steady. He fired like crazy into the woods, even though we could barely see the flags of the two deer leaping away from us. He kept firing; he missed one, but hit the other one – a button buck – and the bullet broke its back, but didn't kill it."

"Oh, no!" exclaimed Lila. She looked up and saw a mixture of disgust and distress revealed in his honest blue eyes.

"The deer went down and started to thrash. It *bleated* like a helpless goat; it was awful to hear. And then the poor thing started to whimper, almost like a *baby*. When we reached the downed deer, my classmate took one look at the bloody mess, and then turned and ran."

Hobart choked up. Lila felt empathetic tears spring into her own eyes. She pressed his hand reassuringly, but said nothing.

He cleared his throat. "The deer was still alive," he went on. "He was looking at me with the saddest brown eyes I've seen. I almost could hear him thinking: *Don't shoot me!*" Hobart paused. "I'd never had difficulty killing anything until that moment. But the deer was obviously suffering, and I knew I couldn't leave him like that for the coyotes. I threw my jacket over his legs—I was afraid if I didn't pin him down he'd slice me with those sharp hooves. I took my hunting knife and slit his throat. I held the deer's head in my lap while his life just slipped away. One moment he was alive; the next he was gone." A hot tear fell from Hobart's eye and landed on Lila's hand. The precious fluid rolled down her arm, cooling as it dispersed. "He was such a pretty little thing."

"Shhhh," she whispered, reaching up and running her fingers through the stiff curls of his hair. "You don't need to say anymore!" But Lila knew that he did not hear her nor feel the light touch of her hand—he was not present in the truck with her; he was still in the woods with the dying deer in his lap.

Hobart lifted his head and gazed into the sublime. *"We reached the old wolf in time to watch a fierce green fire dying in her eyes,"* he quoted. *"I realized then, and have known ever since, that there was something new to me in those eyes—something known only to her and to the mountain."* He drew in a tremulous breath. "Thank God for Aldo Leopold!" he proclaimed. "What he wrote about his experience with the old mother wolf helped me understand my hunting incident in a positive way. There was *something new* revealed to me that day. And I've never hunted; never fired a gun—never killed anything since," he concluded, simply.

Lila could no longer hold back her tears. "Omigod," she said, weeping openly. She groped with her right hand around the cab of the truck until she located his blue bandana. "I didn't know I would need this again so soon!" She wiped the tears from her face and blew her nose.

Hobart ruffled her short black hair. "Thanks for listening," he said, awkwardly. "I never thought I'd tell that story to anybody, except maybe my Dad someday."

"You're a special guy, Mike Hobart," Lila said. Her eyes glowed openly with admiration. She took his hand affectionately.

"Aw, I'm not that great," he said. "I'm just a regular Maine guy." Nevertheless, he was pleased. He toyed with her hand, and his heart began to sing.

"Well, you're not like any guy I've ever known!"

"My Dad's been a big influence in my life. Now, *he's* a special guy!"

"Is he still alive?"

"Oh, yeah; Dad is very much alive!"

Lila felt a deep stirring of grief as Hobart spoke of his father. His words brought to her mind memories of her own beloved father, who had died when she was five years old. She had loved him; and she had lost him. Life was so fleeting! One minute her father was alive, like Hobart's deer, and the next minute he was gone; bringing to an end to life as she knew it—including her innocent childhood.

She trembled at the memories of what had followed on the heels of her father's death—and then thought of that slightly yellowed letter from her mother tucked away in her keepsake box. *I will not let the past affect me! I CAN do this!*

But not tonight.

"It's been a lovely evening, Mike," she said, pulling apart from him with obvious regret. "I don't want to end it, but I think I should go home now. I've got a lot to do before my chickens arrive. Plus Rebecca's coming on Wednesday!"

Hobart experienced a sudden letdown. He had been hoping for … what? A kiss, maybe? But he had told Lila that he would allow her to set the pace and tone of their relationship, and he would honor that decision.

"No problem," he said, easily. He regrouped himself and fastened his seatbelt. Before he put the vehicle in gear, however, he scrutinized her closely. Once again, her demeanor made him think of an abandoned chick searching for its mother. "Don't forget what I told you earlier," he reminded her. "If you ever need someone to listen to *your* deep dark secrets; I'm available."

"Thanks, I'll keep that in mind. But I think I've had enough tears for one evening!"

"Me too," he admitted. "Me too!"

Lila tittered, her peculiar chickadee-like laugh that he loved to hear, and once again all was right with the world.

Chapter 15

· · · · · · ·

The New Arrivals

Lila was not exaggerating when she told the Gilpins she was depending upon Rebecca to manage the domestic affairs of the household as well as the business side of *The Egg Ladies*. She had been so busy working with Mike Hobart to prepare the hen pen for the arrival of the chickens, that she had barely given the house a second thought. Piles of magazines and poultry catalogs were stacked up like plates on the kitchen table and some had followed her like friendly pets into the living room. Lila had transformed the dining room into a makeshift office, and here her laptop and other office accoutrements were holding court on the rectangular oak dining room table. Lila's clothes and personal items were confined to her bedroom, however, that was also the only room (except the bathroom) she had thoroughly cleaned before taking occupation, which was now nearly six weeks ago.

"Place ain't changed much," Wendell said when he visited Lila on Monday morning to check on the time the laying hens would arrive the following day. He surveyed the kitchen and peeked around the corner into the great room, a combination living-dining room. "Good thing I took the newspapers off the furniture so's you'd have some place to sit down."

"You mean, so I'd have a place to put more stuff," Lila said. "I know that's what you're really thinking, Wendell. But don't worry, Rebecca's a GREAT housekeeper. She'll have me whipped into shape in no time!"

"Wal, you know—it's *yore* house," Wendell replied. "I'm jest glad to have someone livin' heah agin." A bashful look came over his good-natured face. "When do you expect yore little friend?"

"Who?" Lila asked. She was not used to hearing the pleasingly plump Rebecca referred to as 'little' and at first didn't know to whom he was referring.

"Yore *little friend.*"

"Oh, REBECCA!" Lila said, catching on. "Wednesday afternoon, thank goodness! Her daughter Amber and some friends are driving the rental truck up with all of her stuff, and Becca's following in the car with her cat."

"Wal, you know, if you need some help, jest let me know," Wendell offered. "I ain't as shaap as I used to be, but I kin still help." Lila's phone *jingled* and Wendell headed for the kitchen door to let himself out.

"Remember, the hens arrive at 10 a.m.," she called after him, as she picked up her phone.

Wendell paused and grinned. "I'll be ovah!" he replied. "Wouldn't miss it for a second helping of Ma Jean's blackberry pie!"

On the phone was Miss Hastings, who was also following up on Rebecca's imminent arrival. Lila filled her friend and neighbor in on the details, and then reminded her of the big day tomorrow. "Don't forget, Mike's going to pick you up around 9:30," she said; "so you'll be here in plenty of time to see the chickens!"

"Dahrrrling, I'll be there with bells on!" Miss Hastings said. "I've got my best duds all laid out, ready to roll!"

For some reason, however, Mike Hobart showed up at the old Russell homestead an hour earlier than scheduled. Lila, who had been excitedly bringing her followers on Twitter up to date with the latest on *The Egg Ladies*, was freshly showered but still dressed in her bathrobe. Her wet hair, slicked back behind her ears, looked blacker than ever and once again reminded Hobart, when she opened the door, of a chickadee's cap.

Lila's heart fluttered wildly at the sight of him. "This is awkward," she said, pulling the pink fuzzy robe closer about her slender frame to keep out the damp chill from the April morning.

"Not for me," Hobart replied. "But I can see how Wendell might be embarrassed."

"You're an hour early, Mike!"

"Yes, but I would have been an hour *late* if I hadn't run into the truck driver with your chickens asking for directions here while I was getting my coffee at Gilpin's."

"Omigod! He's HERE already?!"

"On the way up the hill, even as we speak. Why don't you call Wendell while I run up and get Miss Hastings. Oh, and you might want to put some clothes on, darling."

Hens and Chickens

Lila shut the door, totally flummoxed. *The chickens are finally here!* she thought, doing a little dance on the way to the bedroom. But it was when she was dressing that she registered the other reason why her heart was singing. *Did he just call me DARLING?*

The farmer from whom Lila had purchased the laying hens turned into her driveway only moments after she'd pulled on her Muck™ boots. She dashed outside and directed him to back the truck up to the lower entrance to the hen pen. The chickens, New Hampshire reds, were confined in wire cages stacked three-deep on the truck. Despite being packed generously, only four to a cage, the chickens were understandably excited by their trip up from southern Maine and squawked and jostled for position as though they were passengers on the Titanic.

"Hey, girls! Welcome home!" Lila called to the hens at large. She laughed happily. "Omigod, I didn't know you were so big!"

While the truck backed up, Wendell ambled over the mushy spring ground from Bud's place in a gait slightly faster than usual. He pulled his plastic comb quickly through his hair in a final finish to his morning toilet and returned it to the back pocket of his jeans. "Ain't they shaap-lookin'," he said to Lila, in a voice loud enough to override the cacophony of cackling chickens.

"You think so?" asked Lila, eagerly, seeking reassurance from the veteran chicken farmer. "They don't look too beat up by the trip?"

"Nah, they git ovah thet pretty quick," he said. The truck came to a stop four feet from the lower entrance and Wendell leaned in to examine the birds more closely. "They're jest the size they should be for one year olds," he said; "and they still got plenty of good color." He directed Lila's attention to a particular hen in the cage nearest to them. "Course you want to see thet yellow in them legs; means they still got a lot of egg-layin' left in 'em."

Before the hens were unloaded Lila dutifully paid the farmer, who scribbled her out a receipt on the back of an old grain slip he scrounged up from his truck. By that time, Hobart had returned with Miss Hastings, dressed in her Sunday best.

Miss Hastings was as excited as Lila. "Dahrrrling, I'm so happy for you!" she exclaimed, squeezing Lila's hand. "I knew you'd be much better off up here with us than staying at that stuffy old insurance company in Boston!"

Miss Hastings' words momentarily transported Lila back to that February morning when Rebecca had been fired and she'd walked out on Joe Kelly. It seemed a lifetime ago to her now. "You were so right about that!" she said.

Mike Hobart and the farmer ferried the 25 cages of chickens into the hen pen, where Wendell cheerfully released one bird at a time, tossing them lightly into the rejuvenated coop. Hobart had completely rebuilt most of the nest boxes, and Lila had covered the boxes with a white primer and then painted the entire hen pen with a red-mite paint that was approved for certified organic use. Four new galvanized poultry feeders hung down from the high ceiling like stalactites and were strategically situated near the grain chutes for easy refilling. Two large waterers rose up like stalagmites from the floor of the coop, which was now ankle-deep in a pine-scented mixture of organic sawdust and sweet straw that MOGG regulations required.

After the farmer departed, the four friends gathered in the hen pen with mutual satisfaction to watch the birds adapt to their new home. The newly liberated red chickens fluttered and *squawked* and flew a short distance about the hen pen before flapping to the ground or alighting onto the spruce polls that Hobart had installed in a raised, theatre-seat style for the roosts. The feathers on the large-breasted birds were a consistent chestnut color, except for the short tail feathers, which looked as though they had been dipped in a pail of black paint.

"What DAHRRRLING birds!" said Miss Hastings, who – not much taller than the poultry waterer and dressed in a fringed yellow shawl – looked much like a chicken herself.

"New Hampshire reds are not the best egg-layers," Lila confided to Miss Hastings; "they're more of a dual-purpose breed, both egg AND meat. But they were the only organic flock I could find that was for sale."

Miss Hastings patted Lila's hand reassuringly. "They are simply wonderful, dahrrrling; WONDERFUL!"

"Ayuh, you done good," agreed Wendell. "And look! – you got one settin' in a nest box already!"

While Wendell pointed out the lone setting hen to Miss Hastings, Mike Hobart took the opportunity of the diversion to lean over and place a light kiss on the nape of Lila's neck. She shivered at the feather-weight touch of his lips. "Good job, darling," he whispered.

Lila's face flushed with pride. Tears of joy filled her eyes. She brushed them away with her hand, and sniveled slightly.

"What, no handkerchief?" he said, searching his jacket pockets for his replacement blue bandanna. "This is getting to be a regular habit."

Hens and Chickens

No further work occurred during the rest of the day, which seemed like a merry holiday to Lila. The four friends celebrated the arrival of the chickens by going out to lunch at Ma Jean's restaurant, where they cheerfully shared the particulars of the day's event with several other interested patrons. Word passed around quickly that *The Egg Ladies* of Sovereign, Maine was now open for business. After lunch, each went their separate way. Hobart dropped Miss Hastings at her cottage, then proceeded down to Troy to put together a quote on a post and beam horse barn for a family named Shorey. Wendell went back to Bud's place to work on one of his many tinkering projects.

Lila herself spent most of the afternoon in the hen pen, observing her chickens and photographing them so that she could post new pictures to Twitter. She had provided herself in advance with a small, red plastic pail half-filled with organic scratch corn, and soon found herself overrun with the friendly, *cluck clucking* creatures.

"Whoa! Hold up—there's plenty for everyone! *There's plenty for everyone!*" she cried, feeling like a Mardi Gras float participant dispensing loot as she tossed handfuls of coarsely-ground corn to the milling hens.

Lila hardly slept that night, so eager was she for the arrival of Rebecca to complete *The Egg Ladies* operation. Although Lila had missed her best friend, she also recognized how much she had matured during this time that she had been making her own way in Sovereign. She slept with the bedroom window open several inches – as she had slept every night since the dinner party at Maude's – and since that evening, as Mike Hobart had predicted, the initial solitary peeps from the tree frogs had swelled exponentially into the soothing sound of distant sleigh bells.

Rebecca and the caravan from Massachusetts arrived mid-afternoon the next day. The two friends hugged, and exchanged warm greetings.

"I'm soo glad you're here, Becca!" Lila enthused.

"I can't *wait* to see the house again!" said Rebecca, her pretty face flushed with excitement. "But Amber just wants to see her new bedroom!"

"You get your pick of three upstairs rooms," said Lila, turning to Rebecca's young daughter. Amber, a slim 21-year-old with gorgeous waist-length hair the burnt-brown color of her mother's, was accompanied by two female college classmates. "I haven't been beyond the bottom of the stairs since your mother was here," Lila added.

"Oh, my goodness!" said Rebecca. "That was quite a while ago!"

"Eggs-actly," joked Lila.

Lila respectfully restrained herself while Rebecca gave Amber and her friends a thorough tour of their new home. Rebecca pointed out highlights from every room, such as the huge soapstone sink in the kitchen, the white porcelain claw foot tub in the bathroom, and, of course, the precious copy of Grammie Addie's cookbook shelved in the kitchen cupboard just like in Addie's time. Rebecca's pretty blue eyes shone with proprietary pride as the young people sang the praises of the antique farmhouse and all of its comfortable furnishings.

"It's amazing—just what I'd imagined!" Amber exclaimed, twirling around the cheerful front upstairs bedroom that she had selected as her own. "I can't wait 'til summer!"

Rebecca beamed with satisfaction and pleasure. "You like it?"

"I love it!" Amber pulled her mother down onto one of the twin beds, and wrapped her arms around Rebecca's neck. "I'm so happy for you, Mom!" she cried. She laid her head on her mother's shoulder and closed her eyes. Overjoyed, Rebecca stroked her daughter's hair lovingly.

Lila watched the affectionate interplay between mother and daughter with dueling pangs of loss and envy as she remembered her own mother. She turned away to hide her tears, and a flickering sensation of shame darted out like a hungry flame from her subconscious.

Back in the lock box! she commanded her emotions. *I will NOT let the past ruin my future!*

Lila quickly regained her composure. "When are you done school?" she asked, turning back to Amber.

"May 24th – and I've already got my bus ticket for Bangor! That's the closest city to Sovereign I can get."

"One of us will drive down and get you, if you want," Lila offered.

"Thanks, but I'm pretty used to public transportation."

"Well, don't get TOO used to it, 'cause up here 'public transportation' is catching a ride from a neighbor!"

The little group laughed.

Lila was somewhat disappointed by Rebecca's lackluster interest in the chickens and the hen pen, especially since that had been the focus of Lila's efforts during the prior six weeks. Bemused, she reminded herself that their partnership was likely to be that much MORE successful because of their separate interests. Already, Rebecca was making lists of necessary purchases for the kitchen and bedrooms, and had even

Hens and Chickens

suggested a dinner party – to include Miss Hastings, Wendell, the Gilpins and Mike Hobart – for the following weekend.

Amber and her college friends departed early the following morning, in order to return the rental truck on time and to ensure that they didn't miss any more classes than necessary. Rebecca and her daughter exchanged tearful hugs goodbye, and then Amber clambered up into the truck.

"I'll see you in a little more than a month!" Rebecca cried, as the trio backed out of the driveway.

Amber stuck her head out the window. "I forgot to tell you, Mom – all my friends are following @TheEggLadies on Twitter!" she called.

"Don't forget to text me when you get back!"

Both Lila and Rebecca waved until the empty rental truck disappeared down Russell Hill. The early morning in Sovereign was then still, except for the sounds of awakening birds eagerly going about their work. Three robins hopped eagerly across the side lawn, looking for worms. A phoebe called from a nearby cedar fencepost: *"Phoebe! Phoebe!"* A mourning dove crooned hauntingly from a high limb in the Staircase Tree. The musky scent of spring and a hint of sweet grass filled the soft country air.

Rebecca, feeling the familiar sadness creeping in, took Lila's arm companionably. "Looks like it's just you and me now, *partner,*" she said, with an extra attempt at cheerfulness.

But Lila's thoughts had already wandered off to revisit with pleasure yesterday's light kiss from Mike Hobart and she barely noticed Rebecca's touch. *When will I see him again?!*

"Lila?"

"Mmmm?" she said, feeling a warm spot of sunlight on her back.

Rebecca, whose own chick had just flown the nest once again, turned her motherly eyes back to her friend. With a little shock, she registered the change in Lila – the glow of inner satisfaction that had replaced the hurt and anger; the perpetual smile that replaced the scowl and frown; the happy lilt to her gait that replaced the purposeful stride. This was certainly a far cry from the young woman who had stalked out of Joe Kelly's office in February!

Rebecca had also been reading between the tweets with some accuracy of the developing relationship between Lila and the handsome carpenter. "Hmmm," she said aloud. "Maybe it's *not* just you and me!"

"Maybe not," said Lila, lazily. "Maybe not!"

Chapter 16

·······

Mouse Motel

Lila was awakened in the middle of the night by an awful screech. At first, because her window was open, she thought the noise that disturbed her slumber must have been the blood-curdling shriek of a prowling owl. However, when the ceiling above trembled and the cries continued, Lila realized that the distress was emanating from Rebecca's bedroom directly above her.

Not knowing what to think, Lila tossed the down comforter aside and leaped out of bed. In her flannel pajamas she rushed to the bottom of the stairs, grabbing an antique cane along the way, liberating the crutch from its 40-year hiatus by the corner of the brick fireplace. "Are you alright?!" she called up to Rebecca. She took the stairs two at a time.

"Naooo!" screamed Rebecca; and Lila heard what sounded like a struggle on her friend's bed.

"What IS it?!" she cried, bursting into Rebecca's bedroom, brandishing the maple cane.

Her friend, pale-faced and trembling – long brown hair disheveled – stood upright on the bed in her white cotton nightdress, with the sheet pulled up nearly to her chin. Lila's anxious eyes scanned the room but found nothing out of the ordinary! There was no prowler, no rapist, no terrorist, no marauding vigilantes—not even a wayward bat!

Lila turned her gaze back to her friend in wonder. Rebecca did not appear to be having a nightmare or sleepwalking. "What IS it?" Lila repeated, lowering her weapon. "What's wrong?!"

"There!" shrieked Rebecca, pointing to a dark spot on the painted floor near the stenciled pine dresser.

Lila followed Rebecca's finger and saw—a tiny gray mouse scrunched up on its haunches looking as harmless as a plastic computer mouse! The rodent evidently thought that its odds were diminished by Lila's arrival,

117

however, and took the opportunity to shoot across the floor in a beeline for the door. Instinctively, Lila raised her bare right foot and brought it down with a fierce *stomp*. She felt a warm bulge beneath her sole and knew that her timing had been accurate.

"EEeewww!" Rebecca said, covering her face with her hands. "How *could* you, Lila?!"

"It's just a mouse," said Lila, lifting her foot. Sure enough, the flattened gray rodent lay lifeless on the ginger-colored floor. She leaned down, picked the mouse up by the tail and quickly moved the bitty carcass behind her back so Rebecca couldn't see it. "There's quite a few of 'em around here," she continued. "You'll get used to it."

"I will *not* !" exclaimed Rebecca, opening her eyes and stiffening up for battle. "That, that … *creature* ran right up over me in bed! I will not have mice in the house, Lila. I will not!"

Lila fought back the urge to laugh aloud. "Umm, haha – where's Mr. T?" asked Lila, biting the inside of her lip. "Your cat should take care of these critters in a few days." She glanced once again around Rebecca's neat bedroom. "Where IS Mr. T? I thought he always slept with you?"

Rebecca sheepishly dropped the white sheet she had been holding, and there, curled up in bed with her, was the 13-pound, four-year-old tiger cat. Exposed to the cool air, Mr. T yawned, and rolled over on his back, showing off his spotted belly. The tabby reached out with one white boot and lazily touched Rebecca's bare leg.

This time Lila did burst out laughing. "Haaahaaa! Mr. T is not gonna carry his weight around here, I can see that!" She laughed so hard she had to sit down in the oak rocking chair situated next to Rebecca's window. The cane she had been carrying fell on the wooden floor with a *clack*. Mr. T didn't even flinch.

Rebecca giggled, and relaxed her defiant stance on the bed. "I won't have mice in the house, Lila," she repeated, in a diminished tone. "We've got to do something. I *hate* mice!"

"Oh, I get that," said Lila, taking care to keep the dead mouse out of Rebecca's line of vision. "Haaahaaa! Too funny! I totally get that!"

After disposing of the mouse down the toilet, Lila tried to convince Rebecca to return to her bed for the balance of the night. However, her stubborn friend insisted on holding vigil on the living room couch, covered up with a spare quilt from the blanket chest in Amber's bedroom. The quilt, which had been packed away for decades, smelled like moth balls,

Hens and Chickens

and Lila was glad to return to her own bedroom, where the fresh evening air seeped in from the partially open window.

Lila awoke late the next morning to the tantalizing scent of frying bacon. She hurried into her jeans and oversized sweatshirt, and popped into the kitchen. She discovered Rebecca cooking away and regaling Wendell – who had ambled over early to see how the new hens were laying – with the night's adventures. Lila repressed her greeting and slid into a chair. She gratefully accepted the cup of coffee that Rebecca poured and set on the table in front of Lila without missing a beat in her story.

"And then," Rebecca continued; "the poor mouse tried to escape out the door, but Lila *stomped* on it!"

"Didja kill it?" Wendell asked Lila, with renewed respect.

"With her *bare foot*!" Rebecca answered, not waiting for Lila to reply. She set a plate down for Wendell that contained two cheerful-looking poached eggs on buttered, homemade toast.

Wendell's eyes widened. Lila didn't have long to wonder whether he was more interested in the mouse story or the farm fresh eggs cooked to perfection, as he eagerly picked up his fork.

"It was deader than a dormouse," Lila added, taking a large sip of coffee. Unfortunately, she started to giggle at the memory of Mr. T and some of the hot liquid went painfully up her nose.

"It's *not* funny, Lila!" Rebecca said, waving a slotted spoon at her younger friend. "I won't have mice in the house! I checked all of bottom cupboards in here and found *three* mouse holes and *lots* of mouse droppings! How would you like your eggs cooked, dear?"

"Um, poached, thanks," she said, blowing her nose on a paper napkin. She turned to Wendell and attempted to change the subject. "So, what do you think of our very first eggs?"

Wendell swallowed his initial bite of poached egg and was about to reply when Rebecca interjected again.

"I'm sorry to say this, Wendell," Rebecca said, cracking an egg on edge of the cook stove; "but this place has a major mouse infestation!" She dropped the yolk and white into the pot of boiling water with a *sizzling* splash.

Wendell looked chagrined. He put down his fork. "Wal, you know, I kinda thought there was a problem ovah heah." He looked at Lila almost accusatorily. "Why didn't you say nuthin' earlier?" he asked. "Afore yore little friend got heah?"

Lila swallowed hard. She didn't want to say that the mice weren't a "problem" until Rebecca had arrived – although that was the truth – because she didn't want to risk agitating Rebecca further. "I'll get some mousetraps from Gilpin's today," she said, instead. "What kind do you want me to get, Becca – the sticky ones? Or the old-fashioned snap traps that break their necks? Personally, I prefer the old-fashioned traps – I'd rather get rid of a carcass than have a live mouse stuck on one of those sticky ones watching me and wondering what I was going to do to it."

Rebecca, who was naturally kind-hearted, gave a little shudder. "Can't we just catch the mice alive and let them go?"

"Where?" said Lila. "Let them go outside? So they can just turn around and come right back inside?!"

The toast popped up and Rebecca buttered it silently. She scooped out Lila's eggs and set the plate on the table in front of her. She put her hands on her hips and pouted.

"Wal, you know, I got an ideah," said Wendell, flashing Rebecca a gold-toothed grin.

Rebecca perked up. "What?"

"I kin build a Mouse Motel," replied Wendell. "We kin catch 'em alive and put 'em in the Motel. When it's filled, we kin take the Mouse Motel ovah the river and let 'em go all at once." Wendell scratched his head. "Wal, maybe we better take 'em ovah TWO rivers, jest to be sure they don't git back heah agin."

"Oh, that's *perfect*, Wendell!" Rebecca cried, patting Wendell's arm appreciatively.

Encouraged, Wendell picked up his fork and attacked his breakfast with gusto.

Lila eyed him suspiciously. "You're gonna build a mouse motel? So you can take a bunch of mice all at once and dump 'em onto some other unsuspecting homeowner?"

"Let him finish his eggs, Lila," Rebecca scolded. "They're getting cold! More toast, Wendell?"

Wendell nodded, and wolfed down his eggs. "Wal, you know, we kin let 'em go next to an old dairy farm where there's sure to be plenty of bahn cats."

At the mention of cats, Lila rolled her eyes. "Right," she said. "I do NOT have a lot of faith in cats at the moment."

"But Wendell … isn't it going to be a lot of work to build a Mouse Motel?" Rebecca asked.

Hens and Chickens

"Oh, 'tain't much," he said. "Jest some hardware cloth hooked together in sections, with a door for each room so they ain't quite together."

"How *many* rooms?" asked Rebecca, pausing next to the toaster, two slices of anadama bread in hand. "There are a *lot* of mice in this house!"

"Wal, you know, we kin make more 'n one trip ovah the river," said Wendell. "But I was figgerin' on six or eight rooms."

"Eight would be good," said Rebecca, dropping the bread in the toaster. "We'll still have to make several trips to release the mice, judging by the evidence I uncovered under the counter, and … and last night!"

"Wal, you know, 'twould be a good way for you to git to see some of the countryside. We kin make a little day trip out of it," Wendell suggested, blue eyes twinkling.

"Are you going to put numbers on the doors, Wendell?" asked Rebecca, hopefully. "I think it would be really cute if the Mouse Motel had numbers on the doors."

Lila groaned inwardly. She gulped down the last of her eggs, and took a swig of coffee. "I'm gonna go do my chores," she said, rising from the table. "I can't wait to see how many eggs we get today!"

"We kin have numbers," Wendell said. "I don't see any reason why not."

Lila exited the kitchen without another word. In the shed, she sat down on the wooden gray stool and pulled on her Muck™ boots. "What's more important?" she asked herself, shaking her head in wonderment. "How many eggs we get to SELL? Or … should we have NUMBERS on the doors of our Mouse Motel!"

She grinned and stood up. "Don't answer that, Lila!" she said aloud, and headed for the hen pen. Upstairs in the hen house, she padded her pockets with scratch feed and then tossed several bucketfuls of grain down the chute. Then she put her hand on the metal frame of the spiral staircase, and carefully wound her way down the worn, wooden wedge-shaped steps to see her hens.

"Hello, girls!" she called, entering the coop. Already, the chickens had learned to recognize the hand that fed them, and they came running, leaping and *squawking* up to greet her, a veritable sea of red flapping wings that sent up a thin cloud of sawdust. "Here you go!" She tossed some of the scratch corn onto the floor of the coop and then opened the pint-sized door to the south-side outdoor run, tossing most of the remaining scratch corn onto the grass outside. She laughed joyfully as approximately two-thirds of the chickens dashed eagerly out the tiny door into the sunshine of the spring morning. Lila filled the feeders, and then rinsed and refilled the two waterers.

A soulful-looking hen lingered underfoot as Lila performed her chores. "What do you want, Sweetie?" she asked, schootching down to stroke the chestnut-colored feathers on the chicken's back. "Attention, huh? Want me to tell you you're the cutest little thing going?"

The chicken responded with a happy *clucking*.

"That's what I thought," said Lila dryly, reaching into her pocket. "You just want extra corn!"

Her favorite part of the chores came next – the egg gathering!

Lila lifted Grammie Addie's watermelon-shaped wicker basket from the square-headed iron nail plugged into the old barn boards adjacent to the door of the coop, and then – one by one – she searched the nest boxes for the precious brown "gifts" left behind by the laying hens. She carefully ran her hand over the sweet-smelling sawdust, seeking out the warm spots where the hens had been setting. Within 10 minutes Lila's basket began to get heavy and she calculated she had collected 47 jumbo-size brown eggs! Nearly half the hens were laying again already!

"This is totally awesome!" she exclaimed aloud.

Lila carried the basket of eggs into the cleaning and sorting room, and set it on the work counter that Mike Hobart had built especially for her height. She lightly removed any lingering manure from the brown eggs with sandpaper, and then dipped the eggs one at a time into an organic cleaner and sealer. Lila then sorted the eggs by grade, placing them – pointed side down – into the appropriate molded-fiber egg carton. Grammie Addie had stored her eggs in a wooden egg box the size of a small steamer trunk, however, Lila had found the box impracticable and elected instead to use the more traditional egg containers, purchasing both 12-egg and 18-egg boxes, and 30-cell egg trays, all made from recycled materials.

Lila found herself humming a cheery little tune as she graded and sorted the eggs. She recognized the ditty, having heard it several times on the days that Wendell had worked re-wiring the hen pen. Now, Lila herself burst into song:

> *'When all the world is dark and gray, keep on hoping!*
> *When bad things sometimes come your way, no sense moping!'*

Hens and Chickens

When she was done, Lila removed the packed eggs to the cold storage room, which still contained the built-in wooden shelving from Grammie Addie's day. She stacked the boxes up and double-checked the thermometer to be sure the temperature was cool enough. Then Lila stood back with a satisfied grin and surveyed her hens' efforts of the past two days – altogether she had six gray cartons of fresh eggs ready for sale!

"It's a start!" she said. "I wonder how this place will look a year from now?" She happily envisioned dozens and dozens of organic eggs neatly stacked and waiting for sale.

Lila exited the hen pen through the ground level door on the east side, crossed around the front and leaned back against the south side of the weathered gray hen pen. She closed her eyes and let the morning sun warm her face and eyelids, enjoying the sound of her chickens *clucking* and *squawking* contentedly. A light breeze carried the scent of pine from the nearby woods, as well as the faint *rumble* of an approaching vehicle. Instantly, Lila identified Mike Hobart's truck from the sound of its diesel engine. Her heart jiggered excitedly at the thought of seeing him again. "Omigod," she thought, pushing herself away from the building; "I haven't even showered yet!"

Lila grimaced, and glanced down at her dirty sweatshirt and jeans. She could smell a faint odor of ammonia from the chicken droppings on her boots. She sighed, however, and waved cheerily as Hobart pulled into the drive, alerting him to her presence at the hen yard.

Hobart hopped out of his truck and strode up to greet her with outstretched hands. "Well?" he asked, grasping Lila and pulling her close to his broad chest. His blue eyes shone down at her. "How many eggs did you get?"

"At last!" cried Lila. "A rational human being! I ... I could KISS you!"

"So what's stopping you?" he said, with a twinkle in his eye.

Lila lifted her head and placed a shy, affectionate peck on his freshly-shaven cheek. Her head instinctively sought the security of his warm shoulder, and she closed her eyes. *Peace at last!*

Hobart squeezed her into a strong embrace. "My first kiss from *The Egg Lady* of Sovereign, Maine," he whispered. "I'll never forget it." He dropped a return kiss on the top of her head, and released her. "I've got to run," he continued. "I just got the call from the Shoreys in Troy—they want me to start on that new barn right away! But I wanted to see how the hens were laying, first."

He was leaving already!

Lila quickly covered up her disappointment. "I collected 47 eggs today," she reported. "And yesterday, I got 22. We're in business!"

There was so much she wanted to share with him – so much she wanted to tell him! But Lila could see by the look in Mike Hobart's eyes that he was eager to begin his new carpentry project. So she smiled at him and simply said: "I'm so happy for you, Mike. I want to hear all about the barn you're building."

"I was hoping you would. How does Sunday morning sound? I'll tell you all about it, then."

And then he was gone. And she wouldn't see him again for two whole days!

Chapter 17

·······

Fiddleheadin'

While Lila lamented the fact that she wouldn't see Mike Hobart for two whole days, she was so busy scraping paint and preparing the hen pen for a fresh white coat, that when Sunday dawned she couldn't believe that 48 hours had passed so quickly. Lila awoke at 5 a.m. when the evening's sonorous chorus of peepers was replaced by raucous birdsong. She tossed back the blankets and leaped out of bed. It was a lovely spring day, and Lila raced through her morning chores humming happily. By 9 a.m. she was showered, dressed in a pretty floral print dress and ready for her visitor. Rebecca noted Lila's change in wardrobe with widened eyes and a raised eyebrow, but said nothing.

Lila didn't have long to wait, as Mike Hobart pulled into the yard shortly before 9:30 a.m. He hopped out of the truck and strode toward the kitchen ell where Lila greeted him at the shed door.

Hobart whistled when he saw Lila framed by the doorway in her silky print dress. "Wow!" he said. "Am I glad I didn't tell you in advance we were going fiddleheadin' or I never would have seen *this*!"

"Fiddleheading?" repeated Lila, stepping back to allow him to enter the shed. "Is that some kind of a funky folk dance?"

Hobart laughed, and slid his arm around her waist. Lila only half-heartedly tried to escape. "Nope," he replied. "Fiddleheadin' is an opportunity to get cold, wet and possibly eaten-alive by black flies in order to track down a wild fern that grows alongside streams and rivers, and tastes like an old dandelion."

"Sounds, uh, lovely!" said Lila. She glanced down at her outfit and sighed. "This is the first time I've put on a real DRESS in years—you should have seen the look on Rebecca's face!"

"The effort isn't wasted, let me tell you!" Hobart said, attempting to get his other arm around her waist.

But Lila slipped from his grasp, smiling with satisfaction. "I think I better go put my jeans on," she said, "or we'll never get anywhere today!" She took him by the hands and pulled him into the kitchen. "Here, talk to Rebecca while I go get changed."

"You'll need a sweatshirt," he called, as she disappeared into the bedroom. "And your boots!"

Rebecca greeted Hobart warmly, and offered him a seat at the kitchen table where she was embroidering a chicken onto a new red gingham placemat. "Can I fix you some sandwiches to take with you, Mike?" she asked, hopefully, setting her work down. "It'll only take me a minute or two."

"No thanks," he said, toying with a spool of yellow thread. When Hobart saw Rebecca's crestfallen look, he added; "I happened to mention to Ralph at the store yesterday what I was planning for today, and Maude insisted on packing us a picnic lunch."

"Oh, but you *will* come to dinner next Sunday?" she said, anxiously, settling herself back to her stitching. "Two o'clock. It's our first dinner party and we're inviting Miss Hastings and Wendell, as well as the Gilpins."

"I'll put it in my social calendar," Hobart said, "which seems to be getting pretty filled up this spring!"

Most folks from Away think that summer is the best time of year to visit Maine, but they'd be wrong. Mainers know that the *best* season in the Pine Tree State occurs between Mud Season and Memorial Day—the few weeks of the year during which the state becomes a veritable Garden of Eden; when the flowers, trees, hills, uplands and woodlands awaken and burst into infinite shades of green and when the explosion of yellow forsythia is so bright that it hurts the eye to look at it, but before the serpent opens the door to the Garden and allows in the black flies, mosquitoes and the tourists.

During this peculiar time, while the showy lilacs and fruit trees hold tight to their buds for later May blooms, the untrained eye examining the landscape might conclude that it lacks the postcard perfection summer folks have come to expect from Maine. But those who live here year-round know that when the soft scent of April fills the air it signals not only that one has survived another winter but also that paradise is born anew. The locals know then that the suckers are running upstream in the chilly brooks, and that pockets of crystalized snow rest like fairy

Hens and Chickens

beds deep in the woods, and that the precious fiddlehead fern delicately swaddled in its brown paper wrapping is poking its head up from the black moss-bottomed streambeds only waiting to be picked!

Hobart parked in a certain spot alongside Black Brook (which spot shall remain vague as I have not been authorized to disclose my young friend's secret fiddleheading location). He shrugged on his L.L. Bean® backpack containing his water bottle and Maude's lunch, and lifted two food-grade 10-gallon pails from out of the bed of the baby blue pickup.

Lila's eyes enlarged when she saw the size of the white plastic pails. "You're joking, right?"

Hobart grinned, and shook his head. "Didja think this was a day off, darling?"

The two tramped up the brook's riparian zone through the scrub brush — prolific alders, gray birch, fuzzy pussy willows, flowering shadbush — following the stream up and away from the road. Hobart went first, winding his way around thickets of bushes and trees, tracking the animal trail that skirted the brook and is distinctive of wildlife corridors. He graciously held aside branches of the larger trees to allow Lila to pass so that the slingshot-like stems didn't snap back and slap her in the face. He smiled encouragingly at her each time, allowing her an opportunity to gauge by his glowing eyes the unbounded enthusiasm he felt for the natural world and the pleasure of the task before them.

They hiked for 10 minutes in companionable silence, weaving around skunk cabbage and blow downs, tree stumps and dead wood. Lila gradually discovered that her hearing became more acute as they moved further into the woods, away from the road noise and other sounds of civilization. She began to hear the rush of the black water over the stones in the brook, and the *plash* of the white, lacy spray, which reminded her eyes of Miss Hastings' frilly white blouses. She distinguished the gurgling of sink holes, the trickling of rivulets and the drip-drip-dripping of morning dewdrops. In spots, the water-logged ground *squished* beneath her feet, and a jabbering jay kept them company, flying from tree to tree ahead of them, warning the woodland life with strident calls that they were coming.

They stopped at a widened tableau of land where the stream split up like a search party ferreting out the easiest route down to the bog. Here, curly-headed ferns popped up amongst the puckerbrush and looked more like the antennae of visiting extraterrestrials than something springing naturally from the earthy Maine quagmire.

"Is that them?" cried Lila, pointing to several fronds of fuzzy ferns near the main channel of the brook.

Hobart set down his pails and dropped his pack on a rotted tree stump. "Nope, that's a red fern. The fiddlehead is the ostrich fern," he said. He scooched down onto his haunches and pushed aside a cold, wet blanket of musty-smelling leaves, revealing a clump of darker, daintier ferns hiding beneath. "*This* is what we're looking for!"

Lila dropped down beside him. "But they look EXACTLY the same! How can you tell them apart?"

Hobart plucked the fiddlehead, its stem breaking easily with a little *snap*. He held the fiddle-shaped frond in the palm of his hand so that Lila could examine it. "See the celery-like stem? That's an identifying feature. And fiddlehead stems are deep green, not red," he said. "But most obviously, young fiddleheads have this brown papery covering."

With her thumb and forefinger, Lila lifted the crisp green curl from his hand and turned it over in her own, examining the delicate pieces that made the whole so foreign-looking. The brown paper protecting the frond felt as flimsy as a spider web and flaked off at her touch. "And people eat this?" she asked, dubiously.

Hobart chuckled at the look on her face. "Lots of people—in Maine, anyway," he said. "It's quite a delicacy."

Lila was about to gamely pop the fiddlehead into her mouth to taste it, however, Hobart quickly stopped her. "It's not safe to eat raw," he said. "Although I've certainly eaten plenty raw myself over the years."

"Why not?"

"Bacteria. Nasty stuff like *giardia* and *e coli*. I wouldn't want you to get sick, darling."

"If you're trying to make them even more appealing, it's not working!"

"You'll like 'em cooked," he promised. "Served hot, with plenty of butter."

"Maybe … with lots and LOTS of butter!"

He demonstrated how to pluck the necks of the fiddleheads and then showed Lila a good spot to begin picking. Hobart settled himself at a thick patch of fiddleheads 20 feet away, close enough to keep an eye on her but allowing Lila plenty of room to rove. After half an hour, Lila had picked enough fiddleheads to cover the bottom of her pail but she discovered that Hobart had gathered—nearly half a bucket!

Hens and Chickens

"How did you do that so fast?" she inquired, staring up at him in reverent astonishment.

He grinned and shrugged. "Practice makes perfect. I've been fiddle-headin' since I was old enough to walk."

They continued working their way up the brook, alternating between walking, picking and talking. Upon Lila's encouragement, Hobart described the post and beam barn he was building for the Shoreys in Troy, and Lila shared with him the particulars of Rebecca's arrival and the necessary creation of Wendell's Mouse Motel. By noontime, they were tired, hungry, dirty and wet – but had enjoyed themselves thoroughly gathering two pails full of fiddleheads!

"Let's eat," said Hobart, when they reached a dry, sunny spot next to a height of land near the brook.

"I'm starving!" Lila exclaimed, carefully setting down her pail. She turned her face to the warm April sun, opened her arms wide as if embracing the sky, and breathed in deeply the musty, woodsy air. A pine warbler recently returned from its winter home sent out a slow, musical trill.

Hobart dropped his backpack onto the spongy grass and doffed his baseball cap, liberating his matted curls with his hands. Then he stripped off his sweatshirt, exposing his muscular forearms. He knelt down next to the brook and washed the dirt from his face and hands. Lila followed suit.

Hobart unrolled a thin ground cloth and began pulling out multiple plastic tubs of Maude's picnic for Lila to unpack. Despite the short amount of lead time to prepare, Maude had outdone herself, providing the couple with homemade French bread, soft goat cheese with rosemary and garlic, stuffed eggs (from *The Egg Ladies*, of course), a raw vegetable medley, pumpkin spice cake with cream cheese frosting, and fresh strawberries dipped in chocolate.

"This is an amazing feast!" exclaimed Lila, as she spread the food on the waterproof ground cover and unfolded the napkins and silverware.

Hobart looked sheepish. "I think my good friend Maude is trying to help my romantic endeavors," he admitted.

"Well, not that you NEED it," Lila said; "but this time … it's working!"

After they had consumed as much as they possibly could eat, Hobart lay back onto the ground cloth and pulled Lila gently down into his arms.

"Is this OK?" he asked, his blue eyes plumbing the depths of her hazel ones.

Lila nodded wordlessly, and nestled her head onto his sturdy chest. She closed her eyes and listened to the steady beating of his heart. She felt a thrilling surge of joy at the reassuring *thump-thump-thump* and as she pressed against the comfy cotton of his T-shirt it crossed her mind in a flash that she never would have met Mike Hobart had she accepted Joe Kelly's "promotion" and stayed with Perkins & Gleeful in Boston! She shuddered at the thought of what she might have missed.

"Cold?" asked Hobart, in a concerned tone. He wrapped his arms closer around her.

"Mmmm, no. Something just walked across my grave, that's all," she said, lightly.

"I hope it walked off again," he said. He planted a feathery trail of kisses from her hair down to her nose, stopping just short of her parted lips.

"All gone," she said, closing her eyes and lifting her lips to his, willing him to finish what he started.

In response, Hobart shifted, and deftly maneuvered Lila to the ground beneath his propped up elbow. "So, *now* you like me," he teased, interposing kisses with words upon her upturned face, everywhere but upon her aching lips. "Now, you even want me to *kiss* you, hmmm? Seems like it wasn't too long ago when 'Lila' wouldn't even give a poor guy a break – until after he fitted her friend with a new bra."

"Oh, don't mention that!" she cried. "I was horrible to you; I admit it!"

"But now . . . say that you like me!" he ordered.

In response, Lila cupped the back of his neck with her right hand and guided his head down to meet her hungry lips. He responded passionately, pressing her into the ground with his well-muscled frame. The ecstasy of their union was almost unbearable and Lila nearly swooned.

Suddenly, Hobart pulled away. Lila lay languidly gazing up into his desire-ridden eyes. "What's wrong?" she said, reaching up to pull him back down to her throbbing breast.

"Nothing's wrong, darling," he replied, leaning over and dropping light kisses on her eyelids. "And that's why I'm stopping, before something *does* go wrong!" He sat up.

"Oh, don't leave me, Mike!" she cried, half rising from the soft ground.

Hens and Chickens

"No, no, shhhh; I'm not going anywhere," he said. He lay back down with her, willing his passion to subside.

Lila snuggled closer, with infinite satisfaction. Her euphoria settled down into a steady beatitude. She felt completely safe with him; respected and honored as a woman. Who WAS this man who made her feel this way? How little she knew about him! Except that he was kind, honest, good, generous, patient, thoughtful and hardworking!

"Tell me more about yourself, Mike Hobart," she directed. "How'd you get to be so special?"

"Aw, I'm not that special," he said, tickling her neck with a stalk of dead grass.

Lila giggled. "I don't believe it! You're the first guy I've met in the past five years who hasn't wanted to talk about himself all the time. I don't even know where you're from or what you're doing in Sovereign." She ran her fingers lovingly through the thick curls of his dark blond hair.

"I'm here waiting on you, darling," he whispered, brushing a kiss against the sensitive spot on her neck. "I've been waiting for a long, long time."

Lila tingled with heightened pleasure. Some romantic part of her believed that his declaration was entirely true. But it wasn't enough. "Details, Mike. I want details!"

He lightly stroked her hair. "I'm from The County—Aroostook County; northern Maine," he replied. "A town called Maple Grove."

"Big place, is it? I've never heard of it."

It's about the size of Sovereign. The people there are much the same, too; honest, caring folks. When you first drive into Maple Grove you feel like you're driving back into the '50s. My family has a potato farm just outside of town. It's been in the family for seven generations. Well, eight generations, if you count all my nieces and nephews. My older brother John pretty much runs everything now – he added broccoli to the operation about 15 years ago. But my Dad still puts his 2¢ in from time to time."

"Eight generations!" Lila exclaimed. "I didn't know that was even possible in Maine! I didn't think this state had been settled that long."

"We've been here quite a while," Hobart admitted. "The first Hobart came over to Massachusetts from Norfolk, England in 1642. Our branch of the family moved to Aroostook County in the early 19th century. It's a beautiful place. Lots of land; big fields, big skies. When the potatoes are in bloom it looks like a fairyland, miles and miles of beautiful white blossoms."

"I'd love to see it someday!"

"And I'd love to show it to you, darling. But it's pretty far away—even farther than Boston."

"If you're trying to scare me off, it won't work!"

Hobart felt a glow of pleasure at her words. "Are you trying to get me to kiss you again?"

"Is it work...?" but before she even finished her question, Lila had her answer.

She responded passionately to his probing tongue, eager to lose herself completely within him. She felt as though she had transcended her physical body, joining her spirit with his in a mystical union.

Ah, this was heaven! This was joy! This was paradise unguarded!

Hobart broke away again, breathing heavily. He rolled over onto his back and locked his hands behind his head to forestall temptation. He regarded Lila impishly. "My turn for 20 questions," he said.

"Now?!" she lamented, unwilling to end the rapture.

"Now, darling."

She sighed. "I guess that's only fair," she said, dropping to her stomach and resting her chin on her hands. "Fire away!"

"So, where does Lila Woodsum harken from?"

"Big city, mean people," she said.

"Seriously?"

"Kidding! My Mom was from the big city of Boston but my Dad was from a small town in Western Massachusetts. He grew up on a farm. I used to love to visit my grandparents on the farm when I was little because they had all sorts of ..." Lila broke off and playfully signaled that she wanted Hobart to complete the sentence.

"Cows?" guessed Hobart.

"You're not very shaap, are you?" she teased. "Chickens!"

But Lila's good humor was quickly replaced by a look of sadness. "My Dad died when I was five, pancreatic cancer," she continued; "and my grandparents both died within the next two years, of broken hearts, I believe."

"I'm so sorry, darling," he said.

"My Mom got remarried when I was eight and we moved back to Boston. My life was never the same after that. I never forgot those early

Hens and Chickens

days on the farm, though. How happy we all were! I felt safe on the farm. That's the main reason why, when Miss Hastings mentioned coming to Maine to raise chickens, well, that's why I knew I needed to be here."

"That and you knew I was waiting for you," Hobart hinted.

"If I'd have known that, I'd have come a lot sooner!" Lila cried.

"Mmmhmm," he said. "Nice touch. Boyfriends? Broken hearts left behind in Boston?"

"None," said Lila. She hesitated. "Well, there was this one guy ..."

"I knew it!" he interjected.

"... this one guy, Ryan MacDonald, who WANTED to be more than a boy-FRIEND. But I wasn't interested BECAUSE ..."

"... because you knew I was here waiting for you," he concluded.

Lila giggled again. "You're getting shaaper," she said, tossing a twig at him.

And then Hobart found he could resist no longer. He sat up and scooped her into his arms. "Too bad for him, because you're *mine* now," he declared.

Chapter 18
. . . .
"The Parade Will Go On!"

True love is not just an affair of the heart, it is the embodiment of the divine; a little spark of God enters like the first breath into the souls and bodies of lovers and unites with them in creating a new thing on earth, a new heaven on earth. Love is not lust. Love is not greed. Love is not self-satisfaction or selfishness or sin. Love is sacrifice, and respect, and wanting your beloved to be the best that he or she can possibly be.

In the 20th century, lust and self-love were often confused for the true love of self-less devotion. Unfortunately, self-love leads to a life of misery, meanness and decay. The state of complete satisfaction and self-actualization for which we all long is realized through a life of sacrifice, duty, charity, mercy and disinterested, unconditional, *true* love.

Lila loved Mike Hobart in this manner of love, and she knew that she was beloved by him in return. She floated through the following week in a font of blessed serenity. Her cup was full, and was running over.

Never in her life had she felt so safe, so happy, so secure ... so *beloved*. She had been as a fragile musical instrument sadly out of tune until with his touch, his voice, his goodness, his love she was brought into the perfect pitch of human existence.

These days of true love – first love, in particular – are short in our life, for life itself is fragile; one moment it's here and the next it's gone. But these days are of inestimable value since they are the fountain of youth upon which our ageing and aged selves will return to drink again and again. They are our secret hope, our memories, our hope for the future, for our children, our grandchildren, our great-grandchildren. Once we have been beloved, we know that true love exists – and that knowledge makes all the difference in the world.

Lila had never been loved so selflessly before. Her mother had loved her, in a blinded, motherly fashion. And her father had adored her, but he had died and left her. Tragically, her stepfather had lusted after her, and had used and abused her. As a child, she had been betrayed by life, abandoned by hope, detached from the divine. Her soul had been trapped, tampered with, torn and discarded. Her self was destroyed.

And yet here she was today spiraling high like a kite in the April breeze, swirling and dipping and laughing and feeling the warm sun on her spirit like the kite-flyer feels it on her face and hands. The Goddess in her goodness and mercy gives us a second chance at life, if only we have the courage to reach out and accept the gift that the divine is dying for us to accept!

It would not spoil our story *too* much here if I told you what happened to embody Lila with the courage to give and receive true love, after having been sexually abused as a child. However, it would be putting the cart before the horse and I don't want to risk a derailment in our little tale. Instead, I will just lift up to your attention the fact that something awful had occurred before her decision to move to Maine (as Rebecca had suspected) and in this awfulness was the footprint of the divine – not a *fingerprint* but a *footprint* – for the Prime Mover gives us a path to follow out of every tragedy, if for no other reason than to find our way home. And Lila Woodsum was finding her way home.

"Your phone is off," said Rebecca on Wednesday, when Lila came in from the hen pen. "Miss Hastings called on the landline trying to reach you. She wants you to call her back. By the way, she's definitely coming to the party on Sunday!"

"Did she say what she wants?"

"No, she just called me 'darling' several times, said she'd see me on Sunday and hung up!"

"I bet she wants to know when my baby chicks are coming," Lila guessed.

"When *are* the chicks coming, dear? I've been so busy with my sewing and cleaning – and with Wendell and our Mouse Motel trips across the rivers – I forgot to ask!"

"Next Tuesday. Two hundred of 'em. I'll be busy after that!"

But Lila was wrong. Miss Hastings had telephoned to see if Lila would give her a ride to school on Friday afternoon.

"I'm giving a music lesson to the kindergarteners and first graders," she said, "and Trudy Gorse was going to take me but she's got a TERRIBLE head cold. Would you mind giving me a lift, dahrrrling?"

Hens and Chickens

"I'd LOVE to take you!" said Lila. "I've heard about your 'music lessons' and I've envied every school kid in Sovereign for having YOU as a teacher!"

"Dahrrrling, I'm just an old loose screw, but we DO have lots of fun!" And Miss Hastings burst into peals of laughter.

"What time?"

"I told Mrs. Lakewood – she's the vice principal – that we'd be there by one o'clock."

"I'll pick you up half an hour earlier, OK?"

"Wonderful! Bring a silly hat and a tambourine or a drum or something, dahrrrling – and don't forget to wear your heart on your sleeve!"

"Oh, my heart is already on my sleeve!" said Lila, joyfully.

"A little bird told me THAT and I'm SO HAPPY for you! He's such a dahrrrling boy!"

Amen, thought Lila. 'Darling boy' was an absolutely perfect description of Mike Hobart!

Rebecca was able to locate a slightly-abused bongo drum in Amber's bedroom, as well as a floppy hat purchased 30 years ago for an '80s wedding in which she'd been a bridesmaid. So, Lila was as provisioned as any five-year-old when Friday arrived, and quite possibly as excited.

She motored the short distance up the road in Miss Hastings' old 1964 gray Pontiac LeMans, arriving exactly at 12:30 p.m. She discovered that Matilda had been transferred to a cat carrier for the trip, and loaded the cage into the back seat of the car. Miss Hastings, holding onto her music books and a tambourine, was dressed in her trademark professional black suit with lacy white blouse. She had attempted to confine her wriggling hair into something like a bun, however, the wiry strands escaped and seemed to dance in delight around her ears and temple. Her brown eyes sparkled with enthusiasm and her smile was heightened by glossy red lipstick.

"Let's roll, dahrrrling!" Miss Hastings instructed, as she buckled herself into the familiar front seat. She lovingly patted the leather passenger armrest as though it was an old friend.

Sovereign Elementary School has 87 children, 18 from the combined kindergarten and first grade. The decibel level in the small auditorium was high where all 18 children were sitting cross-legged on the polished hardwood floor eagerly awaiting Miss Hastings and her dancing pet chicken Matilda. A black acoustic upright piano had been wheeled into the room and Miss Hastings began by settling herself onto the piano bench with a flourish and inviting all the children to gather round. Matilda squawked from her cage atop the piano and the children needed no further inducement to scramble forward.

Miss Hastings took powerful possession of the piano, banging out chords as though she was a maestro from the New York Metropolitan Opera and not an 87-year-old spinster with knobby arthritic claws.

"This is the story of the little red hen, DAHRRRLINGS!" she began, in her teaching voice. But then she burst into a sonorous alto, singing the words to the song 'The Little Red Hen' from a green, oversized book, *The Kindergarten Book*. She indicated where the children were to sing along with her, and Lila joined in, quickly seduced by the uplifting sound of the music. They sang:

> *"Cut cut cut ca dacket," – Said the little hen.*
> *"See my little yellow chickens eight, nine, ten."*
> *"Cut cut cut ca dacket, Count them all again.*
> *1,2,3,4,5,6, seven, eight, nine, ten."*

Singing is a physic with an invigorating effect on the human system, a dose of one-part celerity mixed with two-parts celebrity. By the time Miss Hastings had moved through the four piano pieces she had selected to play and sing, the children – as well as the adults present – felt as though they encompassed a chorus from heaven, specially gifted to share good cheer with the world. Matilda cackled and squawked along with the music, hopping about in her tiny cage in step with the tempo of each piece. The atmosphere was electric when Miss Hastings brought the final selection to an end with a thundering crash on the piano.

Lila's heart leapt at the sound. *Omigod, my heart's on FIRE!*

She pressed her hand to her chest to keep her heart from leaping out and dancing on top of the piano with Matilda.

Miss Hastings whirled around on the piano bench and cried: "Who's ready for a parade?!"

Pandemonium broke loose as the children screeched and clapped and shouted their willingness to participate in the musical parade. During the last song, Mrs. Lakewood had surreptitiously wheeled in a three-tiered cart containing various musical instruments, including tambourines, cymbals, drum pads, whistles, kazoos and harmonicas. The kindergarten and first grade teachers had added armloads of colorful hats and scarves,

Hens and Chickens

and the children made a run for their favorite selection of both instrument and costume.

Lila, without any hesitation, donned her pink floppy hat and schlepped her bongo drum under her left arm in preparation for her part in the parade. Miss Hastings nodded decisively to Mrs. Lakewood, who released Matilda from her cage, to the delighted cries of the children. Unfazed, the barred rock hen hopped to the auditorium floor and paused expectantly at Miss Hastings' shiny black pumps.

"Line up behind Matilda!" Miss Hastings instructed. "Line up! And … let's have a PARADE!"

Miss Hastings lifted her legs high and began to march enthusiastically around room, thrashing her arms and jingling the tambourine high in the air. The chicken and the children lurched into a crescendo of musical noise and movement, snaking behind her in a long, strange string of youthful jubilation. Miss Hastings tossed sunflower seeds to Matilda, and the bird snapped them up happily and hopped along proudly like a Grand Marshall. Miss Hastings shouted out encouragement to the children − "Wonderful! Wonderful! Lift those legs higher! Sing, sing, sing, dahrrrlings!" − and everyone within hearing distance of the parade, including the janitor, fell into line singing, dancing, playing their instruments as though bewitched.

"Daadaa, deedum, dum; shake those tambourines and pound those drums!" Miss Hastings cried, wild hair flying everywhere. "Daadaa, deedum, dum, do-opp a DOO! SING, SING! and DANCE and Matilda will dance TOO!"

Blood pumped rapidly through Lila's veins, as she pounded Amber's bongo drum and marched along following the line of children. She sang out, "Daadeedaa dee dum, dum!" in a loud voice, completely unembarrassed. She was a child again, entranced by the undulations of the parade line and the marvelous harmony of the musical clamor.

How does she do it? Lila thought after 10 minutes, feeling herself tiring and running out of breath. *This is why she'll live forever!*

Later that evening, when Lila tried to describe the day to Rebecca, she discovered that the event with Miss Hastings was almost too indescribable for words.

"It was the most magical experience I've ever had," she declared. "Every care I ever had in life, every bad thought, every disappointment just completely disappeared! I was five years old again, but not only that,

I was THE MOST SPECIAL five-year-old the world has ever known! That's the feeling I got so I can't begin to image how powerful it must have been for those kids who actually were five years old!"

"I wish I'd gone with you," said Rebecca, enviously.

"Next time," said Lila. "Next time—you go and take your special place in Miss Hastings' parade!"

"But what if there isn't a next time?" Rebecca worried. "She *is* 87-years-old, after all!"

"Oh, there WILL be a next time," Lila vowed. "Even if I have to learn how to play '*The Little Red Hen*' on the piano myself! The parade will go on!"

And do we know? Can we know? Of the wellspring of unconditional love to which the good-hearted old spinster returned again and again to seek replenishment for her own ageing spirit?

From which sacred waters did she drink to recharge those tireless batteries? From whence sprang her hopes, her dreams, her noble indulgences? Her love of children and chickens?

Might we lift the curtain of Miss Hastings' girlish memories, the holy of holies, as fresh for her today as they were 70 years ago?

My pips, there are some places in this story where I fear to tread! And so Miss Hastings' secret hope remains a sacred mystery to us all.

Chapter 19

· · · · · · ·

Sooner or Later

Let me reassure all the lovers of lovers (and we know who we are) that Lila has not gone the entire week without seeing Mike Hobart. Our handsome hero has stopped by the old Russell homestead most mornings on the way to his barn-building jobsite in Troy (or most evenings on the way home from it) in order to snatch a quick hug, a sweet caress, a reassuring word and perhaps a kiss or two, eagerly bestowed by his sweetheart. Lila's kisses were dropped freely on his face and lips, much like the early petals dropped by the gangly wild cherry, offering not only some amount of immediate gratification but also the promise of many more soft blossoms yet to come. These were delicious moments for Mike and Lila, for the anticipation of seeing our lover is often as sweet as the event itself, adding a sumptuous sugarcoating to our ordinary, everyday lives.

Writing is *not* my vocation but a necessary and often burdensome part of my calling. Thus a cruel slave driver sits on my right shoulder constantly goading me to move forward with our little tale. (Poor Rebecca has been slaving all week to prepare for their Sunday dinner party.) Fortunately, however, the sweeper of the skies and the keeper of my heart whispers in my left ear to proceed slowly; linger *l-o-n-g* in these moments of golden sunshine when love abounds like the song birds in spring, which are legion. *Tomorrow will come with abundance*, this Voice instructs; *but these moments of blissful love are never long enough!*

There is no question which Voice I will obey. And so we lovers of lovers will live vicariously through this sacred moment with Mike and Lila.

I suspect that cynics reading this will cry foul at my weak attempt here at a Time Out. These people know only too well that – sooner or later – when Tomorrow does appear for Mike and Lila, pain will mingle with their love to dull the shine much like rust mars the chrome on a new bicycle. But now, NOW is their moment of unending bliss! And the Voice to whom by sacred vocation I *am* called to listen has given me the power to pin this moment in time simply by the twist of a pen!

The spring peepers on Saturday evening were as charming as sleigh bells of long ago, reminiscent of incurable romance. The air was thick and warm, unusually warm for the time of year. And so the frogs – and the humans – were happy.

"Not a bad ambience, for chorus frogs," said Hobart, drawing Lila down with him onto the wooden double rocker that Rebecca had found in the open chamber above the shed and Wendell had repaired. Hobart was showered and changed from his work clothes into clean jeans and a blue cotton T-shirt. Rebecca had cooked him an omelet and toast, and then shooed the cooing couple out onto the open-air farmer's porch that graced the east side of the old Russell homestead.

Lila giggled. "You shouldn't have told me to look up peepers on the Internet," she said. "I thought they were romantic until I saw how ugly they were!" She chastely moved a respectable distance away from him on the newly cushioned rocker.

"You don't *like* me today?" he asked, feigning hurt.

"Noo, silly; Rebecca might see!" Her hand couldn't resist touching him, however, in order to reassure itself of his physical presence. Of their own accord her fingers buried themselves in the damp curls of his thick, blond hair. A sigh escaped her parted lips at the contact, and she leaned closer.

"Careful, Rebecca might see!" he mimicked. He grasped her wrist, turned it over and placed a light kiss on the sensitive spot at the base of her palm. When this mission was complete, he pulled her hand behind his neck and her slender frame followed in a complete surrender.

She cuddled against his steady chest. He rested his cheek upon her silky hair, breathing in deeply her feminine scent comingled with the sweet evening air. "It'll be dark soon," he said.

"Mmmm," she replied, lazy, lost, content in the moment.

"Then Rebecca won't be able to see," he said, suggestively.

She giggled again.

"I love to hear you laugh," he said, sincerely. "It makes me happy— to make you happy."

She smiled up at him. "Doesn't take much for me, obviously," she replied. "A few frogs and some moonlight."

Hens and Chickens

He kissed the tip of her nose. "Isn't there some old fairy tale about frog kissing and princes?"

"Never heard of it."

"Well, there once was a handsome carpenter that a wicked witch turned into a frog," he began; "and he needed a beautiful young blonde to kiss him ..."

"Blonde!" Lila cried, sitting upright.

Did I say 'blonde'? I meant 'redhead,' of course," he corrected himself. But he must still have been mistaken, because he metamorphosed into a prince immediately after the deliberate kiss of a hazel-eyed brunette.

"There," she said, pulling away to review her princely handiwork.

"Come back here," he said, cupping her neck with his hand, and silencing her lips once again.

Dusk fell like dew. On the porch was the sound of soft sighs and murmurs. In the dining room, Rebecca clicked on a light over the table where she had left her sewing sprawled out before dinner. The bright light spilled out onto the farmer's porch like a square yellow patch on a quilt, narrowly missing the two pair of entangled legs.

Startled, they broke apart. "Phew, that was close," said Hobart, chuckling. "A little more to the right and Rebecca *would* have seen!"

"And I couldn't care less," Lila said, giggling again.

They lay back against the double rocker holding hands. Lila closed her eyes, reveling in her happiness. A surreal feeling of weightlessness filled her spirit. She was setting sail; they were setting sail, together, with an ocean of possibilities in front of them. She could be no place without him because he was the blue water beneath her and the blue sky above her. Now, she was skimming over the water effortlessly, as though her sailing ship had sprouted wings.

"Have you ever had the flying dream?" she asked, curiously, eyes still closed.

"I think I'm having one now," he said.

"No, really?"

He was quiet a moment, toying with the fingers of her left hand abstractedly. "When I was a kid, I did," he said. "Once or twice."

"Tell me about it," she demanded.

"When I was six or seven, I dreamed I was flying across the big potato field next to our house in Maple Grove. It was so real I could feel the wind on my face. I looked down to see where I was, and I saw a white, star-shaped potato blossom directly beneath me – I was looking at it from an aerial point of view, much like a bee or a butterfly – and the blossom had this enormous yellow stamen, I remember. It felt perfectly normal to fly. Then I woke up and discovered it was a dream. What a disappointment!"

"I can imagine!"

"How about you? Since you asked."

"When I was little, I DID fly," she said, firmly. "I know it. I could fly, at least until I was 10. It was a very powerful experience; I needed to fly away."

"Think you can still fly away, my darling chickadee? There was a time when you wanted to fly away from me."

"That was instinct; self-preservation on my part," she replied, honestly. "But now ... now you've got me eating out of your hand!"

"More birdseed, my Matilda?" said Hobart, leaning over to nuzzle her neck.

"Mmmm," she replied. "That 50-pound bag of bird seed was a neat trick!"

"Worked, didn't it?" he said, with some satisfaction.

"Oh, it worked alright!"

Rebecca suddenly switched off the dining room light, and the porch descended once again into darkness. Hobart shifted his 6-foot frame to a more comfortable position on the wooden rocker. As his eyes adjusted to the change in light, he automatically scanned the 10-acre eastern field, where green grass was being transformed into fluid patches of black water by the slow-moving, cloud-induced shadows of the evening. "This is about the time last year when we first saw Tinkerbell in the field," he remarked.

"TinkerBEAU," she corrected, following his gaze. "I'm starting to think your fabled white deer doesn't exist. Rebecca and I look for him every evening."

"You doubt me?" he asked, in mock disappointment.

"No, no, I don't doubt you," she assured him. "But Tinkerbell is keeping a pretty low profile these days. We see plenty of other deer in the field, but no white deer."

"Patience," he said. "If Tinkerbell survived the winter, you'll see him here, first."

Hens and Chickens

They rested in peaceful silence for a few blessed minutes. Hobart spoke first. "Say, did you ever have the kissing dream?"

"The kissing dream! How silly! I never heard of it."

"It goes something like this …" he said, bending his head toward hers.

When their lips met, Lila experienced a translocation of the order of the universe, as though time turned like the tide and began to roll backward. She felt as though she was gaining life by the second, by the month, by the year – as though the antique clock on the mantel in the living room had slipped a cog and was running counter-clockwise. She lost herself in the timeless eternity of his kiss. When he breathed in deeply, she entered his spirit upon that breath and once inside became unable to tell where her Self began and his ended. There was no boundary between them, no bones or skin or sinew like a rock wall separating them. There was no mistrust, only perfect confidence in one another. He loved her; he respected her; he cherished her. What more did she need? Was not this the very embodiment of life?

When temporarily sated with kisses, they lay back against the wooden rocker, his arm tucked protectively around her shoulders. "I could sit like this forever, looking at the stars," she said. "I love how they twinkle!"

"There's Venus," said Hobart. With his free hand he pointed out the radiating white planet. "And Mars … Wow! You can really see why it's called the Red Planet, tonight."

Lila followed his direction, and saw Mars throbbing with a reddish-orange color. The sight of the Red Planet intensified her senses, as though Mars was mirroring her own throbbing emotions and desires. "I've never seen it so red before!"

"Strange, isn't it," he said; "to think how many billions of people over the years have looked up at these same stars and planets?"

"Makes me feel small in a way, but also somehow connected to a much greater whole."

He kissed her fingertips one at a time; soft, sensuous caresses. "You are my whole," he whispered in her ear.

Her heart imploded with exquisite pain. "Oh, oooh!" she cried, raising her lips to seek his once again. "I so need you!"

"Shhhh, I'm here, darling," he said, confidently claiming her breath as his own.

Time continued to roll backward. This provident fluke of nature forestalled Tomorrow, creating for our lovers that sense of unending present bliss.

Cynics, who feel the pain of Tomorrow much like the arthritic feels a coming change in the weather, know that this rapturous moment won't last; for nothing lasts, they say, not even true love. Tomorrow will come – sooner or later – bringing with it heartbreaks of unexpected pain, grief and loss.

But this moment of unending bliss is not lost; never lost! For we keep these sacred moments in our hearts and souls; do we not, my pips? We carry memories of former rapture with us into our daily lives to ward off despair, hopelessness and grief, much like soldiers carry religious tokens into war or pilgrims tote relics along the dusty road searching for hope.

We cannot always live in glory or ecstasy, no more than we can dwell forever in suffering and discontent. Everything in moderation, the sages say.

But let us give Mike and Lila—Tonight! At the very least, this bliss-filled moment! Let us allow *them* a sacred relic to remember all the days of their lives.

This, *this* is the moment when these two souls surrender their secrets to one another. The anima and animus rise up like supplicants, hands raised above their heads, beseeching the heavens to have mercy upon them, conjoin them, hook them to the same yoke and bid them go forward and pull together in the harness.

Let us publish the eternal wedding banns Tonight for Mike and Lila!

Some people believe that it is the Holy Church which joins two souls together via the sacrament of marriage. But let us never forget that Jesus is the greatest fisher of men; and it is God who first casts a wide net upon two honest hearts and hauls them into the same boat to go forward together as one.

But—wait!

Lila, our poor Lila! falters as she climbs up from the ocean into the fishing boat where Mike Hobart's perfect love awaits her. She senses a malevolent shadow from her past rising up from its watery grave – and glances down at Yesterday, which, alas! like Tomorrow, has the awful power to intrude upon Tonight.

Lila shivered. Eternity slipped from her grasp like a fish.

"Cold?" Hobart asked, tucking her more securely into the shelter of his broad shoulder.

But his close embrace was not enough. Unholy ghosts not yet completely laid to rest latched onto the fabric of her consciousness and yanked Lila back to a grim reality. The past had a hold on her that she had not completely left behind!

She hid her face against his chest, and tried not to cry out. *Omigod, he deserves so much better than me!*

And thus ended Mike and Lila's moment of perfect bliss. No doubt the inky demon perched on my right shoulder – and my cynics – are satisfied.

Chapter 20
. . . .
Martha's Lot

Poor Rebecca has gotten short shrift in our story lately, much like poor Martha in the New Testament stories of Martha and Mary (see Luke 10.38-42). While it's too late to redeem Martha from her lowly place in history, we *can* restore Rebecca to her deserved place of prominence in our little tale.

After her arrival in Sovereign, Rebecca worked tirelessly to restore comfortable living to the old Russell homestead and the place responded gratefully to her loving touch, awakening like a superannuated pair of leather boots in the hands of a master cobbler. The wainscoting began to glow like embers in a fire and the windows sparkled with new light, which wasn't all emanating from the rays of the sun.

Old houses react to love bestowed upon them just like old humans do, their creaking joints stretch and strain to meet the affection halfway and they discover that there is a lot more life left in 'em than they had imagined. A state of nervous excitement is created when one first begins to cherish and restore an old place like the Russell homestead. Noises unheard for 40 or 50 or even 60 years are sounded once again: hopeful footfalls, curious doors opening and closing, latches on cupboards clicking with renewed confidence. Even the mice scurry about knowing that – as in this case – their days are numbered, for the traps are baited and the Mouse Motel is ready to go (and has, in fact, made several trips with Wendell and Rebecca over the Sebasticook and Kennebec rivers to relocate the rodents).

In addition to general cleaning and de-cluttering, Rebecca sewed new curtains for the great room, and made up various other comfortable cloth necessities, such as the new dining room place mats, the new cushions for the couch, and the new upholstery for the porch's double rocker. She was a whirling dervish about the place, at once destroying and creating or re-creating the Goode Life that most old farmhouses in rural Maine have offered those brave enough to take on the initial challenge.

Old timers knew how to live, and took care of their comforts. They knew just where to place windows to catch the sun in winter so that they could sit in their rockers and read the Bible. They knew where NOT to place windows, so that the cold northwest blast wouldn't find a way in around the sashes in the wooden frames. They knew where to build the fireplaces and the chimneys, so that they and their large families would be warm and snug and could cook and yet the smoke wouldn't bother anyone. They calculated in advance where their tired old hands would come to rest on the upper level of the staircase so that when they hitched themselves up that top stair at night there'd be a solid wooden grip at just the right spot. They knew that what they were building was not just for themselves, but for those who came after them – and the ones who came after *them*. The old timers who built the Russell place might not have expected Rebecca Johnson and Lila Woodsum to come along to occupy the place, but they knew that the place would still be standing if *someone* came along.

Rebecca had also made a cursory review of the gardens, now long overgrown yet yielding fruits, herbs and flowers, not all of which were planted by the Russells. Some original plantings set good roots or reproduced and "took," as the local slang goes. But other plantings were done by a much more indiscriminate hand, the hand of Mother Nature, which sowed seeds promiscuously and carelessly via the bills of birds and the defecation of wild animals. Thus the lemon balm grew up with the bull thistle and the red bee balm multiplied with the milkweed. One major discovery in the gardens was the presence of rhubarb – both green-stemmed and strawberry. This "find" offered immediate gratification to Rebecca because now she could serve strawberry-rhubarb pie (as well as custard pie) for dessert at *The Egg Ladies'* first dinner party, which was scheduled for Sunday afternoon.

Most of the week prior to the dinner party was necessarily focused on preparations for the big event. Rebecca's silverware, which had once belonged to her mother, was counted and polished. For china, she liberated Addie Russell's "good" dishes from the cupboard over the refrigerator, first examining the plates, bowls and cups for chips and cracks. Satisfied with their condition, Rebecca lovingly bathed each piece of the Johnson Brothers "Woodland Turkey" china set like a precious newborn baby, and calculated how she would set the dining table so that the colorful china with the rotund turkey in the center of the plate would have the most charming effect.

Rebecca enlisted Wendell's aid in examining and re-gluing the oak dining room chairs so that the guests need not worry about falling to the floor in the event of overeating. She scrubbed down the tables and the chairs with large doses of Murphy® Oil Soap (purchased from Gilpin's where Ralph kept a healthy supply on hand) and polished the set with lavender-scented beeswax (discovered in the cleaning cupboard under the slate sink). Floors were washed and waxed; rugs were beaten within an inch of their lives; windows squeaked clean; curtains and tablecloths rendered from whole cloth; and each dangling teardrop and glass *bobeche* on the chandelier was removed, hand washed and lovingly replaced.

Yes, Rebecca had been busy. No wonder that women such as Rebecca champion poor Martha's cause (the worker) and cast a disdainful eye upon her sister Mary (the thinker) in the New Testament tale. Although Jesus had the power to feed multitudes, he more often relied on Martha than upon miracles to provide for himself and his retinue.

And the feeding of hungry souls was important to Rebecca, as it was to Martha. For is not the preparing and sharing of a meal as sacred an act as sitting still and contemplating deep theological questions as Martha's sister Mary elected to do? Rebecca longed to create a meal by which she and Lila could show their deep appreciation to their new friends, those who had been supporting their offbeat hopes and dreams for a new life. Simple, good food over which friends could gather and felicity could be found was Rebecca's order of the day.

Spurred on by the "Woodland Turkey" dinner plates, Rebecca purchased a Bourbon Red heritage breed turkey from a Thorndike farmer for the main course. She naturally elected to complement the meat with Lila's fiddleheads, baked potatoes secured from a grower in Troy, spicy rhubarb sauce (a recipe she would attempt from Grammie Addie's cookbook), stuffing and gravy, Wendell's sweet overwintered carrots, and a variety of pickles from Maine's organic foodie Cheryl Wixson (whom Lila had discovered on Twitter @CWKitchen and whose products were available at Crosstrax in Unity). In addition, Rebecca would bake whole wheat yeast rolls and the two pies for dessert. Altogether, the menu offered as satisfying a Sunday dinner as could be found in any Maine home over the past 200 years.

"We just need to figure out where everyone's going to sit," said an apron-bedecked Rebecca, her pretty faced flushed from cooking, as she contemplated the dining room table on Sunday morning. The scent of the roasting turkey wafted through the spacious old farmhouse.

"Why do we need to assign places in advance?" asked Lila, who had been summoned from her chores for her opinion. "Why don't we just let everyone sit where they WANT to sit?"

"That won't work," Rebecca said, with a small but determined shake of her head.

"Why not?"

"Well, if you don't know, dear, I don't think I can explain it to you. That's just the way it is when you're hosting an intimate dinner party such as this." Rebecca felt slightly taken aback that something so obvious was not known by her young friend.

Wendell, who was hovering in the background as Rebecca's aide de camp, spoke up. "Wal, you know, folks is like dairy cows. They need to know what stall to git into or they gits all mixed up in the bahn."

"Right," said Lila. "Just tell me what to do and I'll do it," she added, bemused.

"Thet's jest it," said Wendell, winking. "Ain't it more comfortable jest being told?"

Now, liking her own way was a cross that Lila had to bear. She didn't take direction well, and she knew it. Therefore, it was with some difficulty that she swallowed back her initial sarcastic retort to the kind-hearted chicken farmer, and smiled sweetly. "Yep," she said. "Sure is."

Heartened, Rebecca began assigning seats. "I think we'll put the two men at the ends," she said. "Wendell, you'll go here," and she touched the pressed-back oak chair at the head of the table nearest to the kitchen. Wendell instantly puffed up with importance. "And Mike will go at the far end of the table."

This new development cut across the grain of Lila's young, feminist spirit. She didn't know much about seating arrangements, but she was acutely aware of the symbolism of placing two men not even FROM the household at the heads of the table. "What about Ralph Gilpin? He's a man!"

"It's not quite the same, dear," said Rebecca, who could easily see the difference between the two single men and the one married man.

"Right," Lila said, dryly. She noted, however, that Wendell was standing straight and tall with his unexpected new authority, and she discovered that she couldn't put a crimp in his posture. And what was the big deal, anyway? Did she really care where she sat or who sat next to whom? As long as she got to sit next to Mike Hobart!

"And I'll sit on this side here, next to you Wendell, so I can have easy access to the kitchen," Rebecca continued. "I'll have a lot of jumping up and down to do and this will keep me out of everyone's way."

"Where do you want me to sit?" asked Lila, beginning to feel more like a small child than the co-hostess of the dinner party.

"I think you should sit down there around the corner from Mike, with young Grayden next to you, and Miss Hastings between him and Wendell—you'll keep an eye on Miss Hastings, won't you, Wendell?"

"Ayuh," he said, with even more importance.

"And then Ralph will sit next to me, and Maude between her husband and Mike."

"I thought husbands weren't supposed to sit next to their wives?" Lila pointed out, with a small amount of sarcasm.

"That's archaic, dear. You've been reading too much Jane Austen. Nobody follows that table etiquette anymore."

Lila groaned inwardly. She actually knew nothing about the etiquette of formal dining appropriate to Jane Austen's era or any other, and immediately elected to secede from the discussion. "Whatever," she said. "I mean, whatever you think is best, Becca."

"Well, then we'll keep Ralph and Maude on the back side of the table with me," Rebecca concluded, happily. And so the seating arrangements for the dinner party were disposed of exactly in the manner that our good "Martha" had preordained.

Following this exchange, Lila retreated to the relative safety and sanctity of her hen pen (where the flapping and fluttering chickens suddenly appeared much more rational) and Rebecca returned to the kitchen to check the turkey. The full-figured bird sizzled in its juices in the propane oven and boasted a tight-fitting brown vest, upon which Rebecca lovingly basted another layer of herbal oil and succulents. She closed the oven and wiped a stray strand of hair away from her moist forehead. Satisfaction filled her senses as much as the scent of roasting turkey filled the air.

"Shore smells good," said Wendell, who had followed her into the kitchen. His eyes widened at the sight of the turkey and his mouth watered. "What else you want me to do afore I go home to change?"

"Do we have enough chairs?" Rebecca inquired, resting lightly back against the counter.

"Ayuh. I counted 'em twice. We got eight, what with thet Captain's chair I brung down from the open chamber."

"And there *are* eight of us ...?"

"Ayuh."

"You're OK with using that chair, Wendell? Or should we give the Captain's chair to Mike?"

"Wal, you know, I'druther Mike had thet chair. I ain't as light as I used to be."

"We'll give it to Mike, then," Rebecca decided, wiping her hands on her apron.

And so the conversation progressed for several minutes, and was in effect a conversation between Rebecca and Rebecca. No detail was inconsequential; nothing escaped her notice, including ice for the water glasses and the necessity of placing multiple salts and peppers on the table for the convenience of the company. Wendell's carrots were inspected for faults; the dough was covered and set near the stove for perfect rising; the pickle dishes were selected with the utmost discernment.

Love can be expressed in manifold ways, not just in the soft crooning and the kisses bestowed on a farmer's porch in the dusk of evening. Love can be seen in the bustle and activity of Rebecca's preparations for her friends, in the way her happy hands melded the flour and lard together and rolled out the pie dough, and in the frequency with which she checked the turkey.

Love can also be espied in the special way in which we serve one another. A car door opened, a helping hand, a proffered favor, a suggestion, a sounding board, a reassuring smile—all of these are indicative of an abiding love and respect. While these actions and others like them might not be noticed in the beginning by the beloved, they will be regarded for their true value in the end as actions are much more enduring and endearing than the spoken word.

Unfortunately, while such signs pointed to the fact that our old friend Wendell Russell was smitten, his affection for Rebecca will no doubt be noted sooner by you, my pips, than by Rebecca herself. Had Wendell taken her into his arms in a grand display and declared his passion, Rebecca would have been startled but she would have understood his intentions. As it was, however, while she was unconsciously grateful

Hens and Chickens

for Wendell's help, she was conscious of nothing more than that he was occasionally underfoot in her kitchen.

Wendell was the shy, silent type. For him and men like him, the spoken word acts more like a lead sinker than a bobber. Language to Wendell was an impediment, like an old boat that won't float. He could no more toss out a pretty phrase than he could throw out the nylon line of an expensive L.L. Bean® fly rod. But give him a few worms and an old fish pole and Wendell will come home with a pocketful of brook trout every time.

Lila was never in doubt of Mike Hobart's feelings, for he was a man born knowing how to declare his affections to a woman. But Wendell Russell, on the other hand, "Wal, you know, I cain't git my tongue rigged up right to ... wal, you know."

And we do know, indeed, how difficult it was for Wendell to verbally express his affections. Unfortunately, Rebecca Johnson did not know. And so Wendell remained in her kitchen underfoot, but hopeful.

"Didja want me to put them things on the table?" he asked, indicating three pretty vintage sets of chicken salt and pepper shakers that Rebecca had stumbled upon earlier in the week, packed away in a wooden box in the open chamber.

"Yes, please, Wendell. Oh, wait! I need to fill those pepper shakers, first," said Rebecca. She stood on tip toe to try and knock down the black pepper container, which was just out of her short reach on the third shelf in the baking cupboard.

"I kin git thet for you," he offered. And then the old chicken farmer actually did lean over Rebecca in an intimate fashion and easily secured the metal container from the shelf.

"Well, oh, my!" Rebecca said, blushing. She settled back down to her 5-feet, 2-inches, necessarily clasping onto Wendell's hefty forearms to steady herself. "Thank you!"

His blue eyes twinkled. "Ayuh," he said, flashing his trademark grin.

Their eyes met. And I think in that moment our good-hearted "Martha" did get an inkling of his intentions.

Chapter 21

. . . .

Lila and Rebecca at Home

The Gilpins were the first to arrive at the dinner party. Young Gray was anxious to check out Lila's John Deere® riding lawn mower, which he would be using to mow the large yard at the old Russell homestead. Seeing a sizeable amount of cash hovering before his eyes, as well as infinite tractor driving, he hounded his grandmother to arrive at *The Egg Ladies'* Sunday dinner party nearly an hour early.

"She said, any time after 1 p.m. would be OK," Gray said. "So, like, what's wrong with 1:01?"

Maude could think of no viable argument, and so she simply gave in to her grandson. "Rebecca did SAY that," she told her husband, who was fidgeting about the house still in his church clothes.

"I ain't got nuthin' better to do here dressed like this," Ralph said; "so we might as well git in the car and go over there!"

Lila greeted them at the side shed door, for which they had made a beeline. Rebecca had left suggestively ajar the house's rarely used West-facing front door, exposing the glass storm door and thus the interior of the pretty formal entryway. However, no self-respecting Mainer would be caught, well, *alive* entering a home via the front door. That august entrance was reserved for accessing the parlor, and therefore closely linked to the bringing in, taking out, and laying out of the dead.

Lila was disappointed to discover that their first guests were the Gilpins, although she quickly hid her disappointment with a warm welcome. Her old ghosts were now safely crammed back in their lock box, and she had been secretly hoping that Mike Hobart would show up early enough to claim a few kisses. Now, however, she would have to wait until dinner was over and all the guests had left before she could once again feel the security of his muscular embrace. She shivered excitedly at the thought of surrendering to his demanding lips.

157

"Cold one, ain't it?" said Ralph Gilpin, stepping up into the shed in time to catch Lila's shiver. He rubbed his arthritic hands together brusquely.

Lila was momentarily befuddled. "What?"

"Say, thet was quite a haul of fiddleheads you 'n Mike got t'other day!"

"Right," replied Lila, instinctively.

Wendell, always on the alert, exited Bud's place as soon as he heard the Gilpins turn into the yard. He sauntered across the way, pulling his comb through his hair and returning it to his back pocket with a practiced move. He followed the Gilpins into the side shed without knocking.

Ralph stopped to greet him. "Hey-ya old timer!" he said, slapping Wendell on the back. "How the Hell are ya?"

Wendell, who was in fact the junior of the two men by 10 years, flashed his trademark grin. "Wal, you know, young fella – I ain't too bad!"

Lila escorted the three Gilpins and Wendell into the kitchen, where she turned Maude and Ralph over to Rebecca's gracious attendance. Then she took the teenager out to the barn to introduce him to the riding lawn mower, being extra careful not to get any grease or oil on her pretty silk dress.

"Wow, it's awesome!" said Gray, examining the 20-year-old John Deere®. "Can I start her up?"

Lila nodded. "Mike's got it going again and sharpened the blade," she said. "You can try it out today, and then maybe come back and mow sometime next week, OK?"

"Totally awesome!"

The lawn mower's engine drowned out the identifying hum of Hobart's pickup as he drove in the yard ferrying Miss Hastings. Hobart and the retired music teacher were thus settled comfortably with the others in the living room area of the great room, beverages in hand, when Lila finally returned to the house.

She paused awkwardly like a schoolgirl, unsure as to how she and Mike Hobart should present themselves to all their friends. He was dressed in fresh jeans and a short-sleeved dress shirt, and looked handsomer than ever. Her heart fluttered at the sight of him.

Hobart, spying Lila, excused himself abruptly from his conversation with Maude, stood up and strode to her side. "You look beautiful, darling," he said, slipping an arm around her waist and pulling her to

Hens and Chickens

him. He kissed her on the cheek. He could not have announced their relationship to their friends any more clearly than had he asked them to stand with them at the church altar.

Lila flushed happily, and the world became rosy once again.

Rebecca marshaled everyone to the dining room table just as the gingerbread clock on the mantle *clanged* 2 p.m. She easily indicated where each of the guests was to sit, and they all pulled out their chairs and settled down like setting hens eager to get to work on the business before them. The cheerful table was laid with Rebecca's steaming feast and many hearts quickened. There was an expectant pause, however, as seven sets of eyes automatically turned to the head of the table, where Wendell was carefully unfolding his cloth napkin onto his lap.

Wendell felt the amplified attention. He looked up and was momentarily flummoxed. He realized that Sunday dinner etiquette required some few spoken words from the head of the table, but his Quaker heritage relied upon quiet not vocal prayer. He recoiled inward, and regretted that he had been so quick to secure the plum post.

Miss Hastings, sitting at Wendell's right hand, leaped to the rescue. "We thank the GOOD LORD for bringing us together here today," she gushed; "and thank our hostesses for providing us with this WONDERFUL food! Amen."

"Amen!" repeated the little group, of which the loudest was Wendell Russell.

The food was passed around with the joking and jostling characteristic of intimate dining, and the meal proceeded under the watchful consideration of an anxious Rebecca. She kept an eye on every dish, noted the piles of food on every plate, and mentally measured the liquid level in every water glass. The first 10 minutes progressed with no remark more scintillating than a few humorous exclamations and directives such as "pass the butter, please." A good deal of quiet attention was paid to eating, however, which is the highest compliment any chef can receive—and Rebecca was gratified by it.

Maude Gilpin, always the consummate hostess herself, shortly initiated the conversation. "Thanks for all those lovely fiddleheads, kids," she said to Mike and Lila, who were both close at hand. "I'm baking my usual fiddlehead quiches for the church fundraiser in two weeks. I'll let you know ASAP how many eggs I'll need," she said to Lila. "Last year I think I used 30 dozen."

"Thirty dozen!" exclaimed Lila. "How many quiches do you make?"

"I baked about 100 last year. I think the two pails of fiddleheads you gathered are enough to do that again."

"Oh, my goodness!" exclaimed Rebecca, dropping her fork and losing her concentration altogether. She was the only one present who truly understood how much work the baking of 100 fiddlehead quiches represented.

"Folks come from three counties to buy one of my Maude's fiddlehead quiches," Ralph said, proudly. He threw his left arm affectionately around his wife's fat, round shoulders. "Thet church would be on life support if it warn't for my Maude!"

"Is that the little white church at the corner?" Lila asked, curiously.

"Only one we got in town," said Ralph. "A white dinosaur, if ya ask me."

"I've wanted to stop in and see that church ever since I came to Sovereign!" said Rebecca. "It's such a lovely old building."

Maude leaned in front of her husband to catch Rebecca's eye. "Feel free to stop into the church anytime, dearie," she encouraged. "The door is always open. It's a quiet, calming place. Sometimes I just stop in so's I can have some peaceful time to myself."

Gilpin guffawed and his grandson tittered.

"How many people go to church there?" Rebecca asked.

"Ain't many," Ralph answered her. "They ought to shut them doors for good, but the townfolks won't let 'em."

"Don't be sayin' negative things, now," Maude chastened her husband. "That church is a piece of our history!" She gathered herself and addressed the table at large. "Most folks don't know it's a Union Church – a joining of the original Quaker, Methodist and Universalist churches we once had in town," she said. "SOME of us are trying to keep it part of our future, too. And to answer your question, dearie, we've got about 150 members, but only 25 or 30 attend like we do on a regular basis."

"Course 'twould probably help if there was a regular minister," Wendell suggested, getting his vocal sea legs again.

"Ayuh," Ralph agreed. "The one we got is only in the pulpit every *other* Sunday."

"She's an itinerant," Maude said, defensively. "She's got other churches to cover. She can't be here all the time, because we can't afford a settled minister."

Hens and Chickens

"That's too bad," Rebecca empathized.

"She sure is an odd duck," continued Ralph; "what with running naked through the goldenrod 'n all!"

Wendell chuckled. "Traffic does kinda pick up on the Cross Road come August, don't it?"

"What's that?" said Lila, intrigued. She looked from Wendell to Ralph, inquisitively. "Why does the traffic pick up on the Cross Road in August?"

"Thet's where the minister lives," replied Ralph. "Come summer she strips down bare-ass naked and goes runnin' through her field of goldenrod like Lady Godiva, only without the hoss!"

"Shushhh! There's children present!" exclaimed Maude.

"I'm 15, Grandma; I ain't a kid."

"Ain't like *she's* a kid no more, neither!" Ralph quipped.

"Well, she's a dahrrrling woman," interjected Miss Hastings. "Her sermons are WONDERFULLY funny. I go almost every Sunday she's preaching just to get a good laugh, even if it IS sometimes at myself!"

"Didja know she's a Quaker, jest like ole Wendell here?" Ralph said to Miss Hastings.

Miss Hastings shook her head. Her rioting dark hair threatened to come unglued and tumble to the table like a dropped can of worms. "I knew there was something special about her!"

"Say, buddy, how'd you like that lawn mower?" Hobart asked Gray, calculating that it was time to turn the table conversation in another direction.

"It's awesome!" Gray exclaimed. "I'm comin' over next Wednesday to mow the yard."

"Kid ain't never used a ridin' mower before. I'll probably never git him to mow our lawn evah agin," grumbled Ralph.

"I will if ya pay me, Grandpa."

Under the watchful eye of his wife, Ralph choked back the sharp retort aimed at his grandson. "Thanks for gettin' the thing up and runnin', Mike," he said, instead.

"No problem. I used to mow lawns for spending money when I was his age."

"Well, dahrrrling," Miss Hastings said to the teenager; "you'll just have to drive that big old rig right up the road to my house and mow MY lawn, too!"

"Awesome!" repeated Gray, quickly calculating in his mind how rich he would become by the end of the summer.

Lila, who wanted to hear everything there was to hear about Mike Hobart's childhood in Maple Grove, was disappointed when the conversation turned away from him. Her mind momentarily wandered off, but she came to, startled, when she felt the proprietary touch of a masculine hand on her right thigh beneath the tablecloth. She flushed with pleasure and glanced at Hobart. He winked, and squeezed her leg. Lila's heart swelled like a tree frog in full song.

The main course proceeded until nearly all the food was abolished. Rebecca and Lila then began a steady stream of removing the plates and serving dishes, and preparing the pies, coffee and tea for the dessert course. Maude offered to help, but when her assistance was graciously declined she turned to keep the guests occupied, respectful of Rebecca's sovereign right to the kitchen duties.

After the hot beverages were served, the custard and strawberry-rhubarb pies were produced with a stack of dessert plates to the open admiration of those present. Rebecca seated herself in front of the pies brandishing a porcelain pie server and expertly began carving up pieces and dishing them out to the expectant guests. She served Miss Hastings first, and then went around the table proffering juicy slices based on the traditional etiquette with which Emily Post adherents will be well acquainted. Rebecca served herself last, and settled back into her chair to enjoy her two slivers of pie.

In the seat next to her, Wendell smacked his lips with satisfaction. "Thet's the best strawberry-rhubarb pie I evah et," he pronounced, earnestly. "Not even Grammie Addie coulda done bettah!"

"Oh, well, my!" Rebecca said, blushing.

Wendell's acclaim was echoed around the table. Maude even went so far as to ask for the recipe, which to Rebecca, still marveling over the 100 quiches, was the highest praise of all.

"Thet custard's pretty darn good, too," said Ralph. "Must be them eggs!" He chuckled pleasantly at his own backhanded compliment to Lila and *The Egg Ladies*.

"I just hope I've got enough eggs for Maude's fiddlehead quiches," Lila said, worriedly. "I'm getting almost eight dozen a day, though, so I should be alright!"

"Just give those hens an extra charge of sunflower seeds and you'll get more eggs than you know what to do with!" exhorted Miss Hastings.

Hens and Chickens

Lila smiled. "I'll need a lot more than 50 pounds!" she replied, her heart skipping happily over the memory of the big bag of sunflower seeds that had brought her and Mike Hobart together.

"I'll help unload 'em," Hobart offered, innocently; and everyone laughed.

Once again, Lila found herself marveling how differently her life would have been had Joe Kelly NOT fired Rebecca, and had she not quit her own job in protest. She said a little private prayer. And then she was even emboldened enough to search for Mike Hobart's hand beneath the tablecloth!

Chapter 22

. . . .

"I Can't Do It!"

When the dessert plates were being cleared away from the dinner guests, Gray eagerly excused himself to return to the youthful delights encompassed by the barn and the riding lawn mower. Rebecca refilled the coffee and tea cups, and the pleasant aromas unconsciously refreshed the spirits of her guests. She reclaimed her seat, and a satisfied silence descended on the little group of adults. It was a sensation not unlike the palpable, heartfelt hush that settles over a quiet, unprogrammed Quaker meeting. One could almost feel the presence of a sacred mother hen gathering the baby chicks under her heavenly wings: *"For where two or three are gathered in my name, I am there among them."*

After a minute or two of comfortable quiet, Miss Hastings spoke up. "That was a WONDERFUL meal!" she proclaimed. "You could even give my old friend Ma Jean a run for her money!" she added, speaking directly across the table to Rebecca.

"Thank you so much," said Rebecca. "Lila and I wanted to take the opportunity to show our gratitude to all of our new friends in Sovereign."

"Absolutely!" Lila avowed. "We couldn't have gotten *The Egg Ladies* off the ground without ALL of you!"

"Hear, hear!" said Ralph Gilpin, thumping the table with his arthritic fist.

"Amen!" added Wendell with religious fervor, perhaps making amends for his earlier balk.

"How does it feel to be back in the old place, Wendell?" Mike Hobart asked, regarding the chicken farmer with curiosity. "Does it seem strange to be here?"

Wendell took a moment for consideration. "Wal, you know, feels pretty good. Course I didn't used to sit *heah* at the table," he admitted. "This was old Pap's spot. And after Pappy died Grammie Addie jest left his chair empty."

Jennifer Wixson

"Where DID you sit?" asked Lila, glancing around the table, attempting to picture the extended Russell family at a Sunday dinner in 1950.

"Wal, right there in yore seat," he replied. "Next to Grammie Addie. She kept me pretty close at hand to make sure I et all my vegetables."

The little group laughed. His reply gave Rebecca an idea, however. "Why don't you tell us a story from your childhood, Wendell," she said, lightly touching his flannel shirt sleeve. "Would you mind?"

Wendell Russell's worn-out old heart did a backflip at Rebecca's intimate touch, and new power surged into his tired battery. "Wal, you know, I don't mind," he said, flashing a gold-toothed grin.

The little group settled back into their seats in anticipation. Hobart, whose left hand was reclining on Lila's leg, reached up and secured hers from where it was resting on the table. The eyes met, and he gave her hand a reassuring squeeze. Lila heard the joyful sound of sleigh bells in her heart.

"Course 'twas pretty hard work 'round heah most of the time," Wendell began; "I never see Grammie Addie sit down 'cept for meals. But every year in May – when the sun got good 'n hot but jest afore the black flies come out – we'd all git dressed up in our Sunday best and take a picnic down to the Millett Rock."

"I'll be goddammed," said Ralph. "I ain't thought of the Millett Rock in 50 years!"

"Shushhh," said Maude. "It's *his* story."

"What's the Millett Rock?" asked Lila, momentarily distracted from Hobart's attentions.

"She's a big ole boulder the glacier left behind on its last pass through, 'bout the size of thet white church down to the corner," Wendell said. "Thet rock's been parked in the woods 'cross the way for 11,000 years, like a broke down tractah no one could git stahted agin. We used to climb all ovah the Millett Rock when we was kids, and Grammie Addie always put on her big ole bonnet and packed us all a picnic to take down to the Millett Rock every May. 'Twas 'bout the only recreation she evah had. She looked forward to thet May picnic more 'n we kids looked forward to Christmas. I kin still see her scamperin' up thet rock in her silk dress jest like a young heifer let out of the bahn after a long wintah."

"We should take a picnic down this year!" Lila said.

"What a WONDERFUL idea!" Miss Hastings concurred.

Wendell looked dubious. "Wal, I ain't shore if we kin git in there now," he said. "She's pretty growed up, what with trees and puckerbrush.

Hens and Chickens

Course it used to be all pasture back then and Grammie Addie rode Charity down, she was ole Pap's favorite work hoss." He looked apprehensively at 87-year-old Miss Hastings.

Mike Hobart instantly picked up the drift of the chicken farmer's concern. "We can make it work," he declared. "I'll go in beforehand with a chain saw and clear a path. A friend of mine has a four-wheeler I can borrow on the day of the picnic, and we'll use his ATV to ferry in anyone who doesn't want to walk. That's if you don't mind me cutting the trees down there, Wendell," he added, quickly.

"I don't mind. She's awful haad goin' but yore shaap enough with a chainsaw to git the job done, Mike," Wendell replied.

A targeted date two weeks away was set for the picnic to the Millett Rock – weather dependent, of course – and the little group chatted excitedly about what to expect and who would bake what and what types of fancy dress clothing should be worn, with Lila suggesting that she and Rebecca wear the old silk gowns she'd discovered in the attic. The mantelpiece clock chimed 3:30 p.m., but still the satisfied guests held fast to their comfortable seats, unwilling to let the agreeable dinner party end. A trio of mourning doves fluttered up to the ground beneath the bird feeder dangling outside the east-facing window, and the purple-gray birds started up a round of mournful *cooing*.

"Who else has a childhood story to tell?" Rebecca asked, her pretty blue eyes roving hopefully around the table.

Lila felt her first stirrings of fear. What if Rebecca solicited childhood remembrances from everyone at the table?! What would she do? What COULD she say?!

"I remember a WONDERFUL story that my father – bless his heart! – used to tell," cried Miss Hastings. "He was tending his strawberry bed one spring when a couple in a flivver drove into the dooryard, wanting to know what the folks in Sovereign were like. 'What are the folks like where YOU come from?' Father asked. 'Oh, they're awful mean; small-minded and mean-spirited!' the man answered. Father thought a moment: "Wal, that's likely what you'll find 'round here,' he replied."

Everyone at the table chuckled, except for Lila. Her breathing had become slightly labored. *Not now! Please, not now!*

"Wait, there's more!" Miss Hastings exclaimed. "The next spring, Father was out planting his peas when another couple drove into the yard, wanting to know what the folks in Sovereign were like. 'What are the folks like where YOU come from?' Father asked. 'Oh, they are the dearest, sweetest folks you ever saw, and we hate to leave, but I just got a job here in town!' the man answered. Father never missed a beat. 'Wal, that's likely what you'll find 'round here,' he replied."

This time the little group broke out into hoots of appreciation and genuine laughter. Miss Hastings eyes sparkled. "Isn't that a dahrrrling story?" she said. "We used to make Father tell that story over and over again when we were kids!"

"Lovely!" proclaimed Rebecca. "Thank you so much for sharing it!" Her eye began roving around the table again, searching for another storytelling volunteer. "Who's next?" she said, encouragingly.

Lila felt the panic viscerally. She swallowed hard and surreptitiously glanced at Mike Hobart to see if he had noticed her rising anxiety. Hobart, however, was busy bantering with Ralph Gilpin, who had suggested the carpenter as the next story-telling candidate.

"Don't everyone speak up at once!" Rebecca said, laughing.

Lila was suddenly hyper-aware of herself, as though she had floated out of her body and was hovering over the table watching the action from an aerial position. It was almost like flying. She recognized the sensation and attempted to quash it, but—*it was too late!*

The door *clicked* softly shut, and a dark shadow loomed over her bed. It was her stepfather! He was standing over her, unfastening his belt. His eyes were glazed over with evil, predatory intent.

A sob escaped from Lila's throat. "Oh, make him stop!" she cried, staggering to her feet. The table swirled around her like a merry-go-round and she noted the concern on Mike Hobart's face as he tilted past, and Rebecca and Miss Hasting … but no one stopped to help her! She rushed from the dining room, hands over her face.

The startled group sat momentarily dazed and befuddled. Rebecca started to rise, but Hobart was on his feet in a split second.

"Let me go," he said, tossing his napkin onto his chair. He strode out of the room on Lila's heels, and Rebecca sank back down into her chair. It never crossed her mind for a second to contest his right to comfort her beloved young friend.

Hobart found Lila sobbing, on her knees in the sawdust, face into the corner of the hen pen. She was cold and dirty, and at first resisted his attentions.

"Shhhh," he whispered soothingly. "It's OK—you're safe." He sank to

the floor beside her and gently lifted her into his lap. She turned her face
to his shoulder and continued to cry. He stroked her hair and back, and let
her sob, her little chest heaving pitifully. Hobart wrapped his arms around
her to keep her warm, and occasionally mumbled inarticulate reassurances.

Lila cries gradually abated, and after 10 minutes ended altogether.
She sniveled and shivered, and made an attempt to gather herself together. *What have I done?!*

A thousand thoughts flew into her head at once, like the swallows
returning to San Juan Capistrano. *I'm not ready for this! He deserves better than
me! Why can't I leave this horror behind me?*

But one thing was for sure: she would NOT ruin his life. She would
NOT!

Lila took a deep breath, in order to calm herself. She felt a sense of
resolute purpose rising within her. *God give me strength to do this!*

Hobart was still holding her tightly, stroking her short hair. "It's OK,
darling," he whispered, again. "I'm here. I love you. Nothing will ever
hurt you again!"

New hot tears, tears of loss, stung Lila's eyelids. She pushed herself
away from him and sat up. "I'm OK, now, thanks."

"Sure? I can get my hankie from the truck," he said, teasingly.

Lila clasped his strong hand and tugged on it to get his serious attention. "I can't do this, Mike," she said, bravely. She felt like throwing up,
but forced herself to continue. "I'm not ready for a romantic relationship. I thought I was, but obviously I'm not."

"But, darling," he pleaded; "whatever's wrong, I can *help* you."

"No, I won't do this to you," she said, firmly. She straightened
up defiantly, like a bent silver birch shaking off its heavy load from a
snowstorm.

"Shouldn't I be the one to decide that?"

She read the distress in his honest blue eyes, and felt his love descend
down to the innermost reaches of her soul. "Oh, Mike!" she said, sobbing. She pressed his hand to her cheek, kissing his palm. "Please, please!
Just give me some space!" she begged. "I need TIME to think everything
through!"

How could he argue with that? He could not!

Hobart's hopes dropped like a ruptured helium balloon. He sighed,
dispiritedly. "Whatever you say, darling," he said. "I just want you to be
happy!"

Lila squeezed his hand in reply.

"I won't give you up," he said softly. He pushed the tousled hair away from her eyes. "I'll wait."

She bit her lip, but could not speak.

Hobart stood up and helped her gently to her feet. He brushed the sawdust from her pretty floral print dress, as tenderly as a father toweling a small child. "I think your chickens are calling your name," he said, generously. "Want me to say 'goodbye' to the others for you?"

Lila nodded, her hazel eyes speaking louder than words the depth of her gratitude.

He smiled reassuringly, and leaned closer. "Remember, I'm very, very good at waiting, darling," he whispered, lips brushing her hair.

And then he was gone, and Lila was once more alone.

Chapter 23

·······

Tinkerbell

How does a young woman live with a broken heart? How does she go about her daily duties? How does she feed her chickens? Collect the eggs? What gives her the strength to get out of bed every day? Put one foot in front of the other?

How do any of us with a broken heart get through our days?

We all do what we have to do. We have no other alternative, unless we want to stop living altogether. But most of us choose not to end our life after the heartbreak occurs – when our home is destroyed by fire or flood, or our child drowns, or our spouse dies, or sickness overwhelms us. Somehow, somewhere, we find the courage to keep moving forward.

The first big loss is always the most difficult. We have not yet learned that loss will be one of the major themes of our lives. We have not learned that we will lose everything and everyone that we have ever loved, because Time marches forward like a terrible marching band that refuses to stop playing. And we must face the music over and over and over again, which is why love – true, honest, selfless love! – is so important to cherish and foster and reciprocate!

Lila *did* get out of bed the morning after the dinner party. She had chores to do and 200 baby chicks arriving the following day to prepare for; chicks that would be completely dependent upon her to keep them alive, and that would require food and water and heat and a special pen. And she was grateful that she had something to occupy her mind so that she wouldn't spend every waking hour mourning the loss of her childhood … and the resulting loss of her love, Mike Hobart.

So Lila stumbled through her day, mechanically performing her duties. The hens greeted her with their usual fluttering, flying excitement, which brought a faint glow to her spirit like that of a dying ember. And the egg collecting, cleaning and sorting served as a soothing physic for her sore heart. That afternoon Lila put the finishing touches on the separate pen, which would house her replacement chicks; filling waterers and feeders, and double checking the warming lights.

Rebecca, in the meantime, had allowed the incident at the dinner party to go entirely unremarked. Mike Hobart had taken her aside Sunday afternoon and briefly described the situation, saying that Lila had requested time for reflection. The motherly Rebecca had wanted to swoop in and rescue her young friend, but Hobart had recommended giving his beloved a day or two to recover on her own before confronting her. His advice tended contrary to Rebecca's own instincts, but she promised she would honor it, for at least the first 24 hours. After that, well, Rebecca was to use her own judgment.

And what about Mike Hobart?

In our anxiety for our heroine, we must not overlook the other major sufferer—our hero. The handsome carpenter was experiencing his own challenges as he struggled through the first night and the next day, laboring over the post and beam barn he was building in Troy. He did not – could not – understand what was causing Lila's grief, but he knew that he loved her, and so he hurt with her.

Hobart's grief was mostly not for himself; his distress was for his love. He thought first of her, felt first for her, wanted the best for her. The fact that he was absolutely sure HE was the best for her did alleviate some of his own personal sufferings. But the competing fact that he was helpless at this point to assist Lila caused him no end of agonizing pain. For it is difficult to watch someone we love suffer and realize that there is nothing, absolutely nothing, we can do to alleviate their suffering.

On Sunday night, following the incident, Hobart considered telephoning his father. However, the two men were so emotionally close that Hobart knew he could not get through the conversation without weeping. In addition, he didn't want to worry his father, who was looking forward to meeting Lila that summer. Suffice to say, a man with a dilemma of the heart – AND blessed with three older sisters – need not look far for emotional support. And so that evening Hobart poured out his troubles in an email to the *youngest* of his three older sisters, with whom he had the closest relationship.

After sending the email, however, Hobart decided it might be uplifting to hear a friendly voice from Maple Grove. Not wanting to spoil the contents of the email to his youngest sister, he elected to telephone his *eldest* sister. Per usual, he placed the call from his cell. Unlike per usual, he connected with fairly clear and steady phone service to Aroostook County in northern Maine.

"Mikey!" his elder sister exclaimed. "It's about time! How IS everything down there?"

"Not so good," replied Hobart. And before he knew it he had also bared his soul to his eldest sister. What else could he do after that but at least send a text message (or two or three) to his *middle* sister? And so within 24 hours the entire town of Maple Grove was buzzing with genuine concern for Hobart, who, as the baby of the seventh generation of potato farmers – and who lived Away – was felt to require particular empathy.

Wendell, our kind-hearted friend Wendell, was also suffering; worrying about everyone involved. On Monday afternoon he drove down to Hobart's job site in Troy and corralled the carpenter. "Wal, you know, she's gonna be a nice lookin' barn when yore finished," he said, after viewing the initial stages of construction and examining Hobart's design plans. "But how're *you* doin', Mike?" he asked, finally getting to the crux of his visit.

"I'm doing," replied Hobart, listlessly, resting on a long-handled spade. "Have you seen her today?"

The "her" was of course Lila.

"Wal, you know, I was ovah for breakfast but she was already out with the chickens. Her little friend said she ain't talkin' much. She's such a little bitty thing, you cain't help but feel bad for her."

Tears came to Hobart's eyes. He brushed them away, but didn't try and hide them from the chicken farmer. "Lila's strong," Hobart replied. "It might take her some time, but she'll bounce back."

"Ayuh, she's pretty spunky," Wendell agreed.

And Miss Hastings telephoned Monday morning – on the landline, not Lila's cell, which was her usual mode of contact with *The Egg Ladies*. Rebecca, who was obviously the intended recipient of the call, answered the phone.

"How IS the poor dahrrrling?" Miss Hastings inquired. "Matilda and I have been so WORRIED."

"She's taking care of the chickens just the same as usual," Rebecca replied. "But she hasn't spoken yet. I'll keep you posted."

"Do! I talked with Maude, and she and Ralph are VERY concerned. We're ALL praying for her!"

And so before long the whole town of Sovereign knew that one of *The Egg Ladies* was poorly, and a mutual sympathy began to be expressed. More than a few silent, as well as vocal, prayers were uttered. The supportive sentiment rose from the small community like the ethereal mist that rises up from Black Brook, dispersing up the hill toward the hen pen. Lila, as she went about her day, gathering and cleaning eggs, felt a slight, inexplicable up-lifting of her spirits.

Who knows the mysterious ways in which love works? Or of the power of prayer? Especially the efficacy of prayers from TWO Maine communities!

Let us never think for a moment that our prayers are wasted, even if they are unwanted. We have nothing to lose by freely sending our silent blessings to the Heavens, and our friends, loved ones and acquaintances might have much to gain. (But perhaps we shouldn't announce our intentions to the recipients of our prayers lest we forget that the bragging rights for the efficacy of prayer surely don't belong to us.)

Rebecca had promised Mike Hobart to keep silent for at least the first 24 hours. And she kept her promise. After that, however, she could contain herself and her concerns no longer.

"Please, dear, can't you tell me what's wrong?" she begged, when she discovered Lila moping in the wooden rocker on the farmer's porch Monday evening. Rebecca sank down beside her younger friend, taking Hobart's customary spot. She clasped Lila's hand affectionately.

"I don't want to talk about it, Becca," Lila said, flatly. But she didn't pull her hand away from her friend. Instead, Lila stared blankly with unseeing eyes out over the expanse of field, which was still a sharp green color despite the onset of dusk.

A phoebe who had been building her nest over the porch light, became momentarily discouraged. The brown bird abandoned the pile of twigs and grass, and *fluttered* away. Two was company but three was a crowd for the perky little flycatcher.

"I know that *something* has been bothering you for a long, long time," Rebecca pressed on. "Ever since your parents' death."

Her friend's words acted as a slight scratch upon the thin veneer that covered Lila's emotions. "He wasn't my father," said Lila, angrily.

"What?" said Rebecca.

"THAT MAN wasn't my FATHER!" Lila said, through clenched teeth.

Hens and Chickens

Rebecca was confused. In all the years she had known Lila, she had never been contradicted when referring to Lila's parents or to the tragic boating accident in late 2009 that had claimed their lives. However, in point of fact, Rebecca realized that she had never even heard Lila discuss her father *or* the accident. Avoidance of the incident had seemed natural at the time the accident occurred, but now Rebecca began to wonder if there wasn't more to the story. "If he wasn't your father, who *was* he?" she asked, finally.

"He was my mother's second husband. She married him when I was eight. My real father died when I was five."

Here was a clue; a small clue, to Lila's unhappiness. But what should Rebecca say now? In which direction should she go?

"I always wondered why you had a different last name. I'm sorry," she added, lamely.

"Sorry for WHAT? That he died?!" A hysterical giggle escaped Lila's lips. "He had no choice."

"No, I don't suppose any of us have a choice when it's our time to go," said Rebecca, thoughtlessly.

"You're soo wrong about that!"

"What do you mean, dear?"

"I don't want to talk about it, Becca," Lila repeated. And once again she clammed up.

Rebecca could think of nothing else to say, so she decided not to push her luck. She settled back against the comfortable cushioned settee and welcomed the pause to rest her own worried soul. The delicate scent of early viburnum blossoms drifted up from the bush nestling against the porch. Rebecca inhaled the sweet, spicy scent, and felt herself relax. How busy she had been since she had arrived in Sovereign! And how much her world had changed since she had been fired from Perkins & Gleeful!

Rebecca's eyes became accustomed to the dimming light and she saw movement in the upper right hand corner of the field. It was not unusual for the wild deer to browse the sweet new grass in the twilight, and Rebecca was glad for the opportunity to sit and watch their peaceful roaming. After a few minutes, however, she distinguished a blotch of white keeping pace with the half dozen brown bodies. Her mind puzzled over the white anomaly amidst the small deer herd. "Goodness!" she exclaimed, piecing the puzzle together. "Lila! I think that's *Tinkerbell!*"

Rebecca's announcement had an electrifying effect on Lila. She leaned forward as though stuck with a cattle prod. "TINKERBELL?!"

"Yes, Tinkerbell—look!" Rebecca pointed to the mysterious white blotch floating slowly across the upper field with the other deer.

"Omigod!" said Lila, almost unable to believe what she was seeing with her own eyes. "It IS Tinkerbell!"

A rush of adrenaline shot through her slender body, and a mass of pent-up emotion followed quickly upon its heels. The sight of the long hoped-for white deer acted as a catalyst, pushing Lila through the anger and denial that had been holding her back. She began to laugh and cry at the same time, expressing years of anguish, loss and grief. "Haahaa, arnnnnn, ahhh, haahaa! Tinkerbell! Arnnn, haha! Oh, oh, oh!"

"Oh, my dear!" exclaimed Rebecca, hugging her young friend to her motherly breast. "There, there," she soothed her; "let it out, let it out!"

Ten minutes passed in this fashion until Lila reached the bottom of her emotional well. She sat back up, and dried her eyes on the sleeve of her sweatshirt. She thought momentarily of Mike Hobart's blue handkerchief and experienced a stab of pain mingled with joyful love. "Thanks, Becca," she said. "I'm OK, now."

"But, dear, can't you tell me what's wrong?" Rebecca implored.

Lila exhaled deeply. "No, I can't. It's too complicated. You wouldn't understand."

Rebecca looked hurt, and Lila immediately felt the sting of her own words. She wouldn't have intentionally wounded her friend for anything! "I'm sorry; I didn't mean that like it sounded," she added quickly. "It's so complicated! It has to do with good and evil, and why bad things happen to good people."

Here was another clue!

Rebecca deliberated over this new information. *Good versus evil?* In her New England born, Congregationally-churched mind, there was only one course of action. "Why don't you go down and talk with the minister of the little church?" Rebecca suggested. "That's what *I* would do."

Lila's spine stiffened at the suggestion. "What can a minister do to help me?!"

Rebecca remained calm. "I don't know, dear, but there's one way to find out. Maude told me that the minister keeps open office hours at the church on Wednesday and Thursday afternoons, just in case anyone wants to drop by to talk with her."

Hens and Chickens

Lila was about to come back with a sarcastic retort, when she experienced a moment of *déjà vu*. Something about this conversation seemed familiar.

She recollected in a flash motoring up to Miss Hastings' house after their first meeting with Mike Hobart at Gilpin's General Store, recalling in particular Rebecca's concern about her treatment of him and of men in general. To her chagrin, Lila also remembered that she herself had resolved that day to gratefully accept Rebecca's motherly suggestions, instead of fighting her like an immature child all the time.

"I'm sorry," she apologized to Rebecca. *"I promise—I'll try to do better."*

Lila fell silent. She gave serious consideration to Rebecca's suggestion that she meet with the local minister. She remembered what Ralph Gilpin had said about the pastor of the little white church: "Come summer she strips down bare-ass naked and goes runnin' through her field of goldenrod like Lady Godiva, only without the hoss!" Despite her doldrums, Lila smiled.

Why not meet with the minister? Why not! What harm could it do?

"Ralph DID describe her as an odd duck," Lila said, decidedly. "I suppose that's as good a recommendation as any."

Rebecca laughed hopefully. "You'll do it?!"

"I'll do it; I'll go down and see the minister. What have I got to lose?"

"Oh, nothing, dear! And you have so *much* to gain!" cried the good-hearted Rebecca.

Chapter 24

. . . .

The Little White Church

The news about the reappearance of Tinkerbell was delivered throughout Sovereign from one household to the next with the efficacy of personal delivery telegrams. After the initial sighting Monday evening, traffic on the Russell Hill Road picked up 10-fold as residents strove to get their own personal glimpse of the fabled white deer. Beat up old trucks with entire families crammed inside motored up and down the road, especially in the gloaming, those refreshingly liberating twice daily spells when Day and Night are so preoccupied changing guard that wicked and wonderful things slip past.

Most of the residents of Sovereign are hunters or come from hunting families and, however conflicted this might seem, they harbor a deep love of nature and appreciation of the natural world in their breasts alongside the killing instinct. They are like executioners who oppose capital punishment, yet still persist in pulling the switch. The affection for the creatures they kill is real, and therefore the sighting of Tinkerbell created enough of a sensation to push Lila and her troubles off the forefront of the local gossip.

Ralph Gilpin accosted Wendell the moment he walked into the general store Wednesday morning. "Didja see that white deer yet?" he asked, excitedly.

"Ayuh," said Wendell, with some satisfaction. "I seen Tinkerbell last night."

"What's she look like?"

"Looks jest like she did last year, Ralph; 'cept bigger, course."

"Maude's takin' Gray ovah to yer place after school to mow the yard," the shopkeeper continued. "Think that deer'll be back this evening? Kid's hopin' to see her."

"Most likely."

Miss Hastings, whose own upper field was frequented by the same roving band of white tail deer, was nearly ecstatic with anticipation. She tugged her Canadian rocker around so that she could keep sentinel at the eastern kitchen window; parking her child-like frame in the chair and hoisting binoculars in lieu of a musket. On Wednesday evening she was rewarded. She immediately dialed Lila on the younger woman's cell. "Dahrrrling, I've spotted her! I just KNOW it's Tinkerbell!" she cried. "OOoo, I can't TELL you how BLEST I feel!"

Lila, much like Miss Hastings, Rebecca, Wendell, the Gilpins and everyone else in Sovereign, felt her own spirits rise as a result of the presence of this enchanting genetic mutation in the local deer herd. The reappearance of Tinkerbell, combined with the arrival the day before of her 200 baby chicks – all alive and kicking – had cheered Lila more than she could have believed possible on Sunday evening after her break-up with Mike Hobart. The combined events didn't satisfy her desperate longing for the handsome carpenter, but they did make the loss of his steady, physical presence easier for her to bear.

On Thursday afternoon, after her chores were attended and she'd gathered the eggs for the second time that day (and after she'd checked on her baby chicks for perhaps the 10th time) a hopeful Lila rolled the 1964 Pontiac LeMans out of the barn. She motored the short distance down the road to the little white church on the corner, intending to keep her promise to Rebecca and meet with—me, the minister of the little white church.

As Maude had said, the church was unlocked, and Lila took a deep breath, swung open the solid wood door and walked in. The interior of the Sovereign Union Church is much larger than you would have imagined from the outside, since it encompasses mostly one large room with an expansive cathedral ceiling and elongated leaded windows that stretch nearly from ceiling to floor. The initial effect is one of uplifting brightness, most likely the intended effect of the town's originators, who painted the walls, ceiling and pews the highly polished white that seems to be a prerequisite of churches in the New England Protestant tradition. One 19th century Maine writer, Lura Beam, has even gone so far as to say about her little white church that from the back pew a visitor might feel as though she was *"well down the throat of a calla lily."*

A burgundy carpet crept up the center aisle and divided two rows of twelve pews, each able to seat eight worshipers comfortably. The

Hens and Chickens

elevated altar bore the traditional empty cross and beneath it the mahogany lectern was situated. The carpet in the foyer was stained and threadbare, and shamefully worn up the distance of the first eight pews from the door; however, the red rug appeared almost plush and new up near the front of the church where no one ever wants to sit, leading one of our members recently to joke that we should turn the carpet around to make it last for another hundred years. An old upright, out-of-tune piano rested tiredly near the choir pews, which were never utilized during these days of sparse attendance.

A pillar candle burned cheerfully on the altar, and its flame flickered in the draughts that chased each other like small children around the church. Lila hesitated, glanced around, and seeing no one, walked halfway up the aisle and took a seat in the right-hand pew facing the altar.

I saw her come in from the vantage point of an open door in the tiny office that a former pastor had cobbled into the front south corner of the church, next to the unisex bathroom (which now fortuitously has indoor plumbing). I was surprised to see Lila, since most young people I know regard churches and organized religion much like our ancestors regarded witchcraft. I knew who she was, of course, although we had never met. I had lived in town long enough to become acquainted with not only my attenders and church supporters, but also almost everyone else by description and personal history. And until the reappearance of Tinkerbell, Lila Woodsum's drama had been the most talked about in Sovereign.

She settled herself into the white pew, which was recently made snug with thick cushions purchased with money raised by Maude Gilpin in our February fundraiser. After a few minutes of Quaker quiet I heard Lila exhale in the restful manner of someone who arrives with a burden – but has found a Comforter with whom to share it.

I've discovered during my many years in the ministry that when a person enters a church looking to commune with the Divine, a third party is not required. Therefore, I rarely put myself forward. If he or she is hoping to speak with a minister or a priest, well, one is more often than not underfoot.

Lila espied me ten minutes later, as she rose and prepared to exit the church. "I saw your light," she said, poking her black-capped head in through the door of my front office. "I didn't know anyone was here."

I pushed my ample frame up from the desk where I was reviewing my pastoral message for Sunday. "I didn't want to bother you," I replied, and introduced myself. We shook hands, and I waved vaguely toward the one gothic-looking chair in the room, apart from my own, which was empty of papers and books.

Lila slid into the proffered seat, and surveyed my extensive collection of theological and religious books, which encompassed three walls of bookcases. "You read a lot?"

"No, they're just for looks."

She tittered, and I was reminded of the perky chickadee.

"Ralph Gilpin said you were different," she said, smiling.

"An 'odd duck,' I believe is the actual term Ralph uses. He doesn't quite know what to make of me, but he shows up every other Sunday when I'm here, anyway. Of course he wouldn't show up at all if it wasn't for Maude – and maybe Gray and Bruce."

"Mmmm," said Lila. I could tell that she was already turning over in her mind how much of her burden she wanted to share with me – and how much would remain with her previous confessor.

"What is it, Lila?" I said. "Something a worn-out, odd duck can help you with?"

She pulled a slightly yellowed, postmarked envelope out of her jacket pocket and handed it across the paper-strewn desk. I took it, with a raised eyebrow, but said nothing. "Open it," she directed. "It was the last letter I ever got from my Mom. She was killed in a boating accident in 2009; along with my stepfather. She mailed the letter on the morning she died."

I did what she told me; I opened the letter. It contained a few short sentences, hand-written in faded blue ink. I read the few words aloud:

"I'm so very, very sorry, darling! He'll never bother you again.
Love, Mom
p.s. I'll always love you."

Wordlessly, I folded up the letter, tucked it back into the envelope and handed it to her.

"She killed him," Lila said.

I nodded. "It appears that way. She probably had good reason."

"He molested me when I was eight, not long after they were married."

"Damn."

"I WANTED to tell her, but I didn't dare. He said he'd kill Mom if I told her. When he'd come to my room at night, I'd fly away, up into the wallpaper, until he was gone. I didn't have a clue what was happening or why. Then, when I was 10, we had a program at school about incest and abuse. I was able to make him stop by threatening to tell my teacher. I still had nightmares, and worried constantly it would start up again; but I made it all the way through high school without anything else ever happening."

As she talked, I felt the rage rising inside of me like a female tigress whose cubs had been violated. But I tamped my emotion back down. "Did he physically hurt you? Have you seen a doctor?"

She nodded. "Yeah, I'm physically OK, but I can't seem to leave the flashbacks behind me. I KNOW that Mom killed him partly because she felt guilty—and partly so I'd have a chance to live a normal life. I don't want her death to go for NOTHING, but I haven't been able to shake the flashbacks since the accident!"

"How do suppose your mother finally found out about the abuse?" I asked.

"When I graduated from college, he and I had a terrible argument," Lila said. "Mom had gone out to get my graduation cake. I wasn't afraid of him anymore. I gave him an ultimatum; I would tell Mom myself when I turned 25, unless he confessed to her before then. I guess he believed me. They died shortly before my 25th birthday."

"Tragic," I said, simply.

"But why, WHY did she have to die?!" Lila wailed. "She never hurt anyone! I should never have given him the ultimatum! Mom would still be alive! Why did she have to go and kill him?!" She put her face in her hands and began sobbing.

I understood Lila's mother perfectly, because – one woman to another – I'd have done the same thing; except maybe I'd have used a shot gun on him. (I'm not the best of Quakers, which is probably why I'm no longer a member of the Religious Society of Friends.) But the challenge now was not to find absolution for Lila's mother, but to find absolution for Lila herself. The poor pip, in addition to bearing the burden of her stepfather's predation, also bore the guilt of her mother's unnecessary death.

I've witnessed many Shakespearean tragedies during my days in the ministry, but never one quite so twisted as this. I wanted to help her, but I couldn't figure out how to untwist her wrong-headed thinking about herself and her role in the family drama. Something was missing from the convoluted equation – not taking anything away from the power of the Divine, but I like to have my own ducks in a row. There was something I couldn't quite put my finger on.

Mother, Father, Holy Spirit, I said to myself. *Give me a clue here!* Mother. Father? Father!

"Where was your *real* father during all of this, Lila?" I probed.

"Dead," she said, tiredly. (I could tell she wasn't going to stay with me much longer.) "He died of pancreatic cancer when I was five."

"Was he a good Dad?"

"My father was the BEST. He was so kind and gentle! Dad used to read to me every night, and when he'd tuck me in, he'd give me a kiss and tell me I was his special little chick. When he turned out the light, I was never scared, because I knew he was there to protect me."

"But then he died and left you to fend for yourself."

Lila's hackles rose. "It wasn't his fault; he died."

"It was no one's fault, except your stepfather's," I said, quickly. "He was a sick, thoughtless, selfish man, who made a lot of people suffer needlessly!"

"I know, I know!" Lila cried. "I've tried to put this whole thing behind me by moving to Maine – and I soo love Mike! – but I don't want to ruin HIS life, too!"

I reflected a moment. She was a spunky little pip, and I desperately wanted to help her; but I still didn't have a clue. She had hit a snag in the healing process, which she herself had initiated by moving to Maine and daring to love again. However, most people know what they need to do to heal themselves, and when I run out of sage solutions, I generally just ask *them.* "So, what do you think you'd need to do – no matter how crazy it seems – to put this whole thing to rest once and for all, Lila?"

Surprisingly, Lila replied almost immediately. "If I could just see my Dad once again! If I could just go back in time and hear him telling me that everything was going to be OK … I'd believe it. But that can't happen," she added, sadly.

"No, probably nn…" I began, but broke off. A chill ran up my spine, and the hair on my arms stood up. A crazy idea overtook me; a simple solution to Lila's problem. Oh, how often we go off the beaten track searching for something that's right under our noses!

"You know, I've got an idea that you're going to get your wish," I said, confidently. "Or something pretty close to it."

Hens and Chickens

"No way!" she said, with a sharp intake of breath.

"Way!" I replied.

"You mean … I'll be able to talk to my father again?!" she said, tremulously.

"I believe you will."

"That's not possible," she said, flatly.

"Not if you think like that, it isn't."

She eyed me like Ralph Gilpin looks at me sometimes, as though I was a few sandwiches short of a picnic. "How?" she challenged. "When?!"

"Patience, patience, Lila!" I counseled. "Have a little faith."

She bit back a sharp retort and silently pondered my words. I could see her turning everything over in her mind. I knew she wanted to believe me.

"Stuff like this takes time," I coaxed. "You're on the right track—you did a good thing moving to Maine. But your spirit needs more time to heal. It could take weeks or even months before you get your wish. In the meantime, just go about your daily life; follow your heart, and all that blather. If you do that, I think your wish will come true. Think you can hang in there a while longer?"

When people *want* to believe, miracles *do* happen.

She tittered jubilantly, as the last of her resistance gave way. Her lovely face flushed with renewed hope and her beautiful hazel eyes sparkled like the city lights of Waterville seen at dusk from Goosepecker Ridge. I could understand why my young friend Mike Hobart was crazy about her!

"Boy, you must really have SOME connections!" she said.

"Oh, I've got connections, alright," I replied. "Sometimes they even pay off!"

Chapter 25

. . . .

A Surprise Visitor

*A*fter her meeting with me at the Sovereign Union Church, Lila was able to steady herself and find equilibrium in her young life. If not outright cheerful at her chores, she was calm and somewhat contented over the next week or two, going about her daily life, caring for her hens and baby chicks, and collecting, cleaning, sorting and selling all those dozens and dozens of eggs. She had built up a steady stream of regular customers who came to the farm to purchase eggs each week, yet she was still able to stockpile the 30 dozen eggs Maude needed to bake those 100 fiddlehead quiches. So our next church fundraiser hauled in enough money to paint the foyer, but, I'm getting ahead of myself. Back to our little tale …

Rebecca was amazed at the dramatic change in Lila when she returned from the church. "My goodness, that minister must be *very* gifted!" she said. "You seem almost … happy!"

Lila offered up a rueful smile. "I can see why Ralph says she's an 'odd duck.' She's certainly NOT what I expected from a minister!"

"What did she *say* to you?" asked Rebecca; however, the instant the words were out of her mouth, she regretted her probing. "Oh, don't tell me, if you don't want to talk about it!" she cried.

Lila debated how much she wanted to share. "There isn't much to tell," she replied, finally. "The minister told me to go about my daily life –*follow your heart,*' I think she actually said – and she told me if I did that, everything would be alright."

"That's it?" said Rebecca, disappointed. She had expected the pastoral session would include assurances that God loved Lila and didn't want to her suffer. Possibly the minister would also give Lila several books to read, Augustinian-type treatises upon the nature of good versus evil. "Follow your heart?!" Rebecca repeated.

"Yep," said Lila. "There was also the usual stuff about having patience and faith, but *'follow your heart'* was the gist of it."

"Oh, my!"

Rebecca felt slightly piqued. Had she been asked for advice, it would have been much more detailed than the succinct *"follow your heart!"* And yet apparently the minister had said what it was that Lila needed to hear!

Over the weekend, disaster struck. A red fox had found a breach in the chicken wire of the outdoor pen in which the laying hens took the air and scratched for bugs. By the time the hole was discovered, the fox had carried off several of Lila's beauties. Missing the few birds – one of which was her pet, the soulful-looking hen she'd named Babette – Lila discovered three freshly-cleaned chicken carcasses not far from the fox's lair, which was situated in a copse of trees behind the barn. On the prior Wednesday, Gray had spied two fox kits jumping and tumbling with each other while mowing the yard and had tracked down the fox's den. He had pointed the baby foxes out to Lila, who at the time pronounced them "totally cute." Now, however, the entire fox family was denounced as "thieves and rodents!"

Lila repaired the hole in the chicken wire, and immediately called a war council for *The Egg Ladies*. "What should we do?" she asked her little group of advisors. "We can't have a family of foxes living right next to the hen pen!"

"Wal, you know, you got thet hole in the fence fixed up and the rest of the fence is all good," Wendell said, reassuringly. Our old friend and former chicken farmer had become a necessary part of the operation, and therefore netted a regular seat at the kitchen table with Lila and Rebecca. "You ain't likely to lose many more hens to thet fox."

"But we can't afford to lose ANY more hens," said Lila. "My replacement chicks won't come on line until this fall!"

Any discussion of what *The Egg Ladies* could and couldn't afford, necessarily worried Rebecca. "Oh, can't you catch them all with your live trap, Wendell?!" she asked, anxiously.

Wendell hated to disappoint Rebecca, but he knew that the Mouse Motel routine wasn't going to work this time. " 'Tain't big enough. Plus thet fox ain't like a mouse—she's too shaap for us to catch. Course, you kin walk right up to them baby foxes and toss 'em into a bag."

"Yeah, we could catch them, no problem," said Lila, with a good deal of feeling. "But the one we need to get rid of is their mother. The vixen!"

Hens and Chickens

"Maybe Mike could scare the whole family away by shooting a gun off next to their den?" Rebecca suggested.

A little jolt went through Lila at the mention of Mike Hobart. She took a deep breath, but said nothing.

"Ayuh, a gun might discourage thet ole mother fox," said Wendell, thoughtfully. "If she figgered 'twarn't healthy for her kits 'round heah she might move out—lock, stock and barrel. Course, I don't hunt. Nevah did. I ain't nevah seen Mike hunt, but he looks like a fella who kin handle a weapon."

Lila, however, knowing Mike Hobart's past hunting history and his present feeling about guns, finally spoke up. "I don't think we should ask Mike," she said. Since both Wendell and Rebecca immediately assumed that this was because of the current suspended state of their romantic relationship, Lila discovered with relief that she didn't need to add any further explanation.

"Wal, maybe we kin git young Grayden to do it, then," Wendell said. "He's been itchin' to use thet new gun his Dad give him for Christmas."

After a few more minutes of conference, it was settled that – if it was OK with his grandparents – Gray Gilpin should be allowed to utilize his 16-gauge shotgun in service of *The Egg Ladies*. Wendell would set up a target for Gray to practice on in an area near the fox den, and from that vantage point he could keep an eye on the hen pen. If the mother fox and/or her kits were spotted in the area, he would be authorized to send a threatening volley into the air over the foxes' heads.

"Them foxes better watch out!" said Gray, when he was dropped off along with his gun after church on Sunday. "I told ya they was trouble!" he added, to Lila.

"Oh, please don't kill them!" Rebecca pleaded.

"He ain't gonna kill nuthin'!" his grandfather pronounced. "He's jest here for some target practice and to git familiar with his gun afore deer huntin' season; right, Grayden?"

"Right, Grandpa," the teenager replied, meekly.

"I'll keep an eye on him," Wendell assured Ralph. He put a friendly hand on Gray's shoulder. "Thet's a pretty shaap lookin' weapon you got there, young fella!"

Mike Hobart, who was driving up the Russell Hill Road for a Sunday afternoon visit with Miss Hastings, spotted the little group and pulled into the dooryard. It was the first time he had seen Lila in a very l-o-n-g week, although he had received regular reports on his sweetheart from both Wendell and Miss Hastings. This first meeting would be necessarily awkward, but he was grateful for what appeared to be a natural opportunity to stop in and visit.

Hobart hopped out of his truck and offered up a general greeting in response to all the others. Out of the corner of his eye he saw Ralph give his wife a meaningful nudge, but most of his attention was directed at Lila, whose bare foot was toying with a pile of sweet-smelling grass clippings in front of her. There was no time to plan a specific course of action, so he simply walked up to her and, without exactly knowing how, shortly found himself holding both of her hands. He racked his brain for something appropriate to say. "Getting a lot of eggs?" he asked, finally.

Lila looked shyly up into his bright blue eyes. "Eight dozen a day," she replied, aware that all the others were breathlessly watching them. Her first instinct when she had seen his baby blue truck pull in the driveway was to run into the house and hide, but the minister's words kept floating through her head: *"Follow your heart, and all that blather."* Well, her heart was right here in front of her, so why would she run away?

Lila felt absurdly happy. "How's your barn coming?" she asked, in return.

Hobart was encouraged by the sparkle emanating from her pretty hazel eyes. He felt the ground slipping away beneath his feet. "Pretty good," he said, lamely.

"I'm so happy for you, Mike! I can't wait to see it."

He attempted to steady himself, but failed. "Getting a lot of eggs?" he repeated.

"Mmmm."

Behind him, Wendell coughed. Hobart realized that there were others in the world and that he was still holding Lila's hands. Regretfully, he let her go and turned back to their friends. They were all seven standing in the driveway – Hobart, Lila, Ralph, Maude, Gray, Rebecca and Wendell – enjoying a "dooryard visit," as it's known in Maine. The warm May sun was shining, breathing encouraging life into man, beast, bird and insect alike. Two bluebird couples were battling over the same bird box and the apple and lilac trees were nearly bursting with buds waiting to bloom. Honeybees hovered over the bright dandelions blossoms, emitting a little *bzzzing* noise each time they picked up and moved to the next fuzzy yellow button. Hobart inhaled a deep breath of fresh spring

Hens and Chickens

air, and regained his equilibrium. "The trusses are coming next week," he said, for the benefit of the group at large.

"Lovely," said Rebecca, who hadn't the least idea what "trusses" were.

"You haven't forgotten our picnic next Sunday, have you, Sweetie?" said Maude. "I'm making a big batch of bread pudding, just for you!"

"Oh, I haven't forgotten the picnic!"

"I seen you been down to the Millett Rock, Mike," Wendell said. "Whatcha think?"

Hobart nodded. He leaned back against the side of his truck and folded his arm. "I went in late Friday afternoon," he replied. "She needs some work, like you said, Wendell, but I think we can get away with cutting out only two or three of those big pines. And I've got a clearing saw that will take care of all those small balsams that grew up in the woods road."

"You got time for thet?"

"I'm gonna take down the pines today, and I'll quit work early a couple of days next week to get the path cleared and the brush cleaned up. By the way, I talked with my friend, and the four-wheeler is good to go!"

"Awesome!" said Gray. "Can I drive it?"

"NO!" said both of his grandparents at the same time.

"Sorry, buddy," said Hobart, winking at the teenager.

"My daughter Amber is coming up on the bus Saturday just so that she can go on the picnic with us," interjected Rebecca. "I'm so happy you Gilpins will finally have a chance to meet her!"

"How old is *she*?" asked Gray, hopefully.

"Twenty-one," Rebecca replied, smiling kindly. "Sorry, Gray!" And the dooryard visit broke up with much good-natured laughter.

Now that the first meeting with Mike Hobart was over, Lila found she could look forward to the picnic at the Millett Rock next Sunday with actual pleasure. Euphoric bouts of daydreaming attended her as she lingered through her daily chores, serving to heighten her anticipation. She thought again of what I had said to her about "following your heart," and my stock in trade went up appreciably.

Who knows where our paths will lead us when we follow our hearts? Sometimes the way tends straight across country, like the old Belfast and Moosehead railroad tracks that once carried the train from the Maine coast to the Sovereign depot (ferrying the Sears® kit house that Ralph Gilpin's grandfather had purchased for his bride). But more often than not the path has more twists and turns than a cow path in a Maine meadow in summer. However, if we truly follow our hearts, what does it matter which way the road goes or even what happens along the road *not taken*? For how is it possible to take a wrong turn when we are in pursuit of our heart's desire?

Rebecca also felt light-headed throughout the following week. In her own modest mind, she attributed this new intoxication to the fact that Amber would be joining them for the picnic. In addition, she was happily refitting three of the long gowns Lila had discovered in the attic for herself, Lila and her daughter to wear to the picnic. However, there was perhaps some additional kindling on her heart's fire, which unconsciously aided in the stoking of Rebecca's internal flame.

By the following Saturday, the day before the big event, the anticipation in the household had built to such a fever pitch that when a knock was heard that afternoon on the front door – that rarely used entryway reserved for the dead – Lila's heart skipped a beat. For a brief moment she wondered if her father had come back to life as the minister had promised, and was now standing on the cut granite door stoop waiting to tell her that everything was going to be OK!

Trembling, Lila swung open the heavy wooden front door, and discovered—Ryan MacDonald, the Perkins & Gleeful corporate attorney, from Boston!

"Ryan!" she exclaimed, clinging to the weather-beaten wooden door for support. She felt disappointed and yet relieved at the same time that the mystery visitor was NOT the ghost of her father, but her former boyfriend. "What are you doing here?"

MacDonald had not been sure of the reception he would receive – his calls and emails with Lila had dwindled to nearly nothing over the past few months – but he held his ground stolidly. "I'm here to see *you*," he replied, a friendly expression in his unwavering brown eyes. "How are you, Lila? May I come in?"

Lila moved back away from the door. Encouraged, MacDonald stepped into the foyer. He was a tall, slender man, looking every inch the polished 32-year-old corporate attorney that he was, from the top of his neatly clipped brown hair to the bottom of his highly polished leather shoes. Even though it was four o'clock in the afternoon, not a hint of facial hair shadowed his smooth cheeks. He was wearing "business casual" per usual for him on the weekends, and was handsome enough to have modeled for GQ magazine.

"Quite a place you've got here," MacDonald continued, glancing around the quaint entryway. "Must be a big change from Boston." He said this as a statement of fact, not as a question.

Lila tittered. "You have NO idea!"

MacDonald peeked into the great room. "Rebecca here?"

"No, she's gone up to the bus station in Bangor to pick up her daughter," Lila said. "I'm sorry; I'm being rude, Ryan. I … I wasn't expecting YOU. Come in and sit down. Want some coffee?"

MacDonald answered in the affirmative, and Lila turned and headed toward the kitchen. The attorney, however, made for an easy chair in the living room section of the great room. Lila stopped him. "Not here," she said. "We sit in the kitchen. That's where we do most of our planning and stuff."

Docilely he followed her through the combined living room and dining room, and into the country kitchen. MacDonald examined the rustic, eat-in kitchen with a raised eyebrow, but said nothing as he took a seat at the kitchen table. Lila drew some water from the tap into the 8-cup enamelware percolator coffee pot and set it onto the gas stove to perk. She dumped a generous amount of aromatic coffee grounds into the basket, placed it inside the pot and *clinked* the cover back on the percolator. Then she pulled up her customary seat at the head of the table.

MacDonald, anxious to fulfill his legal obligations before Rebecca returned, opened the negotiations immediately. "Joe sent me up here," he said. MacDonald's place setting, which was in point of fact Wendell's seat, contained the latest issue of GRIT magazine. He automatically moved the brightly-colored country magazine with a chicken on the cover to one side. "Joe has authorized me, as the company attorney, to make you an offer."

Lila blinked. *Joe who?* "What?" she said. She had moved so far beyond her old life in Boston that she didn't have the faintest idea what Ryan MacDonald was talking about.

"Perkins & Gleeful will pay you *double* your old salary if you come back as Marketing Director," MacDonald continued. "Plus stock options worth a lot of money. It's a very good deal, if I do say so myself, Lila."

When his words finally sank in, Lila burst out laughing. "You mean – go back?! To THAT place!"

MacDonald was disconcerted. "You can't mean that you like it *here*?" The corporate attorney waved his manicured hand in the direction of the black soapstone sink. "This place is a relic from the 19th century! I don't know what you're doing here, but ..."

"Raising chickens," Lila interrupted. "And selling eggs. Organic eggs."

He unconsciously wrinkled his nose. "Surely what Joe Kelly and Perkins & Gleeful have to offer is much more lucrative than that!"

Lila's hackles rose. "Lucrative, maybe, as far as the Almighty Dollar goes," she retorted; "but some things are more important than getting rich in this world, Ryan! I'm happy here; happier than I've been since I was a kid! And there's NOTHING you've got to say or NOTHING Joe Kelly has to offer that would ever make me give this up!"

MacDonald quickly realized he was taking the wrong tack with her, and was aware that if he continued in this direction he would get no-where fast. He was not a high-powered corporate attorney for nothing, and effortlessly shifted direction. "I'm sorry if I offended you, Lila," he apologized, in a humble voice. "It's just so much different here from how I'm used to seeing you that I'm surprised, is all."

MacDonald's words were effective. Lila felt a rush of remorse. "I'm sorry, too," she said. "It's a long way for you to drive to have someone yell at you!"

He smiled, affectionately. "I admit, I *was* kind of hoping for a friend-lier reception." He reached over and took Lila's hand. "We used to be pretty good friends. I thought we might be able to pick up where we left off?" he added, warmly.

Lila felt the ice growing thin beneath her feet. Fortuitously, a quick, familiar rap on the shed door interrupted their intimate moment. "That's Wendell," she said, quickly pulling her hand away. "Door's open!" she called, but Wendell was already entering the shed.

The old chicken farmer stuck his head in the kitchen. His eyes widened when he saw MacDonald, sitting alone at the table with Lila. She introduced the two men, but neither of them made a move to shake hands.

"Where's yore little friend?" Wendell asked, instead.

"She's gone up to Bangor to get Amber," Lila reminded him.

"Course," he said. "I forgot. She comin' back for suppah?"

"I hope so!"

Hens and Chickens

"I'll be back, then," said Wendell. He turned and exited hastily, without any further word or even a parting salutation.

MacDonald shook his head in wonderment over the old chicken farmer. "Who was *that* rustic?" he asked.

Lila explained – or attempted to explain – the special relationship *The Egg Ladies* had with Wendell Russell. But she could tell by the bewildered look on Ryan MacDonald's face that the he wasn't following her. *He doesn't know how many different types of love and friendship are possible in this world!*

"Wendell's not usually like that, anyway," Lila concluded, ineffectually.

But you can probably guess the reason behind Wendell's apparent rudeness, my pips. Our old friend had spotted imminent danger – another fox in the hen house, so to speak – and he hastily made his way down across the road to where Mike Hobart was clearing brush in preparation for the next day's picnic. A few quick words did the trick, and within five minutes of his abrupt exit, a second summons, much more demanding, could be heard at *The Egg Ladies'* shed door.

"Sorry," said Lila. "That's probably a customer to buy eggs; we sell a lot on weekends. It'll only take a sec."

Alas, alas! We know who was at the door!

Within moments, the two suitors for Lila Woodsum's heart were standing face to face! And she was alone with them!

Chapter 26

·······

Picnic at the Millett Rock

"This is awkward!" said Lila, as Mike Hobart and Ryan MacDonald glared at each other across the kitchen table like dogs squaring off over the same bone. The air was thick with testosterone. She grasped the back of her wooden chair with one hand and momentarily covered her eyes with the other hand, partially afraid of what might happen next but also in an attempt to muster her courage. Her heart was pounding and her hands trembled.

But, what did SHE have to be anxious about? She was doing nothing of which to be embarrassed or ashamed! Ryan was only here in Sovereign to make her a job offer and Mike was here—Why WAS Mike here? She peeked at the dirty, sweaty, bedraggled carpenter, who, having cleared brush all day was covered with pine pitch and balsam needles and smelled like the floor of a Maine forest. A small twig stuck out from a patch of matted hair on the back of his head.

Lila spotted the twig, and tittered. "This is too funny," she said. "You look totally silly, the both of you! I wish you could see yourselves—acting like two roosters!"

Hearing Lila's words and tone, MacDonald wavered, hoping his opponent would back down first. But Mike Hobart was not about to surrender. It was one thing for him to wait patiently on the sidelines, as Lila had begged, giving her time to untangle her emotional issues. But he could not – would not – sit idly by while another man moved into his territory! Surely she could not expect him to do *that*!

Hobart, our steady, handsome hero, was an incredibly patient man, as we've discovered during the course of this tale. But he *was* human after all. Therefore, he completely ignored Lila altogether and continued to glower at his opponent!

Faced with such ferocity, MacDonald surrendered the field. He relaxed his stiff stance, and stuck out his hand in a friendly fashion. "Ryan MacDonald," he said. "I worked with Lila at Perkins & Gleeful in Boston. The company Vice President sent me up here to make her another job offer."

Hobart accepted the proffered hand, and squeezed punishingly. Although two inches shorter than MacDonald, he was much more muscular in build. "Mike Hobart," he said, simply, as though the name alone would suffice to explain the significant nature of his relationship with Lila and thus his territorial behavior.

Lila rolled her eyes. "Men!" she lamented, trying to pass the fiasco off with a laugh. Secretly, however, she was thrilled by his jealous protection.

"She's not going back," Hobart stated flatly. His icy blue eyes remained firmly locked on those of his rival. "No matter how much your company offers, she's *not* going back."

"Looks that way," agreed MacDonald. He retrieved his hand from Hobart, shaking it slightly to get the blood flowing again.

"Hello, hello? I'm right here," signaled Lila. "I can speak for myself."

"Lila belongs in Maine!" Hobart growled at his rival.

"I guess she does," said MacDonald.

"She's *not* going back!"

"Nooo," agreed MacDonald.

"Omigod, this is ridiculous," said Lila. She sank down into her chair and burst into tears.

The most effective way for a woman to get a man's attention is by weeping. Something in a man's nature can't resist offering aid to a suffering woman. Let a small child or an old person get run over by a car, and a man might feel badly, but he'll offer up little more than: "Shoulda looked both ways before crossing road!" However, let a woman break down – especially a pretty woman – and a man will drop instantly to his knees.

This was the case with our hero, who awoke to Lila's presence – horrified – as though each of her tears was an accusatory arrow piercing his heart. In truth, Hobart believed he had caused those tears by betraying his promise to give her space—and he actually *did* sink down to his knees before his astonished sweetheart! "I'm so sorry, darling!" he cried, remorsefully. He laid his dirty, tousled head in her lap and clasped her around the waist, almost weeping himself.

And before any of the three knew exactly what was happening, Lila's tears evaporated and she found herself comforting the testosterone-burdened winner of the dog fight! "Shhhh," she said, removing the offending twig from Mike Hobart's hair and brushing the stubborn balsam spills from the back of his sweaty navy T-shirt. "Shhh, it's OK, Mike. You've been working really hard lately!"

A heart-felt sob escaped him. "I don't know what came over me! My Dad would be so ashamed of me!"

MacDonald, who was watching his rival's emotional display in disbelief, suddenly smelled the coffee pot on the stove beginning to perk. "Want me to turn that down?" he suggested to Lila. "Looks like it's about to boil over."

She nodded, bemused. "That is so totally ironic," she said.

And so somehow the roles got reversed all around. The strong became weak, the distressed became the comforter, and the one obvious guest in the house found himself acting as caretaker and host. While Lila soothed Hobart, MacDonald set the egg timer for five minutes, and searched through the cupboards until he found three coffee mugs. He placed them on the kitchen table, and liberated three teaspoons from the silverware drawer. He expertly located the sugar bowl, and secured a pitcher of cream from the fridge.

By the time Rebecca returned from Bangor with Amber and rushed into the kitchen (having been briefed by Wendell first), the odd trio was sitting around the table joking and laughing like … old friends! Rebecca, who had originally championed Ryan MacDonald's romantic cause, was now girded up to do battle for the steady carpenter. Imagine her surprise when she discovered that Hobart himself had invited MacDonald to accompany them on their picnic to the Millett Rock the next day!

"Oh, my goodness!" Rebecca exclaimed. "I go away for an afternoon and the whole world gets turned upside down!" And then Rebecca, the sovereign of the kitchen, sank into the guest chair at the table and meekly accepted a cup of coffee from the hands of Ryan MacDonald, who had never even been in that house before today!

The transmutation and transcendence continued into Sunday, the day of the picnic to the Millett Rock. It was the kind of a day that folks in Maine live for, why some of us elect to stay here and suffer the long dreary winters instead of seeking warmer climes. Those of us who stay know that the agony of our sufferings only serves to magnify the exquisiteness of our spring and summer pleasures.

The sun rose with perfect clemency at 5:30 a.m. and a fresh breeze carried the scent of apple blossoms and lilacs in through Lila's open window. She was the first to awaken, and breathed deeply of the fragrance, almost able to taste the lilacs on her lips. She leaped out of bed, eager to attend to her hens and baby chicks before cleaning up and dressing for the big event. All of the picnickers were to gather at the old Russell Homestead by 10:30 a.m., and Lila, who had several hours of work to do, knew she had no time to waste.

Rebecca, too, was shortly bustling about the kitchen, preparing breakfast for the others. Amber, hearing her mother rise, followed upon her heels. "What's for breakfast?" she asked, lovingly draping her T-shirt clad arms over her mother's shoulders.

"Do you have to ask?" Rebecca said, happily. "Eggs, eggs and more eggs! Just the way you like them!"

By 10 a.m., *The Egg Ladies*, including Amber, were dressed in their long, colorful gowns and matching beribboned floppy hats and were ready to go. Rebecca was finishing the final packing up of her many and varied contributions to the picnic, when Wendell ambled across the way decked out in black pants and a country Western-style black dress shirt with a silver-clipped string tie. He looked a bit like Johnny Cash, handsome in his finery, and he liberally flashed his trademark, gold-tooth grin.

"You look awful shaap!" said Lila, greeting Wendell affectionately. "How do WE all look?"

Lila swept back into a low curtsey, but Wendell's eyes turned automatically toward Rebecca, who, blushing, dropped a quick curtsey of her own. "Wal, you know, you gals look downright good enough to eat!" he proclaimed.

Mike Hobart had brought the four-wheeler and an accompanying utility trailer over the day before, and parked them overnight in the barn. He now arrived in his pickup with Miss Hastings in tow, and presented himself in the kitchen as though nothing out of the ordinary had occurred in that room the day before. He was freshly scrubbed, and looked boyishly handsome in a white cotton shirt, laundered blue jeans and black string tie on loan from Wendell. Miss Hastings was bedecked in her frilly white blouse, and a burgundy-colored crepe skirt that draped elegantly over a neat set of black leather ankle boots, which instantly gave Amber footgear envy.

"Where did you get those old boots!" she demanded, before even greeting the elderly woman.

Hens and Chickens

"Amber!" chastened her mother.

"Don't stop her, dahrrrling! You know I ADORE honesty!" Miss Hastings said to Rebecca, before turning to Amber. "I paid $2 for these boots in New York City in 1952! I think they're going to outlive ME!" She burst into gales of laughter.

The gayety continued and spilled over into the dooryard where it became amplified with the arrival of the Gilpin family. Maude was stunning in an outfit consisting of a silk white gown laced with pink satin ribbons, which seemed to erase 40 years from the doting grandmother and highlighted the beauty of her fat face. Ralph was obviously smitten with his wife, and strutted around her in his Sunday dress, sans coat and with a bright red bandana replacing his necktie, looking very much like a cocky Bantam rooster. Gray Gilpin had been sweet-talked by his grandmother into a pair of black jeans and a green dress shirt, and he likewise sported a red bandana, which, shortly after his arrival at the old Russell place, ended up flapping out of his back pocket like a tail feather on a young jake turkey.

Ryan MacDonald was the last to pull in. Not having the foresight to pack an old-fashioned costume for his mission to Maine, MacDonald, who had taken a room at the Copper Heron in neighboring Unity, should by rights have been the least prepared for the picnic. However, he was not a high-powered attorney for nothing, and therefore MacDonald coaxed his hostess at the B&B into assisting him. She led him to the local Amish store, Community Market on the Thorndike Road, where she outfitted him in the dark pants, sky blue short-sleeved shirt and suspenders that are traditional summer work clothing for the men of this agrarian community – topped off with an authentic Amish straw hat. Wendell had brought over an additional string tie, as a peace offering to the man whom he had once wished back to—Boston, at the very least! And with this jaunty addition to his toilet the little group shortly pronounced that, out of all of them, Ryan MacDonald was the best dressed for Grammie Addie's annual outing to the Millett Rock!

Ryan MacDonald certainly was handsome; there was no denying the fact. Rebecca felt a flutter in her own heart when she looked at the dark-haired, sexy-eyed corporate attorney, and she glanced quickly at Lila to measure whether or not her friend was showing any symptoms of lingering affection. However, Lila's heart was safe from that direction, since she had eyes for no one but Mike Hobart.

But, alas for our heroine! She soon discovered that she herself was safe from romantic overtures from ALL directions! Hobart, still chaffing over his peccadillo of yesterday, chastely refrained from touching Lila or even looking at her! Instead, he hung back in the dooryard, laughing and joking with MacDonald, as though the two had been best friends since childhood. Lila, when she looked at her two suitors, so recently at each other's throat and now acting boyishly like Tom Sawyer and Huck Finn, felt her young heart overflowing with joy and love.

But we must not forget to mention the OTHER guest at the picnic, which was certainly not the least. Matilda, Miss Hastings' pet chicken, *cluck clucked* happily from her cat carrier, already loaded alongside the picnic gear and food into the ATV's utility trailer. Rebecca had sewed a miniature bonnet for the barred rock hen, and the bird was liberated long enough for the seamstress to slip the calico cap upon the hen's inquisitive head. Matilda cocked her head sideways, causing the bonnet to slip back like the bonnet of a young girl tossing her head. The little group laughed with glee at the silly-looking chicken, who, appreciating the attention, hopped around on the grass showing off her new style.

A few minutes before 10:30 a.m., Hobart threw his long leg over the ATV and MacDonald carefully lifted the elderly music teacher up onto the leather seat behind him. Miss Hastings clasped the carpenter's waist with her left arm, and patted him on the shoulder with her other hand. "Let's roll, dahrrrlings!" she cried. Hobart revved up the four-wheeler and the little group of picnickers coalesced behind the tow-trailer, laughing as they strolled across the road down into the green field, which curved down suggestively toward where the pine woods was walking up to meet them. The black and white bobolinks, home from their winter adventure, shot up out of the tall grass like skeet from a skeet shooter, startling Rebecca so much so that Wendell, always on the alert for an opportunity, reached out and took her arm to steady her. He gave her hand a reassuring squeeze, and her pretty face turned towards his with some satisfaction. Their eyes met, and the chicken farmer winked.

Gray dared Amber to race him to the woods, and gamely the college student lifted her long skirts and bolted after his skinny frame. Maude and Ralph, who were meandering along arm in arm, watched the antics of their grandson with obvious pride and pleasure.

Our heroine, Lila, found herself at the end of the parade! Mike Hobart had left her in the dust, without even so much as a backwards glance. Even worse, he had left the field entirely open to his one-time rival, who now graciously offered up his arm to Lila. She took the proffered aid from Ryan MacDonald, laughing happily at the difference a day made.

The sharp, vigorous scent of freshly cut pine and balsam fir greeted the little group when they reached the edge of the woods, where Hobart had hewn a path to the big rock. The smell of the Maine forest filled our friends' senses and they breathed deeply of the pungent nectar. "Ahhh!" expostulated Wendell, who was already walking on clouds with Rebecca on his arm; "ain't thet smell somethin' shaap!"

MacDonald appreciatively inhaled the biting scent of the pine and balsam. "Reminds me of Henry David Thoreau," he said, glancing around the cool woods.

No matter where I am, the sharp scent of pine or balsam always brings to mind the romantic image of the Maine woods, a place Thoreau loved, and that I love, too. When I'm on my deathbed, if someone will just bring me a handful of balsam spills or a sprig of white pine, I know I will die a happy woman!

The Millett Rock, a huge gray boulder the size of the Sovereign Union Church, once had threatened to burst free from the forest floor but has been restrained over thousands of years by gnarled tree roots, lichens, moss, pine branches, rust-colored pockets of pine needles, and grasping saplings. These days the flat-top boulder looks much like Gulliver tied down by the Lilliputians. From a distance the rock looms between several towering pines and appears insurmountable. However, up close, natural hand-holds, foot rests and plateaus present themselves, making scaling the Millet Rock a pleasurable and doable challenge.

Hobart parked the ATV and utility trailer at the bottom of the big rock, and MacDonald quickly abandoned Lila to help Miss Hastings alight. Hobart hopped off the four-wheeler and exchanged significant looks with his former romantic rival. The lawyer nodded his head meaningfully in Lila's direction, and needing no further encouragement Hobart replaced MacDonald at her side.

Before she knew what was happening, Lila was being helped by the handsome carpenter up onto the first level of the rock, and she scrambled for a hand-hold, enjoying the feeling of the rough rock against her bare hand. She flipped her hat back so she could see better, and the hot sun on her head encouraged her onward. Exultantly she clambered up and

up, eager to reach the view from the flat top of the Millett Rock. She
glanced down at Hobart, who was supporting her from below. Their
eyes locked, and Lila was consumed by the ardor revealed in his potent
gaze. She paused, and a wormhole in time opened up. Lila felt as though
he had picked her up, tossed her over his shoulder and strode off into
the bushes with her. She trembled at the touch of his hand on her ankle.

I so love you! she thought.

Hobart's blue eyes darkened as if in response to her heart's murmur.
Lila registered his, *And I love you, darling!* as clearly as though she'd heard
the words aloud.

"Hey, what's the holdup – up there!" cried Gray, from below. The
wormhole closed. Lila giggled joyfully, and scrambled for the top of the
rock.

"Watch the gap in the corner, darling," Hobart cautioned her, pointing knowingly toward a six-inch crevice that threatened to split an ear
away from the northern face of the big rock. My sources tell me that
many a shoe, wallet, plate, fork and ribbon have met their demise in that
crevice over the past 200 years, never to see the light of day again.

Hobart, satisfied that Lila was safe, returned to the bottom of the
rock to help the others scale the heights. By 11:30 a.m., everyone was up
to the top of the Millett Rock, "Oo-ing" and "Ah-ing" over the views,
especially those of the Western mountains, outlined in indigo against the
soft blue sky. Blankets were settled, pillows placed, dead branches tossed
overboard, and the picnic was unpacked. Dainty cut sandwiches, stuffed
eggs, fruit, cheeses, pickles, sweets and other delicacies were passed
around, hand to hand, hand to mouth, joyfully, laughingly, teasingly, lovingly – as though this was the last supper and each of the picnickers was
prepared to enjoy it to the utmost.

No one describes the type of felicity found on top of the Millet
Rock that afternoon better than Ralph Waldo Emerson, who writes in
his beautiful essay, *Friendship*:

> *"We have a great deal more kindness than is ever spoken. (Despite) all the
> selfishness that chills like east winds the world, the whole human family is bathed
> with an element of love like a fine ether…The effect of the indulgence of this
> human affection is a certain cordial exhilaration."*

An hour later, when everyone was stuffed, the group sprawled languidly atop the warm gray rock, luxuriating in the sensation of Emerson's

Hens and Chickens

"certain cordial exhilaration." Wendell dozed off and Rebecca, who had been sitting next to him, gently tucked her shawl under his head.

"Didja evah see such a bread pudding as my Maude's?" Ralph cried, overcome with a rush of love for his wife. He threw his arms around her and squeezed fondly. "She's the best cook evah!"

Maude blushed, but for once she didn't rebuke her husband for "spoiling the mood."

"Hey, no shillyshallying!" teased Hobart, who was stretched out full length and resting on his elbow. He eyed his former employer with unabashed fondness—and not a little envy.

Lila felt her heart take flight at the look of longing in Mike Hobart's blue eyes. *Someday?! Someday!*

"Wonderful! Everything was just wonderful, dahrrrlings!" exclaimed Miss Hastings, from her comfy nest of fluffy feather cushions. Matilda squawked her agreement, and even Ryan MacDonald laughed.

Chapter 27

·······

The Staircase Tree

That night, after the picnic, Lila experienced her worst nightmare since her mother's death. Her stepfather "visited" her during the night, taunting her with words and looks too fiendish and sick for me to describe. Rebecca, who heard Lila's cries from the bedroom above, rushed downstairs in the moonlight and found her young friend weeping softly in bed. "Oh, my dear, what's the matter?" she cried.

Lila sat up, brushing the tears from her eyes. "I'm OK now, Becca," she said, smiling tremulously. "I told him to go away and … he left!"

"He, who, dear?"

"My stepfather!"

"Oh, my goodness," said Rebecca, sitting down on the edge of the bed and clasping her young friend's hand. "*Can't* you tell me about it, dear?"

In response, Lila scooted over in bed toward the open window, making room for her friend. Rebecca, needing no further encouragement, climbed into the antique brass bed that Lila had appropriated from the open chamber for her downstairs bedroom. The tired old springs *creaked* with the weight of the new addition.

"Ooh, I hope it holds us!" Rebecca said. Both women giggled.

Lila drew in a steadying breath, *finally* prepared to share her burden with her faithful friend. However, Amber, hearing the commotion, wandered downstairs and into Lila's bedroom, interrupting them.

"What's up?" Amber asked, sleepily.

"Nothing, dear," replied Rebecca, propping herself up onto her elbow. "Lila's just had a bad dream, that's all."

"Got room in there for me?"

There was a shifting of bodies, a giggle or two and further *creaking* as Amber climbed into bed with the two older women. She cuddled up next to the warmth of her mother, and Rebecca necessarily squeezed closer to Lila to make room for her daughter. The three curled up in Lila's bed like peas in a pod.

Lila sighed, contentedly. "This is so nice," she said. "It's almost like I had sisters!" She felt herself relax. And before she knew it, she dozed off.

The three women slept together during the remaining few hours of the night. More truthfully, I should say that Amber and Lila slept, for Rebecca slept not a further wink. Instead, she lay sandwiched in bed between her daughter and her young friend, listening to their heavy breathing mingled with the sonorous chorus of peepers outside Lila's open window. She reflected upon Lila's words. *"I told him to go away … and he left!"*

Rebecca wondered what Lila's stepfather had done to cause so much anguish in her young friend's life, and came pretty close at guessing the truth. However, in these early hours of the morning she also realized that Lila seemed to be making *progress* in some sort of healing, not *regressing*. It appeared to her now that Lila had been experiencing a kind of emotional and spiritual cleansing since she had moved to Maine. Rebecca began to suspect that *this* was why Lila had never been able to form meaningful romantic relationships, and that the healing was necessary in order for Lila to claim the love and joy that awaited her with Mike Hobart.

Spiritual forces were at work helping Lila heal, and Rebecca told herself that perhaps she should stop trying to direct traffic and concentrate on playing a supporting role. She promised herself (and perhaps a Higher Power) that, come what may, she would not push Lila or finagle events, but simply BE there, BE present; support and encourage and love Lila.

Perhaps that minister DOES know what she's doing! Rebecca thought. *These things DO take time.*

Healing doesn't happen miraculously overnight, except in the New Testament. And this was Lila's life, not a work of fiction; but a dog-gone, dragged out, dumbfounding LIFE.

One of my favorite books is a collection of letters, *Waiting for God*, by the French mystic Simone Weil. (I actually *do* read some of the books on the shelves in my church office.) The title is taken from a recurring theme of Weil's, a translation of a Greek phrase, *"en hupomene"* – "waiting in patience," or "patiently enduring," a neatly turned phrase that means so much more than the literal translation suggests. This is not just everyday

Hens and Chickens

"waiting for bread to rise" or "waiting for the grass to grow." The phrase suggests a hopeful waiting, in expectation of a wondrous event, or the kind of waiting that's necessary during the emotional and spiritual healing process of a friend or loved one, such as Lila Woodsum.

These things DO take time.

The next morning, Lila and Rebecca rose early, abdicating the bed to the slumbering Amber. The two huddled together at the kitchen table in the early-morning light. Over several cups of coffee, Lila poured out her childhood history and the gist of her meeting with me to her faithful friend. The older woman listened quietly through the entire revelation, only reaching out occasionally and squeezing Lila's hand. For her part, Lila was able to relate her entire story with nary a sob or a tear. At the end she was almost cheerful. "The nightmares are terrifying when they happen, because they seem so REAL," Lila concluded. "But afterwards I feel so much better!"

"That's how I feel after a good cry!"

"Eggs-actly," said Lila, wryly. "For my part, I am cried out."

"Oh, it was such a brave and yet *awful* thing your mother did! I wish I'd known what truly happened at the time," Rebecca cried. "I could have done so much more to help you, dear!"

Lila, who was not normally demonstrative, reached out and hugged her friend. "You did everything you could, Becca. And I can never, EVER thank you enough!"

Tears came to Rebecca's eyes, but she said nothing. She was too emotional to talk. She daubed the tears from her face with the paisley cloth napkin at her place setting, which she had recently sewn to match the new tablecloth.

The two friends sat in companionable silence in the cozy kitchen. A soft, spring rain fell outside. Occasionally, the south wind pushed a spray of moisture against the window, and the water dribbled down hitting the wooden sill with a desultory dripping.

"Mmmm, that was a great picnic, wasn't it?" said Lila, toying with her coffee mug. With the elasticity of youth, she had already leaped from the past to the present, wondering how soon she would see Mike Hobart again.

Rebecca smiled. "Wasn't Ryan handsome!" she exclaimed.

"Omigod, he looked so silly in that straw hat! I can't believe he drove all the way up here just to make me that crazy job offer."

"I think there was more to it than a job offer, Lila. I think he honestly wanted to *see* you again."

Lila tittered. "We're not going to have the old 'Ryan cares for you conversation' again, are we?"

"No, no!" Rebecca said, laughing. "I'm not on *that* bandwagon anymore."

"I thought you were backing a different horse these days, Becca. You should've seen the look on your face when you walked in and found the three of us joking around the kitchen table on Saturday!"

"I *was* surprised, I admit. But it was a pleasant surprise. I was expecting rather a different outcome!"

"Ryan never had a chance with me romantically, and I think he knew it. But he's a good friend."

"Poor Ryan! He's a good man, but he's not the man for you, dear."

"Mmmm," said Lila, picturing the handsome carpenter, helping her up the Millett Rock yesterday. Her heart swelled with love as she relived the passion emanating from his bright blue eyes.

"But … are you sure you're doing the right thing, dear, turning down *double* your old salary? It *was* a fabulous offer Perkins & Gleeful made."

"I'm totally sure! THIS is my home, now," Lila proclaimed. She glanced around the kitchen that Rebecca had made so homey with her domestic efforts. "You'll have to take me out of here in a box!"

Rebecca shuddered at the implication of Lila's words. "Oh, don't say that!" she cried. "It sounds so horrible! Besides, we never know what might happen to us in life, what future choices we might have to make."

"Translated from Rebecca-speak: 'We never know when we might fall in love, get married and move to that guy's cabin in the woods.'"

"Not even loosely translated: that *is* what I was thinking!"

Lila sighed. "I'm not there yet," she said, sadly. "Not until I'm sure these nightmares are gone for good. I wouldn't wish 'em on my worst enemy, let alone someone that I so totally love."

"But you *will* tell Mike about … about," Rebecca broke off. She remembered her promise not to interfere.

"Someday, yes. But not now." Lila stared dejectedly off into space. Who knew how much longer it would be?! *Patience, patience!*

After a few seconds, Lila collected herself. Her impish sense of humor returned. "Besides, his cabin is too small," she added with a grin.

"You've been there?" Rebecca asked, hopefully.

Hens and Chickens

"Nooo, I've never actually seen it. He says that's because he couldn't trust himself not to … well, you know. But I think more likely the place needs cleaning."

"I doubt that!"

"Mmmm; but I know where he lives…"

"You do?"

"Yep. He showed me the dirt drive to his place the night he and I had dinner with Maude and Ralph. Some morning, I'm gonna sneak over to his cabin and crawl into bed with him."

"Lila!"

"Omigod, you are soo easy to tease, Becca!" said Lila, throwing her arm around her friend's shoulder affectionately.

"Totally," agreed Amber, yawning, in the doorway. "Mom is SO easy. What's for breakfast? I need a big meal before I head back to Boston."

"EGGS!" cried Lila and Rebecca in unison.

For his part Mike Hobart spent a reinvigorated night floating on a cloud of hope. He didn't understand what Lila was suffering or why, but he recognized that she had made some small progress during the week that they had been apart. She had asked for time to sort things out, and it appeared even a short period of time had been efficacious. Lila seemed happier, more peaceful, and more at ease with herself and with him at the picnic. Certainly, that was love he had seen in her eyes! He began to calculate how much more time she might need before he could once again press his suit.

Hobart thought it was fair that Lila had asked for time. But he also thought it was fair that he make the most of any opportunity that happened to come his way. He was a patient man, and he would wait for her to invite him back to her side. But he would also ensure that his "side" was as attractive as possible!

He had planned on the next rainy day when he wasn't working on his barn project to finish a surprise gift for *The Egg Ladies*, which would celebrate the opening of their business. On the prior rainy day, he had started to carve a simple wooden *"Organic Eggs for Sale"* sign to hang off the Staircase Tree at the end of the driveway. Today, he would finish the sign—and carve his secret weapon: wooden pegs that inserted into the bottom of colorful *papier-mâché* chickens that the kindergarteners and first graders had crafted for Miss Hastings after her last "music lesson." The wooden pegs would affix the chickens, one hen to a step, into the

Staircase Tree. Hobart knew that the unusual folk art creatures setting like hens in the tree would be an eye-catching addition to his sign.

Hobart wasn't sure now whether or not the "chicken on every step" idea had originated with him or Miss Hastings. He had poured out his troubles to Miss Hastings over tea the prior Wednesday afternoon. "I'm willing to wait for her as long as it takes," he had declared; "but I can't sit around doing nothing while I wait!"

"That's the spirit, dahrrrling!" Miss Hastings gushed, leaning over and patting him on the arm. "All's fair in love and LOVE!"

At that point, the retired music teacher had suggested Hobart follow her into her studio where 18 *papier-mâché* chickens were setting on top of her baby grand piano and in various chairs around the room. Miss Hastings admired each chicken, pointing out particular quirks that signified each child's rendition of Matilda. Hobart looked at the heavily varnished, unrealistic yet charming renditions of Miss Hastings' pet chicken and mumbled a few well-meaning remarks.

"Take it from this old hen, she won't be able to resist these colorful chicks!"

"But what would I do with them?"

"Dahrrrling, step up, STEP UP your wooing! Put them where they'll make a good FIRST IMPRESSION!" And Miss Hastings went off into peals of laughter over the double entendres in her words.

By the end of the day Monday Hobart had made good use of the rainy day AND the sun was beginning to shine. Hobart had finished the pegs and had also cut holes into the bottoms of the *papier-mâché* chickens so they would be easily removed from or inserted onto the pegs. The step tree had 12 steps, so six of the chickens would be in reserve at any time and could be rotated or replaced as necessary. Lila could switch them on a whim and store them all in the barn during inclement weather and winter. Now, Hobart only needed an opportunity to hang his sign and drill the peg holes into the 12 steps. After that, he could set the colorful chickens on their new nests. But he needed time when Lila was away from home, and Lila rarely left her hens and baby chicks for long.

Once again, Miss Hastings came to the rescue. She invited Lila up to tea on Thursday afternoon. Hobart had calculated that he would need two hours to do the work, but Miss Hastings managed to keep Lila from her afternoon egg collection and from checking on her baby chicks for closer to *three* hours by playing an extended selection of Chopin's works on the piano for her guest.

Hens and Chickens

Entranced, Lila lost track of time. "I can't believe it's almost five o'clock!" she exclaimed, glancing at her phone when Miss Hastings had finally finished playing. "That was so amazing!"

"Dahrrrling, I'm just an old loose screw, but I still LOVE to perform!"

Lila thanked Miss Hastings, kissed the old lady goodbye and exited the antique cottage hastily. She had arrived on foot, and now set out to hike the half mile back down the hill in the moist warmth of the late afternoon sun to the old Russell homestead. A chipmunk followed her part way atop the old stone wall lining the road, *squeaking* and *chirping*. A downy woodpecker was *rat-a-tat-tatting* the bugs out of a nearby apple tree, and two blue jays in a nearby white pine and a quorum of grackles on the telephone wires were in a fierce competition to out-*caw* each other. The hot sun had burst open the top blossoms of the apple tree, and Lila inhaled their sweet scent as she strode down the hill.

When she reached her driveway, the most amazing sight greeted her: the steps to the Staircase Tree were filled with a wondrous display of colorful hens and chickens! Hanging from the tree was a brand new carved wooden sign: *"Organic Eggs for Sale."* The net result looked like something out of a colorful children's picture book.

"Wow!" exclaimed Lila, hand to her heart. Despite the fact that only four days earlier she had declared herself to be "cried out," Lila felt tears of joy spring to her eyes. She recognized the author of this delightful display!

But where was he?

Lila glanced around, pulse quickening; expecting (and secretly hoping) that Mike Hobart would step out from behind the old maple tree. Alas, her sweetheart was nowhere to be seen!

When Hobart had completed his mission, he returned to his cabin in the woods. It was enough for him simply to give Lila joy. There would be plenty of time and opportunity – he hoped – to share joy together in years to come. Now, as much as he wanted to share her delight with his handiwork, he didn't need to take advantage of her transitional state. Hobart had confidence that Lila would return to him when she was emotionally ready. He just hoped it was sooner rather than later!

Rebecca and Wendell had no such impediment as Mike Hobart, however. Therefore, Wendell was keeping a sharp eye out for Lila's return from the kitchen window. "Heah she comes," he reported, when he spotted her black head of hair bobbing down the hill from Miss Hastings' house.

He bustled Rebecca out the door and they reached the Staircase Tree not long after Lila had discovered Hobart's surprise. "Whatcha think?" asked Wendell, grinning.

Lila examined the colorful *papier-mâché* chickens perched on the steps of the Staircase Tree with delight and wonder. "It's so amazing! Where did Mike GET these crazy chickens?"

"From the kindergartners and first graders," replied Rebecca. "They're supposed to represent Matilda. The students made them after your visit. Aren't they adorable?"

"Too much! And that sign? It's perfect!"

Wendell nodded in satisfaction. "Ayuh, Mike's got a good eye and he's pretty shaap with them woodworking tools."

"But WHY did he leave?" Lila wailed, once again glancing around for our hero.

"He didn't want to take advantage of you, dear. But he said he would stop by tomorrow after work, if it was alright."

"Oh, it's more than alright!" she exclaimed. Lila once again beheld the Staircase Tree with perfect happiness and satisfaction. A notion came into her head as she looked at the tree, though, and she turned back to the old chicken farmer. "There's something I've been meaning to ask you, Wendell..."

"What's thet?"

"What gave you the idea to carve steps in this old limb in the first place? It's soo twisted!"

"Oh, 'twarn't me. These steps been heah goin' on 10 years now. Nobody knows who done it; and likely nobody ever will."

But for once, Wendell was wrong. There are *some* folks from Sovereign who know the imp responsible for — and the story behind — the Staircase Tree. But perhaps that is fodder for another tale ...

Chapter 28

· · · · · · ·

Brood Hens

Friday morning dawned with the ominous darkness and heavy muggy air of an impending thunderstorm. For the first time during that spring the natural light emanating from the tall windows in the hen pen wasn't enough, and Lila switched on the electric lights. The chickens seemed overexcited and irascible, and when Lila opened the pint-sized door to the outdoor run, more birds than usual remained in the coop than exited to the grassy pen. One of the New Hampshire reds, normally a good-natured breed of bird, even refused to abdicate her nest so that Lila could collect the eggs on which she was setting. The hen actually sprang halfway up from the nest box like a jack-in-the-box, nipping Lila's hand painfully with her sharp beak.

"Ouch!" cried Lila, pulling back, momentarily startled.

The hen glared at her. She shifted her chestnut-red body and settled her tail-end firmly down over the nest of eggs. She ruffled her feathers protectively, sending up a dry spray of sweet-smelling sawdust.

Lila hesitated. The fierce look in the hen's eye was off-putting, and she wasn't sure she was up to what could be a nasty battle between bird and human. Lila recalled that the chicken had claws as well as a beak. She would no doubt win the battle, but at what cost to her hand, arm and maybe even eyes?

Fortunately, Wendell had ambled across the way for breakfast per usual, and Lila went up and collected the old chicken farmer from the kitchen. He carefully followed Lila back down the tight spiral staircase into the hen pen.

Wendell regarded the setting hen ruefully. "Ayuh, she's gone broody," he said. "Thet's jest what I thought."

"What's that mean?" asked Lila, worriedly. "Is she sick?"

"No, she ain't sick. She wants to raise up a brood of chicks. Some chickens got thet natural motherin' instinct bred out of 'em by the scientists, but New Hampshires still make pretty good brood hens."

"But is having a brood hen a good thing or a bad thing?"

"Wal, you know, she ain't gonna raise up no chicks outta them eggs!" pronounced Wendell, grinning. "You ain't got no roostah."

"Right," said Lila. She shifted slightly and the hen cocked its head in order to keep a wary eye on her. "Should I keep her? Will she still lay eggs?"

"Probably not. If Grammie Addie was heah thet hen would go into the soup pot. She'd grab thet chicken by the scruff of the neck – jest like a small dog – and haul her outta thet nest box so quick thet hen'd think she was nevah in there." He demonstrated a quick grab and thrust motion and the broody hen was momentarily distracted from Lila to eye Wendell suspiciously. "Course, you ain't Grammie Addie," he added, unnecessarily.

Lila vacillated. She knew she should cull the broody hen from her laying flock; however, she wasn't ready to relegate her *first* hen to the soup pot!

The good-hearted Wendell, understanding the deliberation that was occurring in Lila's breast, spoke up again. "Course, 'twas me, I'd jest stick some fertile eggs under her to see what happens. You ain't got nuthin' to lose and you might git some baby chicks from it."

Wendell's words reinvigorated Lila. "Hey, that's a pretty neat idea! Where can I get fertile eggs?"

"Wal, Trudy Gorse has got roostahs—she's got them Araucana hens that lay blue-green eggs. Some folks really like them Easter-egg-colored eggs."

"Maybe I'll go over and see Trudy this weekend," Lila mused. She was eager to secure the fertile chicken eggs to begin the experiment with the broody hen, but she didn't want to be absent from the homestead that afternoon since Mike Hobart had promised to stop by after work.

"Ayuh. Want me to change them eggs out for ya when you git 'em? No sense bothering the old gal now."

Rebecca hallooed down the spiral staircase, interrupting them. "Lila—Maude is here for her eggs!"

"Coming!" Lila called up. She turned back to Wendell. "I'll change the eggs out when I get the new ones," she continued, hastily. "Maybe the hen won't be so feisty if she sees me GIVING eggs to her instead of TAKING eggs from her!"

Wendell grinned. "Wal, jest let me know if you need me."

Lila retrieved Maude's four dozen eggs from the cold storage room, and wound her way carefully back up the spiral staircase. She discovered that Rebecca had invited Maude inside while she waited, and Lila removed her offensive-smelling Muck™ boots before entering the cozy kitchen. She wasn't surprised to discover that the two older women were already knee-deep in conversation over a steaming cup of tea.

"And then Bruce said he'd email for sure when he found out," an exuberant Maude informed Rebecca. "He's on Skype with Grayden but he hasn't said anything to *him* yet."

"I'm sure he wouldn't want to get his son's hopes up only to be disappointed," said Rebecca.

"Oh, no!"

"Here they are," said Lila, setting the four gray cartons of eggs on the counter.

"Thanks, Sweetie," Maude replied to Lila, barely skipping a beat. "He never writes like that unless he's sure about it," she continued confidentially to Rebecca. "I think Bruce is coming home from Afghanistan, this time for good!"

"Oh, wouldn't that be wonderful!" cried Rebecca. She was grateful her little chick was still close by and not off at war in the trenches of a foreign country, like Maude's son Bruce Gilpin.

Lila automatically tossed a stick of pine into the wood cookstove. The black cover *chinked* as she returned the cast iron round to its nest on the stovetop, and a sliver of gray smoke escaped and permeated the kitchen. The sound, the scent, the impending thunderstorm were all unnoted by the two women setting at the table.

Lila realized she was invisible as well. She smiled as she conceived that the two older women were much like her brood hen, lost in a world of their own, a world in which the hatching, raising and rearing of chicks was paramount. Normally, Lila, who was in a different stage of womanhood in her young life, would shrug this off. Now, however, she contemplated them with a growing sense of wonder and longing.

She thought of Mike Hobart and felt an ache deep inside her, an ache that only he could fill. The yearning grew like a vine, thrusting itself up from her womb to her heart. *Someday? Someday!*

I WILL get beyond this! I WILL have a normal life!
Lila thought of what I had said to her about her real father. Sadly, she shook her head. *That will never happen. I'll never be able to talk with him again But, if only I could! How much I would have to tell him!*

"I'm bringing Grayden over after school, Lila," said Maude, interrupting Lila's reverie. "He wants to do some more target practicing, if that's alright with you, Sweetie."

This turn in the conversation reawakened Lila to the present. "It's more than alright!" she exclaimed. "I saw that fox again yesterday, so I'm glad Gray's coming!" Lila heard a rumble of thunder and glanced out the window at the darkening sky. "But it could be pretty nasty this afternoon," she added.

"Well, I won't bring him if it's raining, or if it's thundering or lightning at all."

"Oh, no; that wouldn't be safe," agreed Rebecca. "We haven't lost any more hens since he's been target practicing, though, and we *do* enjoy having Gray around!" She twisted in her chair toward Lila. "Would you like a cup of tea, dear? Maude and I are having a nice little chat."

Lila hesitated. She wanted to pull up a chair and join the two mothers, but she didn't feel comfortable crashing the party just yet. *Someday!*

"I've got to finish my chores," she replied. "I'm behind schedule—I haven't even collected all the eggs yet."

Rebecca laughed. "I didn't know we had schedules around here! I thought that's why we left corporate America!"

Lila grinned wryly. "You're right, as usual, Becca. I think I'm almost as tough a boss on myself as Joe Kelly was to us at Perkins & Gleeful."

"That's probably why he fired *me* not *you!*"

The three women laughed roundly. Despite their entreaties, Lila returned to the hen pen to finish her chores. Rebecca refreshed her guest's tea, and the two women continued their conversation. After all, Rebecca had not yet had her turn to crow about her own little chick!

Maude, a grandmother as well as a mother, understood the requisite give and take among brood hens. "When does Amber finish school?" she asked, politely.

"May 24th – she's got two more finals and one paper to write, and then she's done. I can't wait!"

"Is your daughter looking forward to the summer here? I would think it's quite a change from where you lived in Boston."

Hens and Chickens

"We used to live in Roxbury," Rebecca corrected lightly; "but you're right, it's very different! Amber is the one that got us into this whole organic thing, though, so she can't wait to get here and become one of *The Egg Ladies* permanently!"

"I thought she looked right at home during the picnic. She's such a pretty girl!"

Rebecca's feathers fluffed up with motherly pride. "Amber *is* lovely, if I do say so myself!" She was about to remark how glad she was that Amber was thin where she herself was plump, when she recalled Maude's rotund figure—and stopped just in time. "I love her waist-length hair," she added, instead. "I'm glad she never cuts it."

"Does she have a boyfriend?"

"Oh, not yet! She's much too young—she's only 21."

"I was married by the time I was her age," said Maude, succinctly.

Rebecca paused a moment for a quick mental calculation. "Me too!" she exclaimed, laughing in wonderment. "But things seem so different these days."

"My son Bruce got married young. He was 19 when Grayden was born so he's only 34, now."

Both mothers were silent a moment, reflecting upon the merits of their own special chicks. And if the truth were known, both were experiencing very similar thoughts.

I'm glad Amber is too young for Bruce Gilpin! Rebecca thought. *Otherwise, an Afghanistan war veteran might appear very romantic!*

While Maude was thinking, *I'm glad Bruce is too old for Amber Johnson! Otherwise, a pretty young thing like her might seem very attractive!*

"I don't regret that Bruce had Grayden for a minute," Maude said, finally; "but I wish he hadn't married the boy's mother!"

Rebecca was slightly shocked at this pronouncement from the old-fashioned Maude. "They're not still married now?" she asked. She knew very little about Bruce Gilpin's history.

"No, no. She's gone through two other men since him, and had a child with each of them. When she moves on, she leaves the child behind."

"Oh, my!"

"Bruce has primary physical custody of Gray, but of course we've practically raised him since Bruce joined the Guard after 9-11. Would you like to see a picture of Bruce?"

Without waiting for a reply, Maude *clicked* open the gold locket she regularly wore around her neck, and proudly held up the color photo of her son that was framed inside.

Rebecca leaned forward to admire the dark visage of Bruce Gilpin in his military garb. "He's very handsome," she said, truthfully.

"He takes after my side of the family," explained Maude. "He looks just like my younger brother, Peter. There's not a Gilpin bone in his body!"

Rebecca realized that the conversation had switched back to Maude's chick, and she smiled inwardly. She, too, understood the necessary give and take of brood hens!

By the time Lila completed her egg collecting, cleaning and sorting, Maude had departed. She found Rebecca in the dining room, where her motherly friend was already back at work on her latest sewing project. A bolt of burgundy cloth was unrolled on the dining room table and Rebecca was pinning a rectangular paper pattern onto the stiff cloth.

Lila switched on the light over the dining room table. "Want some light?"

"Tharmnks!" mumbled Rebecca. She straightened up, and removed several straight pins from her mouth. "I wondered why I was having trouble seeing today."

"It's dark out—that storm will be here before we know it. Is Maude still planning on bringing Gray over after school?"

"Unless it's raining. Maybe the storm will pass by us?"

Lila shook her head. "I don't like the way the wind is whipping. It blew out one of the window panes in the hen pen."

"Did you get it fixed? Should we call Wendell?" Rebecca asked anxiously.

"I patched the glass back in with some putty. Those windows will eventually need to be replaced, though."

"Will it cost very much? I have some extra money, if you need it," Rebecca offered.

Lila regarded her friend with surprise. "I thought you saved all your unemployment money for Amber?"

"This is *extra* money. I've been doing some sewing," she said, indicating her work. "This is a set of dining room curtains for Miss Hastings and I sewed a tablecloth and napkins for Maude. Plus I hemmed three pair of pants for Ralph and sewed up two holes in his shirts."

Hens and Chickens

"You are really into this homesteading thing aren't you!"

"I love to sew," Rebecca said simply, her pretty blue eyes glowing. "Fortunately for me, it seems that nobody *else* does! I was saving the money for Amber's school books next year, but if we need it ..."

"We don't need it, thanks. We've barely touched my mother's life insurance money, and the eggs are selling really well."

At the mention of Lila's mother and the money her daughter had collected from her awful death, Rebecca shuddered. Her pretty face clouded over. She pictured a woman not much older than herself sitting down to write that last terrible letter to her daughter. What must she have felt as she sat there – hand trembling, tears falling! – knowing that she was giving her own life so that her young chick would have a safe, new life!

But Rebecca knew, with the true instinct of a brood hen, that there was nothing she herself would *not* do to save her own baby chick!

Chapter 29

· · · · · · ·

Tinkerbell Redux

Later that same muggy afternoon, Mike Hobart was wrapping up work on his post and beam barn – daydreaming about his sweetheart and wondering how Lila had liked the *papier-mâché* chickens – when his phone identified an in-coming call from Gray Gilpin. The handsome carpenter was packing his tools neatly into the stainless steel tool box on the back of his truck, but he stopped to answer the call. At first, because of poor cellular reception, Hobart had difficulty understanding the teenager. A thunderstorm threatened, plus he was working in a remote field in Troy.

"Gray? I can barely hear you," he said, speaking loudly although he knew it wouldn't make much difference. "Hold on, buddy, I'll get up in my truck."

Hobart swung his muscular frame up into the bed of his pickup, and from the extra height was able to net better cell reception, enough to distinguish a faint sob on the other end of the line. "Gray, are you OK?" he asked, worriedly.

"I shot Tinkerbell!" the boy cried. "I can't find him! I'm in the woods and I think I'm LOST!"

Hobart, standing in the bed of his truck, felt as though someone had whacked him in the gut with his wooden-handle spade. Momentarily confounded, he sank down onto the side of the truck bed. Gray Gilpin, the darling of his grandparent's eye, was somewhere in lost the Sovereign woods! And he claimed to have shot the white deer?!

Hobart heard another sob. "Stay calm—it's gonna be OK, buddy," Hobart instinctively reassured the teenager. "Tell me what you see around you!"

The woods behind the old Russell homestead edged up against a wilderness area the size of a small city. Much of the heavily forested area was owned by the town of Sovereign, which had acquired nine large

223

woodlots, hundreds of acres each, through tax liens during the Great Depression. Timber was harvested over the years and the area was open to public use, including hunting. Mike Hobart had become familiar with the wilderness area during his first year at Unity College, before his "Aldo Leopold" moment in the very same woods.

"Tell me what you see, buddy!" Hobart repeated, standing back up in the truck bed as his mind went into high-gear. He put his left hand over his opposite ear so that he could hear the teenager better.

"Well, I see a lotta trees …"

"What kind of trees?" said Hobart, glancing around at the hardwoods that lined the seven-acre field in which he was working. "Poplars? Birch? Pine trees? Do they have leaves on 'em?"

After a few minutes of similar questioning, Hobart was able to picture in his mind with a fair amount of accuracy the area from which Gray Gilpin was calling. "OK, now *stay put*, buddy," he said. "I know where you are and I'll be there in about 20 minutes. Whatever you do, if you see Tinkerbell *don't* go near him, O.K?"

"Grandpa is gonna be REALLY MAD at me!" Gray sobbed. "I didn't mean to kill Tinkerbell; it was an accident!"

"It's gonna be OK!" Hobart repeated, jumping down from the bed of his truck onto the matted grass in the field. "No one's gonna be mad at you, Gray! Just don't go near that white deer!" He flipped his phone shut, hopped into his truck and roared the pickup to life.

As Hobart swung onto Route 9/202, his own misbegotten hunting incident, now more than a decade old, flashed through the handsome carpenter's mind. He shuddered at the imminent danger facing Gray, not from the pending spring thunderstorm, but from a dying deer with a fairytale nickname! Hobart knew from personal experience just how dangerous a wounded deer could be, how deadly those hooves could slash. Unwittingly, Gray Gilpin could be sliced to death by Tinkerbell in a matter of seconds!

Hobart sped north up the black-topped road, contemplating as he drove whether or not he should alert Gray's grandparents. It was a dicey call. He knew that the moment Ralph and Maude were told the news that their grandson was lost in the woods both of them would become overwrought. Their anxiety would not only slow Hobart down, but also might lead Ralph to insist on accompanying the carpenter in search of Gray.

Hens and Chickens

No, it was best to go it alone. Hobart made one quick side trip, however. He stopped at his cabin and picked up his hunting knife, as well as the long-forsaken high-powered hunting rifle and ammunition given to him by his father on his 18th birthday. Hobart quickly resumed his mission.

At the Sovereign end of the Jewell Road, Hobart pulled off onto a muddy, rutted logging road from which the town had harvested wood the previous season. He switched on his truck's 4-wheel-drive and careened along the soft road, tires spitting clods of wet dirt in his wake. He drove much faster than usual about a mile back into the deep woods. The road ended in a circular open space where lumber was yarded out of the woods, and Hobart threw his truck into park next to a pile of weathered gray timber remnants. According to his calculations, Gray was about 300 yards into the woods to the north. He heard thunder rumble ominously in the distance and knew he didn't have much time before the storm broke—and it would be much more difficult to find the teenager.

As he exited the pickup into the sticky warm air, Hobart felt a few fat raindrops on his bare forearms. He tied the knife's leather sheath to his belt, expertly loaded shells into the rifle and slung the gun over his shoulder by the strap. He attempted to call Gray on the cell phone once again, but this time there was no reception.

Hobart surveyed the thick woods and quickly selected a course through the area in his mind. He strode valiantly into the thicket, eyes and ears on a hunter's high alert. "GRAY!" he called. "Can you hear me? G-R-A-Y!" His heart pounded, and adrenalin pumped through his body. Every now and again, he stopped his forward motion in order to listen.

At first, all Hobart heard was the eerie *howl* of the wind whipping through the tall pines. The woods was unnaturally still except for the wind. The birds had already taken cover in preparation for the storm and the normally plentiful squirrels and chipmunks seemed to be in hiding. After a few moments of listening, however, Hobart was rewarded. The buffeting breeze teased him with a faint human voice: "Here ... I ... here ... am!"

"Stay put, buddy!" he yelled, in the direction of the voice. "I'm coming!"

Hobart picked up his pace, crashing through low-hanging dead pine limbs with his shoulder and thigh. In an effortless move, he swung the high-powered rifle down from across his back and hoisted it up to his waist into a hunting position. He didn't know where Tinkerbell was, but if Gray had followed the wounded deer into the woods, it was a good bet that the deer was lying – maybe dying – nearby.

Hobart spotted a flutter of movement through the trees the distance of a football field ahead. He narrowed his eyes and distinguished Gray jumping-jack waving at him in a small clearing near a mixture of fir and hardwood trees. Out of the corner of his eye he also spotted a corresponding movement – a white blotch rose up from a thicket five yards to the right of the teenager. Hobart raised his gun to his shoulder, saw the flailing white deer in his rifle's scope, and pulled the trigger. Tinkerbell dropped and Gray uttered a startled, high-pitched cry.

"Stay away from him!" Hobart yelled. "He might not be dead!"

Hobart dashed through the snapping underbrush the remaining yards to where the famous white deer of Sovereign, Maine lay, motionless. He pulled the knife from its sheath, but there was no need for it. Tinkerbell was dead. Only then did Hobart feel regret at destroying the beautiful animal.

His first concern, however, was for Gray. The youth was gazing at the dead deer with a look of horror on his face. He was glued to the spot as though in shock. Hobart dropped the knife and reached for the teenager, clasping the boy to his sweaty, muscular chest. "Gray, thank God you're alright!"

Gray burst into tears. "I didn't mean to shoot Tinkerbell – it was an accident!"

Hobart comforted the sobbing youth. "I know, buddy. Hey, it's gonna be OK!"

"I was just tryin' to scare the fox! I shot over her head, into the woods, and the next thing I know I heard a cry and … and it was Tinkerbell! I tried to track him but I got confused and tired. That's when I called ya."

Hobart pushed the teenager's skinny frame out so that he could address the youth face to face, man to man. "You did the right thing, Gray! But now we have to keep on doing the right thing—we need to tell your grandparents. And the game warden."

Gray groaned. He pulled away from Hobart and wiped his eyes and nose on the sleeve of his red flannel shirt. "Grandpa's gonna kill me! And what'll Miss Hastings say? I shot Tinkerbell!"

"If I know Miss Hastings, she'll be much more concerned about *you* than she will about Tinkerbell. Someday there'll be another Tinkerbell in Sovereign—but Miss Hastings knows that there'll never be another you."

Hens and Chickens

The teenager cheered up at Hobart's words. "Ya really think there'll be another white deer someday?"

Hobart smiled at the youth. "I can almost guarantee it," he said, reassuringly. "Listen, the game warden's a buddy of mine—maybe he'll let us bury Tinkerbell in the Pet Cemetery?"

"That'd be cool. I'll do the diggin'," Gray offered, seriously. "Grandpa says I need to take responsibility for my actions."

"Good man. That's what I was hoping you'd say."

By the time Hobart and Gray reached Gilpin's General Store a half an hour later, however, Gray's resolution was flagging. "Can I just sit out here?" he begged. "I don't think I can face my Grandpa now."

"You can't put it off for long," Hobart pointed out. "You'll have to go home for supper!"

Gray grimaced. "I know, I know. But at least Grandma will be there, then!"

Hobart calculated that it was probably best for him to deliver the news to Ralph Gilpin by himself. That would give the old shopkeeper time to cool off after hearing Hobart's account of what happened. Plus Hobart was aware that if Gray *wasn't* present, he would have more of an opportunity to direct what could otherwise be an emotional scene between grandfather and grandson.

"OK, buddy," he said, opening the truck door. "Wait for me here."

Fortunately, no one was in the store when Hobart walked in. Ralph greeted him with chipper enthusiasm per usual, until the carpenter opened his budget of news. Then, the skinny shopkeeper grasped onto a nearby shelf and made a strange articulation. However, Ralph made no further comment until Hobart was done with his tale.

"He ain't hurt?" Ralph asked anxiously, when Hobart finished speaking.

"Nope; just a little ashamed and embarrassed. But he did the right thing, calling me and staying put. And he's gonna help me bury the deer."

"Make him dig the goddamm hole himself!"

But Hobart had seen the tears in the old shopkeeper's eyes and recognized that Ralph's anger was an attempt to cover other, stronger emotions. "Yep," he replied, smiling. "He'll have to do the digging. I've only got one spade."

"You're a good man, Mike," said Ralph, releasing his grip on the shelf in order to give Hobart an affectionate slap on the back.

"And Gray's a good kid, Ralph. But maybe he better take that hunter's safety course sooner rather than later!"

Gilpin grimaced. "Kid's gonna be the death of his grandmother!"

At Ralph's insistence, Hobart used Gilpin's landline in the store's back office to contact the game warden. The warden, after hearing the tale, allowed that Hobart and Gray could bury the white deer in the town's Pet Cemetery. "I'd like to get a blood sample to look at those genetic abnormalities," said the game warden; "but the state doesn't have money for that. So just go ahead and put the deer in the ground."

Hobart was about to exit the store, when Tom Kidd popped through the double glass doors. Hobart nodded at his former Unity College classmate but attempted to push past him without speaking. *Of all times to run into the Organic Kidd!*

"Hey, hey Hobart—whaddaya say?" Kidd said, reaching out and catching the carpenter by the arm.

"I'm in a hurry, Tom," Hobart replied, necessarily stopping. He shook off Kidd's grip and put his hand on the glass door to exit.

"Oh, yeah, I bet you are! Too bad about that white deer," Kidd said, lewdly.

Hobart felt his heart stagger. "*What* did you say?!"

Kidd gestured with his head toward the parking lot. "I saw Gilpin's grandson sniveling out there in your truck and asked the kid why he was crying. He told me he shot your precious *Tinkerbell.*" Kidd pronounced the deer's nickname with a sneer.

Hobart groaned in his spirit. *Poor Gray felt badly enough as it was about killing Tinkerbell, without having Tom Kidd going around telling tales!*

Hobart selected his course of action in a split second. "*I* killed Tinkerbell," he said, forcefully.

"Aw, you know I don't believe THAT, Hobart. You're too lily-livered to kill anything these days."

"I don't lie. You know *that* from firsthand experience, don't you, Tom?"

Kidd winced. Hobart's words had struck a nerve. His right hand absently fingered his fawn-colored goatee. "What proof ya got?"

Hobart repressed his anger. "Follow me," he said, tight lipped. He led the Organic Kidd out to his truck, stopping next to the bed. He flicked back the ground cloth that was covering the stiff white carcass of Tinkerbell, taking care to expose only the deer's head and upper shoulder, and not the bloody gash in the hind quarter from Gray's shotgun shell. The deer's brown eyes stared glassily into space. A slight smear of bright red blood was clearly visible against the milk-colored fur at the deer's neck where Hobart's rifle shot had entered. Hobart pointed to the clean round hole that only a high-powered rifle could have made. "Do you need a ballistics test or will you take my word for it now?"

Kidd stepped away from the truck as though the pickup contained hazardous waste. "Jesus! Hobart—why'd ya shoot it?!"

Hobart flipped the tarp back over the dead deer. "I've got nothing else to say, Tom."

Kidd shook his head. "You're fucked, buddy! You're *fucked!*"

Without a further word to his former college classmate, Hobart hopped into the cab of his truck, where Gray sat watching and listening in bewilderment. He backed up and sped off, leaving Tom Kidd standing in Gilpin's parking lot, eyes agog and mouth open so wide that he almost netted a passing carpenter bumblebee, racing home before the thunderstorm broke.

Chapter 30

· · · · · · ·

The Devil Tries for a Toehold

Lightning streaked across the darkening sky as Tom Kidd idled his charcoal-colored pickup in the parking lot at Gilpin's General Store. He took a deep swig of beer from the pop-top can resting on his leg, reflecting upon what he had just witnessed—the dead white deer in the back of Mike Hobart's truck. As he sat and drank the bitter brew, Kidd thoughtfully parsed every word of his prior conversation with Mike Hobart.

"I killed Tinkerbell."

"Aw, you know I don't believe THAT, Hobart. You're too lily-livered to kill anything these days."

"I don't lie. You know THAT from firsthand experience, don't you, Tom?"

It was this last statement by his former college classmate – a question, actually – that was like wormwood to Kidd: *You know THAT from firsthand experience, don't you Tom?*

"Fucking Hobart; rubbing it in my face!" Kidd swore aloud. He rubbed the fainéant goatee on his chin. His brown eyes narrowed and a sadistic grin came over his sallow face. "Well, buddy; ya just gave me the opportunity to knock ya off your white horse once and for all! I've been waiting a LONG time for this. Payback's a bitch," he added.

Thunder crackled overhead. A hostile breeze whipped a dead branch into the windshield of Kidd's truck. The Organic Kidd put the truck into gear and tore out of the parking lot at a high rate of speed, sending the branch flying to the pavement.

Kidd sped north on Route 9/202, stomping on his brakes at the last moment when he reached the turn-off to the Russell Hill Road. A heavy rain finally began to fall and pelted the windshield and roof of his vehicle. Kidd automatically switched on his windshield wipers, and the *splish-splash* of the blades increased the tempo of his already racing heartbeat. He chuckled fiendishly.

For those of you who have *not* already untangled the mystery behind the Organic Kidd's mission to knock our hero from his white horse, let me share with you the fact that Tom Kidd was none other than the Unity College classmate, the beginning hunter, with whom Hobart experienced his "Aldo Leopold" moment. It was Kidd who fell victim to buck fever; Kidd who thoughtlessly pulled the trigger again and again; Kidd who wounded the young deer but could not kill it; Kidd who turned and ran when he discovered the bloody mess that his sick behavior had caused.

On the other hand, our hero was the one to clean up Kidd's mess; Hobart put the deer out of its misery; he ignored Kidd's pleas to keep the incident a secret (he refused to lie about it); and reported the hunting infraction (shooting the skipper without a proper permit) to the authorities. Both men had been fined $500 for the infraction, and had lost their hunting licenses for a period of one year.

We know the effect the incident had on our hero: Mike Hobart never killed or hunted again, until today. However, the incident had an entirely different effect on the Organic Kidd, who had waited nearly 12 years for his revenge.

But it wasn't just revenge alone that drove Tom Kidd. For years, he had been disgusted by the integrity and graciousness of Mike Hobart, who had never even alluded to the hunting incident with Kidd—until today. Misery loves company, and Kidd – a miserable, selfish, worn-out soul, more depleted than a hundred year old Maine cornfield – had been longing to bring Hobart down to his own base level for more than a decade. Finally, Kidd thought he saw an opening. And he wasn't going to waste it.

"Hey, hey, *buddy*," Kidd said sarcastically, accelerating up the road toward the old Russell Homestead; "whaddaya think your little BABE will say when *she* hears the news?!"

Both Rebecca and Lila were in the kitchen when Tom Kidd knocked on the shed door. Lila greeted him at the door amicably, if unenthusiastically. She had learned to tolerate the Organic Kidd during the organic certification process of *The Egg Ladies*. She invited Kidd into the shed, where he shook the rainwater off his dark green slicker and tossed it over a wooden peg. Kidd followed her into the kitchen, and took the proffered seat at the table.

"I'm going out to pick some rhubarb for sauce for supper," announced Rebecca, untying her apron.

Hens and Chickens

"Wear a raincoat," Kidd suggested, pleasantly. "It's pouring out."

"Oh, I'm not afraid of a little rain!" Rebecca said, and excused herself.

"What's up?" said Lila, taking her customary chair at the head of the table. "Is there something else I need to do for my certification?"

Kidd put his elbows on the table and leaned closer, eyeing Lila familiarly. "I'm just checking on your new chicks," he lied. "Making sure ya got 'em by the time they were two days old."

Lila recoiled from his nearness. She started to rise up from her seat in order to lead the Organic Kidd out to the hen pen and show him the 200 replacement chicks. He stopped her with a touch of a tapered hand. Lila instinctively jerked away from his moist, warm touch.

"I don't need to see 'em," he said. "Your word is good enough for me, Lila."

Lila sank back down. "The chicks were a day old when I got them," she reported. "They're about two weeks now. I haven't lost any."

"Hey, good for you! Death sucks; I know that from personal experience!"

Lila raised a dark eyebrow, but said nothing. She waited patiently for Kidd to say what he had to say, and leave.

Kidd flicked a strand of wet black hair back over his shoulder. "Yeah, it's too bad about that white deer," he added, mysteriously.

Lila stiffened. "Are you talking about our white deer, Tinkerbell?" she asked, coldly.

"Lila, *Lila*—that's not very friendly."

"What ABOUT Tinkerbell?"

Kidd smiled in satisfaction—the fish had taken the bait. "Hobart shot that poor thing. Killed it."

"I don't believe it," Lila stated, flatly.

"I saw the deer myself in the bed of his blue pickup 15 minutes ago. Deader than the proverbial doornail!"

Lila felt her anxiety rising. "There must be some mistake."

"Oh, there's no mistake. Hobart needs money. Everybody knows he hasn't had much carpentry work since the Recession started. Jesus, he's so broke he even sells fiddleheads! The hide from that white deer alone oughta bring him about $5,000."

Lila clenched her fists beneath the table. "I don't believe you," she repeated, in a fiercer tone.

"Hobart told me himself, *Lila*," said Kidd, fire flashing from his dark eyes. "Plus he had Gilpin's grandson with him; you can ask the kid."

Rebecca returned to the kitchen at that moment, shaking herself off and laughing ruefully at her rain drenched clothing. She placed a basket half-full of rosy-red and green rhubarb stalks on the counter next to the soapstone sink. "Phew, that was a bit wetter than I thought!" she exclaimed.

Lila turned to her friend. "Did you see Gray?" she said, tersely.

"Gray's gone," replied Rebecca. "His grandmother must have picked him up before it started to rain. I'm going upstairs to change out of these wet things!"

The blood drained from Lila's face. She felt sick to her stomach. Her world seemed to be crashing in on her. *Mike killed Tinkerbell?! How COULD he?!*

Rain pelted against the kitchen window. The lights dimmed. Thunder cracked overhead.

Kidd leaned closer to whisper in her ear. Lila smelled and felt his hot beer breath against her cheek. His thick lips brushed against her hair. She tried to pull back, but was frozen; transfixed! *Please, God! Not NOW!*

"*Lila, Lila*," Kidd taunted softly. "Ya can ask Hobart yourself. Ya know he never lies!"

When Rebecca returned from changing out of her wet clothes, Lila was alone at the kitchen table. Rebecca started to speak, but her young friend rose up with a strangled cry, startling her.

"Lila, dear, what's the matter?" Rebecca asked. She was shocked by Lila's changed appearance—her face was white, her hazel eyes abnormally large and her nostrils flared slightly. The motherly woman instinctively reached out to comfort Lila, but the younger woman pushed her away.

"I've got to go; I'VE GOT TO GO!" Lila cried.

"Where, dear? What happened! What did that organic man *say* to you?!"

But Lila appeared to be in a frantic daze. She raced to the shed, pulled on her Muck™ boots and rain jacket, and slammed out the door. The next thing Rebecca knew her friend was speeding out the driveway in Miss Hastings' old '64 Pontiac LeMans, without one further word of explanation!

An hour later, Mike Hobart was sitting in the same spot from which Tom Kidd had spewed his lies to Lila. Hobart, soaked from the thunderstorm, was drying his wet, grimy face with a cotton hand towel that Rebecca had given him. His jeans were muddy from helping Gray bury the deer and his boots were not only muddy, but bloodstained. Instead of going home to change per usual, he had elected to drive straight to the old Russell homestead. He suspected that his former college classmate might attempt some type of nefarious retaliation, and Hobart wanted to see Lila as soon as possible, so that he could tell her himself of Tinkerbell's demise.

"Sorry about the floor," he apologized to Rebecca, handing the dirty towel back to her. "I was in such a hurry to see Lila, I forgot to take off my boots. Is she in the hen pen?"

"Nooo—she just left. You missed her by about ten minutes."

"Where'd she go? Up to Miss Hastings'?"

Rebecca hesitated, unsure what would be the best way of breaking the unsettling news to Lila's lover. "I'm not sure *where* she went. She was acting very strange."

A sick feeling washed over Hobart. "What do you mean *strange?*" he demanded, gruffly.

"She looked like she'd seen a ghost," Rebecca replied. "I don't know what that organic man said to her, but it must have been something *awful.*"

Hobart's handsome face turned ashen beneath his tan. "Tom Kidd was here? Already!"

Rebecca nodded. "Sitting with Lila, right where you are now. I went upstairs to change my clothes – I got wet picking rhubarb in the rain – and when I came back down, he was gone and Lila was, well, almost wild."

"Did you hear *anything* Kidd said? Anything at all?!"

"Not a word."

Hobart put his head in his hands. "He told her! Of course he told her! *What must she think of me?!* "

Concerned, Rebecca sank down into Lila's chair at the head of the table. She didn't know what was going on, but her caretaker instincts recognized a soul in need. "Lila loves you, Mike," she said, touching him reassuringly on the shoulder. "You *know* that. I know that. Some *lie* that man told her isn't going to change the fact that Lila loves you!"

He groaned. "It wasn't a lie. I killed Tinkerbell." And then in between shaky breaths Hobart related to Rebecca the events of the afternoon as they had unfolded.

Tears came to Rebecca's eyes as she listened to his tale. "Oh, no! Not Tinkerbell!"

"I had no choice!" he sobbed.

"Oh, I know; I know! Gray could have been injured or killed!" Rebecca shuddered at the thought.

"But you can bet that's not how Tom Kidd told the story to Lila!" Hobart exclaimed. He groaned again. "*What must she think of me?!*"

"Oh, Mike! Surely you've got more faith in Lila's love than *that*?"

"Faith? What is faith?!" Hobart cried. "God knows I've tried to help Lila, but she can't seem to break free from something in her past! And now … THIS?!"

Rebecca, who now knew every detail of Lila's past, was silent for a moment. "She's getting better," she said, finally.

"I thought so, too. But this – *this* might set her back! Who knows what terrible spin Kidd put on Tinkerbell's death!" He buried his face in his arms and burst into tears.

Rebecca bit her lip. She agonized in her mind whether or not she should tell Hobart anything. Perhaps Lila had gone down to see her new confidante, the minister of the Sovereign Union Church? Perhaps this unusual behavior even had something to do with what the minister had promised Lila: that she would see her deceased father again? Rebecca didn't understand it all herself, but, bizarre and unsettling as the suggestion was, Lila obviously had faith that seeing and talking to her real father would help her put her past behind her.

But … Rebecca recalled her own promise to herself not to interfere. In addition, Lila had certainly not authorized Rebecca to share her personal story with anyone, not even Mike Hobart. In fact, Lila herself should be the one to make the disclosures to him. No, Rebecca could tell him nothing. She could only wait – patiently – and hope that whatever was occurring for her young friend, the end result would be positive for Lila *and* for this very deserving young man who was now weeping at her kitchen table!

"There, there dear," said Rebecca, soothingly. "Try not to jump to conclusions. Let me just call Lila on her cell and we'll find out where she is."

She stood up, went to the kitchen wall phone and dialed Lila's number. A few moments later, a musical sound was heard from the dining room. Lila – normally attached at the hip to her phone – had left the electronic device behind on the table, next to her laptop!

Hens and Chickens

At that point, I think, Rebecca herself began to wonder herself if Lila WAS coming back.

Chapter 31

·······

Hens and Chickens

We've reached the *denouement* of our story, where Good triumphs over Evil and where we discover that – once again – the Devil's attempt at a toehold in Sovereign, Maine is not successful. This is the point at which (before I conclude our little tale) I clamber up onto my soap box, er, into my pulpit, and deliver a defining pastoral message, which is necessarily one and the same as the moral of our story. For by now you know that your storyteller is none other than the itinerant Quaker minister who leads the Sovereign Union Church every other week, the "odd duck" who runs bare-assed naked through the goldenrod in August.

If I were you, I'd flip ahead at this point, and skip the sermon. However, knowing that human tendency to want to skip the medicine, I've deliberately inserted into this chapter a very important clue as to how Lila is liberated forever from the clutches of the Devil and the nightmares of her childhood. Alas, the clue will be revealed *only in this chapter!*

If you *do* choose to stay with me here, my pips, I promise my preaching will be brief...

I was born in the 1950s on a dairy farm in Winslow, Maine, when such farms were a dime a dozen (I counted seven dairy farms on our road alone) and the Grange, the Order of the Patrons of Husbandry, was still a thriving affair. We lived in an extended nest; my parents, grandparents and great-grandparents, three generations of dairy farmers right in a neat row on the Garland Road—*boom, boom, boom.* If you can find a more perfect place to grow up and a more wonderful situation into which to be born, I'll eat my precious, ratty, 1,044-page, New Revised Version of the Bible given to me when I was eight by the pastor of a Congregational church.

Jennifer Wixson

My favorite person was my grandfather. He was kind, gentle, loving – much like Lila Woodsum's father – and he doted on me. I tagged along when he called the Jersey cows home to the barn to milk in the afternoon: "Here cows, c'mon cows. Come, come!" And I hung out with him in the barn, which was my favorite place to be in the whole world. I loved the smells of sweet hay and sour milk, and was mesmerized by the hot *splash* of cow urine and smelly *splat* of cow manure that erupted during feeding time. I loved being anywhere with Grandfather, but especially in the barn with the cows, because just *being* there with him was so satisfying an experience!

When I was six, my father decided to improve his own family situation. Dad had seen the writing on the wall for Maine's small dairy farms (in the '50s there were 51,000 herds of dairy farms in Maine; today in the Pine Tree State there are 304). He elected to pursue higher education as a vocation by which he could feed his growing family. So we split from the extended family, sold our farm and moved away from the nest. Friends, I never recovered from that loss.

My grandfather died less than a year after our departure from Winslow. I never saw him again. I wrote letters and colored pictures for him almost every day. But I was seven and a half. I didn't even know what death was. I didn't know that one day you could be holding hands with someone you love – or calling the cows in to milk with him – and that the next day he would be gone; never to rise or smile or love me again.

The system really needs work. But I haven't thought of a better one to replace it, yet—and believe me, I've tried.

After that, the old folks in our extended family (and there were a lot of them) started dropping like flies: my great-grandfather, two great-grandmothers, grandmother etc. etc. Finally, I was left with one living grandparent—my mother's mother. Now, this particular grandmother – let us call her "Gram" for short – had nine grandchildren, of which I was her least favorite. The six boys, of course, ranked highest, followed by my girl cousin, my older sister and then—me.

I was 21-years-old when it came to me like a vision, high on a hilltop in California, that if I wanted to return to Maine and re-experience living in the family nest amongst the hay fields and the balsams and the white pines – if this was my heart's longing, passion and delight (and it was) – then I had better hurry home to the Pine Tree State because only Gram remained; and she wasn't getting any younger.

Hens and Chickens

To make a long story short, I called up my grandmother and asked if I could live with her. She debated my request for about a week, and then allowed that I could move in with her, into the old brick homestead in Norway, Maine, which has housed various members of our extended family for eight generations (of which she was the fifth generation and I was the seventh). She didn't like me very much (I was a know-it-all) and I didn't like her very much (she was imperious and demanding), and we grated on each other like a stone in a shoe. But she needed me (she was a lonely divorcee) and I needed her (I was a lonely kid) and so we stuck it out.

She showed me where and particularly *how* the silverware was to be sorted *just so* in the tired out old pull-drawers, and I mowed the lawn, stacked the firewood and hung the clothes out on the clothesline to dry. She baked biscuits and perked coffee on the woodstove, and Gram and I would sit in the warm kitchen in quiet satisfaction in the afternoon stuffing our faces with hot Bakewell Cream biscuits smothered in cow's butter and dripping with raspberry honey. Food prepared with love for the satisfaction of another person offers up a proof of that affection that speaks louder than any word, practically shouting "I love you!" without any need for sound to pass through the vocal chords.

Gram was wild over plants, flowers and trees. She introduced me to every one of the half dozen ancient apple trees still standing in the hillside orchard and explained how these weathered friends were started from pips – from seed – and not from grafts of proven rootstock like modern-day fruit trees. "They never knew what they were getting when they planted pips," she said, "but they were grateful for every piece of fruit, no matter how flawed." Gram's affection for heritage apples rubbed off on me and living with her was when the word "pip" became incorporated into in my everyday vocabulary.

Much like the old Russell homestead, Gram's place was populated with other types of trees: red maples, willows and white pine. Flowering shrubs that had been planted by generations past also littered the yard, serving as a continuously expanding, living legacy of my ancestor's love for the place. My grandmother and I cared for all of it, but my grandmother had a pet garden of her own that we added to the mix during my tenure with her. In this newly-established garden on top of the stone foundation of the old the barn (which had burned down before she was born) Gram lovingly tended several succulent flowering plants of

241

the *Crassulaceae* family, known to all gardeners as *Hens and Chickens*. This interesting and unique plant resembles a large, setting hen that shortly gives birth to several smaller succulent satellites—the "chicks" of the *Hens and Chickens*. The family of plants multiply over time, as the chicks grow big and become hens themselves, throwing off their own new set of *Hens and Chickens*.

Over the 13 years that I resided with my grandmother, the families of *Hens and Chickens* we planted expanded their numbers exponentially. And, in much the same exponential fashion, Gram and I came to admire, respect and love – truly *love* – one another. Even now I shake my head and marvel at how close we became over the years, much like shoes and socks. I think I knew more of Gram's secrets than I did my own!

When I received the phone call telling me that she had suffered a stroke, I raced to the hospital, thankfully in time to find Gram conscious and talking on the gurney to the nurses. I knew she wasn't going to die, because she had survived so many bouts with death before. "Howzit going, Gram?" I asked. "Well, to tell you the truth, my pip," she said, affectionately; "I've had better days!" She fell into a coma shortly after that, from which she never awoke. Ten days later she was gone, the last of her generation to leave me.

More than 20 years have slipped away since Gram's death, and I'm now one of the older generation myself, one of the grown-up hens with my own special chick, a daughter that I named "Nellie" after my Gram. And during this time the *Hens and Chickens* in my grandmother's flower garden have increased to marvelous proportions, and many of them have made their way into my own special garden at my home on the Cross Road in Sovereign.

I love to weed my own *Hens and Chickens*, just like I weeded Gram's garden 30 years ago, because with these special succulents I've spied so many truths about myself, about Life, and, most importantly the power of Good over Evil. With the maturity that comes from the telescoping of time, I realize now the amazing power of Love. We need never, *ever* fear Evil, my pips, as long as we are willing to risk loving one another!

The irony of my story – and the moral of it as well – is this: had my grandfather not died young, I never would have experienced this loving relationship with Gram. After his death, I was a young chick searching for a replacement for his love, seeking a home, someplace to roost. And that urgent need I felt to love and to be loved led me to an old mother

Hens and Chickens

hen, worn out by time and circumstances beyond her control in life, but who saw in me a new hope rising, a new chick pushing up out of the black soil. And so the two of us hooked up, and the rest, my friends, is history.

Our young heroine Lila has found a man who is steady and true; and there is not a better man in the world than Mike Hobart. However, that is not enough for her. Like me, Lila is searching to replace the love she lost as a child, the love of her father. Will she ever be able to fill this void? Will she ever find a safe and loving place to roost?

Ah! I know for a fact that finding such love is possible! For my life is proof positive that when a baby chick goes searching for love, a hen is surely somewhere to be found.

However, not everyone is blessed with visions from mountaintops, as I was in my youth. Sometimes hungry orphan chicks and tired old hens need a little help connecting with one another. That's where the power of love comes in … that and the everyday miracle of modern communications. Where there's a will, there's a, well—Twitter.

So on Lila's behalf, after the Good Lord had done her healing work, I sent a Direct Message to one of my Tweeps up in Maple Grove, in northern Maine. And now, my pips, you have your clue.

Chapter 32

· · · · · · ·

"Come and Let Me Love You"

To know where our heroine has absconded to and why, we must go back—back to the snug country kitchen in the old Russell homestead, where the rain is splattering against the single-pane windows and Lila is still sitting at the table with the Organic Kidd. In order to follow Lila's footsteps, we must pick up where the Devil leaves off …

The blood drained from Lila's face. She felt sick to her stomach. Her world seemed to be crashing in on her. *Mike killed Tinkerbell?! How COULD he?!*

Rain pelted against the kitchen window. The lights dimmed. Thunder cracked overhead.

Lila put her head in her hands. Kidd leaned closer to whisper in her ear. She smelled and felt his hot beer breath against her cheek. His thick lips brushed against her hair. She tried to pull back up, but was frozen; transfixed! *Please, God! Not NOW!*

"Lila, Lila," Kidd taunted softly. "Ya can ask Hobart yourself. Ya know he never lies!"

He never lies.

Something within Lila shifted. She sprung back up like a winter birch dropping a heavy load of snow. "NO!" she proclaimed, loudly and fiercely. "I don't believe you for one minute!" She was so forceful she almost startled herself.

Tom Kidd jerked away from her as though struck by lightning. "Jesus, lady," he said; "you don't have to yell at me!"

"Get out! GET OUT OF MY HOUSE!" She was trembling now; standing and glaring at the Organic Kidd in righteous indignation. Her nostrils flared in anger.

Kidd stood up and backed slowly toward the door. "I'm going; I'm going! Jesus Christ!"

"Don't ever come back here again! EVER!"

He turned and scrambled out the shed door, leaving his raincoat behind. Kidd jumped into his truck and roared out of the driveway. "What a whacko!" he expostulated to himself. "She's perfect for Hobart!"

Lila slowly sank back into her seat, still trembling. Her mind quickly sifted through the facts at hand – Tinkerbell was dead and Gray Gilpin, who had been target practicing in back of the house was suddenly missing – and Lila pieced together the scenario almost exactly as it happened. When she came to the conclusion that Mike Hobart had been forced to kill the white deer from some sort of necessity, she experienced a surge of empathetic anguish for him. *What MUST he have felt?! What pain he must have suffered, pulling that trigger!*

To kill again when he had sworn that he would never kill again?! Oh, Mike! My darling!

I need to go to him now. NOW!

Lila rose up with a strangled cry.

"Lila, dear, what's the matter?" Rebecca asked.

"I've got to go; I'VE GOT TO GO!" she cried.

She raced to the shed, pulled on her Muck™ boots and rain jacket, and slammed out the door. She pushed Miss Hastings' old '64 Pontiac LeMans harder than it had been pushed in decades as she barreled across town, over to the North Troy Road. The rain came down in buckets, but Lila didn't notice. She peered determinedly ahead as she drove, swerving off onto the dirt drive where she knew Mike Hobart's cabin was located. Through sheets of rain, she spotted his baby blue pickup parked beneath a towering pine tree, near a neat-looking cabin.

He's home! Lila thought, in exquisite relief.

The cabin door, knotted pine with wrought iron hardware, was open a fraction of an inch. Without stopping to knock, Lila rushed inside. "Mike, darling!" she cried. "I'm here; I'm HERE my darling!"

He was sitting in a Windsor-style rocking chair by a roaring fire in a stone hearth. He pushed himself up from the chair at the sound of her voice. Lila started toward him with a little joyful cry, hands outstretched and—stopped short.

It was Mike Hobart … but it was NOT the man she knew! It was Mike Hobart *in fifty years!*

In a flash, Lila noted that the dark-blond curls through which she loved to run her fingers were now completely white; the twinkling blue

Hens and Chickens

eyes were wrinkled and watery; and the firm lip of the man that she loved, trembled slightly. It was Mike Hobart—but it was NOT Mike Hobart! "Oh-my-God!" she said, moving in amazed wonderment towards him across the smooth wood floor. "Mr. ... Hobart?!"

He slowly came forward to greet her, a delighted smile lighting up his blue eyes. He stooped from age and from the physical labors of a long life on a potato farm in northern Maine. He held out thick-veined, curled arthritic hands. "You must be Lila!" he exclaimed. "Mikey's told me so much about you! I feel like I already know you, my dear. Won't you come and sit with me?"

Mikey?

She took his shaky, outstretched hands in a daze, and allowed him to escort her back to the opposite chair by the blazing fire. She sank down onto the edge of the matching Windsor rocker, never taking her eyes from his weathered face. It was a friendly face, an honest face, a loving face.

"Where's Mike?" she asked, completely befuddled.

"I don't know, my dear. I just drove down from Maple Grove, myself. I was hoping you could tell *me* where he is. I've only been here long enough to get the fire going." Mr. Hobart's bright blue eyes emanated good humor and kindness.

Instinctively, Lila glanced around the cabin. The knotted pine dwelling with exposed posts and beams was exactly what she would have expected from Mike Hobart. His home was sparse, neat, attractive in a masculine way. Two pair of wood and leather snowshoes decorated the wall by the stone fireplace and pictures of white tail deer, black bear and moose hung on the walls. She could smell the scent of him all around her and her soul was filled with an intense, physical aching for him.

She suddenly recollected his father, and turned back to Mr. Hobart. "I'm sorry, I'm being rude," she said, attempting to shake herself back to normal. "Did Mike's Mom come down with you from Maple Grove?"

"Hasn't Mikey told you yet?" he asked, softly. Mr. Hobart read her answer in her eyes. "His mother died from complications giving birth to him. Mikey was quite an unexpected gift! Margaret was 44 when we found out she was pregnant and I was nearly 50! The three girls were grown and almost gone, and we were thinking more of grandchildren than children at the time. But, God has a sense of humor, I guess," he added, sadly.

"I'm so sorry!" said Lila, tears springing to her eyes. "He's never mentioned his mother, only you. Now, I know why!"

Mr. Hobart breathed in deeply, and let out a long, tremulous sigh. A log shifted on the fire and sent up a sprizing spray of orange sparks. "He feels responsible, I think. He never says so, but that's what I think. I raised him by myself. I did the best I could—the girls helped, of course, but they had lives of their own to live."

"He's an amazing guy. I love him!" Lila blurted out.

"I know you do, my dear," said Mr. Hobart, leaning over and patting her hand. "And I know he loves you, too. I miss him terribly, but we're still very close. I know Mikey had to move away from me, in order to become his own man. But he's been down here a long time; a very long time! I was hoping he'd come back to Maple Grove one of these days, and bring me back a pretty little daughter to love." The old man hesitated. His thin hand trembled. "Will you come and let me love you, Lila? Will you come back to Maple Grove and be my pretty little daughter?"

Will you come and let me love you?

Lila's parched heart responded greedily to the proffering of love from this old mother hen. "Yes!" she cried, sinking onto her knees on the braided rug in front of his chair. "YES!" She put her head on the old man's lap and burst into tears.

"Oh, my dear!" he exclaimed, patting her back and lightly stroking her silken black hair in the familiar comforting fashion for which *he* had so longed. "Shhhh; everything's going to be alright!" His blue eyes filled with tears, and he coughed a little to clear his throat. "We'll be just fine now, my dear, won't we? *All* of us!"

Mike Hobart, who wasn't always the "shaapest" of suitors, finally figured out where Lila had gone to and why. Half an hour later, he reached his cabin. He saw Lila's car parked out front, but in the pouring rain failed to notice his father's matching baby blue pickup.

He burst into the cabin calling Lila's name. He broke off when he beheld a beaming Lila sitting in front of the hearth holding hands with—his father! He stopped dead in his tracks. "Dad!" he exclaimed, astonished.

The exultant old man rose from the rocker, pulling a radiant Lila up to her feet by his side. He gave her an affectionate squeeze. "I've done the heavy lifting for you, my boy!" Mr. Hobart crowed. "Lila's said 'Yes!' You don't even need to get down on your knees!"

Hens and Chickens

Hobart shook his head in amazement. He attempted to process his father's words, but could barely fathom the fact that his father was here and not in Maple Grove. Fortunately, the glorious look in Lila's eyes revealed all. "Lila?" Hobart said, wondrously, opening his arms to his beloved.

Mr. Hobart released her, and she flew to him like a chickadee to a pine tree. He embraced her hungrily. "My darling!" he cried, crushing her to his muscular chest and pressing multiple kisses upon her face and hair. "My *darling!*"

She lifted her chin and her eyes begged for the fulfillment of his kiss. Hobart didn't hesitate. He accepted her offering, claiming her as his own. She was his own; his Lila! Was there ever a more perfect name than *Lila?*

And that, my pips, is how our little chick finally came home to roost.

Chapter 33

· · · · · · ·

Conclusion

Since now you know my peculiar position as sacred confidante in the community, you might also suspect the truth: that there have been many different sources for this little tale. All of my sources, however, have given me permission to share their stories—Lila, especially, is hoping that her personal history might help others find the courage to seek and secure happiness despite similar childhood trauma. So let us take a moment and follow this tale to its many happy endings...

While Lila, Mike and Mr. Hobart were making merry in Mike's little cabin in the woods, celebrating the couple's informal engagement, the rain let up on the other side of town and the sun made a bold run at dispersing the remaining thunder clouds on Russell Hill. Wendell Russell had watched from Bud's place as first the Organic Kidd, then Lila, and then Mike Hobart had sped out of the driveway. Never one to miss an opportunity, he calculated that Rebecca was finally alone, a situation which had been difficult for him to engineer. Wendell ambled hurriedly across the way, pulling his black plastic comb through his hair and returning it to his back pocket.

He rapped quickly on the shed door in his familiar fashion and let himself in. Rebecca was on her hands and knees in the kitchen cleaning up the mud and water from Mike Hobart's dirty boots. She sat back onto her haunches at the sound of his knock.

"Come in, Wendell!" she called, but he was already poking his head through the inner door.

"Lila gone?" he asked, wiping his feet on the rug and stepping inside the toasty country kitchen.

Rebecca absently dropped the dirty sponge back into the bucket of cleaning water. "Yes! I don't know *what's* going on here! Things are getting curiouser and curiouser!"

Jennifer Wixson

"Ayuh, thet happens in Sovereign," Wendell said, chuckling. He reached down and helped Rebecca to her feet. He set the pail to one side, next to the soapstone sink, so that it wouldn't get knocked over.

"Tinkerbell is dead! Lila's missing! That organic man was here, my goodness! Would you like some rhubarb sauce? I just made it!"

"Ayuh," Wendell said, pulling up his usual chair at the table.

Rebecca served him a large helping of the rosy red sauce, and he admired it with obvious enthusiasm. She poured out two cups of tea from the boiling water in the nickel-plated tea kettle that was hot on the cookstove, and set the steaming cups at each of their place settings.

Rebecca sank down with a sigh into her chair across the table from him. She watched with fond satisfaction as the old chicken farmer devoured with gusto the big bowl of her rhubarb sauce. "You know, there is something I've been meaning to ask you, Wendell," she said, fingering the handle of her teacup.

"What's thet?"

"Why is it you never use my name? You call 'Lila—Lila' and 'Mike—Mike' but I've only ever heard you refer to me as 'yore little friend'?"

Wendell grinned, his charming, gold-toothed grin, and reached across the table, securing her hand from the teacup. "Thet's 'cause I was waitin' 'til I could call you 'Mrs. Russell,'" he said. "Think I might?" He winked.

Rebecca, our modest, old-fashioned Rebecca, did not even blush! Instead, she giggled like a schoolgirl. "Oh, I think you might!"

He leaned across the table – she met him halfway – for an affectionate kiss. And then Wendell and Rebecca finished their tea in companionable silence in the kitchen of the old Russell homestead.

Our young lovers, Lila and Mike, were married in June at the Sovereign Union Church. What a crowd we had that day! The entire Hobart clan motored down from Maple Grove in Aroostook County and what with husbands and wives from the seventh generation and children and grandchildren from the eighth generation, the Hobarts filled up most of the pews on *both* sides of the little white church, although it was obvious to all that more of the family elected to sit on the bride's side of the aisle than the groom's! Poor Lila, who had no family of her own, was overcome when she entered the church in her lovely white gown to discover that Mike's family was determined to show to Lila and to the world that she was part of *their* family now.

Hens and Chickens

Lila's side was also represented in the church by steadfast friends such as Ryan MacDonald, Miss Hastings and the Gilpin family. Cora Batterswaith, "Queen Cora," held court among a little group of Lila's former coworkers, including Shelly Thompson, who had helped Lila pick out the outfit for her mother to be buried in, and Carl Esler, who had held Lila's hand through her mother's funeral service. Queen Cora had been invited because of her single act of kindness to Rebecca that last day at Perkins & Gleeful—she had helped Rebecca carry her things to the car. Joe Kelly, that "tight-fisted twit" (as Miss Hastings still describes Lila's former boss) was *not* invited.

Lila was walked down the aisle by our old friend Wendell Russell on one side of her, and by her new father on the other. Her handsome, steady hero waited for her at the altar and I've never performed a wedding service for a man more in love, nor a more deserving man, than Mike Hobart. Patience, selfless love and a sense of humor had won him his prize.

The wedding service was short and sweet, and the guests decamped to the old Russell homestead, where Rebecca and Maude Gilpin had prepared a wondrous feast for the wedding celebration. Mike's older brother John gave a toast, officially welcoming Lila to the Hobart family. It was a glorious, joyous day; one that us Sovereign folk won't soon forget.

A few weeks later, I performed the wedding service for our other *unmarried* lovers, Wendell and Rebecca—a small ceremony at the old Russell homestead. After first paying off the mortgage to Wendell, Lila gave the deed to the place as a wedding gift to her faithful friend and her new husband, so now Rebecca's name, her rightful name – Rebecca Russell – is finally recorded at the registry. Like all of us, Lila recognized that Rebecca belonged in Sovereign, in the house that she had brought back to life. Wendell, the old chicken farmer who had once dreamed of bringing the *farm* back to life, suddenly found himself an official proprietor of *The Egg Ladies*. He discovered that he was NOT too old after all to take over Grammie Addie's operation! Plus he had plenty of help from his devoted wife and the newest egg lady, Amber, whose organic propensities had perhaps instigated the whole Maine adventure.

This summer, Amber has been staying at Bud's place, to give her parents some privacy during the early days of their marriage. However, a proposed late August visit from Ryan MacDonald is being talked about, so at least one of the three upstairs guest rooms will once again be pressed into service at the old Russell homestead. An excursion to the Maine coast that will include the Gilpins, Miss Hastings, the Russells, Amber, and Ryan MacDonald has been planned during MacDonald's visit, and this time they have even invited yours truly!

Our *married* lovers, Ralph and Maude Gilpin, celebrated their 53rd anniversary in June, at which illustrious event Ralph took care to assure the couple's guests: "She's *still* my bride, though!" Gray Gilpin took and passed his hunter's safety course in July. Despite the Tinkerbell incident, he *will* be deer hunting this fall with the new shotgun his Dad gave him last Christmas. Gray is hoping that his father will return soon from the war in Afghanistan, an event which some of us know for a fact will soon come true and for which Maude Gilpin has prayed every day during the past 10 years. Sometimes – if we have patience, hope and faith – we *are* rewarded with our heart's desire! But perhaps the imminent return of Bruce Gilpin is fodder for another tale …

The Organic Kidd is still floating loose in our area, although he's officially stationed in Unity, at the MOGG certification office. He hasn't shown his devilish face again at the old Russell homestead, however, Lila did receive the official certification for the egg business in the mail not long after Kidd's *last* momentous visit.

Miss Hastings – the town's beloved Miss Hastings! – is alive and kicking, along with her pet chicken Matilda. Miss Hastings has planned another trip to the Sovereign Elementary School for this fall (this time Rebecca will accompany her) and has been practicing on her piano the songs the children will be singing during her next "music lesson."

Mike Hobart's father, once too proud to accept offers of assistance from his children, is now regularly to be seen squired about Maple Grove in a 1964 Pontiac LeMans by his new daughter-in-law, of whom he is unabashedly proud. In a private moment after the wedding ceremony, Mr. Hobart had given Lila the keys to the old family homestead in Maple Grove, which was in effect giving her not only his home but also his heart. "Sorry, Mikey," he said, jubilantly; "if 'whither thou go, I go' is still in effect, you're coming home to Maple Grove!"

And that's how Lila Woodsum – who only six weeks before her wedding had proclaimed that she would need to be taken out of the old Russell homestead in a box! – ended up in Aroostook County, in northern Maine, where she and Mike now abide with her beloved father in the homestead that has housed seven generations of Hobarts. Lila

Hens and Chickens

has taken over the marketing of Hobart Farms, the family potato and broccoli business, now run jointly by John and Mike Hobart. Lila and I follow each other on Twitter, and she tweets regularly of her new family's adventures in Maple Grove. Just a few days ago, in early August, in fact, Lila sent me a Direct Message saying that they were expecting a new addition to the eighth generation of Hobarts!

Those hens and chickens have a way of multiplying, my pips, as time marches along!

Now, have I forgotten anybody?

Ah, yes, *me*!

I was fortunate enough to secure additional itinerant ministry work this spring and early summer with the First Universalist Church of Norway (Maine), which was my Gram's church. In addition, I also filled the pulpit for their sister church, the West Paris Universalist Church. There I preached about Good versus Evil, and the importance of un-conditional, self-less, downright honest *love*.

Since all three churches are closed for July and August (and since my daughter, Nellie, is spending her summer break touring Australia with a friend), I've had plenty of time to write down this story—a little tale about hens and chickens; pips and peepers; love, and well, *love*. As I glance out the leaded-glass window of my church office, I see that the goldenrod is about to burst into glorious bloom, signaling that it's almost time for my annual naked skedaddle through the field next to my home on the Cross Road.

Some of you might wonder *why* I strip bare-assed naked and trot like Lady Godiva ("only without the hoss") under the hot August sun through the fuzzy golden blooms. Why, my pips?

I run in the natural state – the state in which God created us – to re-mind myself that we 21st century pips do NOT need to isolate ourselves from the joy that we need to thrive. Our hearts and heads and souls and bodies belong *together*—not cleaved apart like freestone fruit!

I run naked through the goldenrod to show that I'm not powerless! That what *is* doesn't necessarily have to *be*!

And, last (but probably not least) … I run bare-assed naked through the goldenrod to give the good-hearted folks of Sovereign something to talk about!

The Sovereign Series

By Jennifer Wixson

The Sovereign Series, a three-volume work of fiction by Maine farmer and itinerant Quaker minister Jennifer Wixson, introduces the mythical town of Sovereign, Maine (pop. 1,048), a rural farming community where "the killing frost comes just in time to quench all budding attempts at small-mindedness and mean-spiritedness." Notable for the good-hearted nature of its citizens, Sovereign produces such lovable characters as the old chicken farmer Wendell Russell and the town's retired music teacher Miss Hastings, both of whom weave in and out of the pages of *The Sovereign Series* like beloved friends dropping in for a cup of tea.

Visitors to Sovereign partake in the felicity that abounds in the 10-mile-square settlement of rolling pastures and woodlots, whether whilst sharing a picnic with our little group of friends at the Millett Rock or wandering with a lover beside Black Brook. Readers, like the residents of Sovereign, become imbued with "a certain cordial exhilaration ... the effect of the indulgence of this human affection." – Ralph Waldo Emerson

The Sovereign Series consists of three titles:

Hens and Chickens (White Wave, Aug. 2012) – Two women downsized by corporate America (Lila Woodsum, 27, and Rebecca Johnson, 48) move to Maine to raise chickens and sell organic eggs—and discover more than they bargained for, including romance! *Hens and Chickens* opens the book on Sovereign and introduces the local characters, including Wendell Russell and Miss Hastings, as well as the handsome carpenter Mike Hobart and the Gilpin family. A little tale of hens and chickens; pips and peepers; love and friendship, *Hens and Chickens* lays the groundwork for the next two titles in the series.

Peas, Beans and Corn (White Wave, 2013) – Afghanistan war veteran Bruce Gilpin returns home from the front to restart the old pea canning factory in Sovereign, fixing to can local organic produce. His newly developing romantic relationship with Amber Johnson (Wendell Russell's step daughter) leads him to the organic movement, but also leads him into hot water with his parents (Ralph and Maude Gilpin), as well as with Amber's mother (Rebecca Russell), all of whom oppose the match. When Bruce's ex-wife (and the mother of his son Grayden) and the handsome corporate attorney Ryan MacDonald arrive in town, the situation in Sovereign becomes even hotter!

The Minister's Daughter (White Wave, 2014) – Unlike the previous two books in the series, which are narrated by the minister of the Sovereign Union Church, this little tale is told by the minister's daughter, Nellie Walker. Picking up where *Peas, Beans and Corn* leaves off, *The Minister's Daughter* is a story of love and loss; remembrance and letting go; holding fast and moving on—and closes the final chapter of *The Sovereign Series*. As we say "goodbye" to our old friends from Sovereign in *The Minister's Daughter*, we are once again reminded of the importance of unconditional love, "the fountain of youth upon which our ageing and aged selves will return to drink again and again." As we sit with Nellie Walker watching the Sovereign sun set for the last time, we know that the sun is rising elsewhere with new hope.

For Foodies

Food plays a vital role in all three books of *The Sovereign Series*. As author Jennifer Wixson says in Chapter 31 of *Hens and Chickens*: "Food prepared with love for the satisfaction of another person offers up a proof of that affection that speaks louder than any word, practically shouting 'I love you!' without any need for sound to pass through the vocal chords."

Sovereign folks buy (or grow) local foods produced with love by their families, friends and neighbors. Here are a few sources for readers who might like to share some of their delights:

1. Cheryl Wixson's Kitchen: *"More Maine Food on Maine Plates"*
http://cherylwixsonskitchen.com/
Organic foodie and sister to the author of *The Sovereign Series*, Cheryl Wixson's mission is to put more organically-produced Maine food on Maine plates. Inspired by her childhood growing up in a family of Maine women farmers and cooks (who utilized the best local ingredients), Cheryl's company continues the tradition by offering fine pasta and pizza sauces, pickles and relishes, and secret family recipes, such as *Una's Hot Water Gingerbread.* You can also follow her on Twitter @CWKitchen

2. Original Bakewell Cream – *"It's not just for biscuits anymore!"*
http://www.newenglandcupboard.com/bakewell-cream.php
Bakewell Cream is a gluten-free leavening agent that produces a lighter, flakier, biscuit and better tasting baked goods. Those who try it (including Cheryl and Jennifer Wixson's ancestors) have become loyal customers for life. This is a made-in-Maine product that is a staple of most Maine households. Their famous biscuit recipe is included on every can, and the company has a renowned Bakewell Cookbook with great baking recipes.

3. The Maine Organic Farmers and Gardeners Association (MOFGA)
http://mofga.org/
MOFGA, which is nothing like MOGG (the Maine Organic Growers Group) represented by the wily Organic Kidd in *Hens and Chickens* (apologies by the author), is a wonderful organization that helps Mainers grow and source local organic food. MOFGA also sponsors the annual, totally awesome Common Ground Country Fair (always the 3rd weekend after Labor Day at the MOFGA fairgrounds in Unity). If you've never attended the Common Ground Country Fair, you should!

4. Crosstrax Deli, Depot Street, Unity, Maine
http://www.unityme.org/food.htm
A great place to purchase locally produced foods, Crosstrax Deli proprietor Monica Murphy supports local agriculture. Create your own sandwich to take-out, or sit down and enjoy a taste of Maine in the charming town of Unity, the epicenter of the local food movement.

Special Places and Churches

Like many Maine writers, Jennifer Wixson draws inspiration from the natural world around her, and as a child was heavily influenced by special places in her life, including the rolling pastures, woods, frog ponds and vernal pools discovered on the family land situated in Norway and Winslow, Maine. Her ancestors' 19th century family homesteads, as well as her own post and beam home in Troy, Maine, served as a composite for the old Russell homestead in *Hens and Chickens*. In addition, the Ralph and Eva Luce homestead in Troy served as the inspiration for the hen pen (and was at one time home to 400 laying hens).

In addition, the following church communities (information taken from their websites) have played an important role in the development of *The Sovereign Series:*

1. The First Universalist Church of Norway (Maine)
http://www.norwayuu.org/new3/
The First Universalist Church of Norway, Maine, was founded in 1799, and is the oldest continuously existing Universalist church in the state of Maine! Our building, listed on the register of historic places, was the original location of Town Meetings in Norway and has served as a symbolic and literal anchor of Main Street.

2. The West Paris (Maine) Universalist Church
https://sites.google.com/site/wpuniversalist/home
Welcome! We are a small church located in the foothills of Western Maine. We invite you to join us for our Sunday Worship Services at 9 a.m.

3. The Winslow Congregational Church (UCC)
http://www.winslowucc.org/about-us
The Winslow Congregational Church has been ministering to this community and the world since 1828. We are committed to exploring and expressing the gospel of Jesus Christ, and providing worship, Christian nurture, and opportunities for ministry for all who join with us.

Other Works by Jennifer Wixson

1. *A Frost Pocket of Goodness* – eBook, April 1, 2012
An unorthodox and irreverent pastoral message delivered to the unpretentious First Universalist Church of West Paris (Maine) April 1, 2012, by itinerant Quaker minister Jennifer Wixson. Like much of Wixson's writings, the sermon casts a twisted theological slant on modern day issues with roots set deep in Maine history and nature. This pastoral message is actually the basis of Chapter 4 in *Hens and Chickens*, the first novel of *The Sovereign Series*.

2. *We Are All Pilgrims Here* – eBook, January 17, 2012
Six thought-provoking pastoral messages delivered to an off-beat New England church (the First Universalist Church of Norway, Maine) by itinerant Quaker minister and farmer Jennifer Wixson. Each pastoral message includes the literary and religious readings that precipitated it. Although each is a complete message on its own, the sermons – much like a symphony – evoke movement, a spiritual Pilgrimage, toward a denouement of Hope.

Pastoral messages include "The Spirituality of Place," "A Kernel of Gratitude," and "The White Rainbow."

$1 from the sale of each eBook is being donated by the author to the First Universalist Church of Norway, Maine.

3. *Learning to SOAR! – A Guide for People Who Want to Create Their Own Recovery Programs* (White Wave, September 1993)
When first published, *Learning to SOAR!* was a revolutionary and much-welcomed approach in the field of addiction and recovery. The book, which documents Jennifer Wixson's personal journey of recovery from alcoholism, asserts not only that complete recovery is possible, but that also addicts have the right and responsibility to create their own recovery programs.

Still sober 24-years later, Jennifer Wixson "has blazed a trail through the wilderness for the rest of us. Her optimism is contagious and inspiring." — Harriet R., former addict

Jennifer Wixson

Maine farmer, author and itinerant Quaker minister, Jennifer Wixson writes from her home in central Maine, where she and her husband (fondly known as the Cranberry Man) raise Scottish Highland cattle. A Maine native, Jennifer was educated at the School of Hard Knocks, and also received a Master's degree in Divinity from Bangor Theological Seminary.

You can follow Jennifer's adventures @ChickenJen on Twitter.